THE GAME
Nothing Is As It Seems

HEATHER NOËL

THE GAME: Nothing is as it seems
Expanded Edition

Heather Macauley Noël

Publisher: The Giving Game Foundation

© 2016 by Heather Macauley Noël

ISBN-13: 978-1534733510

For my daughter, the real Amelia.

*"Visionary Fiction speaks the language of the soul.
It offers a vision of humanity as we dream it could be."*
Jodine Turner

INTRODUCTION

In 1995 I self-published the original version of this visionary fiction story called <u>Children of Light</u>. I was going to sell it out of the trunk of my car, but instead I had a baby! And since I had no idea how to market books, I solved my problem (5,000 books stored in my garage) by giving them away to a variety of charitable organizations – all in one week!

Over the years, I wanted to create an updated e-reader version of <u>Children of Light</u> and while I was at it, I wanted to weave in some information passed down by a remarkable woman from Russia named Anastasia. Her teachings have been recorded in a series of books called the <u>Ringing Cedars of Russia</u> and I wanted to make the ideas more accessible by framing them in a fictional story.

I've tried to do this twice and each time the book morphed into something I wasn't expecting! I called the first version <u>Parallel Worlds</u> and you're about to read my second attempted rewrite!

So, depending upon your perspective, this book is either a rewrite of <u>Children of Light</u> or a rewrite of <u>Parallel Worlds</u> – or, it's a combination of both storylines from a brand new perspective!

Luckily for me, it's now the wild, wild west of publishing! I don't have an editor or a publisher to tell me that I can't mix-and-match and put together a new storyline (and that totally thrills the renegade in me!)

For those of you who have already read <u>Children of Light</u> or <u>Parallel Worlds</u> I hope this version will take you on an even more thrilling adventure! (I also hope that you, too, will become a renegade by the time you're done reading!) Below are the original endorsements. ~ Heather Noël

"Heather Noël represents a welcomed new addition to the great storytellers of the human spirit."
~ DEEPAK CHOPRA, M.D.

"... a thrilling fantasy-adventure that opens the heart and mind, and takes the reader on a journey of infinite possibilities."
~ JACK CANFIELD

"... powerfully enlightens us on universal truths: God's consciousness as the ultimate reality; Love – its essence; and Forgiveness the pathway. A masterpiece!"
~ BRUNO CORTIS, M.D.

"... a parable of the evolution of consciousness. If you let it, it can profoundly transform your life."
~ LEONARD LASKOW, M.D.

*"All the proofs, all the truths of the Universe are
preserved forever in every human soul."*
Anastasia

CHAPTER 1

How strange it was to be seventeen and facing death.
The tranquility of the desert night with its vast array
of glittering stars and the merest crescent moon belied the
imminent danger of hypothermia. There was little comfort
in the fact Amelia wouldn't be dying alone. She barely knew
the boy sitting by her side. Matthew had been chosen as her
hiking partner by their geology teacher, but they'd never really
spoken until that day.

It started as a weekend camping trip to Canyonlands
National Park with eleven other high school seniors. They had
left Friday at noon, and after three hours on paved roads and
another bumpy hour down a dirt path, their old yellow school
bus rumbled into their campsite spewing noxious black clouds
of exhaust that quickly dissipated into the crystal clear evening
sky of southern Utah.

Amelia never would have considered herself lucky to be
the least experienced hiker in the group until the next morning
when their geology teacher, Mrs. Caldwell said, "Amelia I
understand this is your first time hiking in the desert. Matthew
will be your hiking partner since he's the most experienced and
knows the terrain well."

Though she didn't know Matthew, Amelia had noticed

him at school on her first day. He was tall and athletic with dark hair, ruddy cheeks and grayish-blue eyes. Despite his obvious popularity he was a bit shy and unassuming as well – she thought that was the nicest thing about him. Amelia tried not to look overly thrilled, but inside she was jumping up and down. On principle, she typically ignored guys who were too good looking, and that went double for guys whose families had lots of money. But since he was her assigned partner, she considered it more of a *God's-will-type-of-thing*, so a small inner-celebration was in order.

Mrs. Caldwell then looked directly at Matthew and in a strong, authoritarian voice she added, "Be sure you're back on time," which seemed to imply that he had the tendency to show up late and she would be holding him personally responsible for Amelia's well-being.

By mid-day it was seventy degrees, the sky was clear, deep blue and so incredibly immense. They hiked through fields of coarse grass, sage, and prickly pear, and along dried stream beds gathering rock samples for their class. They'd scrambled up and down over rugged outcrops that looked like megalithic statues; frozen waves, rising and subsiding in the vastness of the high desert – an indelible reminder that this had once been an ocean floor.

The trail wove through the desert disappearing into a jumble of cliffs and ravines then reappeared in the massive presence of red sandstone walls laddered with cool crevices and fissures. As they emerged from the dark interior of the canyon labyrinth and sat down just a few feet apart, Matthew took off his sunglasses as he slumped down onto the warm red rock surface to rest. It was the first time Amelia had seen him up close.

Though it made no sense at all (and she wouldn't admit it in a million years) when he looked at her she felt as if she had known him forever. Matthew smiled and not only did Amelia suddenly realize she'd been staring, she was instantly mesmerized by the fact that he had dimples and, as if she had no will of her own, she stared a bit longer.

"Yeah I love it here," he said warmly.

Amelia pulled her knees close to her chest. Ironically, her backpack had the initials YOLO (You Only Live Once) displayed across the front but something about the last few minutes was bringing that concept into question. What if people actually live more than once? And if she was somehow remembering the *feeling* of Matthew - could he remember her as well?

After a few moments of reflecting on the fact that her day just kept getting better and better, Amelia opened her eyes and turned her head to see Matthew smiling at her as he handed her a bottle of water.

"We need to get going," he said and though she nodded in agreement, and admittedly was an inexperienced hiker, it seemed unnecessary to rush. Matthew pointed to a trail in the canyon below and said, "That's a much nicer trail than the one we're supposed to be on. Do you want to take that one instead?"

"Sure," said Amelia, enjoying the fact that he had asked her opinion since she wouldn't have known the difference between one trail and another.

As they descended into a deep canyon labyrinth, time seemed to stand still. Surrounded by earthen walls, Amelia could only see the vibrant sapphire sky overhead with no indication of the sun's proximity to the horizon. Emerging from the enclosed space, a profound and hypnotic beauty appeared before them, the sun falling slowly toward the horizon, washing deep oranges and fiery reds over the land.

They stood staring for a moment and then as if awakening from a trance Amelia said in a slight panic, "Matthew will we make it back on time?"

"Don't worry I know this trail really well. We'll make it!" Matthew sounded confident but Amelia noticed a certain urgency in his walk.

Wherever the land was fairly flat they ran instead of walking.

They scrambled over boulder fields in their gradual ascent to the top of a high mesa where red rock canyons rose majestically above the desert floor. Slanted rays drenched blazing red rock walls with golden light and shadows lengthened across the canyon skating along the desert floor. The air was slightly cooler now, but didn't breathe what was yet to come.

As it grew darker Matthew stopped and said, "Hold on a sec," as he dug through his pack. "Shit! I forgot my glasses!"

"I can lead, do you have a flashlight?" said Amelia nervously.

A guilty look passed over Matthew's face. "I don't. I was thinking this would just be a day hike, I didn't think to pack one."

"It's ok," said Amelia, "let's just keep going."

Until this point Amelia felt confident that Matthew would take care of everything, and if there was an emergency he was a really fast runner and could have made it to the camp for help. But now it was up to her to get them safely back. Anxiety blooming in her chest and flowing into every cell of her body, she took the lead, running from one rock cairn to the next. With iron legs she climbed steep cliffs, the muscles in her thighs shaking with the effort. She tried jogging through the fields but could manage no more than a fast walk.

The sky was now dark purple, the evening clouds were brushed over with shimmering gold, but there was just enough light to see the cairns up ahead. Despite exhaustion Amelia tried to run as fast as she could from one cairn to the next. Then suddenly the horizon turned a soft sable bringing to light three glittering stars and a new moon dangling by an invisible thread at the edge of the horizon. In moments the sky and land had become one. It was too dark to safely go any further.

Amelia's heart was frantically rushing in her chest and roaring in her ears as a roiling, swirling feeling made her too dizzy to walk. Sitting side by side, she and Matthew silently watched more and more stars float out of the velvety darkness. As the temperature quickly dropped, Amelia pulled on her sweater. It was oversized, warm and cozy, and though she knew the warmth wouldn't last for long she immediately felt better.

Digging through her pack, she handed Matthew half of her peanut butter and jelly sandwich.

"Thanks. I'm starving," he whispered gratefully.

Within minutes the soft evening breeze was edged with a hard chill.

"How cold do you think it's going to get tonight?" said Amelia, as she emptied out her backpack then fumbled with different ways to fold it.

"It'll probably drop below freezing." Matthew paused then added slowly, "Do you know what that means?"

Amelia knew the answer but she was desperately hoping Matthew might have something in mind a little less drastic than *death-by-stupidity* – the leading cause of death between the ages of 14 and 24, a statistic regularly quoted to her by her father. Of course she had ignored him as he was just being her dad. But now she was beginning to realize how easy it was to become a statistic.

"We could die from hypothermia," said Matthew his voice low and apologetic.

Amelia involuntarily gasped a stuttering breath as tears silently streamed down her cheeks. "Don't you think they'll look for us?"

Matthew moved closer and put his arm around her.

"I'm sure they will," Matthew said. "They'll drive into town or wherever they can get a cell connection and call my dad. He'll fly down in his helicopter and use the search light, but they'll be looking at Canyon Rim which is nowhere near here."

"Wow, your dad flies his own helicopter?" asked Amelia lightly, hoping to change the topic.

"Yep," said Matthew in an exhausted tone making it clear he didn't particularly like his father. "He learned to fly in Africa. I call him *the great white hunter* because he goes on safaris every year and now we have the heads of dead animals hanging all over the walls of his study."

"Oh," said Amelia, not really sure what else to say.

"Yeah," said Matthew with a slight laugh. Then he drew Amelia closer and said, "I'm sorry. It's my fault," his voice guilt-ridden. "I never should have taken you off the trail."

Amelia knew he must be as frightened as she was; feeling worse even, because he felt responsible for her.

"It's okay," she said squeezing his hand, "it was my choice too."

As the night grew colder the stars appeared razor sharp. Amelia's body, tingling and numb, began shaking uncontrollably as the freezing air penetrated her bones, a fierce, constant pain drawing out the little warmth left in her body. And though Matthew moved to sit behind her, wrapping his arms tightly around her, she felt herself sinking into the blackness of the night sky, drowning in stars as numerous and cold as falling snow, her body encased in ice, eyes wide open staring. Nothing seemed to exist but infinite galaxies of light and color blooming in her mind, pulling her forward with greater and greater intensity into an empty void of nothingness.

Suddenly, enveloped in darkness and with all the air squeezed out of her lungs, Amelia traveled at lightning speed down a long tube composed of dense grey light. With a whipping jolt she found herself sitting in a dimly lit room on a cold linoleum floor, gasping for breath.

As her vision cleared various shapes gradually began to emerge - a thin, flimsy mattress coupled with a faded, grey wool blanket, and a well-used pillow, all of which were lying in a neat pile on a cheap plastic bed frame screwed tightly into the floor. A piece of reflective metal was embedded in the wall above a small, rust-stained sink and next to it sat a toilet with no lid. A gloomy light was cast by a single bulb in the ceiling encased in a metal cage. High in a corner a solitary security camera swiveled slowly back and forth systematically scanning the room. That was it... there was nothing else. No pictures, no windows, just white-washed cement walls.

After frantically pulling on the handle and beating on the

door, it was obvious no one was coming to help her. She tried yelling and waving her arms at the camera, and though she was certain she was being watched no one responded as she anxiously paced back and forth like a caged animal. Finally, Amelia gave up, sat down on the decrepit little bed, crossed her legs and slowly leaned back against the cold wall.

Taking a deep breath she closed her eyes and began to vividly imagine herself outside of this strange room. Instantly she felt her *essence* completely pull away from her body until she was floating close to the ceiling. From this vantage point she could see herself below sitting motionless on the bed wearing green scrubs.

Amelia floated along the ceiling, then through the wall and further on into a brightly lit hallway lined with doors that looked just like hers. She continued on and soon found herself in a large community room. The television seemed fairly new, but the couches, tables and chairs appeared to be at least twenty or thirty years old. As she drifted through the open doors leading to the Intensive Care Unit she immediately saw Matthew lying in a hospital bed, unconscious and on life-support. She gently floated in to see him, but quickly realized he was in a coma and unaware of her presence.

Unconcerned, she floated back out of the ICU and returned to the community room. This time she noticed a middle-aged woman with deep brown eyes and black, curly hair streaked with grey, dressed in green scrubs and fluffy, pink slippers. There was a deck of cards sitting on the table in front of her and as Amelia floated closer the woman looked directly at her.

"Sit down my dear, I'm Itzel. I've been expecting you," she said hooking a chair with her foot and pushing it away from the table.

Amelia sat down. Without a word Itzel shuffled the deck and spread the cards out face down in a perfect arc on the table.

"Do you know you're playing a game? Do you remember asking me to do this for you a long, long time ago before you were even born?"

Shaking her head Amelia said, "I don't know what you're talking about."

"It's alright," said Itzel, "Just remember it's all a game. Now go ahead and pick three cards, one at a time."

Amelia obediently pointed to a card and Itzel flipped over the Death card. The picture showed Death himself portrayed as a skeleton wearing armor and holding a black flag with the Roman numerals XIII in white. His horse was carefully stepping over a dead man, woman and child, all lying on the ground in that order. Standing in front of the horse and rider was a bishop dressed in yellow paying homage to Death.

With an inexplicable, penetrating look Itzel said, "You cannot resist Death nor conquer it. The white horse is a symbol that Death is the ultimate purifier like the sun that dies at night and is reborn every morning. It means you can die and be reborn fresh and new.

"But notice this card is upside down so the meaning is also reversed. Sudden, unexpected change is coming and you must know that everything within you will resist that change. Death always includes transformation, but if you refuse to change you will be trapped, stuck in limbo. Do you understand?"

Amelia looked at her blankly. Some hazy, distant part of her did understand, but she said nothing.

"Pick another card, darling."

Amelia pointed to The Hermit which was also turned upside down. The card depicted an old man with a flowing white beard and shoulder-length white hair dressed in a long, grey cloak standing alone on a snowy mountaintop with a dark, bluish-grey sky in the background. He carried a staff in his left hand and held aloft a lantern with a glowing six-pointed star in the center.

"As you can see this card is reversed, but in the upright position it is a symbol of wisdom and the sharing of knowledge with others. More than anything it represents a deep awareness of yourself – an awareness that can only be gained through isolation.

"But the meaning is reversed, which means you will not choose to be alone or go within, your isolation will be unwelcome, forced upon you. There will be a separation from someone you care for deeply and it will bring you overwhelming emptiness and pain if you resist. But notice The Hermit wears the grey cloak of invisibility and in this very moment you are invisible to everyone but me, so there is potential here IF you don't resist what is now happening."

Without being asked Amelia pointed to a third card and was immediately relieved to see that finally one of the cards was upright, until she saw it was The Devil. The card portrayed a Satyr, an unappealing creature part man, part goat with large horns sprouting out from his head and gigantic vampire bat wings emerging from his back. From his feet protruded bat claws rather than the typical toes or hooves and he was perched high above a man and woman – both naked with tiny goat horns sprouting from their heads and goat-like tails as well. They were chained to the podium where the Devil sat and also chained to each other.

"This doesn't look good," said Amelia shaking her head.

With a sigh Itzel said, "Yes, this one is challenging, no doubt."

"This IS just a game, right?" said Amelia uncertainly.

"Yes, my dear, you are playing a game," said Itzel reassuringly.

"Okay – go ahead and tell me what it means," Amelia sighed.

"This card represents an actual person who, like a bat, sucks the life out of his prey. But in this case it's not blood, but energy. He takes the life-force of others, believing that the end somehow justifies the means. There is something about him that is irresistible, almost hypnotic. He may actually use hypnosis to get what he wants and those that come near him are easily held within his power. The inverted pentagram above his head signifies dark intent and black magic."

"Is there anything good about any of this?" asked Amelia doubtfully.

Itzel raised an eyebrow and said, "Well, look here at the man and woman. It appears they're being held captive against their will, but if you look more closely you can see the chains around their necks are loose and could easily be removed. This means they're voluntarily in bondage."

"This is the good news?" said Amelia impatiently.

"It means you have a choice. This is actually the most important card for you to understand. On the one hand you'll meet a man who embodies these things, but unlike the repulsive picture on this card you may feel strangely drawn to him, he may be ultra-charismatic, he may have certain characteristics that are much like your own. In other words he won't look like a devil. But he will mirror to you all your hopes and fears.

"It will be easy to feel like his victim, easy to blame him for what happens to you. But if you believe that to be true, you *will* fall completely under his control. You'll transfer your energy over to him and he will become more powerful while your energy becomes more and more depleted."

"But I thought you said we're playing a game," said Amelia, feeling frightened and confused. "This doesn't sound like any fun at all."

"The trick to this game is to remember it's all YOUR game. And you have a choice; you can play it according to someone else's rules or play by your own rules. You can get caught up in their *version of reality* or you can choose to remain in your own."

"Have we done this before?" said Amelia blinking. "I've dreamt of you before haven't I?"

Amelia's body began shaking uncontrollably then suddenly, both Itzel and the room dissolved into complete darkness.

CHAPTER 2

S tartled back into awareness Amelia realized that Matthew was shaking her. Teeth chattering, his voice low and urgent he spoke in stuttering breaths. "Amelia our core temperatures are dropping, we have to find a way to make the most of our clothing and everything we have."

Slowly Amelia began to process where she was and what was happening. She could no longer deny the facts. No one knew how to find them. No one would be coming to rescue them. They would either find a way to survive together or they would die.

This stark realization was accompanied by an electric jolt; suddenly Amelia's mind was sharp, clear, and focused. A seemingly unrelated memory popped into her mind: Amelia was thirteen years old, giggling with her friends at her birthday slumber party on the subject of the *Siberian Survival Method*.

Amelia never knew whether it was just a joke or the truth, but it was the only thing she could think of, so setting aside any feelings of embarrassment and speaking as best she could despite her own chattering teeth, she said, "I think we need to be skin to skin. My sweater is huge – we can both fit into it. So you put it on, unbutton your shirt so my back will be against your chest and then wrap the sweater around me."

"Okay," said Matthew, "first let's put our backpacks together so we can lie on our sides. It won't be very comfortable, but it might help."

They were so cold it was difficult to move let alone arrange their packs in the dark while trying to find a spot that was as level as possible. It felt like diving naked into an icy pond when Amelia took off her sweater. With completely numb fingers she unbuttoned her shirt and put it on backwards.

Matthew quickly put on her sweater, unbuttoned his own shirt and with a bit of awkward fumbling in the dark they managed to reposition themselves so they were skin-to-skin with Amelia's sweater wrapped around them both. Had Amelia been on her own she would have felt the discomfort of the uneven, rocky ground, lumpy backpacks and the annoying zipper digging into her hip, but every ache and pain dissolved into the warmth of Matthew's bare chest pressing solidly into her back, his strong arm wrapped tightly around her waist.

"Are you okay?" he whispered his voice deep, but shaky from the cold.

Amelia firmly placed her hand over his. "Yes," she said nodding slightly.

Even with the needling cold pricking every part of her, Amelia was only aware of Matthew's warm skin, his chest rhythmically rising and falling with each breath; his heart beating all the way through her body. She wanted to dissolve into that moment and float forever along the waves of light passing silently between them.

Amelia's body began to feel a bit warmer, but it wasn't yet midnight. With at least six or seven hours left to go she knew survival was impossible. What was it about time? It was so inconsistent – badly behaved, even. In the late afternoon time had moved so quickly, zipping by when they desperately needed it to slow down; and now it was moving agonizingly slow – heavy as stone. Time seemed more like an obstinate child: whatever she wanted from time, and the more she wanted it, time would do just the opposite.

Tomorrow the sun would continue shining, the world would go on just as it did every other day – night dissolving into day and back into night, endlessly cycling, seasons irresistibly recurring, but all of it would exist without them. How was that even possible? They were only in high school. Weren't they allowed to make mistakes? How could life be so unfair?

With Matthew's arm still wrapped tightly around her, his heart beating steady and slow, time dissolved into that moment. In fact, the entire world was dissolving into that moment. No one and nothing else existed – just the two of them. Amelia gently took Matthew's hand from her waist, placed it over her heart and placed her hand over his.

Then suddenly, the ground beneath her disappeared as an electric charge pulsed through Amelia's body and a blazing beam of golden white light drew her up into the sky. The world was frantically spinning, breaking apart into countless shining pieces as if stars were being flung into the heavens. It was so beautiful! Amelia could hardly breathe. How had she missed this?

Everything was vibrating. Every cell in her body, every atom on Earth, every star and galaxy, everything seen and unseen was pulsating – singing a song as ancient as time itself. As if she contained the sun, light radiated out from Amelia's heart and from every cell in her body.

Matthew could feel it too and whispered, "What's happening? You feel so warm."

Electricity ran through Amelia's body as she shook her head unable to speak. Trying to make sense of what she was experiencing she opened her eyes.

"Matthew," she whispered urgently, "Look!"

Before them stood a golden-haired child; a little girl no more than ten years old with radiant skin, rosy cheeks, full red lips and vivid blue eyes. She was barefoot, wearing a simple white dress with a wreath of wildflowers in her hair. Though she carried no light, and certainly wasn't glowing from within, they could see her clearly while still unable to see each other or anything else.

At that moment Amelia and Matthew both felt warm and comfortable as if the cold from only moments ago was nothing more than a dream. Though there was no apparent source of light, everything around them was lit by a soft, gentle glow that seemed like a combination of late dusk, pre-dawn, and a full moon all rolled together as one.

The child smiled sweetly and said, "I'm Äsha." Then heading down the path she added, "Come on…this way!" as if she was about to lead them on some grand adventure.

Not only did she act as if nothing unusual had occurred she seemed completely oblivious to the fact that Matthew and Amelia were still lying on their sides cocooned together in Amelia's sweater.

Blinking and looking around trying to make sense of everything, Amelia quickly unbuttoned the sweater they'd been sharing, wriggled out of it, then sat up and tried to get her bearings. Matthew sat up as well, pulled off the sweater and handed it back to her. Though she was not the least bit cold, Amelia hurriedly put on the sweater rather than try to figure out a way to gracefully turn her shirt back around and button it. Hastily, they both jumped to their feet, grabbed their backpacks and rushed to catch up with the curious little girl.

Barely able to feel her feet touching the ground, a strange tingling current flowed through Amelia's body as if she was floating. And though she was bursting with questions nothing came out of her mouth as they followed the girl down the trail.

Finally Amelia found her voice. "Are you an angel?" But before the girl could answer she added breathlessly, "Are we dead?"

Äsha continued walking but turned her head to address Amelia. "I'm not an angel. And you're not dead," she said lightly.

"But it's not cold anymore… and it's still dark, but we can see. How's that possible?" said Matthew incredulously.

"You're both fine," said Äsha reassuringly. "You're just in another part of the program, what you might think of as a different dimension," she added as if they knew exactly what she was talking about.

"What other dimension? What program are you talking about... the geology class we're in?" Matthew asked, studying the girl intently as she turned to look at him.

"Oh my goodness," said Äsha in a sweet, sympathetic voice, "I'm afraid I've gotten way ahead of you. This may be difficult to understand... well actually it's not difficult to understand, it's just that you obviously don't remember anything and you wouldn't believe me if I told you." She stopped walking and then surveying them both, she said, "What I have to tell you might be a bit shocking, so maybe we should sit down for a moment."

"We don't have time to sit down," said Amelia urgently, "we have to get back to our camp. People are worried about us... they're out searching for us!"

Kindly, yet pragmatically Matthew said, "Whatever it is you have to tell us... maybe we could just keep walking back."

"Oh, I'm afraid you don't quite understand. Maybe it would help if you were to think of this as a parallel world," said the girl hopefully.

Matthew and Amelia looked at her blankly.

Asha thought for a moment. "In this parallel world that you're now in it's warm instead of cold... right? Well... your friends and the people searching for you are in the world where it's cold," she said, appearing rather pleased with herself.

"What are you saying?" said Matthew.

"I'm saying that if you went back to your campsite," said Äsha slowly, "no one would be able to see you. No one would know you were there."

They stared at her silently trying to assimilate the gravity of their situation.

"So we *are* dead," said Matthew quietly.

"No!" said Äsha throwing her head back laughing. "Okay,

I'm just going to say it! There….Is….NO….Death! There never has been death and there never will be death. You will never die. Death only exists in the eyes of the beholder.

"Oh dear, I wasn't really planning to start there," said Äsha sheepishly rolling her eyes, "I was thinking I would break you both in a bit more slowly to that idea.

"Okay, listen… what I'm about to tell you is…well… it's something that's known throughout the universe, but it's the biggest secret on Earth. It explains absolutely everything about so-called life and death, and it answers all unanswered questions and scientific anomalies…every senseless thing, every terrible act, even the deepest sadness – all of it will make perfect sense.

"But first, repeat after me – *Imagination is more important than knowledge.*"

Silence.

"I don't mean in your heads – say it out loud," said the girl encouragingly.

Amelia and Matthew looked curiously at each other then back at Äsha.

"Imagination is more important than knowledge," they repeated perfunctorily.

"Part two," said Äsha. "No matter what I tell you…no matter how unbelievable it may seem, simply say to yourself, *This is a possibility.* You don't have to believe what I am telling you, just give the idea some *breathing room*," Äsha added taking a deep breath. "*This is a possibility*… Are you ready?"

Amelia nodded vigorously, hoping Äsha wouldn't change her mind and suddenly decide it was time for breakfast, leaving them hanging.

"Here's the big secret."

Matthew and Amelia stared at her wide-eyed, mouths slightly open and breathless with anticipation.

"Earth and everything you experience here is a virtual reality."

Äsha looked expectantly at the pair as they sat stunned,

staring back at her blankly.

"In fact Earth was created to be the Ultimate Virtual Reality Game in the Universe, we just call it The Game," said Äsha enthusiastically. "It's the most challenging game ever created and it's definitely not for the faint of heart!

"You've spent your entire life playing this game, but in reality, Earth isn't your home. It's simply a place where everyone goes to play and have experiences that they couldn't have anywhere else in the Universe.

"Shall we sit down now?" said Äsha nodding.

In stunned silence Amelia and Matthew sat down next to each other facing Äsha.

Of all the things Amelia expected to hear in that moment, the idea that she was playing a game – that anyone could think of life on planet Earth as simply a *game* – was the most ludicrous thing she'd ever heard. It was one area where *this is a possibility* absolutely, positively did not apply. Not to mention the fact that something on the scale of planet Earth would be impossible, even for God. Well, maybe not for God, she thought, but why would God create a virtual reality game? Was it just to keep His creation entertained?

"There's no way," said Amelia skeptically, "if this was a computer program then everything in it, every blade of grass, every raindrop, snowflake, grain of sand, every sunrise and sunset, not to mention every human being and every event throughout history, would have to be programmed into the game."

"Not only that," said Äsha unflinchingly, "EVERY possibility… on every dimension, including parallel worlds and alternate realities, and things you've never even heard of before! And not only is EVERYTHING programmed, The Game has been around for billions of years and will continue for as long as people want to keep playing.

"Of course there are some cultures that understand your world better than others. For instance, in India they call life on Earth, The Maya… they see life as an illusion – which is true, but it's not the whole picture. And the aboriginals in Australia call it The Dreamtime, which is also on the right track. But very few people have ever guessed that Earth and everything happening here is a game.

"If you think about it neither of you could have ever comprehended the idea of a virtual reality game if we were having this conversation a hundred years ago. So an *illusion,* or a dream, would be about as close as you could get."

"But how could we be playing a game without knowing it?" asked Amelia.

"You're born into the game. But before you're *born* you choose your parents, your name, your date of birth, and of course your physical body, it's your avatar," said Äsha. "You agree to *forget* who you are, where you came from, as well as any previous games you've played and most importantly, the fact that you're playing a game at all.

"Every game you've ever played is recorded and stored in your DNA, so occasionally people do remember portions of games they've played before... and I'm only telling you this because it can be a little confusing. Most people don't have a visual memory of past games, but sometimes they have feelings that come up that can't be explained."

Amelia had the feeling Äsha was trying to tell them something, but she couldn't begin to imagine what she was talking about. Despite that, Amelia decided to put logic aside and just play along, surely this was some kind of a made-up story typical of a ten year old.

"So just like with any game, I could decide to play anyone I choose and be *born* at any time in history," she said. "I mean, I could be Benjamin Franklin or Cleopatra but then so could countless other people, right? How would that work? We can't all be the same person?"

"Of course you can," said Äsha, her eyes sparkling. "Think of it this way – no matter how many times you play a computer game, you never play exactly the same way, right? So every time you play it's a new and different experience. Or think of it like a dream. Millions of people could dream they were Cleopatra or Ben Franklin and every dream would be unique – people wouldn't be competing with each other to play the part.

"In the same way, each time you are *born* into The Game you create a new timeline. So there could be an infinite number of *parallel versions* of Cleopatra or Benjamin Franklin and each version creates its own unique history so to speak.

"Remember, EVERY possibility already exists. Every time someone plays they tap into a new *version of reality* that has never been played out before."

"You're talking about infinite parallel realities," said Matthew, his scientific mind finally letting go of what was or was not possible. "But what about Amelia and I for instance – is there another *version* of us that went back to the campsite before dark or a version that died?"

"Yes of course," said Äsha. "All possibilities already exist. You can't think of anything or come up with a scenario that isn't already part of the program."

"So you're saying that of all the fictional books that have ever been written or ever will be written – all the stories are actually true in some alternate or parallel reality – and the author just tapped into that reality when writing the book?" asked Matthew shaking his head doubtfully.

Äsha smiled and nodded her head yes, vigorously.

Over and over Amelia said to herself *'this is a possibility, you don't have to believe any of it, it's just a possibility,'* but everything in her wanted to rebel.

"I know this should be mind-expanding and all," said Amelia, sighing heavily, "but it's just confusing. I mean, if it's all programmed how does it work?"

"Prior to being *born,* you program your gifts into your DNA. These are gifts you've earned or developed in previous games," said Äsha. "You also program your challenges and the people you want to *play* with during the course of your life. Some people will be your challengers and others will be your supporters, but usually you are playing with people you've played with before in previous games – or what you might think of as previous *lifetimes* – and that's why you sometimes feel you already know someone you've just met, for better or worse! You program *everything* you want to experience... even a few *exit points* where you can *die* out of the game if it just gets to be too much."

Amelia glanced at Matthew wondering if he had recognized her the way she had recognized him, but he was intently focused on Äsha and didn't look in her direction.

"Another reason you may feel that you recognize or remember someone you've never met is because your *PFI*, personal frequency-ID, remains the same through every game, whether you are male or female, a child or an adult," said Äsha matter-of-factly. So even though your conscious memory is wiped clean, much like reformatting a computer hard drive, all frequencies of every player remain unique, but you can only identify each other through an intuitive sense or feeling – there will be no logical reason for what you feel."

"But without a computer where does the program exist?" asked Amelia thoughtfully.

"Your human body isn't just your avatar, it's a living bio-computer. The program runs very much like a binary code that turns on and off, but rather than a computer that's plugged into electricity, your bio-computer is *plugged in* to your feelings," said Äsha.

"But if this is a virtual reality and my body is my avatar then are you saying that I'm not real?" said Amelia reaching up to tap both of her shoulders with her fingertips.

"I'm saying," said Äsha slowly, "that YOU are NOT your body. If you were your body, every time you cut your hair or trimmed your fingernails, a part of you would be lost."

Deep in thought Matthew suddenly held up his hand like a guard at a cross-walk. "Wait! Wait a second," he said firmly. "You're right, none of this makes sense... and in a strange way it's also the only thing that does make sense. But the idea that this is a virtual reality game is a little too perfect.

It explains away every conceivable anomaly because anything and everything is possible."

Äsha nodded. "Well, that's how the truth works. In your world every scientific theory gives way to new theories. Theories you believe today will all change in time. Truth is simple and unchanging. Anything that *explains away every conceivable anomaly* is the nature of Truth."

"I still don't understand the part about your feelings and the binary code," said Matthew, somewhat perplexed.

""Well it's a little more complex than you might imagine because it's an interactive program," said Äsha, "but in the simplest terms think of it this way - instead of ones and zeros turning the computer on or off - your feelings are your navigation system. On corresponds with positive emotion. Off corresponds with what you might call negative emotion or fear. Think of it like the feeling of yes or no or the feeling that you are safe or unsafe.

"If you think back to your hike there was most likely a moment when you felt unsafe, a niggling feeling that you should head back, but you talked yourself out of it."

Amelia knew immediately what Äsha meant as she thought back to the exact spot on the trail when she started feeling unsafe. It was just the smallest hint of a feeling and it didn't make sense at the time. If she had been alone she might have acted on the feeling, but she didn't want to say anything to Matthew since he was an experienced hiker and she was not.

"So you're saying that when the binary code is switching on or off you feel safe or unsafe," said Matthew deliberately. "And if you don't act on that feeling of being unsafe it just gets stronger and stronger until you do something about it?"

"That's it exactly!" said Äsha genuinely pleased. "But it can also happen over longer periods of time – days, weeks, even years – it just depends on how important it is for you to respond quickly and how long it takes for you to get the message and take action.

"Of course sometimes there's no warning at all, not even a

whisper. And when there's no warning, no feeling that you're unsafe, that's because the event is an important part of what you have programmed for your lifetime experience."

Amelia shook her head. How could any of this possibly be true? What was this child playing at? Äsha was so convincing, maybe she was a pathological liar.

"Even if this is all true," said Amelia, fearful she was being deceived, but still trying to be polite, "there are a lot of people looking for us right now and we really don't have time to talk about this. We need to let someone know we're alright."

Äsha was quiet.

Amelia looked at her skeptically and said, "That is, of course, unless we really are dead."

"You're not dead," said Äsha firmly, "you both programmed everything you're experiencing now before you were born. This is just an opportunity to learn how to navigate The Game at a more advanced level."

"Well, I find it hard to believe that I would *program* myself to be here – wherever *here* is – and that I'd want to learn about some unbelievable game that no one else has ever heard of and no one would even believe rather than just going back to our friends," said Amelia, shaking her head. "It just doesn't make sense."

"It would make sense if you knew what was coming," said Äsha knowingly.

"Well then tell us what's coming," said Matthew pragmatically.

"That's not for me to say," said Äsha quietly. "I'm only here to teach you how to navigate The Game more effectively. It's your choice whether you stay and learn, or go back to your own dimension."

"You mean we can go back right now?" said Amelia hopefully. "And it doesn't matter that we supposedly programmed all of this?"

"You have free will, Amelia. No matter what you programmed prior to your birth, the prime directive of The

Game is, *Thy will be done*," said Äsha.

"Well then, it is my will to go back!" said Amelia with conviction.

"And so it is," said Äsha softly.

Her body seemed to shimmer for a moment and then she disappeared.

CHAPTER 3

Instantly it was pitch dark and freezing cold again.

"Oh my God, what have I done?" said Amelia shaking and terrified.

"It's okay," said Matthew calmly. "Did you notice that Äsha led us down a trail that got us off of the plateau? We're on level ground now. It will be slow going, but we can't fall off a cliff, so we'll make it. And even though it's cold, my core temperature is warm now... is yours?" asked Matthew.

"Yes," said Amelia, pulling her sweater tightly around herself.

"We're really not that far away from our campsite, don't worry," said Matthew taking her hand. "Even if we don't make it back before it's light, at least this way we can keep moving. We'll be alright... I promise."

Matthew suddenly stopped and said, "Amelia, look!" He turned her slightly and she saw a bright white light appearing out of the darkness.

"Oh my God, it's a helicopter!" said Amelia excitedly. "Is it your dad?"

"It must be," said Matthew staring at the approaching lights.

"Do you think he'll see us?" said Amelia breathlessly.

"Well, there are no trees nearby and my father knows how to do a sweep. We just have to stand here and wait," said Matthew confidently.

As they stood patiently waiting the helicopter appeared brighter and sounded louder than Amelia would have expected, but then again she had never been rescued at night in the desert. Finally the light swept across them and a large helicopter landed on the flat, sandy ground about twenty feet from where they were standing. But instead of Matthew's father emerging, two soldiers jumped out of the doorway dressed in standard military flight suits and helmets with boom mics.

"Are you both okay?" yelled one soldier over the tumultuous sound of the chopper blades.

Matthew and Amelia nodded vigorously.

"Come with us!" he yelled.

Ducking down Matthew and Amelia ran with the two men and were both helped inside. They climbed in between two rows, four seats in each row facing one another. Amelia and Matthew sat facing forward with both soldiers directly facing them. One of the soldiers, a man in his fifties with a square jaw and intense, dark eyes, indicated that they should put on the headsets which were hanging above their heads on their seats.

"You're okay now," he said confidently as he nodded his head.

"How did you find us?" said Matthew, speaking through the attached microphone.

"We just kept looking," he said.

The helicopter rose swiftly into the air and then spun around nearly 180 degrees and began flying in the opposite direction.

"Are you taking us back to our campsite?" asked Matthew apprehensively.

"No, we have other instructions," said the soldier loudly.

"What do you mean… other instructions?" asked Matthew still somewhat concerned.

"We're headed back to the hanger… that's all I know." Then with a slight smile he added, "We're just the rescue team!"

Relieved, Matthew said, "Is this a Black Hawk?"

The soldier smiled and nodded. "Yep… it's a UH60."

Amelia looked at Matthew and he smiled at her.

"I know a bit about helicopters," he said shrugging.

"I'd say so," said Amelia returning his smile.

In silence they flew for half an hour or so, but Amelia wasn't really sure about the time because there was nothing to see except the interior lights reflecting off of the windows. Finally the helicopter dropped straight down as if it was about to land, but instead, it seemed to be flying slightly above the ground. Amelia still couldn't see anything, but she noticed the sound seemed to be echoing back to them as if there were walls on either side of them.

She wanted to ask Matthew if he knew what was going on, but she felt self-conscious knowing that the soldiers could hear her as well. A few minutes later her questions were answered when they landed. As she climbed out, Amelia saw that they had flown directly through a massive manmade tunnel and were now in an underground hangar surrounded by walls reaching up at least fifty feet high.

"This way," said the dark-eyed soldier as he and a couple of others accompanied them to an electric humvee.

Amelia looked anxiously at Matthew.

"Where are you taking us?" said Matthew cautiously.

"I don't know, kid, this is just a hangar," said the man. "You'll be taken to someone who will explain everything."

He then held the humvee door open for Amelia. Cautiously, she climbed in and looked uncertainly over her shoulder as Matthew followed and sat next to her. A driver was waiting along with two armed soldiers in the seat behind them, all were dressed in black jumpsuits and wearing headsets with microphones. The moment the door closed there was a clicking sound as it locked automatically. Amelia had an uncomfortable, claustrophobic feeling knowing they were now locked inside with no way out.

The vehicle moved to the opposite end of the hangar and then sat silently idling in front of a pair of thick, wide metal doors spaced a few feet apart from each other. Hovering in front of the doors was a bright yellow hologram that seemed almost like clear glass, displaying the word CAUTION in bold letters.

A moment later the yellow band of light disappeared as the doors raised slowly, revealing a deep, wide cavern enveloped in darkness. The vehicle plunged into the abyss, down a steep hill and past high rock walls. The exterior darkness only amplified the eerie sound of wheels droning against strangely smooth pavement and the air whooshing ominously by as the walls climbed higher on either side of them.

Amelia leaned against the window, stark, still and about to panic when she noticed the darkness above seemed to be changing. She couldn't quite make out what was happening but she saw ridges and strange shapes where it was smooth before. Points of light began to appear, multiplying by the moment, becoming brighter, as if they had just driven straight outdoors. She was astonished to realize she was seeing an azure sky filled with clouds overhead and the strange shapes were actually buildings at least four stories high.

The soldiers were communicating through their headsets, but Amelia couldn't make sense of what they were saying.

Leaning toward Matthew she whispered in his ear, "How is this possible? Where could we be?"

Matthew held her hand, shook his head and replied, "I have no idea, but we didn't fly for very long... we'd still have to be somewhere in the Utah desert."

"Could your dad have anything to do with this?" said Amelia nervously.

"No," said Matthew, "my father isn't involved with the military... at least not that I know of."

Needling points of anxiety pricked Amelia from within. As her body began to tremble she took long, deep breaths willing herself to stay calm. She wanted to talk to Matthew but the fact that the soldiers sitting behind her might overhear anything she said caused a feeling of panic to rise up from her chest and tighten around her throat, censoring anything she might say.

Uneasily she focused her attention outside of the vehicle as they traveled down a well-planned grid of wide streets that seemed to have been designed specifically for transporting large machinery and building materials. Suddenly the drab, grey buildings were bathed in what appeared to be real sunlight and she was stunned by the feeling of warm sunshine on her arm.

As they drove, weaving in and out through a quiet whir of electric vehicles, Amelia was both frightened and fascinated. Without knowing why she tried to commit as much as possible to memory but soon everything was a jumble as they moved past large interior spaces, unbelievable in their size and complexity, and on into the center of the city.

They drove past a park where wildflowers dotted the grass with little bursts of color. Overcoming her fear, Amelia whispered to Matthew in astonishment, "Could this be a military base?"

Speechless, he could only shake his head.

Along the roadside trees swayed green and leafy with birds singing and flitting about in their branches. Rustic looking wooden foot-bridges spanned creeks and waterfalls. And then just as Amelia had decided there couldn't be anything more surprising than what she had already witnessed, they passed a wide opening where she saw a theatre towering thirty feet above a sports arena, as if the theatre was some type of strange giant peering over the top of the stadium intent on watching a game.

When they left the city everything seemed like an endless system of tunnels and security panels that flashed from red to green as they moved through computerized check-points displaying security cameras. Amelia couldn't fathom the size and scope of the facility, not to mention the fact that it had been built in secret.

They passed a freshly dug tunnel with a surface so smooth it appeared to be glazed. Inside the tunnel a boring machine moved at a snail's pace, like a huge, steel-encased worm with a team of 35 men sealed inside of its enormous belly. Next, they passed sealed tubes containing shuttles and passengers and a sign that read: "To Los Alamos: Connections: Area 51; Page, AZ; Creed, CO; Carlsbad, NM."

"Did you see that?" Amelia whispered as she glanced over her shoulder to see if the soldiers were listening - but as far as she could tell they weren't showing any interest.

"What?" said Matthew staring back at the signs.

"Those signs... are they military bases?" said Amelia puzzled.

"Not that I know of... except I have heard of Area 51," he said.

Matthew paused and then whispered into Amelia's ear, "Maybe they're secret underground bases."

"This can't be good," she whispered, shooting Matthew a fearful look as they drove along a large corridor covered with signs in universal symbols rather than words printed in plain English.

"I know," Matthew whispered tersely, "why would they need universal symbols rather than signs in English?"

A bright green light flashed above large elevator doors as they slowly opened. Their vehicle pulled inside and Amelia immediately noticed security cameras looming overhead. They descended two levels then their vehicle drove slowly down a passageway that stopped at a hospital entrance. Once inside they were quickly escorted down a large hallway that lead to a separate wing of the hospital and on into what appeared to be a common room. Amelia noticed several men and women sitting around the room in green scrubs as one of the soldiers walked up to the nurse's station and she pointed down the hall.

"This way," he said dogmatically as he led them to a conference room and opened the door. "Take a seat. Someone will be with you soon."

Matthew and Amelia walked hesitantly through the door and sat next to each other at a long, dark wooden table with matching, padded chairs.

Though they were alone Amelia whispered, "What are we doing here? This is obviously some kind of top secret facility, why would they bring us here?" Then grabbing Matthew's arm she said, low and guarded, "I know this sounds like some kind of conspiracy theory… but what if they don't let us out?"

Before Matthew could answer a woman in her mid-thirties with dark, short-cropped hair and hazel eyes entered the room. Unlike most of the people in the facility she was wearing a business suit, a white shirt with a black jacket and pants rather than a military jumpsuit.

"My name is Trevor Tulney," she said briskly as she sat down across from them. "I'm a civilian, but I do live and work here. I'm sorry I wasn't able to meet with you sooner to explain what's been happening and why you're here.

"Last night at 22:00 a synchronized series of terrorist attacks took place. The immediate damage has been caused by nuclear weapons detonated on the San Andreas fault line in the San Francisco bay area, but two other areas were also targeted; Yellowstone National Park and a relatively unknown, but very vulnerable part of the Utah desert not too far from here," Trevor said bluntly without a hint of compassion.

Matthew and Amelia stared at each other in shocked disbelief as she continued.

"Your teacher and the students in your class were safely evacuated but by the time we found you two this facility was the closest and safest place we could bring you due to the threat of an imminent eruption. Just after your arrival this facility went into lockdown."

"I don't understand," said Matthew interrupting. "You're saying that terrorists targeted a national park and the desert?

That makes no sense."

"Beneath Yellowstone Park and this desert are two active super-volcanoes," said Trevor with a hint of annoyance. "They're the result of magma in the mantle rising up from a hotspot and pooling beneath the crust unable to break through. Rather than having a single cone volcano, calderas exist below ground, like a cauldron, so you can't see it until it breaks through the surface of the land and erupts.

"We were able to detect and stop the attack on Yellowstone, but obviously, not the attack here," said Trevor.

"I've never heard of an active volcano in Utah," said Matthew looking at her skeptically.

"The Utah caldera has been dormant for over 600,000 years, but just like Yellowstone Park it's been an active hotspot for a while," said Trevor, the tone of her voice making it clear she didn't appreciate being questioned. "Until last night our geologists believed the Utah caldera wouldn't erupt anytime soon so no reports were published in an attempt to protect businesses that rely on tourism.

"However, after the underground detonations occurred we found asphalt melting for thirty miles along a road that runs directly across the caldera. Now, there's a chance that nothing will happen… that it will just remain a hotspot, but we need to wait until we're completely sure before we send you home."

"But we saw trains and signs for destinations that are far from here… couldn't we just take a train and get back home from there?" asked Matthew.

"Lockdown means no one goes in or out," said Trevor seeming much more like a hardened military officer reminding them about rules and regulations than the civilian she claimed to be. "We can survive indefinitely in this facility, but we can't handle the influx of the thousands of people who would want to take refuge here."

"Does that mean our families are in danger?" said Amelia anxiously.

"At this time your families are fine. We'll get word to them that you're both here, and I'm sure they'll be relieved to know that you're in the safest facility in the world," said Trevor in a failed attempt to lighten the heaviness in the room.

"But what if we could talk to someone in charge and convince them to let us leave… then could we go to another base?" said Amelia. "I mean, I saw a train leaving when we were coming here."

"I'm sorry," said Trevor in a tone that was slightly more human and less like an automaton, "it's just protocol. There are no exceptions to the rule. The train you saw was just transporting people to other parts of this facility."

"How big is this base?" asked Matthew.

"It's big," said Trevor, clearly unwilling to be more specific.

"Now, there's no need to worry about anything just yet," said Trevor with a strange intensity that belied her unspoken suggestion that they remain calm. "We can live here underground until the threat is fully assessed. In the meantime, we've already received an influx of personnel so I'm afraid this hospital psychiatric ward is the only place that can accommodate the two of you at the moment, but there's no need to worry."

"Don't worry?" Matthew blurted out. "This place is massive! You're telling us that the only two beds in this entire facility are in a psych ward? Seriously?"

"Due to current events and the massive influx of personnel… every bed has been taken and as you may well imagine," she said shortly, looking directly at Matthew as if she was daring him to ask more questions, at his own peril, "your personal accommodations are not high priority at the moment.

"Our hospital beds are already filled with the sick or injured…" said Trevor in a tone that carried the underlying message they were lucky to have a place to stay at all. "No one in this ward has ever been violent. I promise you, everyone here is completely harmless, many are just here because there's no one to care for them and this is all we have to offer."

Trevor then continued on as if they were military recruits in boot camp rather than a couple of scared teenagers completely out of their element.

"You're safe, but you'll both be here for a while, so when we're finished a nurse will give you a brief physical exam and then you'll be given ID cards and scrubs. Tomorrow when we have your weight and measurements you'll receive military issue clothing.

"You'll each have your own room. You don't have to worry about being in a psych ward at night," she said, putting the word *psych* in finger quotations, "all doors are locked, but you have your own intercom and staff members who are always available in case of an emergency or if you need to go to the bathroom. Sleeping pills aren't required, but if you have trouble sleeping you'll be given non-prescription pills.

"In the meantime, both of you are now part of this community so you'll take aptitude tests tomorrow morning. Then you'll either be placed into job training, or you'll be given further testing if it becomes clear that you have a specialized talent or ability."

"Wait!" said Matthew impatiently, "you're telling us that our country is in the midst of a massive, terrorist attack and you want us to take aptitude tests? Are you kidding?"

"Young man," said Trevor flatly, "no one here is entitled enough to sit around watching events unfold on television - everyone is trained, everyone has a job and everyone works. And since neither of you showed up with a job application in hand… you are going to take aptitude tests so you can work. Now, have I been clear enough?"

Matthew and Amelia both nodded.

Trevor's beeper sounded and after checking her message she said, "I have to go now. When you exit this room turn left, you'll see the common room on your right and the cafeteria at the far end of the hall. It's only open for one hour at each meal so be there on time or you'll miss out. In the common room all rules and regulations are posted and everything that applies to the patients applies to you as well."

As she walked briskly toward the door she turned and added, "Wait here for the nurse. I'll see you both tomorrow," almost as if she was closing a business deal.

When the door closed behind Trevor Amelia said angrily, "I can't believe how indifferent that woman is… she acted like this massive terrorist attack and potential super volcano was just another day at the office. I mean, thank God our families are okay… but still, doesn't it seem weirdly calm here?"

"I know," said Matthew confused, "you'd think everyone would be running around, freaking out, but no one seems upset."

"So what do you think?" said Amelia breathlessly, "do you think there could be a super-volcano eruption right here in Utah?"

"The super-volcano doesn't make sense," said Matthew slowly, "I mean it's a definite possibility in Yellowstone – there's all kinds of evidence already… it's just a matter of time. But I haven't heard anything about an active caldera here in the desert."

"Do you think it's something the government would keep secret?" said Amelia, placing her hands on her knees, hoping Matthew wouldn't notice her hands trembling.

Matthew took a deep breath and said, "Well, it's possible. It wouldn't be easy to see it coming until it's too late."

"How bad could it be?" said Amelia.

"A super-volcano is nothing like anything you've ever seen," he said heavily. "The last eruption here in the Utah desert was 5,000 times larger than Mount St. Helens, and the lava covered 12,000 square miles and in some places it was 13,000 feet thick."

"Do you think that could really happen again?" said Amelia anxiously.

"Well, you can't rule it out," said Matthew.

"How long do you think it will take before they decide that the volcano isn't going to erupt? I mean, I know you couldn't possibly know that for sure... but what do you think?" said Amelia hoping for even the smallest amount of good news.

"Oh, I don't know," said Matthew, "my best guess is that if it hasn't erupted, or gotten worse over the next two to three weeks, they'll probably open things up and let us go home."

Amelia nodded and smiled slightly. "Okay, I could live with that," she said optimistically.

The door opened and a stocky male nurse in grey scrubs with freckles and curly, ginger hair appeared.

"Right this way," he said as he held the door open for them.

As he ushered them to an adjoining hospital wing for their physical exams, Amelia said, "Excuse me, but is there any way we can contact our families? Or is there a way to get a message to them so they know we're alright?"

He spoke politely and said, "I'm sorry, there's no unofficial communication during lockdown, but I'm sure your parents have been notified." Looking at her sympathetically he added, "I don't make the rules. I know it seems unfair, but here we all have to live by them."

Amelia and Matthew were shown into separate rooms for their exams. Their dirty clothes were taken and they were given green scrubs and security passes which they wore around their necks on long, black lanyards. The passes displayed their name, weight, and a specific barcode that allowed for different levels of security.

After her exam was complete, Amelia was sent to the common room where she sat anxiously waiting for Matthew. There were only a handful of patients present, most of them middle aged, but there was one man who immediately stood out. He was quite elderly, his hair was white and he shuffled around the room looking at the floor quietly muttering, "Minus 74 point 85 16 16... Minus 102 point 59 zero 33 zero."

Amelia suddenly had a strange déjà vu feeling, but even that wasn't quite it. It was more a feeling she couldn't identify – familiar yet somehow the context was different. Then she noticed a woman sitting by herself at a table. Against all odds

Amelia recognized her immediately when she saw the woman was wearing pink slippers. But even so she couldn't remember how she knew her until Matthew entered the room and sat down next to her.

"Matthew," Amelia whispered emphatically, "I dreamed this." Then she stopped as she realized she had also dreamed that he was in a hospital bed unconscious.

"There are some things that still don't make sense," said Amelia taken aback, "but see that woman sitting over there by the television? I remember her."

Matthew looked at the woman then back at Amelia and said, "How much of your dream do you remember?"

"Enough to tell you I don't think I was dreaming. I think I was here," she said, her mind racing.

"How's that possible?" said Matthew earnestly. "Wait. Forget I said that. How would we explain anything that's been happening to us?"

"I know! I feel like I'm in some kind of a weird reality show and there are hidden cameras and microphones all over the place." Amelia suddenly stopped. "Oh shit!" she said as she flipped over her security pass looking for a small microphone, but nothing was there. "Oh my God, look at me, you'd think I *belonged* here."

"It's okay, Amelia…" said Matthew gently, "I think it's safe to say we're most likely in some level of shock." Then looking at the woman again he whispered, "What do you remember about her – anything?"

"I know I sat with her at a table and talked to her. It's weird… maybe it was a dream," said Amelia confused.

"Well, somehow you must have been seeing the future," said Matthew at a loss.

"But what does it mean?" said Amelia shaking her head.

A very masculine looking, young female nurse with short cropped blonde hair approached them and said, "Dinner will be served in just a few minutes. I'll show you to your rooms and then we'll go to the dining hall." As they walked down the hall she added, "For your security, your bedrooms are locked at 22:00 hours and will automatically unlock at 06:30, breakfast is at 07:00. Everything you need is in your rooms – toothbrush, toothpaste, soap etc. You can sleep in your scrubs and you'll receive fresh clothing tomorrow."

"Amelia, your room is 102 and Matthew, yours is next to hers... 104," she said, indicating their rooms with a wave of her hand as they passed by without stopping. "Showers are at the far end of the hall. Men and women alternate, so read the schedule to know when it's your turn. Alright then, come this way for dinner," she said in a businesslike, though not unkind manner.

Standing in line at the cafeteria Amelia whispered to Matthew, "This seems like a combination of our high school lunch room and what it's probably like in prison."

"Good thing the food's labeled, otherwise you'd never know what you're eating," Matthew shot back under his breath as Amelia suppressed a laugh.

No one was particularly friendly. Women with hairnets and white uniforms served the most unappealing, overcooked food. There was nothing fresh, and nothing looked particularly edible, but Amelia wasn't hungry nonetheless.

After being handed their trays of mystery food, Matthew and Amelia sat down at a table next to a wall and picked at their plates. Everyone in the cafeteria was fairly quiet and subdued except the old man who was still muttering, "Minus 74 point 85 16 16... Minus 102 point 59 zero 33 zero," as he shuffled along with an attendant carrying his meal tray.

When the man reached Amelia's table he stopped and glared at her. The attendant tried to grab his elbow and redirect him to another table, saying soothingly, "Come, come, Admiral Byrdie, someone is already sitting there, you can sit over here."

The old man refused to budge and stared angrily down at Amelia, raising his voice as he said furiously, "Minus 74 point 85 16 16... Minus 102 point 59 zero 33 zero."

Matthew moved toward the wall and Amelia scooted down the bench next to him and then said to the old man, "It's okay, you can sit here. I'm sorry, I didn't know this was your seat."

With that Admiral Byrdie sat down and said sweetly, "Minus 74 point 85 16 16... Minus 102 point 59 zero 33 zero," as if he was politely thanking her.

Amelia was filled with questions and suppositions to share with Matthew, but she felt self-conscious without knowing why. The old man was clearly harmless, and she really didn't have anything to say that would get her into trouble, at least that's what she hoped, but still she was more comfortable sitting quietly and just observing the others in the room.

During the course of the meal Amelia noticed that the old man needed help from time to time. He reminded her of her grandfather who'd had a stroke, and she found herself automatically helping him to reach his glass of water, or she would pick up a piece of silverware as it clattered to the floor, but she quickly learned to wipe it off with her napkin before giving it to him, otherwise he would insist on eating from the dirty silverware. Other than that he paid no more attention to Amelia than if she had been one of the attendants.

After dinner, *It's a Wonderful Life* was playing in the common room and seemed like a strange choice to Amelia given the recent traumatic events. But maybe no one in the ward knew what was happening. Sitting next to Matthew on a well-worn couch she watched the movie and quickly gathered that it must have been Admiral Byrdie's turn to choose as he took it all in with glowing eyes and in complete silence, as if he'd never seen it before and was trying to take in every word.

It was popcorn night but the old man paid no attention. He was glued to the screen, his lips mouthing the words of each and every character. Amelia brought him a bowl of popcorn and set it on the table next to him.

"This is for you if you want it," she said kindly.

To her surprise he looked into her eyes with perfect clarity and whispered so softly she had to bend down to hear him.

"I'm not crazy," he said genuinely. "When you get inside go to the library."

"What do you mean inside? Inside where? What library?" Amelia whispered, confused and completely surprised that he suddenly seemed so lucid.

But the old man had already turned his attention back to the movie and was mouthing the words of one of the characters as if he had not said a word. Amelia quietly puzzled over what the old man had said to her. Was he just crazy, or was there something he was trying to tell her? Finally, she gave up trying to figure it out and focused upon the movie. This was a favorite Christmas film she watched each year with her parents, she always cried, but it was even worse this time because she didn't know if she would ever see them again.

When the movie ended Admiral Byrdie was once again muttering his favorite sequence as Amelia took his bowl, put it in the tub and then returned to him.

"Can I help you up?" she said, waiting for his permission.

He looked at her with perfect clarity and nodded. Once he was standing Amelia tried to release his arm, but he put his hand over her hand making it clear he wanted her to walk with him.

As they walked down the hall, Matthew on one side of her and Admiral Byrdie on the other, the old man dropped his head downward and said quietly so that only Amelia could hear, "You'll be going inside. You'll know you're there when you get there. You must go to the library or all will be lost."

CHAPTER 4

J ust before Amelia arrived at her room a sudden wave of panic washed over her as she remembered the bedroom from her dream. Thankfully her room was nothing like the vision. It was white, simple and quite ordinary with sterile, linoleum floors. It could have been a small college dorm room, except for that it had no windows. The little room was less prison-like than she'd expected, but the bed frame was plastic and screwed into the floor just as she remembered from her dream. There was something mirror-like embedded into the wall, but there was no sign of either a toilet nor a sink, and this brought some relief knowing they'd have to let her out sooner or later.

At 10 p.m. the doors automatically clicked shut. She heard the lock sliding quietly into place and ending with a slight click as the overhead light faded into a soft nightlight. Amelia sat on her bed unable to sleep, her body exhausted but her mind racing. Finally, she got up and paced around the room thinking about everything the old man had said to her. Try as she might, she couldn't come to a single successful conclusion. Even when she thought about Äsha and the idea that all of this might actually be a virtual reality game, it still made no sense.

Äsha said that feelings navigate the game, but what could she possibly feel that would change what was happening? The idea was crazy. Still, there was a part of her that wished she had stayed longer to listen to what Äsha had to say.

At last she flopped down on her bed, closed her eyes and in the silence of the still room suddenly became aware of every sound around her. Amelia could hear the footsteps of someone walking slowly up and down the hall, most likely one of the nurses or an attendant, perhaps, making their nightly rounds; briefly stopping to listen at each doorway.

Though Amelia shifted back and forth between dream state and reality, she never realized that she had fallen asleep until she suddenly woke to her room literally shaking beneath her. Jumping out of bed, convinced it was an earthquake, she pounded on the door to be let out. But no one came. No one was in the hall making rounds and she couldn't hear a sound. She rushed back to her bed and slid underneath it breathing heavily. Then she heard a voice.

"Amelia, is that you?" said Matthew quietly from the other side of the vent.

"Did you feel that?" she said anxiously.

"The earthquake?" said Matthew. "Yeah I couldn't get anyone to let me out so I got under my bed."

"Oh my God, so did I," said Amelia panicked. "I couldn't get out either."

Another tremor shook the floor, but it wasn't as severe this time.

"Matthew?"

"Yeah."

"Do you think it's safe to talk here?"

"I think so. I doubt they have microphones under our beds," said Matthew lightly. Then more seriously he added, "Is there some reason you're afraid?"

"I just don't know. I mean, everything Trevor said made sense… but why would they bring us here. We're not special or important," said Amelia puzzled.

"We are a bit *different* if you think about it," said Matthew thoughtfully.

"What do you mean?" said Amelia as she reached for her pillow and tucked it under her head.

"Well, I've been thinking about this… and I agree, why would they bring us to a place that is so top secret there's not even a rumor about something like this existing? And, like you, I was thinking that we're just a couple of high school kids, why would the military even get involved in finding us? What makes us different?"

"I don't know what makes us different" said Amelia trembling slightly.

"Don't you think the timing is a bit odd?" said Matthew pensively. "I mean, we're not really sure what happened to us. Did we die and come back to life? Were we really in another dimension? If so, where did we go… and how did we get there? And even more importantly… how did we get back?"

"But if they didn't know we were lost, then how did they even know where to come look for us?" said Amelia.

"That's my point… this place must be *beyond* top secret," he said concerned.

"That's what I was thinking too," said Amelia uncomfortably, "the question of why they brought us here isn't nearly as important as… why would they let us leave?"

"I know," said Matthew, "that's all I've been thinking about."

"How do we even know they're telling us the truth about the terrorist attacks," said Amelia. "I never felt anything last night, did you?"

"No, I didn't feel anything either," said Matthew. "But it is possible, given the fact that the caldera could be over fifty miles in diameter that the detonations were too far away for us to feel."

"Maybe," said Amelia, "but I think if it's real they'll show some footage."

"And if they don't?" said Matthew.

"Well, I just won't believe it until I see it," said Amelia definitively.

"I'm with you," said Matthew. "But even if we see the footage, there are still a lot of unanswered questions."

"I know," said Amelia, "and I think we need to be careful… especially with what we say to each other."

"Yeah, I agree," said Matthew.

"I wish we could stay and talk, but I don't want anyone to get suspicious," said Amelia.

"You're right," said Matthew, "how about we just meet here quickly if we ever have an emergency."

"Okay," said Amelia, "goodnight, Matthew."

"Goodnight, Amelia," Matthew said in his low, musical voice that made her want to throw her arms around him and kiss him.

Amelia climbed back into bed, but all she could think of was Matthew only a few inches away. And then quite suddenly Amelia found herself in a familiar dream. She saw the psychic woman with her cards spread out on a table, but it was as if she was trying to see her way through a dense, grey mist.

At last she fell into a deep sleep only to wake up moments later with the bedroom light shining painfully in her eyes. Blinking and feeling as if she'd been drugged, Amelia slowly sat up as she heard the door automatically unlock. She wanted nothing more than to stay in bed, but clearly, that wasn't going to be an option.

Outside her bedroom door she found a duffel bag with army boots, a few t-shirts, a light jacket and cargo pants, among several other things. Amelia dressed quickly, but from the moment she walked out of the bedroom everything seemed surreal. Artificial lights, artificial people, and artificial food – nothing was real.

Matthew sat down next to her at breakfast and though they were both careful with their words he reached out and held her hand reassuringly for a few moments.

After breakfast, a nurse escorted them into the conference

room. "Your tests have your names on them," she said as she stood waiting for them to take their seats. Amelia sat down across from Matthew.

"You may begin," said the nurse as she sat down.

Amelia flipped her test over expecting to see a straightforward series of questions, but this test was like nothing she would ever have imagined.

The top of the test page read:

1. Your target's identifier is: TABF.

2. Close your eyes, relax, breathe deeply, and empty your mind. Relax into the emptiness for a few moments. Imagine the window of your mind is black and continue holding this image.

3. Think of the target's identifier: TABF. Say the letters over to yourself. Empty your mind. Now write down any colors, shapes, temperatures, textures, movement, or other characteristics that come into your mind. Sketch what you see, do not try to identify it.

4. Close your eyes and quiet your mind again. Write down anything you sense or see beyond the physical description or image you have drawn.

Amelia looked up from her test to see how Matthew was reacting, but from what she could tell without staring or asking him directly, it appeared he was answering some very complex science or math questions.

At first Amelia was inclined to raise her hand and ask if she'd been given the wrong test, but then she wondered if that was part of the testing process – would she raise her hand or not? She decided to answer the questions and see how it all played out. She looked down at the test again. Your target's identifier is: TABF.

Amelia had no idea what that meant, so she took a deep breath and thought TABF, TABF, TABF while trying to keep her mind as blank as possible.

Immediately she saw an image of an icy, flat plane that dipped in at the center. Amelia was glad she had the option of drawing what came to mind because she didn't know how to describe what she was seeing. After drawing what she saw, she closed her eyes and waited to see if anything else would come to her.

Instantly she had the *feeling* of an ocean, but not an ocean with gentle waves on a sandy, tropical beach, which is what she would normally have imagined. Instead this feeling was of a desolate and frigid ocean filled with towering icebergs splitting off and collapsing into the sea. But then, just as if she had ascended to the top of a mountain peak and was now heading down the other side, the feeling shifted. The cold disappeared and she was surrounded by lush green grass and trees, something utterly impossible if she were actually viewing the North Pole or Antarctica.

Amelia remembered she was simply supposed to describe feelings and visual images. She hadn't been directed to make sense of what she saw so she wrote down her perceptions to the best of her ability and then waited for Matthew to complete his own task.

A few minutes after they had completed their tests, Trevor entered the room. She casually sat close to them and said, "Thank you for taking these tests, I know this may seem like we're rushing to get you both involved, but you'll find it far easier to adjust if you have something to do that will keep you busy. You'll have your results at dinner and your temporary job assignments will begin tomorrow. Ultimately you'll have the opportunity to try other jobs and you can also volunteer for research projects.

"Do either of you have any questions?" said Trevor.

"I do," said Matthew. "We haven't seen any news about what's happening."

"Well, that's because it would be too shocking for many of the patients here," said Trevor.

"But we're not patients," said Amelia, "and we'd like to see what's going on."

"Yes, of course," said Trevor understandingly as she stood

up and walked over to a large flat screen television on the wall. She grabbed a remote control and said, "I want to caution both of you that this might be very upsetting, are you sure you want to see it?"

They both nodded.

Trevor turned on the television and dimmed the lights as Matthew moved around the table and sat next to Amelia. A moment later a newscast flickered onto the screen. The images were horrific. Some of the clips were filmed on personal, handheld cameras, some were filmed by news crews or from high above in a helicopter. What they saw was inconceivable. Mass hysteria was sweeping through San Francisco. No one could leave the city. Cars crashed into each other. The Golden Gate and other major bridges in the bay area dangled lifelessly above the water they were meant to traverse. Traffic was wedged together in city streets, gas pumps were empty, highways were totally blocked with people desperate to leave as buildings exploded into flames in the background. There were clips of massive earthquakes tearing apart the San Andreas fault line, collapsing everything in its wake.

Fighting back tears, Amelia closed her eyes unable to take in anymore of what was on the screen. A deep aching in her throat and chest threatened to overwhelm her at any moment.

"Are our families still okay?" said Amelia, feeling it was a bit selfish to even ask under the circumstances, but she needed to know.

Sympathetically, Trevor said, "This is all happening in California. As long as there's not an eruption here in the desert your families should be fine."

Amelia sighed in relief as Matthew moved closer and wrapped his arm around her. She buried her face in his chest and cried, barely able to breathe as the weight of all she had seen clutched at her throat like a noose around her neck.

"Why don't you two spend the day doing whatever you want... I know this is a lot to take in," said Trevor understandingly. "Rest up and get a good night's sleep. I'll meet you at the nurse's station in the morning."

Matthew nodded silently as Amelia sniffled, "Okay."

After Trevor left Amelia looked up at Matthew teary-eyed and said, "I was totally wrong," shaking her head. "It's all happening… I saw the time-stamps and everything."

"I know," said Matthew helping her stand up and walk to the door.

As they walked down the hall Amelia mustered a weak smile and said, "I think I need to have a meltdown by myself… okay?"

"Of course," said Matthew gently. "I'll see you at lunch."

"Okay," she said ducking into her room and closing the door tightly.

Curling up on her bed Amelia cried herself to sleep. She slept through lunch and would have slept on through dinner, but a nurse gently woke her.

"Even if you're not hungry, sweetheart, you'll need to get your work assignment for tomorrow."

Amelia nodded, sighed and struggled her way out of bed. She didn't wash her face, brush her hair or even glance at a mirror, she just stumbled down the hall to the cafeteria feeling dazed and more lost than she ever thought possible. If everything Trevor had told them was true, what was next? What would become of them?

After dinner, an attendant handed Matthew and Amelia the results of their aptitude tests. Both results concluded with 'Further Testing: Level 4.'

In a low voice Matthew said, "What do you think this means – *Further Testing?* What was your test like?"

"My test?" said Amelia. "It was strange… I was supposed to empty my mind and imagine something…"

"Like what?"

"I don't know exactly, there were these letters – TABF. The test said the letters were the *target identifier* – whatever that means. I was supposed to think about the letters, empty my mind and see what came into my imagination. What about you? What was your test like?"

"Nothing like yours, that's for sure," said Matthew shaking his head. "Mine was just one sentence. It said, *Using quantum mechanics, proves that things are thoughts.*"

"Seriously?" said Amelia incredulously. "What did you write?"

"Lights out in fifteen minutes," said a voice over an intercom.

"I'll tell you later when we have more time," said Matthew hastily standing up, "it's the last chance for me to take a shower." Amelia stood up, he gave her a hug and whispered, "If you need to talk, just climb under your bed, tap on the vent and we can talk."

Amelia smiled and nodded, and as she watched him walk down the hall she felt eternally grateful that she had somehow managed, under the strangest of circumstances, to find a true friend. They barely knew each other and yet she felt comfortable with him, exactly as she had felt when she saw his eyes for the first time. It wasn't some odd coincidence. No matter where they were or what was happening he made her feel better. Even through a wall vent, he was a great listener and he always had something intelligent to say, or he would quickly admit anything he didn't know. And he laughed so easily Amelia couldn't help but laugh with him, and somehow, even in this strange place she felt at home with him, as if nothing could go wrong as long as he was there.

Women only had use of the showers in the mornings so Amelia washed her face, brushed her teeth and went to bed. Every part of her was exhausted, yet somehow her mind just wouldn't shut down. She tried jumping-jacks, pushups, sit-ups, and finally ended up just pacing around her room. When none of that worked she sat on her bed with her back up against the wall and tried deep breathing.

She wanted to talk to Matthew through the vent, but she didn't have anything that actually qualified as an emergency. In truth she just wanted to hear his voice, but she didn't want to bother him. Amelia knew a bit about meditation so she practiced focusing on her breath moving in and out of her body. Gradually she felt a bit calmer and then without trying she found herself somehow *floating* outside of her body and looking down at herself from the ceiling.

It felt so familiar, as if she had done this before, but that wasn't possible. Yet she had a clear memory that she had once floated through the wall and out into the hall. The moment the thought occurred to her, Amelia found herself doing just that, floating down the hall and into the common room where she saw a woman sitting alone at one of the tables.

"Come, my dear, no one will hear us talking," said the woman quietly.

Amelia looked at the nursing station, but no one seemed to notice their presence. "Are you outside of your body like me?" Amelia asked.

"Things are seldom what they seem," said the woman. "The Devil is getting closer. In this you have no choice. He has NO MORE POWER than you. He cannot take your power, but you will give it to him willingly. In fact, you will insist on it."

Bright lights awakened Amelia, but this time the dream was clear in her mind. She hurried to the cafeteria to try to talk to Itzel, but the woman didn't show the slightest bit of recognition and seemed unwilling or unable to speak.

Disappointed, but not totally surprised, Amelia got in line for breakfast and found herself standing behind Admiral Byrdie as he struggled with his tray. The attendants were all busy with other patients so she carried his tray and helped him get coffee, cream no sugar and then set the tray down in his usual spot. Matthew was nowhere to be seen so she sat down next to him at the table and the old man mumbled the sequence that Amelia had now practically memorized.

Then quite unexpectedly he put a napkin over his mouth and said quietly, "There's a place you'll be safe, remember this… Minus 74 point 85 16 16… Minus 102 point 59 zero 33 zero. Testing. Testing. Don't forget. News. No, no, no… not happening, not real, no, no, no. Minus 74 point 85 16 16… Minus 102 point 59 zero 33 zero. … you'll be safe… go to the library."

He then looked around cautiously and underneath the table he handed Amelia something that felt like a rather bulky pocket watch.

"Don't look now," he whispered into his napkin. "Don't let anyone know you have this. Watch out for cameras. Keep it with you always. Go to the library."

Then he stood up leaving his coffee and uneaten breakfast and tottered away muttering, "Minus 74 point 85 16 16… Minus 102 point 59 zero 33 zero."

Matthew never came to breakfast but showed up in the common room just as Trevor arrived. He and Amelia exchanged glances, but they didn't speak as Trevor motioned to them from the doorway to join her.

"Your ID tags have been programmed to give you clearance for Level 4. However, you'll always need to be accompanied by myself or someone else that I appoint. You're both coming with me today. Right this way," she added as she pulled open one of the swinging glass doors and then followed behind them.

Trevor ushered them to a small electric transport vehicle somewhat like the type of large golf cart used inside airports, one with no doors and enough seating for several people. As they whisked down the hallway, the object Admiral Byrdie had given Amelia was burning a hole in her pocket. She was sitting behind Trevor so she stuck her fingertips into her pocket and tried to figure out what he could possibly have given her.

It seemed to be the size and shape of a pocket watch, but much thicker, as if something was contained inside. As she felt the surface one side was smooth and the other seemed to have something inlaid around the outer edge and in the center, and also some type of engraving, but it wasn't deep enough for her fingertips to get a sense of what it might look like.

All the while they were being automatically scanned as they zipped past checkpoints, quietly moving from hallways to stone passageways and finally onto a massive elevator.

At Level 4 they disembarked from their vehicle, their IDs were scanned and they were weighed, then they walked down a wide hallway lined with metallic double-doors. Trevor stopped at a large, highly polished wooden door, stepped out of the vehicle and knocked three times.

"Enter," said a man's voice.

Trevor opened the door and said succinctly, "They're here."

"Good, I'll be right there."

To Amelia's surprise, a tall, elegantly dressed man in a tailored grey suit stepped through the door. He appeared to be in his late forties with short cropped, thick, ginger hair, light skin, full lips and striking green eyes. She thought he looked more like a model or an actor than a military man.

"Hello Matthew and Amelia, I'm Thomas," he said informally. "Matthew, you're coming with me, and Amelia you'll go with Trevor."

Then, Thomas turned to Trevor and said quietly, "Use the Montauk Chair for her test."

Nodding toward Amelia and Matthew, Trevor said tersely, "Excuse us for just a moment." Then stepping aside with Thomas she said under her breath, "Sir, it's impossible to know how she'll respond to the chair," her voice low and insistent, "you can't put someone untrained in a device like that, there's no way of knowing what could happen."

Taking her arm and walking slowly away from Matthew and Amelia, as if it was nothing more than a stroll and an informal chat, Thomas said quietly, but firmly, "I want her in that chair. Tell her you're testing her abilities in regard to remote viewing. Do not tell her anything about the history of the chair, just that she needs to focus only on your instructions."

"But sir, you don't know what she might do accidentally," said Trevor with genuine concern.

"If you tell her what to think that's what she'll be thinking about," said Thomas calmly. "She's a teenager. She's not calculating. She doesn't have the mentality or the intent of those who've tried to destroy the chair in the past."

"I understand that sir, but if she's as psychic as you think she is," she said glancing nervously at Amelia, "you don't know what she'll pick up on. There are parts of this chair that came from the original one. How do you know what she'll see or feel?"

"Placing her focus on remote viewing is the safest way for us to find out. No more discussion. Just report the results," said Thomas briskly as he turned in the opposite direction and proceeded to walk back.

Though Thomas and Trevor were walking toward Matthew and Amelia they were out of earshot so Amelia whispered to Matthew, "Did you notice his suit?"

Matthew nodded, "My father has hand tailored suits like that from Italy. The shoes are Italian leather too."

"What do you think it cost?" said Amelia.

"Everything altogether? Probably around fifteen thousand dollars… maybe more," said Matthew.

"Doesn't that seem odd for a man working in a military facility?" said Amelia, unable to overlook the disparity between Thomas' clothing and the various uniforms worn by everyone else.

Matthew looked at her and nodded, but said nothing as Trevor and Thomas approached.

"We're all set," said Thomas amiably, "right this way, Matthew," he added with a sweeping gesture.

"You're with me," Trevor said with a slight smile and a cordial nod in Amelia's direction.

As they walked quietly down the hall Amelia puzzled over what was happening. Trevor's voice had sounded a bit strained, as if she was unhappy about something but was still trying to appear as if nothing was wrong. That in itself wasn't unusual, what bothered Amelia was the feeling that their argument had something to do with her and the test she was about to take.

Amelia tried not to worry as she followed Trevor into a laboratory with thirty foot ceilings, a glass observation booth containing high tech instruments, and what appeared to be a very intricate looking control panel. Outside of the booth in the center of the room was nothing but a large metallic, golden armchair with a square base and no legs sitting flat on the floor. There were footrests for her feet and the seat, back and arms of the chair were padded except for a space where it seemed her hands were meant to rest.

"This is the Montauk Chair," said Trevor, her voice a bit strained. "Have a seat."

Unsure of what was about to happen Amelia's heart beat in anxious anticipation as she tentatively sat down on the chair which turned out to be surprisingly comfortable and cool beneath her touch, its large arms reaching out in front of her.

"Is this chair painted with real gold?" asked Amelia trying to relieve her nervousness.

"No… the chair is made out of gold," said Trevor. "Of course there are many other components, but everything you see is solid gold."

An unidentifiable energy flowed through Amelia's body causing her to feel a bit lightheaded.

Standing next to her, observing her reactions Trevor said, "At the end of the chair arms you'll see indentations for your fingers. Your fingers need to be spread out slightly and held consistently in that position. For this reason I'm going to connect these clamps just above your wrists so you don't accidentally move your arms." Noticing Amelia's discomfort she added, "Don't worry, you won't be trapped… this is for your protection."

"My protection from what?" said Amelia, feeling frightened and confused while keeping her hands in her lap.

"You're here because your test revealed that you have remote viewing capabilities," said Trevor patiently. "We gave you four letters which corresponded to an image that you would not normally recognize or consciously understand. You described it more accurately than our trained viewers," she said with a hint of admiration in her voice. "So we're going to skip some of the initial training, and we're just going to see if we can identify your capabilities.

"The chair will enhance those capabilities and information will come to me directly through your contact with the chair."

"I don't understand," said Amelia, still feeling a bit apprehensive, "how does it work?"

"Well… if you were an aerospace engineer with a background in cognitive neuroscience I could just barely scratch the surface on how the chair works," said Trevor with a smile. "But what I can tell you is that the chair is experiential. So even though you won't understand how it works… you'll have your own experience and then we can talk about it if you have any questions," she said lightly. "Are you ready to get started?"

Amelia nodded. She was still a bit anxious, but now she was also intrigued about what kind of experience she would have.

As she pressed a button the clamps automatically connected securely just above Amelia's wrists. "I'm going to ask you to focus on three different scenarios; one now, one later today, and one tomorrow morning," said Trevor. "But unlike your first test, this will be experiential. It won't appear to be in your imagination in fact it may feel quite real to you. You may feel as if you've actually moved through time and space and it's most likely you'll feel as if you're physically present in each separate scenario.

"If none of that happens, don't worry. I just don't want you to be frightened if you find yourself *someplace else*," said Trevor in finger-quotes. "You'll still be sitting right here, but the technology embedded in this chair will cause you to think differently.

"Now… because we want to see your capabilities, I'm not going to give you any training or explain very much about each scenario. I'll give you only what you absolutely need to know and you must use your own intuition to guide you through the rest. One thing I can tell you is that we want you to report exactly what you see. Don't try to understand what you're seeing because much of it won't make sense.

"Are you feeling relaxed and ready to go?" said Trevor encouragingly.

Amelia shrugged and nodded slightly.

"All right. This test is to find out whether or not you have remote viewing capabilities beyond what you showed us in your first test. As I said, the chair will amplify your abilities and you may actually feel as if you are physically in another place. So don't be frightened. No matter where you seem to be or how real everything appears, you will be unseen and untouchable. Also time will be different. You may feel that you are in a scenario for quite some time, but just like a dream, you'll only be gone for a short period of time. Do you understand?"

Amelia nodded.

"The program will bring you back automatically, but if something goes wrong simply think or say, *Go Back* and you'll find yourself here in the chair." With a nod of encouragement she said, "Okay, I'll be in the booth."

Trevor closed the door, sat down in a chair in front of a panel of lights and then the lights around Amelia dimmed and something about the glass seemed to change because Amelia could no longer see into the booth. At first she felt uncomfortable sitting in the dark, but gradually her eyes adjusted and she realized there was a dim, golden glow emanating from the Montauk Chair.

Amelia thought nothing was happening, but then she saw a slight golden shimmer in the air, and in the next moment it was as if room had been swallowed in darkness and her body was no longer seated in the chair.

CHAPTER 5

Instantly, Amelia became aware of the scent of pine and though she had never smelled this particular fragrance in her current lifetime – she knew she was in a Siberian cedar forest. Her eyes slowly opened to a steel-grey sky marked with the waning light of last night's stars like softly glowing pinpricks in a domed carnival tent.

Cotton-candy clouds, pink in the reflected light of the predawn sun, infused the forest glade with a tender glow. Amelia was lying on a soft, fragrant cushion of pine needles, beneath massive ancient trees that towered over her, but she wasn't alone. All around her young men were sleeping in this woodland world wrapped in capes to ward off the crisp night air.

As she reached up to push her hair away from her eyes she realized her hair was cropped short and she knew she was a woman pretending to be a man. Amelia realized she wasn't just seeing all of this remotely, she was actually there seeing the world through the eyes of her previous avatar, Sasha. Amelia was amazed by the strength and energy in her avatar-body and how alert and quick her mind felt.

As Sasha, Amelia found herself experiencing everything

from emotions to physical sensations exactly as it was playing out for Sasha. And though Amelia was aware of everything happening, she wasn't emotionally involved, it was more like being a silent observer watching events as they occurred.

Sasha heard a whistle. It sounded like the early morning trill of a songbird, but all the men instantly and silently leapt to their feet. In moments horses appeared and stood patiently in front of their riders. Sasha scrambled to her feet as her horse, a sturdy buckskin with a long, black mane and tail appeared before her bobbing its head up and down while eyeing an apple on the ground.

Two swords lay on the ground next to her. Sasha placed the swords in the belt around her waist, one sword on each hip, then held out the apple for her horse. The horse dropped its head to take the apple from her hand and in one fluid motion she swung her leg over the horse's neck – and as it raised its head Sasha slid effortlessly onto its back.

Riding bareback the men and Sasha left the campsite without a word. The majority of the men were in their twenties but a few were in their teens so her lack of facial hair wasn't noticeable. All of the men knew Sasha was a woman and respected her, she was simply hiding this fact because she didn't want to stand out in battle.

For generations the Vedruss had lived in peace, but war had been thrust upon them. Less than a hundred men had spent the night on the outskirts of a small village and though the sun had not yet risen children ran out to greet them with wreaths woven from a variety of fresh herbs.

A little girl running alongside Sasha reached up to hand her a wreath. Sasha smiled warmly and thanked the girl as she slipped the wreath over her forehead in the same fashion as the rest of the soldiers.

A few minutes after leaving the village they came to the edge of a flat rock plateau. Below was a broad expanse with a river running languidly through it. A gentle breeze sprang up out of nowhere blowing the softening night sky into a softer blue. The pink clouds had turned into vanilla cream and hovered high in the firmament reflecting the golden tones of the morning sun shimmering at the edge of the horizon. This time of year the meadows were speckled with colorful fragrant wildflowers, but instead of the wind-swept scent of grass and flowers a sickening burnt odor overwhelmed Sasha's senses.

The soldiers all dismounted and crept to the edge of the precipice then lay on their stomachs to observe the view below. Horror seized Sasha and took her breath away. A deep unimaginable sorrow overwhelmed her as she looked down at a small village freshly torched to the ground with smoke spiraling from ashen heaps that had once been homes and gardens.

Just beyond the wreckage extending as far as the eye could see the landscape was dotted, not with wildflowers, but with tents and battle equipment crushing the delicate beauty of the once pristine land.

Over a thousand horses were in the cavalry and hundreds more were there for pulling the heavy equipment. Campfires were burning and thousands of soldiers were milling about, but they didn't seem to be preparing for battle.

The Vedruss people had no cities, but they had a vast number of settlements that extended throughout what is now known as Russia. Mystical accounts of a lost civilization, a Shangri-la of sorts, referring to the Vedruss' remarkable health and longevity and the extraordinary flavor, size and color of their produce had gained the ear of the Caesar himself.

Hoping to avail himself of this acclaimed fountain of youth and expand his empire in the process, Caesar sent an elite Roman legion of five thousand highly trained warriors to Russia. They set up their camp a mere stone's throw from the first small settlement they came to.

A homing pigeon had delivered the news to Sasha's village -- the Imperial Roman Army had burned down the nearby settlement. The village elder had been locked in a cage and the villagers had been shackled as slaves for their fearless refusal to feed the dark forces of Rome with food from their gardens. Shortly thereafter Roman military runners arrived with a message stating that each village was to send representatives to pay tribute to the most powerful country of all. Those unable to pay would be taken into slavery or die.

On the appointed day when all the elders were expected to gather at the camp the last thing the commander-in-chief expected was ninety young men, including Sasha in disguise, walking into camp at dawn leading their horses. Though they had no armor, helmets or shields it was obvious from the swords at their sides that these men were prepared to fight.

The young warriors all stood quietly in front of a large carpeted podium adorned with red silk fabric trimmed in gold. On the dais stood a throne and a massive metal cage where Rasa, the Vedruss elder, was imprisoned like a giant bird with nothing more than a bowl of water.

Duty-bound, the commander, well dressed but completely disheveled with his black hair at odds with his head, climbed the steps and wearily flopped on the throne with a cluster of red grapes in his hand. One foot was propped on the velvet cushioned pedestal while his other sprawled out as one who had indulged his senses excessively the night before and had no business seeing the sun prior to noon. With a yawn and a loud belch he surveyed the men apathetically.

Much like a fat cat toying with a mouse the commander tossed grape after grape at Rasa through the bars of the cage while indulging in his egocentric discourse. "Rasa, I've ordered the elders of your settlements to pay tribute and hear the decrees of our Emperor. Where are they? And why are these lads here?" he added throwing another grape through bars. "Stand up when I speak to you!" he commanded.

White haired Rasa appeared to be no more than forty, but in fact he was well over one- hundred years old. When he stood up in his cage, he was impressively tall, even amidst the elite warriors standing on the platform. Though pitifully thin, he was nothing like a man starved and mentally beaten into submission: Rasa's blue eyes were blazing and his passion was palpable.

With calm certainty belying the apparent hopelessness of his situation Rasa responded in a surprisingly relaxed manner as if he already knew the outcome. "The elders know what you want. They don't like you and they've decided not to meet someone they don't like. You are here to do battle. These lads look ready to fight." Then looking directly at the young men he added, "Is that so?" The young man leading the group gravely nodded in agreement.

"This is absurd!" bellowed the commander – thinking of what a waste it would be to end up with a bunch of dead bodies instead of slaves for the emperor. "Old man, these lads will listen to you, tell them to surrender now and I'll spare their lives. They will become slaves, but at least they won't die senselessly."

Rasa addressed the men. "As you know, these forces are unequal to your own."

The commander relaxed a bit in the knowledge that Rasa would talk some sense into these impetuous young men and whispered to a guard to prepare for the prisoners.

The elder continued, "My sons, your thoughts move swiftly – I ask that you spare the lives of these men. Do not kill them all. Teach them to put down their weapons and forever turn away from the games of war."

Exasperated, the commander barked, "You have just ordered the death of all these men! I'll give the orders now!"

"It's too late. They understand what I've asked… and they won't kill you."

Before the commander could respond the young warriors leapt onto their horses and galloped at full speed toward the main camp. The commander ordered a detachment of archers to shoot and though they were ill prepared for the moment they finally dispatched a round of arrows. But just as the arrows came within range the warriors jumped off of their horses and ran beside them as the arrows shot past, a hissing blur just above their heads.

As soon as they got close to the Roman troops the Vedruss soldiers split into two groups. One group circled around the troops that had gathered together and the other group, which Sasha was in, began cutting through the troops that were still hastily trying to come together in the midst of unforeseen chaos.

From childhood all Vedruss children played games and created artwork with both hands. They were not only equally adept on both sides of their bodies, but this also developed both hemispheres of the brain equally causing their minds to be lightning fast. There was nothing considered more important in the world of the Vedruss than the ability to accelerate their thinking. They knew that no opponent, no matter how powerful, could outmaneuver one who could think more quickly.

Unlike their Roman counterparts who used ten percent of their mental capacity at best, the Vedruss accessed one hundred percent of their intellectual abilities. In so doing they could send and receive information telepathically: This was as natural to them as it would be for someone to speak their own native language.

To understand the speed of the Vedruss thought imagine a bullet coming toward you. To a slow moving mind the bullet moves with invisible speed. But if your mind moves more quickly than a bullet then from your perspective the bullet would appear to be in slow motion. This is why people often describe an accident as happening in slow motion – their mind has departed the confines of the body and is observing the event from an unencumbered mental perspective; hence, the appearance of the event taking place slowly.

Still running on the ground with a sword in each hand and without armor to slow her down, Sasha was able to disarm or wound her opponents without so much as a scratch on her body. Yet she wasn't a trained warrior. None of them were. But as children they grew up playing sword games followed by the more complex versions they played as adults where they relied on telepathy to outmaneuver their opponents.

While the Romans were hearing words, *your thoughts move swiftly... I ask that you spare the lives of these men,* the Vedruss elder was simultaneously projecting mental images which were seen clearly by all the young warriors. For the warriors it was much like viewing a mind-movie and being shown exactly how the entire battle would play out. Every Vedruss warrior saw himself and the other soldiers in this mental movie and instantly knew exactly what to do.

Even before she began fighting Sasha knew they didn't need to kill anyone. The images in her mind sent by the elder showed disarmed and wounded troops littering the battlefield and subsequently stopping the reserve soldiers from making any headway or taking over for the original troops.

In her mind's eye Sasha saw her group cutting its way back to the tent of the commander-in- chief and taking him hostage. This was exactly what they did. They put a gunnysack over the commander's head, tied it at his waist and threw him over the rump of a horse. In the meantime Sasha released Rasa the elder from his cage and gave him a horse.

Communicating to his troops through mental imagery, the young commander of the Vedruss showed his warriors how they would get the commander out of the camp. Following the projected images they created a protective oval with the commander-in-chief at the center. But rather than return the way they had come they pushed forward until they'd passed through the throng of soldiers. Sasha paid no attention to the fact that she was surrounded by seasoned soldiers twice her size. She focused on each one as if she was playing a game.

In the same way that modern day children and adults play baseball or soccer, Vedruss children and adults played a game with a sword in each hand. The sword tips were dipped in vegetable dye and the point of the game was to tag your opponents with the dye without harming them. The highest points were awarded not for tagging spots that were fatal, such as the heart or throat, but places that were the most difficult to access, such as fingertips or toes. As children they learned to play one-on-one, but as adults they played all at once – sometimes one against many and sometimes in teams.

Having practiced this game her entire life Sasha's mental focus caused her to be flawlessly accurate and utterly unafraid. From the point of view of an observer it would appear that all of the Vedruss had eyes in the back of their heads, but in fact they knew how to go out of body while fighting.

Imagine sitting in a class and listening to a teacher while daydreaming at the same time – it's like being two places at once. In a similar way the Vedruss were fighting while *daydreaming* that they were high above the battleground observing everything that was happening – except in their case they were seeing exactly what was occurring. And they were capable of seeing what was coming as if it was a battle scene playing out in slow motion.

Each one also held the mental image of themselves and all the other Vedruss warriors safely on the other side of the battlefield galloping away. Exactly as they'd envisioned it they all jumped on their horses and galloped to the top of a nearby hill. All of the young warriors, except two watchmen then jumped off their horses and lay in the grass with their arms outstretched falling immediately asleep while their horses grazed nearby.

This may seem like something that could never happen in real life – because most people rarely experience anything in the way they pictured it in their minds – but in fact, this is part of Russian history that has been maintained in such strict secrecy that there are only a handful of people alive who know this is true. The Vedruss practiced a form of white magic that disappeared from the Earth thousands of years ago.

True white magic is harmless – this form of magic cannot be tainted or used selfishly, it simply won't work unless the intention of those performing the magic is for the highest good of all. This is why Rasa the elder said, *'I ask that you spare the lives of these men. Teach them to put down their weapons and forever turn away from the games of war.'*

By asking all of the Vedruss warriors to intend the highest good for all, knowing that the Roman soldiers were simply doing their job and following orders, Rasa was activating ancient white magic, which allowed the direct transmission of assistance from the unseen realms.

But the battle wasn't over yet.

Back in the Roman camp the officers were blaming each other for the colossal fiasco that now ensued. Without their commander-in-chief they argued about who should take charge and what should be done next. At long last after much arguing and deliberation it was decided they would send the majority of their cavalry – nearly a thousand troops – after the Vedruss with a few hundred in reserve following at a distance.

The moment the troops began leaving the camp a Vedruss watchman blew his horn waking the men and Sasha. Now well rested, thanks to the time wasted with all the internal chaos at the Roman camp, they immediately jumped up and began running alongside their horses.

It took some time, but the cavalry gradually began to catch up. When the Romans were nearly upon the Vedruss they sounded their battle horn. The Roman soldiers whipped and spurred their horses—already frothing at the mouth from the strain of the riders and all the armor being carried—into a full gallop. But at the same moment the Vedruss stopped running, jumped on their horses and galloped easily ahead.

The Roman soldiers, fully ignited by their close proximity to the Vedruss, kept whipping their horses onward trying to close the ever expanding gap between them. Finally they slowed down as their commander realized there was now an impossible distance between them.

The Vedruss stopped and gave the Roman commander and Rasa fresh horses. Once again they dismounted and rested while the horses grazed. During this time the Roman cavalry pressed on without a break or water for their horses. At last the Romans spotted the Vedruss not too far ahead. Again their battle horn blasted and the cavalry whipped their horses into a gallop.

Springing into action the Vedruss ran alongside their horses, only jumping on to gallop away when the Romans were a little more than an arrow's shot behind them.

At this point the frothing cavalry horses, beaten to exhaustion, began falling to their knees; some horses fell over dead, pinning their riders underneath them.

At last, the Roman cavalry commander called, *All Rest!*

But it was too late. Horses were lying all over the field, and those that had not succumbed to fatigue were shaking from the energy expended.

The Vedruss warriors suddenly spun around and bore down on the fatigued cavalry. The Roman soldiers had no horses and though they tried to retreat back to the reserve cavalry it was hopeless. Many fell to the ground in exhaustion after a vain attempt to run in their armor. The few that were able to fight were wounded or disarmed by the Vedruss, but the Vedruss didn't touch the soldiers who had fallen.

Finally, seeing all the Vedruss fresh and well rested with a sword in each hand, the Roman cavalry dropped to their knees, placed their swords on the ground in front of them and surrendered.

The Romans anticipated the wrath of the Vedruss, but instead the Vedruss dismounted, removed the wreaths from their heads and applied the grass and herbs to stop the blood flow from the wounded soldiers. Attending to their wounds the Vedruss spoke to the Roman soldiers about a way of life in harmony with man and nature, and without war.

On the battlefield, the commander-in-chief was safely returned to his regiment.

At the same time, Sasha was applying some of the herbs from her wreath to stop the blood flow from a gash on a young Roman soldier's head. Without a word he looked at her as she spoke soothingly to him and dressed his wounds.

He was tall, deeply tanned, and very rugged looking for one who was barely twenty, but his eyes were deep, liquid brown. It seemed to Sasha as if he could see right through her; and she felt strangely weak, though she wasn't tired.

There was a deep familiarity about him which made no sense. Sasha knew she'd never met him before, yet when it was time to move on to the next soldier she felt a gripping feeling in her heart about leaving him, as if she was somehow meant to know him. She hesitated and looked into his eyes searchingly as he returned her gaze.

Finally the Vedruss' horn blew calling all of them together. Sasha gathered with the other Vedruss warriors, but she couldn't help looking back to see the Roman soldier. Much to her surprise he had removed all of his armor and was walking away from the battlefield, following the Vedruss at a distance.

That night as the Vedruss camped out under the stars Sasha wondered about the soldier. She fell asleep staring up at the stars wondering who he was and why he seemed so familiar.

CHAPTER 6

I n the next moment Amelia was aware of herself sitting in the Montauk chair as if she had never left it. According to the clock on the wall only a minute or two had passed, or was it the next day?

"Very good. That's enough for now," said Trevor, her voice impassive, as if she was a school teacher telling the students to put down their pencils at the end of a test. "Before we break for lunch I'd like you to record everything you can remember. Are you feeling a bit dizzy?"

Amelia nodded.

"Don't worry… that's perfectly normal," said Trevor casually. "Just take a few deep breaths, stay where you are and when you're ready just start talking. Everything you say will be recorded and by the time you're done you'll feel back to normal. Later on you can let me know if you have any questions."

Amelia had total recall of everything that had happened to her as Sasha, down to the smallest detail, and though she dutifully recorded her experience she had the feeling in the pit of her stomach to not fully reveal how much she actually knew. Instead, she described her experience as if she was a detached observer doing her best to recall a dream. But a part of her was quite sure she had just re-experienced a game she had once played.

"Okay, that's fine," said Trevor when Amelia told her she couldn't remember anything else. "We'll break for lunch. You'll be eating here on Level 4 with Matthew and we'll resume afterward."

Trevor pushed a button and the clamps around Amelia's arms released. "By the way, you're not to mention anything you see or experience here to anyone else, including Matthew. Understood?"

Still feeling slightly dizzy Amelia stood up carefully as Trevor took her arm and helped her out of the chair. "Yes," said Amelia nodding.

The Level 4 dining hall seemed more like a restaurant than a cafeteria. There were stained glass windows that appeared to be lit by real sunlight. Of course, Amelia knew that was impossible since they were deep underground, but even so, just the idea that it looked like sunshine made her feel a little better.

Waiting at a table, Matthew smiled and waved to Amelia as she walked through the door. She quickly joined him and found a large salad was waiting for her.

"How'd it go?" asked Matthew.

"I can't begin to describe what happened, but even if I could, I'm not allowed to talk about it. Sorry," said Amelia wishing more than anything that she could talk to Matthew and tell him everything.

"What kind of tests are they doing with you?" asked Amelia quietly as she leaned in toward Matthew. "Are you allowed to talk to me?"

"Well, no one said I can't talk," said Matthew in a low voice, "Thomas just sat there talking to me. He asked me questions about quantum physics and then out of nowhere asked if I'd been in an alternate reality or if I'd had a past experience that I couldn't explain."

"Really? That's weird," said Amelia as she took a bite of her salad.

Matthew nodded, "And then he asked if I knew that Earth is actually a virtual reality."

"What did you tell him?" asked Amelia, completely stunned.

"Well, I told him that I was pretty sure that you and I had been in an alternate reality or a different dimension… definitely something we couldn't explain. But here's the strange thing, when I said that I'd *heard* that Earth is a virtual reality, guess what he said?"

Amelia shook her head.

"He said, *'Prove it!'* Not like he didn't believe it. In fact, I think he believes that it's true. I don't know. Maybe he wants me to prove it to myself," said Matthew shaking his head.

"That's crazy! Why would he ask you to explain something that's clearly impossible?" said Amelia, puzzled.

"Well that's just it… I've been thinking about all this stuff and I believe there's more *proof* that this IS a game than there is proving that it's not."

"I don't understand," said Amelia, "how could you possibly prove this is all a game?"

"Well, to explain that I'll have to give you a quick lesson in physics."

"You mean, like, before I've finished my salad?" she said laughing.

"I'm up for the challenge," said Matthew grinning. "Okay… first I have a question for you. Can you tell me what *visually obvious facts* people believed a few hundred years ago that are now known to be untrue?"

"Uh, well, people believed the Earth was flat… and stationary. Oh, and that the earth was the center of the universe with the sun, stars and planets orbiting around it," Amelia added, pleased with herself.

"Right. But even though we know the truth today, isn't it still hard to conceive of the fact that the Earth rotates at 1,000 miles per hour and we're moving through space at 66,000 miles an hour?"

Amelia nodded. She never could remember those statistics and they boggled her mind every time she heard them.

"I'm just pointing out how crazy the world is because you're going to need an open mind for this next part."

Amelia did an informal salute and said, "Okay! Mind open and ready."

Matthew smiled and said, "Everything you see around you seems real and solid, right?"

Amelia nodded.

"But if you go down to the atomic level, the nucleus is the only solid part of the atom. Now get this. If you took all the nuclei of every person on the planet and put them together it's the size of a single grain of rice. And if you put together the nuclei of the entire planet it's about the size of a sugar cube!

"And the distance from the nucleus to the electrons is proportionately the same distance as from Earth to the stars. So everything that seems to be solid is actually 99.999% empty space."

"Wow!" said Amelia, genuinely impressed.

"You're not even finished with your salad yet and it's already starting to sound like a virtual reality right?" said Matthew laughing. "And here's what Einstein said. *Matter is energy whose vibration has been so lowered as to be perceptible to the senses. There is no matter.*"

"Einstein said there is no matter?" said Amelia, finding it difficult to get her head wrapped around the idea.

"Yeah," said Matthew nodding. "But wait, it gets better!" he added, sounding like a salesman on an infomercial. "There was this experiment where scientists set up a camera to observe electrons, and they acted like particles. But when no equipment was used to observe the electrons, they acted like waves and particles simultaneously. And the only logical explanation the scientists could come up with was that the electrons somehow *know* when they're being watched."

"Okay, that's really weird! How is that even possible? It's not like an electron can think. I mean, electrons are just pretty much pure energy, right?" Amelia narrowed her eyes and said, "Oh, I bet I know what's coming," as if Matthew had been pulling her leg.

"Really?"

"Yes!" said Amelia goofing around. "I bet you're going to tell me that not only are electrons smart enough to *know* they're being observed – they even know what you're thinking!"

To her surprise Matthew pondered this for a moment. "Amelia, for someone who has trouble understanding quantum mechanics, that's an excellent point."

"Really? I was just kidding," she said giggling.

"I know," said Matthew nodding vigorously. "But you're right! If electrons have the *intelligence* to know they're being observed – why wouldn't they know what you're thinking? I never thought about it that way. My mind just stopped where the experiment stopped. But what you just said ties in perfectly with what Äsha told us about how our thoughts and feelings create our experiences.

"But here's the thing... I thought she meant that our thoughts and feelings affect how we see things. Like the way people perceive things differently. You know, like a farmer being happy when it rains, while at the same time someone on a picnic is annoyed – same event, different perception.

"But what if that isn't what Äsha was talking about? What if she was talking about cause and effect? Physics has proven that energy has consciousness, and that *that* consciousness is linked to *our* consciousness and then it somehow responds to human intentions."

"Wait a second, you said the electrons responded to intentions. I'm confused," said Amelia, unconsciously chewing on her lower lip.

"Oh, sorry, the intention part came up in a later experiment. You see, once the scientists knew that electrons were simultaneously acting as waves and particles they discovered that whenever the electrons were being observed they would show up according to the intentions of the person setting up the experiment. If the intention of the scientist was to see electrons as particles, the electrons would show up as particles, but if the intention was to see the electrons as waves, they showed up as waves."

"So the electrons do know how to read your mind!" said Amelia amazed. "Do you think maybe the electrons are trying to communicate?"

"I don't know. But here's what I'm thinking, Amelia," said Matthew as if he had just discovered a new planet. "What if thoughts and feelings actually cause energy to slow down to the point that you can instantly see matter – you know, like the things and people you see every day?"

"But what if some energy moves slowly and other energy moves fast and that's just how it's always been?" asked Amelia.

"You've heard of Einstein's theory of relativity... E equals M C squared?" said Matthew.

Amelia nodded.

"Well that equation is saying that when matter moves at the speed of light... squared... it turns into pure energy. So if you think about it, the opposite must also be true. When energy slows down enough it appears as solid matter. And I think that energy has to be... well... not just intelligent, but what if energy is Intelligence itself?"

"You mean like some big, cosmic Universal Intelligence?" asked Amelia incredulously.

Matthew looked at Amelia a bit sheepishly and said with a quirky smile, "That's really weird isn't it?"

"Well it's a lot to get your head around, that's for sure," said Amelia, trying to be supportive.

"I know it sounds totally crazy! But think about it, *'Matter is energy, whose vibration has been so lowered as to be perceptible to the senses.'* But Einstein never tells you what causes the energy to be lowered. What would cause energy to slow down? For there to be an effect there has to be a cause. And remember how

Äsha said that every possibility already exists?"

Amelia nodded, hoping she would be able to keep up with wherever Matthew was headed.

"Well, it doesn't make sense if you're thinking about a game that has to be programmed in advance with every detail down to a grain of sand and you can play the game at any point in time throughout millions or billions of years. But if your thoughts and feelings cause energy to slow down and *show* you a world that matches your own beliefs and perceptions…"

"You mean like The Game's prime directive, Thy will be done."

"Yes. And that's how the game-world could materialize while you're playing The Game! And it's totally customized to you. It's your game," said Matthew with subdued enthusiasm.

"Okay… let me make sure I get what you're saying… so there's this *Universal Intelligence* that's everywhere… connects everything… and IS everything… and because energy responds intelligently to your thoughts and feelings – whatever you believe causes energy to slow down and the effect is that you see what you believe. Is that right?"

"Basically… yes," said Matthew concisely. "Amelia, I think quantum physics has actually tapped into The Game program itself without realizing it. Of course the scientists don't know it because they're all about proof. But really, think of how phenomenal that is!

"It would be like you playing a computer game and then you discover your avatar can drill down through the Earth, right into the level of the program itself. And if you happen to understand programming, you could have your avatar go in and change the program itself – then you could create and play any game you choose."

Slowly Amelia said, "Okay… but how do you know what's real?"

"Remember when you were talking to Äsha about your avatar body and you asked, *'Are you saying I'm not real?'* Do you remember what she said?"

"Yeah," said Amelia, "she said *you are not your body…*"

"Exactly. You are the player, you're not the avatar on the screen. The avatar does what you tell it to. But think about it in terms of The Game. If you are not your body, then your thoughts can't come from your brain."

"But where do my thoughts come from if it's not from my brain?"

"Are you the thought or the thinker?" said Matthew slowly.

"Well, I guess I'm the thinker," said Amelia, feeling a bit lost.

"If you are not your body or your mind then you must be the one who has the body, the one who has the mind. Doesn't that imply consciousness? Remember Äsha telling us that we are born into The Game? If we're not bodies that have learned how to think and be intelligent, there's only one other choice. We would have to be consciousness, thought-force, Universal Intelligence that has created a body."

As if he'd been part of their conversation all along, Thomas walked up to their table and said, "The 99.999% space you mentioned earlier is known as the unified field. Unified means coming together which implies form; field means interest… thought. Unified field, then, is thought taking form and this *thought-form* shows up as your body and the world around you, otherwise known as The Game.

"This so-called *empty space* is actually full of intelligence and because it isn't in a physical form, it's also full of potential." With a smile, Thomas said, "Well done, Matthew." Then looking at Amelia he said congenially, "I'll leave you to finish that salad."

As soon as Thomas was out of earshot Amelia leaned toward Matthew and said, "How did he know what we were talking about?"

Matthew shrugged and shook his head.

"Does he talk like that all the time?"

Matthew whispered, "Well, yes… he's a scientist, but he also says some really bizarre stuff."

"Like what?"

"Well, today we were talking about quantum physics and proving that Earth is a virtual reality and suddenly he was rambling on about diamonds being the hardest substance in the world and perfectly clear, and that if you had a glass wall, ten inches thick, it would have a green tone to it. But if you had a diamond wall ten inches thick, and no light reflecting off of it, it would be completely invisible – and then he said that the program is everywhere, and just like a diamond it's invisible too, so you see right through it."

Amelia laughed, "What does that mean?"

"I have no idea," said Matthew. "He just rambled on saying he knows the secret to how the program works, and that nothing is good or bad from its own side... everything is simply empty."

"Everything is empty? Do you think he's depressed?"

"No. He just talks like that," said Matthew shrugging. "I mean he looks at me as if I'm supposed to understand but I really don't."

Amelia laughed, and then looking past Matthew to the entrance of the restaurant she waved her hand and said, "Trevor's waiting for me... I've gotta go." Amelia stood up and said, "Let me know if you hear anymore Thomas-isms."

"I will," said Matthew laughing. Then taking her hand and pulling her toward him he said, "Maybe we can *vent* tonight and you can talk too."

Amelia smiled and nodded.

Returning with Trevor to the lab, Amelia once again sat in the Montauk Chair. Though it was beyond strange, it was also quite thrilling.

"Can I ask a question?" said Amelia thoughtfully as Trevor pushed the button for the clamps.

"Of course," said Trevor quickly.

"How did I end up viewing that one particular woman, Sasha, at that specific time? I wasn't imaging anything... the chair just seemed to deliver me to that spot."

"The chair has multiple functions," said Trevor, as if she was required to answer Amelia's questions, but had no desire to discuss the matter. "It can function according to your ability to image events or timelines, but it can also be programmed to recognize a specific frequency that you might think of as a specific time, day and place."

"So you chose the place I went to?" said Amelia, trying to come up with the best possible questions so Trevor would continue giving her answers.

"Not exactly," said Trevor. "You have your own frequency and the Chair can search out your frequency at different times in history."

"What do you mean, different times in history?" said Amelia at a loss. "Are you saying you believe in past lifetimes… and that I was seeing myself thousands of years ago?"

Trevor looked at Amelia for a moment as if measuring her capacity for mental comprehension. Then something in her face changed and she said, "Do you know you're playing a game?"

CHAPTER 7

Bewildered, Amelia said, "Um... well... kind of. I mean, I've heard that Earth is a virtual reality, but I don't really understand what that means."

Trevor's face softened as she smiled slightly and said, "Not many people do. Can you get your head around the idea that your body is your avatar?"

"Yes."

"Then do you understand that you are not your body?"

"Yes," said Amelia hesitantly.

"Good. Think of it this way," said Trevor. "You... your unique frequency... can be tuned in to, just like turning a radio dial. I can set the Montauk Chair program to your frequency and then add the date and time... and the chair will locate you."

"So, the woman I saw... Sasha... she was my avatar and that was me playing that game?"

Trevor nodded.

"So where are you sending me this time?" asked Amelia.

"I don't know... I only program in the date and time."

"Well, how do you decide that?" said Amelia curiously.

Trevor paused as if trying to decide if she could divulge

the information. "Thomas decides everything in regard to the Montauk Chair. Now that's all I can tell you," said Trevor with a bit more kindness than usual.

Amelia had a head-full of questions, but she could tell that Trevor wasn't going to say another word. So she sat and waited to see what was next, but this time there was no shimmering golden light or disappearing room.

Her eyes opened. She was sitting on soft grass with morning sunlight sparkling on the pond in front of her. As if she had suddenly awakened from a dream, Amelia couldn't make sense of what she was seeing. Yet somehow she knew she was in her Sasha avatar again, but it was years later because her hair was now down to her waist. As she observed her surroundings Amelia could feel that this was her home in her game-lifetime as Sasha.

On one side of the pond was a forest with majestic cedar, birch, aspen and spruce trees. In another direction wildflowers grew amidst a small vegetable garden with a beehive. In the distance was an orchard with bird cherry and wild apple trees filled with fruit. Just beyond the orchard was a long fence composed of raspberry bushes which surrounded the property. The delicately scented air was fresh and cool.

In the next moment Sasha heard running through the forest. A barefooted five year old boy wearing a light woven tunic and trousers shot out of the woods hotly pursued by a wolf. The boy ran up the side of a tree, pushed himself off with his legs and somersaulted over in a back flip. Landing on his feet he ran off in the opposite direction laughing as the wolf's inertia caused her to continue running past the tree.

Smiling the lad strode up to her and said brightly, "Mama Sasha, I have a present for you!" He dug into his pocket and produced a ripe, red apple which he handed to her.

"Thank you Alexei," said Sasha tousling his curly, strawberry-blond hair as she looked lovingly into his sparkling green eyes.

At the same moment the wolf snuck up and licked Alexei's

hand. Laughing he cuffed her on the neck and shot off in the direction of a huge cedar tree. He ran up the side of the tree and somersaulted as he had before, but this time the wolf knew what to expect. Before he reached the tree she slowed down and then sat on her haunches until he hit the ground, then she licked his arm and took off.

Alexei tried over and over again to outsmart the wolf, but he couldn't. Finally he flopped down next to Sasha utterly frustrated. Kindly, his mother said, "Alexei, first you need to train your thought. You have to think through any moves you're going to make... actually try to feel them before you do them."

"But I've already done that Mama," said Alexei hopelessly.

"Well, sweetheart," replied his mother, "it's not just your thought – you have to take into consideration what the wolf is thinking. See it in your mind and then act accordingly."

First Alexei tried running twice as fast, but the wolf was quicker and no matter what Alexei did the wolf knew the trick and could anticipate what was to come.

Finally he walked up to his mother, looked her in the eye and said imploringly, "Can you give me a hint?"

"Before you can even ask a question, the answer must already exist."

Alexei kept staring at her. "In order for you to ask the question... *What is two plus two?* ...the answer four already exists. If you think there's no answer to your problem then you can't find the answer. But if you realize that an answer already exists and if you'll think more quickly... you'll discover you can think faster than the wolf. And when you do she won't be able to catch you."

Suddenly Alexei's face lit up. He dashed headlong toward the tree with the wolf only a few feet behind him. As he approached the tree the wolf slowed down to wait for him to leap into the air and somersault off the tree. Alexei did leap into the air, but this time his body passed within an inch of the trunk and he kept running while the bewildered wolf sat wondering where Alexei had gone.

Alexei came back glowing. "I got it! I thought quickly for myself, but I had to think more quickly than the wolf could think for herself – and then I put it all together at just the right time! The wolf will never be faster than me again!" He then took off and performed a whole series of tricks. The wolf was completely unable to catch him.

Finally Alexei sat next to his mother and said confidentially, "I know you have a secret – will you tell me now?"

Sasha laughed and looked proudly at her son. "Yes."

"Today's the day isn't it?" he added enigmatically.

"Yes it is my darling," said Sasha warmly. "Come lie next to me and we shall go together as our second-selves."

Lying in the fragrant grass they held hands and Sasha felt the warm sensation of leaving her body, but there was no sense of movement, she was instantly standing with her son in a place she remembered well. They were on the very same cliff where she first saw the Imperial Roman Army and the Romans had returned – this time there were at least ten thousand troops spread across the valley as far as the eye could see.

"They look like ants," said Alexei lightly. "Is this the same army the Vedruss warriors fought?"

"Not exactly," said his mother. "They are from Rome, but these are different men."

"How do you know some of them aren't the same?" Alexei asked curiously.

"That is an excellent question, Alexei," said Sasha smiling as she looked deeply into her son's eyes. "Well, after the battle we formed a group... there are several of us who now keep track of what's going on in Rome."

"Is it dangerous?" asked Alexei wide-eyed.

"No sweetheart," said Sasha comfortingly, "it's not dangerous at all. We never leave the forest, we go to Rome as our second-selves so we're invisible to the Romans, but we have access to everything from conversations to secret communications."

"So how do you know that none of the soldiers down there were here before?"

"When the army left after the battle we took turns tracking the commander until he led us back to Rome. We listened to everything he told Caesar. Not one man was willing to go to war... even the commander himself refused to ever fight again.

"When the commander left, Caesar ordered every man in the battalion to be sent to a different part of the empire and each soldier was ordered to never speak of what happened or else they would be killed.

"For generations a diary had been passed down from one Caesar to the next. I saw it myself. In the diary he warned the future Caesars to leave the Vedruss alone. But when Caesar died his successor saw him as a coward and decided to try again – but to be on the safe side he doubled the size of his army."

"So you knew they were coming?" said Alexei wide-eyed.

"Yes we've known for quite some time," said his mother warmly. "It takes a long time for an army to get here."

"So what are we going to do?" said Alexei enthusiastically. "Are the Vedruss warriors riding into battle again? Can I watch?" he added hopefully.

"No, something much better than that," whispered Sasha secretively. "It's just going to be you and me."

"Really!" said Alexei hugging his mother. "So what's the plan?"

"I'm going to pretend to be your big sister," said Sasha, as if she was unwrapping a gigantic present for him, "and we're going to deliver a message to the commander-in-chief of the army."

Alexei lit up as if every wish he'd ever dreamed of had come true in that moment, "Mamochka, people always think you're my sister!" he squealed, jumping up and down in delight.

"I know," said his mother smiling, "that's what made me

think of it."

"What about Papa? Will he be back in time to join us?" asked Alexei hopefully.

"No darling, your papa has been talking to many people… and those people have been helping us spread a special message to all of the Vedruss settlements."

"I bet Papa will be disappointed that he can't join us," said Alexei glumly.

"But think how proud he'll be of you," said Sasha smiling brightly at her son.

Alexei beamed as he thought of his father and said, "When do we go?"

"Let's get our ponies and go now," said his mother.

In the next moment they were back in their bodies. Alexei whistled loudly, two distinctly different sounds. In moments a pony and a small horse came galloping down a path from a meadow bordering the forest. Each pony had a slender rope at the base of its neck, just above their withers. They stood attentively waiting, but still managed to playfully nip each other like a couple of squabbling children whenever possible.

Whistling to his pony, a plump, dappled-grey mare appeared beneath a tree swishing her tail as Alexei swung down from a branch and landed squarely on her back. Sasha jumped nimbly onto her own steed, a bay pony almost as tall as a horse with a broad chest and rump, and round belly.

Except for the fact that her hair was now long and in braids Sasha could easily have passed for a young boy as she did several years earlier. Imitating the dress of Vedruss children she wore a simple knee length tunic belted at the waist and she had woven flowers into her braided hair. Sasha was so petite and small breasted she appeared to be no more than eleven or twelve years old – riding a large pony added to the illusion.

In a satchel that lay across her pony's withers Sasha had packed water, fruit, and a small bottle of oil that had been pressed from pine nuts and herbal flowers. Using nothing more than the string around their pony's necks, Sasha and Alexei rode quietly through the forest until they were just above the Roman camp, but still hidden by dense undergrowth.

They left their ponies and set off at a quick pace on a trail leading downhill to the edge of the meadow, now buried beneath Roman soldiers and equipment. As they walked Sasha spoke quietly to Alexei. "All you have to do is keep saying that we're here because our parents are busy at a festival… so we're here with a message for the commander. If anyone tries to talk to me, and I have to respond, start arguing with me. Keep saying that you're the one who's supposed to deliver the message. The less I talk the better," his mother added with an inscrutable smile. "The Romans won't expect us to know their language…"

"But Mama, we can speak and understand any language… can't they?"

"No darling."

"You mean their parents only speak to them in one language… they don't grow up speaking in all different languages the way that we do?"

"Well, most people only speak the language of their own country and that's why they would never think that we would know a language other than our own. We will understand everything they say, but they'll assume we know nothing. So don't use too many of their words.

"But when we talk to the commander, here's what you'll say. *'Our parents are too busy to come. But they want you to know there's a storm coming and you need to go and never come back.'* Can you remember that?"

Alexei nodded his head vigorously, barely able to contain his enthusiasm for getting to play such a fun game.

Before they reached the meadow a Roman soldier stepped out from behind a tree with his sword drawn yelling, "Halt!" Seeing they were only children he motioned for them to go back up the path.

Instead of obeying Alexei yelled loudly, "Message for commander… We…" he added putting his palm to his chest, "have message. Commander. Message!"

Alexei played his part with such conviction the soldier finally took them into the camp. Sasha held Alexei's hand and just like siblings they jostled and pushed at each other, a pinch here an elbow there. They made faces at each other and when one would get ahead the other would try to take the lead without getting into trouble with the guard.

One part of her was playing with her son while holding an image of herself as eleven years old. Another part of Sasha, her second-self, was floating above the Roman camp taking in everything that was being said, done or thought.

Sasha knew she was being perceived as a young girl by the soldiers who saw her; she could easily read their minds. She also saw a dark cloud looming in the distance. In her mind Sasha focused on the cloud then imaged it right above the camp, beckoning for it to come closer.

Though there wasn't even a hint of a breeze the cloud formation began to move. If any of the soldiers had been looking up at the sky they might have wondered why the massive cloud was so dark amidst such a clear blue sky.

Finally they reached the platform outside the commander's tent. From within they heard the commander bellowing, "What is it now? I sent out orders for the elders to pay tribute! You're telling me they sent a couple of CHILDREN?"

Standing massive in the doorway of the tent, looming menacingly above Sasha and Alexei, a tall, cloaked man with a stern, ominous face surveyed the children sphinx-like from beneath dark, jutting brows. Bright sunlight glinted harshly on his hawk-nosed face as he hissed to a soldier, "When they've delivered their message we'll take them as slaves."

Then with an angry sweep of his arm he seized his cloak and swung it dramatically round as he strode menacingly up to the children. With a haughty smirk he said scornfully, "Your parents were supposed to come and pay tribute. Tell me little girl why have they sent two children?"

Sasha stood with her head down and peered up at the man

as if she was extremely shy. "Our parents are busy…"

"Wait! Wait!" yelled Alexei, "I'm supposed to give the message. It's my turn! You got to give the message last time!" Back and forth they squabbled as ominous, roiling black clouds drew closer and closer.

"STOP!" bellowed the commander.

Alexei looked questioningly at his mother as she gave him a slight nod.

"Our parents are too busy to come…" he said decisively. "They're at a festival. But they want you to know there's a storm coming and you need to go and never come back again."

In that moment several things happened. Sasha pulled the bottle of oil out of her pocket and poured it on Alexei's head and her own head. The repulsive odor was so repugnant the commander and the guards surrounding them took an involuntary step backwards. The black cloud formation was now hovering directly over the camp blocking the sun causing everything to darken as a deep disturbing hum vibrated through the camp.

Suddenly screaming and yelling could be heard throughout the camp as the commander and soldiers were attacked by millions of bees as they descended upon every person and creature in the area. Soldiers tried to tear off their armor as horses bucked and reared, pulling out the stakes they were tethered to and galloping away unencumbered by armor or riders.

In the ensuing pandemonium Sasha held Alexei's hand and they slipped away unnoticed. Despite the wild chaos in the camp Alexei's piercing whistle caught the ponies' attention. Galloping down the path, across the meadow and into a safe pocket around Sasha and Alexei created by the stench of the oil that they had now wiped onto their arms and legs, the ponies skidded to a halt. Sasha helped Alexei onto his pony and then jumped onto her own. No one tried to stop them as they galloped through the camp and into the woods. Finally, they reached the cliff and could see the valley below.

Alexei surveyed the frenzied chaos at the Roman camp and said grimly, "Now they look like mad ants."

"Yes they do!" Sasha agreed, looking at her son proudly.

"I bet that Caesar person will think twice before sending his soldiers back here again!"

"I'll bet you're right," said Sasha smiling broadly, ruffling her son's hair.

That night as a full moon rose above the tree tops and shimmered over their pond, a tired, but ecstatically happy Alexei fell comfortably asleep in his mother's welcoming arms as she sang him a lullaby. Just moments later a horse and rider emerged from the dappled moonlight on the forest path and into clear view. A tall, handsome, powerful looking man dismounted and embraced his wife while kissing their sleeping son on his head.

No words were necessary. As his second-self he had seen everything that had happened that day, and from this perspective there were thousands of invisible Vedruss who had communicated their desires to their bees. Though the Vedruss as their second-selves were invisible to the Romans, the bees saw them clearly and each hive followed its master, in some cases for many, many miles, until they converged at the outskirts of the camp and created a massive *cloud*. Then all the Vedruss combined their thoughts with Sasha's image of the bees hovering over the camp and the cloud moved accordingly. Though the Romans never saw them, the Vedruss were prepared to show up in physical form if anything had gone wrong on the battlefield or if Sasha and Alexei had been taken captive.

Alexei's proud father laid the sleeping boy on his chest and wrapped his arm around Sasha, kissing her tenderly as nature sang its nighttime lullabies and moonlight sparkled diamonds on the dew-tipped grass.

CHAPTER 8

Amelia found herself back in the Chair, feeling torn between two worlds. She dutifully recorded what happened, but once again she felt frightened and told the story as if it was no more than a hazy memory.

On her way to dinner Amelia thought about the fact that the Roman army had been defeated by the Vedruss – not once, but twice – and yet these events had never been recorded. She knew that her lifetime as Sasha took place in Russia during the time of the Roman Empire, but she'd never read anything about the Vedruss or even the Russian people that far back in history; which seemed odd given that there was historical information about every other culture.

How could an entire race be wiped clean from history as if they'd never existed? And who in the world was powerful enough to rewrite history and make an entire culture vanish into thin air?

At dinner she sat quietly listening to Matthew. On one hand she was dying to talk to him, but on the other she felt relieved she didn't have to explain anything or try to make sense of what was happening to her.

When they returned to the ward, Amelia felt relieved

instead of imprisoned when it was time for bed. She had been waiting all day long to just be alone with her thoughts and feelings – even if it was confusing, at least she didn't have to make sense of anything or try to put her thoughts and feelings into words.

She was about to take off her cargo pants when she remembered the object Admiral Byrdie had given her. Inconspicuously she touched it in her pocket, but she was afraid to look at it since she was under constant surveillance. She thought of climbing under her bed, but then it would look even more suspicious if she did so a second time to talk to Matthew. So she decided to wait until he got back from his shower and in the meantime she flopped down on top of her bed.

Despite everything, Amelia suddenly felt more relaxed than she had in days. As she took a deep breath and closed her eyes images of her life as a Vedruss dominated her thoughts and she imagined herself floating naked in her pond looking dreamily up at the sky. And then she was there.

At first she thought she was having a lucid dream, but as she looked around she knew she was somehow visiting her Russian home, and not as a remote viewer. She was feeling the delicious contrast of the cool water below and the warmth of the sun on her skin from above. And this was happening without the Montauk Chair or programming or anything else.

Amelia wondered if she was teleporting or if she had somehow managed to be two places at once. As she floated in the pond a voice drifted through her mind saying, "Imagination is everything."

Before she knew it bright lights were shining in her eyes and she was waking up in her room the next morning. She had perfect clarity. It wasn't a dream, but how had it been possible without the Chair? Was her avatar body capable of finding her frequency and then taking her to a past-game location on its own? Could avatars actually have that level of programming?

And then she remembered the strange message.

"Imagination is everything." What did that mean?

Suddenly she realized she had missed out on talking to Matthew through the vent. At first she wanted to rush to breakfast and apologize to him, but she desperately needed to wash her hair, among other things, so she skipped breakfast and hurried into the shower room. The apology would wait and this would give her more time to think.

Amelia carefully hung her pants inside the shower and then hung her towel on top, just to be on the safe side. She considered pulling the object out of her pocket and getting a good look at it, but then it occurred to her that there could be a hidden camera. The thought was unsettling, but the shower was hot and she decided it was too late to worry about whether or not someone was watching her naked body.

Even though she skipped breakfast, Amelia still had to hurry to meet Matthew and Trevor on time. Matthew shot her a questioning look and she whispered in his ear, "I'll tell you later," as they started walking with Trevor down the hall.

Silently they walked down the hall together and when they arrived at Thomas' office Trevor knocked on the door.

"Enter!" a voice boomed.

"Wait here," she said as she opened the door, stepped inside and closed the door quietly.

"Sir…" Trevor said immediately, "we can't put Amelia in the Chair again. She is too powerful and undisciplined."

"Yes, I know," said Thomas impatiently. "She's very impressive. She's exactly what I'm looking for."

"She has to be trained," said Trevor with conviction.

"Just give her some direction… she'll be careful if she knows it's her own life on the line," said Thomas dismissively.

"I'm not talking about what she would do consciously. It's what she might do without realizing it. She's too sensitive," said Trevor fervently.

"Nonsense! Look at what she's done with no training at all. She's the first person to go into another dimension and return to this dimension with her memory fully intact. I need to see what else she's capable of," said Thomas impatiently.

"Sir, I'm afraid this girl may pick up information from the Chair itself. Even though you've rebuilt and re-engineered the Chair, *things happened,*" Trevor said emphatically, "and what if she picks up on that without realizing what she's doing?"

"No! She needs to be in that chair TODAY!" said Thomas loudly. Then lowering his voice he added, "Trevor, please sit down a moment, we need to talk."

Trevor sat stiffly in a chair facing Thomas.

"We're out of time," said Thomas. "We've hit a layer of molten rock and now we're forced to use the Tesla device."

"Are you serious? That thing nearly flattened an entire block in Manhattan," said Trevor horrified.

"Yes, and no," said Thomas calmly. "We've been using that device, but we also discovered plans for something much more powerful."

Trevor sat back in her chair and narrowed her eyes, "After the New York *incident,* Tesla told reporters that he had the technology which could… and I quote, *'split the Earth in two.'* Please tell me you're not dabbling with this."

"Well, maybe it could split the Earth in two, but we know how to control the device," said Thomas as if this was child's play and he already had everything under control.

"Really?" said Trevor unbelieving. "You do know that Tesla had to shatter his first device with a sledge hammer to *turn it off.*"

"Trevor, it doesn't matter," said Thomas irritably, "we've got it under control. We're making our way through the molten layer, but we need to be sure the cavern exists at the exact coordinates. Remote viewers have seen it, but I need boots on the ground."

"Sir, we're not at war down there."

"Not yet."

"What do you mean by that?"

"It's classified."

"Can you tell me why this cavern is so important?"

"The cavern is connected to a tunnel system that's vital to the work we're doing."

"Then why send a teenage girl?"

"Because she's the only one who's ever managed to travel between dimensions with her mind intact."

Trevor sighed and said nervously, "Can I at least tell her what's happened in the past?"

"Absolutely not!" Thomas roared. "The last thing you want to do is plant some fearful image into her mind. Especially of something you do NOT want her unconsciously materializing into this reality," said Thomas vehemently as he stood up.

"Nevermind, I'll do it myself," Thomas added as he strode to the door with Trevor hurrying to catch up.

But the stormy look on his face transformed instantly as he opened the door for Trevor and stepped out with her into the hallway. Looking directly at Amelia, Thomas smiled charismatically and said, "I'll be working with you this afternoon."

Then looking at Matthew he said evenly, "Trevor will be escorting you to your testing area today on Level 5. And this will be the last day of testing for both of you. Tonight you'll receive your aptitude scores and then decide where you'd prefer to work."

Although Trevor was trying to hide her discomfort, Amelia knew something unexpected had just occurred. She seemed anxious when Thomas announced he'd be testing Amelia, but she was even more upset when he told her to escort Matthew to his testing area. The moment he said Level 5, it seemed as if Thomas had delivered a coded message and Trevor was unhappy about the direction she was supposed to take.

However, she was disciplined and said briskly, "This way, Matthew," as she walked swiftly down the hall.

Walking to the lab with Thomas, Amelia said bluntly, "Are you going to try to make me be a remote viewer?"

"Of course not, Amelia," said Thomas warmly, as if he was her best friend. "Aptitude tests show us how high you can go at this moment in time, but if you want to wash dishes, or work in the commissary, or change bed pans in the hospital, that's totally up to you."

Amelia knew she should feel relieved, but she still didn't trust him. Her mind tried to convince her that she was just upset about other things and that she had no reason to distrust Thomas. He had always been kind and polite. He was probably the reason that they were all taken in to the base and saved from whatever was going on with the terrorist attacks. She knew it was just a feeling, it wasn't logical. But the feeling suddenly reminded her of Äsha talking about the program switching on and off. It was that unsafe feeling she felt when she and Matthew were hiking and they needed to turn back. But under the circumstances there was no turning back and nothing she could she say or do.

Thomas pushed open the door to the lab and held it for Amelia as she stepped inside.

"Amelia, please have a seat," said Thomas, casually indicating the Montauk Chair. "I'm going to be very honest. You are an extraordinary young lady. For years I've been trying to find someone who could physically enter another dimension – that's what happens when you travel through time and space, you move out of your own dimension and into another.

"Only one other person has managed to go into another dimension and return, but he had no memory of where he had been. Others have gone, but haven't returned. And we don't know why. We don't know if they lose their memory going between dimensions or if something happens and they're killed. But regardless of the reason, no one has ever returned.

"Though we didn't intend for you to physically go into another dimension, you've done it twice and you returned with your memory fully intact. I've been waiting for you Amelia, for over twenty years!" said Thomas encouragingly.

Amelia was grateful this was her last test and she was already making plans to do anything other than remote viewing, or whatever it was that she was actually doing. Washing dishes was starting to sound like a much better option, at least it would be calm and her heart wouldn't be in her throat.

"This is the final test you're required to complete. You'll be perfectly safe, you won't be going anywhere, but there are a few things you need to know. It's imperative that you do not allow your mind to wander. I know things can pop into your head, but do not focus on anything except what I'm telling you.

"This test is in two parts. First, I'm going to tell you to imagine something. I want to see how easily your thoughts can materialize things. I know you can unconsciously create," Thomas said smiling, "but can you consciously create?

"The second part of your test will not require your imagination. I have the Chair programmed to create an image in your mind so you won't be going anywhere with your physical body. You'll be right here in this room, perfectly safe and protected. I simply want you to tell me what you experience. I promise you'll be in that chair the entire time."

"And do you promise, this is the last time I have to do this?" Amelia asked cautiously.

"I promise. Scout's honor," said Thomas smoothly as he walked into the observation booth and firmly closed the door.

As he dimmed the lights Thomas spoke gently over the intercom, "Empty your mind and imagine a rose."

Amelia took a deep breath, closed her eyes and imagined a pink rose.

"Open your eyes."

Amelia opened her eyes and there on her lap was a pink rose, exactly as she had imagined it, slightly between a bud and a fully opened rose. Blinking, and filled with astonishment, she grinned at Thomas. He smiled broadly and nodded encouragingly.

"Now hold out your hand and imagine an apple," he said.

Amelia held out her hand, closed her eyes and began imagining an apple. At first she thought of a red apple, but then changed her mind and thought of a green Granny Smith apple instead. Instantly she felt an apple in her hand. When she opened her eyes it was half red delicious and half green Granny Smith. Amelia burst out laughing and looked up to see that Thomas was equally amused. She then bit into the apple on each side. It tasted exactly as she had imagined.

"Wonderful, Amelia!" said Thomas enthusiastically. "Now, this is the final part of your test. I've programmed the chair to show you someplace unfamiliar. It isn't in another time or a different dimension, so you have nothing to fear. You just need to relax, you won't feel any discomfort."

Amelia suddenly felt raw terror gripping her heart and throat. Her eyes flashed open and she realized she did have a choice.

She jumped up from the Chair and yelled, "No! I'm not doing this! You don't know what can happen! I know you don't! I'd rather wash dishes and change bedpans!"

Amelia ran to the lab doors and flung them open, only to find armed guards barring her way. She whirled around to face Thomas, who was now striding across the floor like an extremely displeased parent.

"Before you decide to leave there's something you need to see," said Thomas sternly as he shut and locked the doors.

He tried to take Amelia's arm, but she pulled away. "Don't touch me!" she hissed. "You said I'd have a choice!"

"And you do. You just need all of the facts before you decide. Come with me," he added as he guided her into the observation room.

On the wall above the control panel was a video of Matthew, unconscious in a hospital bed with a ventilator, a breathing tube and a central venous line.

"Many lives will be saved or lost depending on whether or not you cooperate," said Thomas sternly.

"What have you done to him?" Amelia screamed.

"I didn't want it to come to this, Amelia," said Thomas unsympathetically, "but this is important. What I'm asking you to do is vital to national security and maybe even to the survival of humanity."

"WHAT… DID… YOU… DO… TO…HIM?" yelled Amelia, furiously.

"He's in a medically induced coma. He'll be fine if you cooperate," said Thomas succinctly. "Now, I will admit I haven't been totally honest with you. The Chair *is* programmed to take you someplace. I didn't tell you because I didn't want you to be frightened. The Chair responds to your feelings, so it's important that you relax. I promise you'll be perfectly safe when you arrive, but you do need to return as soon as possible. Just say, '*Go back*,' as usual."

Amelia stood glaring at him furiously.

"My dear, there are always difficulties for medical coma patients waking up after three days. The longer he's in this coma the more he'll become addicted to the morphine and other drugs going into his system. Now, you need to sit down in the Chair and cooperate," he said as if she were a child and he was putting her in time-out.

Livid, Amelia flew out the door of the observation room and sat down in the Chair. She heard the booth door shut and then watched angrily as Thomas fiddled around with settings on the control panel. As Amelia sat fuming, angrier than she had ever been in her entire life, she closed her eyes, clenched her fists and suddenly saw an image in her mind of an immense, hairy beast, at least fifteen feet tall with razor sharp teeth. She imagined it rampaging through the lab tearing everything to shreds, ripping Thomas and the soldiers from limb to limb. It was the most horrifying thing she had ever imagined and yet it gave her a sense of immense satisfaction at the same time. She smiled at the thought.

But her amusement was short-lived as she became aware of an ungodly stench. Opening her eyes Amelia saw an enormous creature, fifteen feet tall bent down and leaning in toward her, its eyes burning and its mouth wide open, ready to sever her head from her body. Petrified, unable to breathe, Amelia sat perfectly still, looking helplessly towards Thomas as he pressed a button.

Instantly she felt as if she was about to start dreaming. It was that feeling of being between two realities, aware of both her waking reality and passing into the dream state, yet not fully in one place or the other. She knew the creature was there, but her senses couldn't detect it. Everything was suddenly still and silent, as if the creature had moved on into the next moment in time without her.

Infuriated, the monster wildly grasped at the empty air where Amelia's body had been and then tore apart the chair, ripping the wiring to shreds.

But Amelia saw nothing. She was no longer in the Montauk Chair.

CHAPTER 9

A melia suddenly found herself in complete and total darkness, nauseous from the adrenaline pumping through her body. The deafening silence was only broken by her rapid breathing and the roaring beat of her heart. Desperately and cautiously she felt the ground around and beneath her. It felt smooth and cool, definitely some kind of natural rock surface.

"Is anyone here?" she screamed, dizzy and disoriented.

"Is anyone here? Is anyone here? Is anyone here? Is anyone here? Is anyone here?" the cavern echoed back.

From the continuous echoes she knew she was in an immense space, and yet it felt as if the walls were collapsing in around her.

"HELLO!" she screamed.

Nothing.

A spasm of terror tightened in her chest as an intense jolt of panic sent shockwaves through her body. Shaking in fear, Amelia's brain screamed for her to run, but there was nothing she could do. She couldn't even imagine where she was or why she had been sent here. There was no air movement and not a single sound. No water dripping. No insects or flutter of bat wings. Nothing. Only the sound of her frantically beating heart.

"Go Back!" she yelled.

But she wasn't surprised when nothing happened. She didn't know exactly what had happened in the lab, but she knew that she wasn't going back the way she came.

"Hello!" she yelled again as tears flooded her eyes and a sick, anxious feeling churned inside.

No one was coming for her and there was no way back.

"I'm here," whispered a familiar child's voice out of the darkness.

"Äsha?" said Amelia, bursting into tears of relief. "Is that you?"

"Yes, it's me," said Äsha gently touching Amelia's arm.

Amelia grasped her hand, "Thank you, thank you for coming to get me!" Then she reached out, fumbling a bit in the dark as she hugged Äsha. "I'm so sorry I didn't listen to you when you told me to stay and learn how to navigate The Game. I've messed up everything," she sobbed miserably.

"It's all right," said Äsha soothingly, "it's not too late, but we need to hurry. You can't go back the way you came and we have a long way to go before we can get out of here. Hold my hand, I'll lead you."

"How did you find me?" said Amelia relaxing a little.

Äsha giggled, "I'm tuned into you like a radio station. Most of the time I don't intervene, because it's your game... but you and I had a prior agreement..."

"Prior... you mean, like, before I was born?" said Amelia, still trying to get her head around the concept.

"Yes. We agreed that I would only intervene if you would certainly die without me." Then with a laugh Äsha added, "But anything short of certain death, at least from the perspective of The Game, and you're on your own."

"Well, that's strangely... comforting... I guess," said Amelia tentatively. "How can you see in the dark?"

"Well, most humans don't know this, but your entire body is capable of seeing... it's just that you've only developed your eyes. The energy of light is a form of communication that you understand. But the energy of darkness also communicates, and I perceive darkness just as easily as you understand light.

"But it's not as dark in here as you think!" said Äsha encouragingly. She stopped for a moment, let go of Amelia's hand and then put her hand on Amelia's shoulder to steady her in the dark.

"Try closing your eyes and cover them with your hands," she said. "Wait about twenty seconds and then open your eyes with your hands stretched out in front of you, fingers spread."

Amelia followed Äsha's directions and saw the darkness created by her fingers with a faint grey hue outlining each finger.

"I see it!" Amelia said excitedly, "But where are we?"

"We're deep inside Earth's crust," said Äsha matter-of-factly.

"But then where's the light coming from?" asked Amelia as Äsha led the way along a descending pathway. "Is it shining in through a cave entrance somewhere?"

"No. We're nowhere near a cave entrance," said Äsha, "in fact, we're miles below the deepest part of the ocean."

"But then why is the temperature so comfortable?" said Amelia thoughtfully. "I thought it would be really hot miles underground."

"We're deeper underground than humans on the surface have ever experienced, and this is what the temperature is here – it's very mild," said Äsha. "Right now, we're heading into a zone of light that shines through the crust. The deeper we go the lighter it will become."

"But how will we get out if we're going deeper?" asked Amelia, puzzled.

"Don't worry, there's a way out," said Äsha confidently.

"Can we go any faster?" said Amelia desperate to get back to Matthew. "I mean, how did you get to me so quickly?"

"I thought of you… and my body followed," said Äsha, as if this type of thing happened every day. "It's sort of like the Montauk Chair, but I don't need anything mechanical. I know this may sound hard to believe, but every human being is capable of traveling through time and space, and even into parallel worlds or alternate realities with nothing more than their imagination and will."

"You mean traveling in our minds… like an imaginative thing?" said Amelia confused.

"No. I mean your avatar-body is capable of going anywhere in the universe by means of teleportation. That's how I came to you. It's like Think-and-Go," Äsha said laughing. "You can even bi-locate, which means your physical body can be in two places at once."

"How do I do that… I mean, teleportation?" said Amelia.

"Well, every human avatar-body possesses these abilities… in potential. Think of the way an acorn has the potential to become a mighty oak tree. But before that can happen, the acorn has to be planted in fertile soil, and then receive enough water and sunlight to sprout and grow.

"It's the same for you, but in your case the fertile soil is your consciousness – your thoughts and feelings… especially your feelings. The more powerfully you feel something the more you'll see it in your experience."

"I still don't understand that," said Amelia frankly. "I mean, I believe what you said. I've heard of yogis in India teleporting, so that must mean I have the potential to do it too, but that doesn't mean I can just make it happen."

"Well it all has to do with what you believe in the most," said Äsha. "Think of what you really, really believe – without doubt. For instance, think of some things that anyone in the world might believe in?"

"I don't know…" said Amelia thoughtfully, "um… God… gravity… myself… night and day."

"Perfect!" said Äsha, "Now I'm going to tell you something you believe in more than any of those things."

"Really?" said Amelia taken aback.

"Yes!" said Äsha confidently. "Imagine you're walking

down a narrow path in the woods and you come face to face with a grizzly bear. I can promise you would believe in that grizzly bear more than you ever believed in God or gravity or yourself or anything else!"

"Oh, well that's true!" exclaimed Amelia laughing.

"You see the things you believe in more than anything else, are the things that you fear. If you believed you could teleport as strongly as you would believe in that grizzly bear, you could go anywhere in the universe instantly!"

"But how do I stop being afraid?" said Amelia hopelessly. "I'm afraid to be here and I'm afraid to go back. I'm afraid that if I manage to get back it won't matter because there's nothing I can do. It's a military installation for God's sake! I have no power. I can't change anything, but I can't just leave Matthew there to suffer... or die."

"Okay, sit down for a minute," said Äsha sympathetically.

"Alright," said Amelia, grateful to rest.

"Now close your eyes and feel how powerless you are."

"It's so dark I don't even have to close my eyes," said Amelia glumly. "And I don't have to try to feel powerless, I am powerless."

"I understand," said Äsha kindly. "Now, I'm going to show you how to navigate the program more effectively. Wait. Let me put it this way... you're always effective. You've mastered the ability to get the things you *do* want... and the things you *don't* want. But I'm going to show you how to get more of the things you do want.

"This will work with any feelings – anger, resentment, fear... it doesn't matter. But for now think about feeling powerless."

"Well that's easy enough," sighed Amelia, sure that she was doomed to failure.

"When you think about being powerless, where do you feel it in your body?" asked Äsha.

Amelia put her hand on her chest and said, "Right here in my heart."

"Okay, now drop the label – the word, powerless… and just feel the physical feeling in your chest. Can you feel that it's just energy?" said Äsha.

"Yes."

"Now breathe," said Äsha slowly. "Take your time and imagine breathing right into that place in your body."

Amelia took a few deep breaths. With each breath she felt the energy slowly breaking up. It took a few minutes, but gradually the feeling became weaker and weaker until it completely disappeared.

"How is this possible?" said Amelia mystified. "I don't feel that tightness anymore. I mean, it's weird, but I actually feel okay."

"Think of animals in nature. When they're afraid they respond with 'freeze; fight or flight' but in a few minutes they shake it off and go on with their day. Humans are just the opposite… they hoard their fear – they hold it inside and sometimes hang onto it their entire lives. Of course, there's nothing wrong with holding on to fear – it's your game, you can do whatever you want, but keep in mind that your beliefs determine your experiences."

"That seems way too simple," said Amelia shaking her head.

"Well, it is simple, but it's not easy," said Äsha simply. "You have to be willing to give up believing in things that frighten you."

"I can do that," said Amelia, standing up and dusting herself off.

"Do you think you could do it if there was a snake in front of you right now?" said Äsha.

"Oh my God!" said Amelia fearfully grasping Äsha's arm so tightly the little girl yelped.

"I'm sorry! I'm sorry! I didn't mean to hurt you. Do you see a snake? Is there really one right here?" she said in utter panic, trying to see in the dark.

"Amelia, there's no snake. I just wanted to help you see that it's all easier said than done. It has to be your will to think and feel differently, and it takes practice. Old habits die hard, as they say." Äsha took Amelia's hand and said lightly, "Come on, we're getting closer."

"But since you teleported here to get me, couldn't you just hold my hand and teleport me out of here?" said Amelia hopefully.

Äsha giggled, "I'm not Superman. If you're walking, I'm walking."

"Of course... I understand," said Amelia. "It's just that I need to get back to Matthew. They have him in a coma and if I don't get back to him in three days, I don't know what the drugs will do to him. I don't even know if they'll keep him alive!"

"If you don't want to get stuck in worry and fear... or repeatedly experiencing things you don't want, just practice focusing on what's here in this moment."

"My fear about what might happen to Matthew IS what's here in this moment."

"Okay, try it again. Where do you feel the feeling?"

"I feel sick to my stomach."

"So what's next?"

"What do mean... I'm supposed to breath into the feeling?"

"You don't have to do anything... the question is just whether or not you want a different result. Remember, I told you The Game's prime directive is *Thy Will Be Done?*"

"Yes..." said Amelia hesitantly, "but if you care about people you worry about them."

"You can absolutely choose that. You can be anxious, worried, fearful or even feel victimized. But *you* are the one who's *asking* to feel more of that. It's really simple. If you feel afraid or worried, you're not in this moment – you're either focused on the past or the future."

"Yeah, but one time I found a snake under a picnic table. Believe me, I was in the moment and I was terrified!"

"Were you really terrified about that moment... or were

you worried about the future?"

"Oh…" Amelia said thoughtfully, "well I guess you're right."

"Focusing on your breath is an easy way to bring your mind back to the moment. And breathing is just… well, it's always a good idea to breathe!"

Theoretically Amelia agreed with Äsha, but it wasn't easy to take her thoughts off of Matthew and what might happen to him. She did try breathing, but she forgot about it rather quickly because it literally took all of her focus to just keep walking in the dark without tripping or falling.

It was slow going and finally they had to stop and rest. Äsha offered Amelia water from a handmade leather flask with the faint scent of beeswax and then handed her some strange food that tasted like fruit but it was quite firm and not at all juicy. Part of the skin was smooth like the cap of a mushroom, but other parts felt like the gills on the bottom of a toadstool.

"Are you ready to keep going?" said Äsha earnestly.

"Oh yes, I'm feeling better and better, actually," said Amelia, amazed at how different her body was beginning to feel. "Breathing this air feels wonderful."

As they continued walking the darkness gradually turned milky and Amelia could finally walk by herself without holding Äsha's hand. The light in the cavern was diffused and emanating from everywhere around them, glowing equally in all directions. It reminded Amelia of dense fog illuminated by sunlight, but it wasn't opaque, the light was glowing yet at the same time perfectly clear.

Rising up through the darkness the forms of stalactites, stalagmites, and saline incrustations reasserted themselves on the walls and high ceilings of a massive cavern. But oddly there were no shadows – everything was softly and uniformly lit as if the light were passing through silk.

"Where is the light coming from? How is it even possible when we're so deep underground?" asked Amelia, utterly fascinated by this phenomenon she was now experiencing.

"It's sunlight. It just has different characteristics than you've been led to believe. When sunlight strikes the Earth's surface some of the light is reflected, but most of it passes through the Earth in an altered state, such as you see here. We call it revitalized light, or rejuvenated darkness," Äsha said merrily.

"But what is it exactly that *revitalizes* the light..." said Amelia slowly, "... or rejuvenates darkness?"

"The same thing that will revitalize you as we continue our journey," said Äsha sweetly. "At this depth the cavern air has a unique life-force that supports and maintains everything from sunlight to plants to human beings who wander in at these depths. No illness exists here. If you had a fatal illness, it would completely disappear in this atmosphere within hours. All caverns at this depth contain the same atmospheric gasses."

"Why haven't I heard of it before?" asked Amelia, puzzled.

"Because most humans haven't yet been deep enough underground to experience any of this. Even Thomas doesn't know what's actually down here. He's been working hard to explore these depths based on legends that he believes are plausible, but no one has ever returned to the base to confirm what he suspects. That's why he's rather desperate for you to make it back."

"I don't care whether he's trying to help people or not... he's selfish and mean and not a very good person," said Amelia angrily.

"He plays The Game his way... you play it your way," said Äsha in a neutral tone.

"Well, it wasn't my choice to come here, he forced me to come here... he put Matthew in a coma. I hardly think that's me playing it my way!" said Amelia indignantly.

"One of the things that keeps The Game interesting is that you have no idea what you've agreed to with others before you were born," said Äsha mysteriously.

"I would NEVER agree to what's been happening to me!" said Amelia vehemently.

"Sometimes what's happening doesn't make sense in the moment. But there may come a time, if your mind is open enough to see, that you'll realize every moment has its own unique perfection, whether you like it at the time or not. You don't know what you're here to do or who you're here to be, and neither does anyone else. So why not lighten up? You might even have some fun!"

Amelia was feeling a bit annoyed to have a ten year old talking to her as if she was her mother instead of a kid, but she didn't feel like arguing so she just changed the subject.

"Does it ever get dark down here?" said Amelia.

"Nope!" Äsha replied. "There's always light somewhere on the surface."

"I don't feel tired or thirsty or hungry at all... is there something in the air?" asked Amelia.

"Well, the air does play a part of that," said Äsha. "But your body is also slowing down. You're no longer in need of your heart and lungs working at full capacity the way they did on the surface. What you think of as gravity is changing as well. You'll find that your movements will become almost effortless the more we descend."

Amelia was bursting with questions, but at this point the cavern narrowed into a small tunnel only ten feet high by three feet wide. They walked through the glowing entrance into a vast chamber rising hundreds of feet high and filled with snow white alabaster pillars four to five feet in diameter. But as she stepped fully into the chamber and looked up, Amelia realized the pillars were not made of stone but were quite alive and capped with umbrella-like covers, looking like colossal toadstools.

These toadstools weren't brown or grey as they were on the surface. It seemed as if the sunlight was passing through a prism bringing with it every primary color of the rainbow to this stunning wonderland: Red, orange, yellow, green, blue, indigo, violet, along with delicate blends of these colors as well. However, each individual hue was so luminous and brilliant they were barely recognizable compared to common surface colors, which now seemed muddy and heavy in comparison. Amelia noticed that many of the colored caps were marked with white diamond-shapes, circles or other geometrical patterns.

Looking around she saw that some of the stems were deep crimson, blue or green, all standing in straight rows as if they had been purposely planted in perfect symmetry. She touched one of the stems expecting it to feel slightly cold and clammy, just as a toadstool in the forest might have felt, but it was wonderfully warm, velvety-soft, and surprisingly fragrant.

"Are these poisonous like the little ones we have on the surface?" asked Amelia.

"No, not at all. Here they grow in perfect conditions. Nothing ever changes. There is no pollution... the temperature, the minerals they feed on and the water they need – everything stays constant. So they are... well... perfect!"

Amelia walked up to a bright red toadstool that was only four feet tall and said, "Hmmm, this is so odd. It smells like strawberries."

"Taste it," said Äsha grinning.

Amelia gently tore off a small piece of the toadstool and said, "It tastes just like a strawberry... but like, the best strawberry I've ever had. How's that possible?"

"Well, you're not surprised that an apple, a strawberry, and a rose have the same color – why be surprised when flavors are the same?" said Äsha enthusiastically. "The various colors of these plants are recognizable from colors you've seen on the surface, why shouldn't you recognize the flavors as well?"

Amelia hurried over to a golden toadstool with round, white spots and said, "This one tastes like pineapple!" And then rushing to an indigo blue stem she inhaled the fragrance of fresh blueberries. "If I didn't know better I'd say I was dreaming!"

"This is where these plants are meant to grow and live. That's why they're so phenomenal," said Äsha, gently stroking a soft, white stem.

Amelia wanted to stay and explore this grown-up fairyland, but she knew she had already lost all sense of time and she needed to get back if there was any chance of saving Matthew. After walking a brief distance they entered a cavern with brilliant, sparkling crystals; monstrous and cube-shaped, a foot or so in diameter. It seemed as if the crystals had been stacked one on top of another creating a wall here and a cliff-face there. Some of the stones were smaller, so Amelia bent down to pick up a square crystal the size of her hand.

"Lick it," said Äsha.

Amelia licked it and said with surprise, "It's salt!"

"Yes, this is a dried salt bed from what used to be an underground lake," said Äsha.

Amelia thought for a moment, then asked, "But how could an entire lake evaporate if we're this deep underground?"

"It couldn't and it didn't," said Äsha logically. "The water travels to the surface and comes out as a fresh spring."

Amelia was sure there must be an interesting science lesson on its way, but before she could ask any more questions they suddenly came to a broad chasm that stretched out for what seemed like miles in all directions. Amelia tentatively approached the ominous ledge, complete with a sheer cliff that loomed over a barely visible cavern floor far below. Amelia let out a frustrated yelp. There was literally no way down, no way back, and no way across.

CHAPTER 10

"What do we do now?" asked Amelia in a complete panic.

"Let's jump down," said Äsha lightly.

"Very funny," said Amelia laughing awkwardly. "You can teleport, but if I jump I'll break my neck."

"No you won't," said Äsha confidently. "Jump up and see what happens."

Doubtfully, Amelia jumped half-heartedly, and with no effort at all she found herself bounding a full six feet into the air, then landing lightly back on her feet. Her face was a curious blend of shock and utter delight.

"See what I mean?" said Äsha smiling brightly as she stepped off the cliff. She fell as slowly and softly as an autumn leaf on a warm, still day. Arriving gracefully at the bottom she called up to Amelia encouragingly, "Come on, you'll be fine."

Even watching Äsha wasn't enough to remove Amelia's fear, so she practiced breathing into the hollowed out feeling in her stomach. Amazingly, the energy began to soften. Amelia took a deep breath and as she stepped off the ledge, reminded herself that Äsha was right there if anything were to go terribly wrong. She drifted down, practically weightless, and though it seemed completely impossible, it was happening and there was no arguing with reality. When Amelia finally touched down she was so excited she skipped and hopped with joy, which under the current conditions translated into soaring leaps and bounds across the canyon floor.

All feelings of fear and hopelessness vanished, and in a matter of minutes she was running up the sides of the canyon walls and pushing herself off, bouncing off the ground and with only the slightest effort she was flying a full ten to twenty feet into the air. Amelia had never felt happier or more alive and free in her entire life. She and Äsha leapt over chasms with no effort. Amelia then skipped down a declining slope that went on for miles and miles, but she felt completely energized and not the least bit tired.

"How is this possible?" said Amelia, laughing with joy.

"What you would call *gravity* is changing," said Äsha knowledgeably.

Finally, the cavern opened up and there before them stretched a vast lake that seemed to reach out into infinity. The water looked as smooth as glass. There was absolutely no movement upon its surface, not a single ripple, and Amelia could see the rocks lying below the water's surface just as clearly as the rock ceiling overhead. There were surface reflections, but no shadows. Everything glowed softly causing the water to look like nothing Amelia had ever seen.

"This is extraordinary," she said smiling at Äsha. "The lake is lit from above, below, and all around."

Grinning, Äsha said, "Well, it's no more extraordinary than the sun shining in the first place!"

Amelia laughed, "I guess you're right!"

They walked around the lake until they came to a metal boat. Without the slightest effort Äsha easily picked up the boat and placed it in the water, even though it was many times her size. She stepped into it, then directed Amelia to follow and sit at the stern facing the bow. Their bodies were so light they barely caused the boat to move when they climbed in and sat down. Amelia's back was to the shore as she watched Äsha slowly and carefully turn a small lever resting on a part of the boat that projected up from the hull.

There was no movement and nothing seemed to be happening, so after a few minutes Amelia said, "Is there a problem? Is there something we have to do to get the boat started?"

Äsha laughed and said, "We've been on our way since the moment you sat down."

"What?" said Amelia incredulously. "That can't be right. We haven't been moving at all."

"Look over your shoulder. Do you see the shore?"

Amelia whipped around and saw nothing but miles and miles of water with no shoreline in sight. Amelia laughed. "I don't understand. We don't have oars or wind or even a motor. How is this possible?"

"We're moving on a *current* of Earth's electromagnetic energy," said Äsha.

With no feeling of movement, the velocity increased each time Äsha touched the lever, until at last the boat rose almost completely out of the water like a bird skimming over the surface.

With no shore in sight Amelia couldn't estimate their speed. She found a tissue in her pocket, tore it in half and threw a piece into the air. "If we're moving fast, why isn't there any wind?" asked Amelia as the tissue fell softly to her feet.

"There's a protective shield in front of our boat. It's invisible, and its shape causes the wind to move around us without slowing us down," said Äsha.

"How fast are we going?"

"About 900 miles an hour," said Äsha as if this was a normal occurrence. "Normally friction would heat up a metal boat and become a big problem at this speed, but the lake below us keeps the boat cool and we're almost as light as air!"

At this point Amelia's mind couldn't comprehend another thing. The lack of gravity made no sense, but of course she was witnessing this herself and it made her wonder how many scientific theories were completely erroneous. At last, she found a pillow and blanket under her seat and curled up in the bottom of the boat, her thoughts drifting away until she fell soundly asleep. When Äsha finally awakened her, she had no sense of time whatsoever. She didn't know if she had been asleep for days or hours or just a few minutes.

Stepping out of the boat and onto the shore Amelia saw a slanting sheet of light that appeared fan-shaped off in the distance. She could see nothing beyond that light. But as she and Äsha bounded quickly across, approaching the rim of the rock floor, Amelia saw the light was streaming in from below – as an immense break that stretched across their path. It appeared to be limitless, bottomless, and springing up from what seemed to be a fissure in the Earth.

They walked a bit farther and stood on the brink of the chasm, staring out into the brilliant, shimmering light. The light didn't dazzle Amelia's eyes – rather it possessed an indescribable beauty, illuminating everything in all directions. If love could take form, she believed this light would be *that* form.

As Amelia peered over the edge, wondering what they would do next, Äsha said, "Below us is a hollow in the Earth and the light is actually reflecting up from the space below… and that's where we're headed.

"Amelia, look," said Äsha pointing.

Amelia turned in the direction Äsha indicated and saw a ship covered in ice and snow, floating in the distance, its sails full as it moved swiftly in the wind.

"Is that a mirage?" said Amelia filled with wonder.

"No. It's real. Everything on Earth has an *imprint* in another place and every event is recorded."

"But how are we seeing a ship?"

"Well, matter is *reproduced* in a so-called vacancy. What you see is like unseen pages where all events are recorded. As that ship sailed over the ocean above us, it disturbed a current of energy, and left an impression – sort of like a holographic image of the ship on a zone beneath it that's parallel with the spot where we are."

"We're seeing a holographic version of that ship? That sounds crazy!"

"No more crazy than *Things are Thoughts*, or the idea of subatomic particles that can be waves and then turn into particles depending on your focus!"

Amelia laughed, relieved to be distracted from the *leap-of-faith* she was about to take.

"Are you ready to jump?" said Äsha smiling and holding out her hand.

Amelia's heart was in her throat as she grasped Äsha's hand and said, "I'm ready," as they stepped off the cliff together.

Amelia threw her arms around Äsha fearing they might lose each other as they fell into the abyss and then closed her eyes tightly, afraid to see what was coming.

"Open your eyes," said Äsha encouragingly, "you have nothing to fear."

Amelia peeked out of one eye and then opened both eyes.

"You can loosen your grip, I promise you can't lose me," said Äsha laughing.

"Oh, sorry!" said Amelia apologetically.

Though she didn't let go immediately, she loosened her grip more and more until she finally let go, and with her arms outstretched felt as if she was flying. The wind moved gently past her body and through her hair, but it wasn't too loud or cold or uncomfortable. Even the light surrounding her was peaceful and calm. Amelia discovered she could easily move any part of her body.

Äsha spoke loudly and said, "The wind that's blowing now will lessen… The faster we fall the more the atmosphere is decreasing… it will completely disappear in just a few minutes."

As predicted, the air movement ceased and Amelia felt as if she was lying in bed – perfectly supported, comfortable, and resting.

"We're still moving at a phenomenal speed, but the atmosphere is no longer the same. That's why there isn't any friction." Then as if reading Amelia's mind Äsha added, "Don't worry. We'll slow down long before we reach our destination."

Amelia understood the concept of the atmosphere disappearing, but from an experiential point of view it felt as if she was no longer moving. At first she thought she was dreaming, but then she realized she was wide awake and still falling through space. Yet it felt more like floating on a cloud with absolutely no sense of time. She felt deliriously happy and completely at peace. It was as if she didn't have a care in the world.

"Äsha, can I ask you a question?" said Amelia dreamily.

"Of course."

"Well, I had this experience…" said Amelia slowly. "I was in the Montauk Chair and I don't really know why… but I was sent back… twice… to a time when I was living in Russia."

Nodding her head, Äsha said, "I can see all of your Vedruss lifetimes."

"Oh good!" said Amelia, grateful she wouldn't have to explain everything in detail, but also wishing she could see things the way Äsha did.

"Well, here's the thing… I really loved it there, and if I'd had a choice and no family or friends… I wouldn't have wanted to come back," said Amelia. "I just keep thinking about it all the time and wishing it was real. I mean, not that it wasn't real, but it's not real now… it's not even possible now. And it makes me sad, because the way the Vedruss lived… well… it would solve every problem on Earth. But no one even knows they existed… and even if I tried to tell people no one would listen."

"You don't need anyone to listen… you can create that way of life all by yourself," said Äsha confidently.

"Oh, you don't understand. There are so many laws… and there's no such thing as free land and no one lives that way anymore."

"Amelia, when you think about your life as Sasha, how do you feel?"

Amelia thought for a moment and said, "I feel... excited... it's sort of like when I've seen the first two parts of a trilogy... and I know I love it... and I love all the actors... and I've been waiting a whole year to find out what's going to happen.

"It's that kind of excitement. And even though I know it was thousands of years ago... I miss it. I really do. Why can't people live like that if they want to?"

"Anyone can live like that if they want to," said Äsha. "In fact, you're already starting to create that."

"Well, maybe I'm teleporting or having unusually vivid dreams... but I'm pretty sure it's just in my imagination," said Amelia, shaking her head.

"You're not just imagining something," said Äsha, "you're feeling what it's like to be there, right?"

Amelia nodded.

"That means you're in the process of creating your own version of that reality."

"But it no longer exists," said Amelia disheartened.

"Okay let's step back for a moment," said Äsha patiently. "This is the most important thing for you to remember. Your feelings create everything that happens to you... including the physical world around you.

"You first begin to understand the binary code when you feel safe or unsafe and act accordingly. But the binary code also responds to the feeling of yes or no... or you could think of is as love or fear.

"So when you imagine your life as a Vedruss and have that feeling of love and excitement that you described – you're telling the program 'Yes' I want to create this. And the more vividly and consistently you feel it... the more powerfully you'll create it.

"But when you focus on your world... the people, the politics, the corporations... you see it as solid and unchanging... your idea starts to feel hopeless and then you worry that what you want can't possibly happen or that it's not happening fast enough… or maybe you're afraid that you're not doing it right.

"Well, when that happens… when you worry… you are actually causing the program to create more of what you don't want."

"But if it's such an intelligent program," said Amelia exasperated, "why doesn't it understand what I don't want?"

"Because the program doesn't perceive right or wrong, good or bad… it only responds to focus. And that brings us back to Einstein," said Äsha grinning, "*Imagination is more important than knowledge*… so be sure you are imagining what you want… not what you don't want.

"And remember, there is no one on Earth who's powerful enough to stop your imagination. Of course, they can try to convince you that you're just making-things-up that don't matter… but it's up to you whether you believe that or not.

"Oh, and one more thing, you will never know how anything is going to happen… that's part of the fun and games of it all! So don't worry about it. Everything has a way of working itself out.

"And on that subject," said Äsha happily, "we're getting very close to our destination!"

"I'm feeling gravity again," said Amelia excitedly. "What's happening?"

"This won't be easy to understand because of what you've been taught, but we're entering the Inner-Earth," said Äsha, "but that isn't quite accurate. This Earth is more like a parallel Earth."

"What do you mean?"

"The continents are exactly the same as your continents on the surface, except this *Inner-Earth* is on a different dimension – it's a parallel reality. The atmosphere changes between dimensions and allows your body some time to adjust. It's a lot like deep sea diving. Your body has to acclimate to the change in pressure.

"Between the two dimensions is what you might call a zero-point - which is the energy that remains when all other energy is removed from a system."

"I don't understand," said Amelia.

"Imagine you're a fish that can breathe underwater with gills or air with lungs. Now pretend air is one dimension and water is another dimension – zero-point would be the moment where you could no longer use your lungs, but you can't use your gills yet either.

"So we've been moving through third-dimensional energy and it was gradually resolving to zero-point where there is no atmosphere, in fact, there is no air in zero-point."

"Well, then how did we manage to breathe?"

"You gradually stopped needing to breathe – didn't you notice? In this moment your heart isn't beating either."

"How can I possibly be alive?" said Amelia, then with a shock she added, "Am I still alive?"

"What do you think?" Äsha laughed, "of course you're alive! In fact, don't you feel more alive than before?"

Amelia shook her head, "I don't understand. I don't need to breathe, my heart doesn't need to beat – and I feel better than ever!"

"Think of it like this. Imagine you're lying in bed in your 3D world. As you start falling asleep your breathing slows down and so does your heartbeat – that would be like moving toward zero-point. And the next thing you know you're in a parallel reality, what you would think of as your dream... where you have no heartbeat and you don't breathe."

"But that's a dream!"

"Well, you've been *educated* to call it a dream. But what if you're a multi-dimensional being? What if you're actually a cosmic-superhero capable of coming and going between dimensions all the time?"

"A cosmic-superhero?" said Amelia laughing. "Oh, I'm just sure!" she said with joking sarcasm.

"I've been trying to tell you – faulty education! You're going to be completely shocked when you discover the truth about your entire existence! And I don't mean the simple fact that you're playing a game – I'm referring to the most common, fundamental things you believe about life on Earth.

"But that discussion will come later!" said Äsha laughing. "Let's get back to what's happening. We've moved through zero-point – where you felt nothing – and now we're gradually acclimating to air and atmosphere on the *other side* of zero-point. It's as if you're now using your gills instead of your lungs. Does that help?"

"Well, sort of," said Amelia, still trying to get her head around the idea. "Are you saying that this *zero-point* is shared by both dimensions?"

"Yes! That's it exactly! It's sort of like *the nothing* that's really everything."

Amelia shook her head and sighed, "Oh… I'm lost again."

"Stop trying to use your mind – it's highly overrated!" said Äsha grinning. "Use your imagination as you think of the space… the *nothing* between words – without it, nothing would make sense. Or the pause in music that makes a composition transcendent – it's the *nothing* that's everything! Or imagine the moment between breathing in and breathing out.

"So think of your journey from one dimension to another as an exhale followed by an inhale. They are different, yet connected – one cannot exist without the other, and they both share the same zero-point. But the *world of the inhale* is quite different than the *world of the exhale*. Yes, the lungs are the same, but the function is completely different."

"Was that analogy supposed to make it easier for me to understand?" said Amelia now in somewhat of a panic as a sheer grey cliff loomed larger and larger in front of them. "Nevermind! It doesn't matter! How are we going to stop without crashing into that cliff?!" she yelled anxiously.

"Have you noticed that we've begun moving toward that cliff in a way that would be impossible without propulsion?" said Äsha calmly.

"Yes! How's that possible?" said Amelia nervously.

"I'm simply using the power of my mind," said Äsha succinctly. Amelia looked even more petrified. "You can try it yourself! All you do is WISH to move to the right and see what happens!"

Amelia wished to move to the right and was stunned to see the distance between them widen.

"Now, wish to go in a circle around me!" said Äsha.

Amelia obeyed and she circled easily around Äsha, laughing with delight. Then Äsha pulled a crystal out of her pocket and threw it into the air. The crystal floated right alongside her as if she was sitting down and had placed it on a table beside her.

"Now, call for the crystal, tell it to come to you!"

Amelia did and the crystal floated to her, landing right in the palm of her hand. Never in her life had she been more surprised than in that moment.

Äsha laughed and said, "Things are thoughts! That's why thoughts influence things! Or maybe it's thoughts influencing thoughts!"

"Are you just trying to confuse me?" said Amelia laughing.

They still had quite a distance to travel before arriving at their destination so Äsha yelled, "Think of how strongly you would FEEL if you were face to face with a grizzly bear. Now WISH with that level of intensity that we move rapidly forward toward our destination. We'll unite our energies and do this together which will be far more powerful than what we could ever do alone."

Amelia looked at where they were headed and intensely wished to be there. The distant cliff was suddenly so close Äsha yelled, "STOP! We're coming in too fast! Make a wish that we are motionless!"

They slowed immediately and came to a halt, hovering in mid-air just ten feet above the land.

"Now, wish to land slowly and with control," said Äsha with her arms in the air as if she was gracefully conducting a symphony through the last few measures. They moved gently through the air and landed softly on a grassy bluff.

Looking around Amelia saw a clear, broad river and a dense forest of evergreens off in the distance with trees so magnificent and immense she thought they must be thousands of years old. Amelia reached out and excitedly hugged Äsha.

"Thank you! Thank you!" said Amelia, relieved to be in one piece. "Do you know how long we've been gone? Which way do we go now?"

Äsha smiled sweetly and said, "Amelia do you remember the agreement I shared with you? The one where I said I would save you only if you were facing certain death?"

"Yes," said Amelia tentatively, suddenly afraid to hear what Äsha was about to say.

"Well, I've done that, and now you're perfectly safe. There is absolutely nothing and no one here that would harm you."

"No. Oh no, please don't go. I'm begging you. Please stay with me. I can't do this without you!" Amelia pleaded desperately.

"Yes, you can," said Äsha gently. "Trust yourself. It's time for me to go. But listen to me carefully – there is nothing I've told you that you didn't already know."

"What do you mean?"

"You carry everything you will ever need to know within yourself. Every aspect of The Game is programmed into your DNA. As long as you have a body you have the tools and the know-how to play the game. It's no different than the way you create your own dreams."

"What?" Amelia exclaimed. "Wait a minute, what are you talking about?"

Äsha laughed, "You create your dream-world every night, why is it so hard to believe that your avatar body creates and projects your waking-world as well?"

Amelia shook her head. "Okay that's WAY over my head! But even if that's true it doesn't solve anything," said Amelia frantically. "And how does that tie into *feelings running the program?*"

"Did you know researchers discovered that you could be dreaming you're sitting in a wheelchair, paralyzed, but if you wake up for just a moment, realize all is well, and fall back to sleep... you would still be sitting in the wheelchair, but you would no longer be paralyzed?" said Äsha as if they were chatting while having tea and crumpets.

"Okay... that's interesting," said Amelia slowly, "but it doesn't really help."

"Well, actually, that concept works exactly the same way in The Game. You just have to learn how to wake up."

Amelia narrowed her eyes, "Okay, I'll bite... how do you *wake up*" she said in finger quotes, "while you're in the program?"

"You just focus on what you want to be real, rather than what you think is real," said Äsha pragmatically.

Laughing Amelia said, "Well that sounds very Pollyannaish... that would never work in my world!"

"That's because you're still sitting in the wheelchair believing that you're paralyzed. I'm giving you the answers, but I can't give you the faith to believe in what you don't see."

"Well, as they say, seeing is believing... scientists don't believe in anything they can't see or prove," said Amelia somewhat sanctimoniously, "that's just how human beings are."

"You can't see love or prove its existence, but you believe that love exists," said Äsha, "and the more you believe in the existence of love... the more you see a loving world.

"As Pollyannaistic as this may sound," said Äsha with a grin, "to wake up... all you do in response to any problem is say to yourself, *'All is well.'*"

"How could that possibly work?" said Amelia skeptically.

"Well, think about the dreamer who falls back asleep. In her dream she's still sitting in the wheelchair, she still believes the dream is her true reality, but she subconsciously remembers FEELING that all is well.

"That feeling... the conviction that all is well actually

causes the dreamer to experience an alternate reality or timeline where all IS well. Remember, every possibility already exists… so not only is the dreamer no longer paralyzed in her dream, she has no memory of ever being paralyzed in the first place. So the rest of her dream is going to go quite a bit differently than the way it started!"

"So… you're saying that all I have to do is say, *all is well…*" said Amelia doubtfully.

"No matter what's happening," Äsha interjected.

"And I'll eventually find myself in another… timeline…" said Amelia unconvinced. "It sounds nice, but it's totally unbelievable. For one thing, just saying *all is well* isn't the same as FEELING that way."

"Still, it works, whether you feel it or not… whether you believe it or not… it just works," said Äsha matter-of-factly. "But you'll never know unless you try.

"Besides it's the first step to the new science you're going to discover." Äsha clapped her hand over her mouth, then with a guilty look she winced, took her hand away and said, "I wasn't supposed to tell you that."

"What? Tell me what?" exclaimed Amelia.

Äsha observed Amelia for a moment and said, "Well… most players keep this type of thing a secret from themselves until they discover it on their own, but if you're sure you want to know…"

"Yes! Whatever it is," said Amelia, "tell me!"

Excitedly, Äsha said, "There's a new science that's ready to be discovered in The Game – a science that will surpass all other sciences… and you signed up to be the pioneer of that science… because only a player in a human avatar can make any changes on Earth."

Amelia's mind was racing. She could imagine the slight possibility that some new discovery, a really simple one, might pop into her mind even though she wasn't very interested in scientific things. But the idea that she would discover a science that would surpass all the other sciences – that was just crazy.

"Okay…" she said hesitantly, "what's it called?"

"Pollyannaology… The science of being excessively and unreasonably optimistic," said Äsha smiling broadly.

Amelia burst out laughing. "Oh, so I'm going to be Earth's first Pollyannaologist!"

"Yep! Just think about it," said Äsha laughing, "you don't need any funding, you don't need any proof of the truth," and then with a mysterious look in her eyes she added, "and you don't even need to mention it to anyone. That should make you pretty unstoppable!"

"You're not kidding are you?" said Amelia.

"Nope," said Äsha.

"You actually believe this will work?" said Amelia, unsure whether she should laugh or cry or just feel sorry for Äsha if she ever decided to actually play The Game.

"Absolutely. It will change your world. And it's simple."

Amelia sighed.

"How much easier can it be?" Äsha continued. "Look, pretend you're the one dreaming you're in a wheelchair, paralyzed."

"Okay…" said Amelia knowing Äsha wouldn't stop until she joined in with her little game.

"When you wake up, two things happen… you are no longer focused on the problem because you KNOW for a fact that all is well. You're not worried either. No one worries when all is well… right?"

"I guess so… but I think YOU are the Pollyannaologist, Äsha, I really do." Then rolling her eyes Amelia added, "Okay, I give. How many times do I say it?"

Clapping her little hands excitedly, Äsha said, "Keep repeating it until you are no longer focused on the problem."

"But what if I don't really believe what I'm saying?"

"It requires no belief at all."

"But what about thoughts and feelings creating my experiences? If I don't really FEEL that *all is well*… then how could it work?"

Whispering secretively Äsha said, "I've just told you the cheat-code to the entire game program... it bypasses everything."

"Well, if it's really that simple," said Amelia, hoping to call her bluff, "why didn't you just tell me that in the first place?"

"What? And miss out on all the excitement you've been having? Where's your sense of adventure?" said Äsha as she began floating into the air.

"Wait!" yelled Amelia frantically, "Don't leave me... I can't do this without you! I don't even know where to go!"

Äsha continued floating upward and yelled, "Go down to the river! Any boat will pick you up and give you a ride for free!"

"Free?" said Amelia.

"There is no money where you are... you'll see!" And then like a mother, rather than a ten-year old she added, "Keep breathing... All is well!"

Äsha gently floated up past the cliff, and as she hovered over the abyss, she yelled out, "Don't worry, someone will be along to help you on your way! Sometimes you just have to rely on the kindness of strangers!"

Äsha then pretended she was swimming through the air doing the backstroke.

"And don't forget you're never alone! There's nothing I know that you don't know – you already know EVERYTHING... Just the way you like it!"

Äsha appeared smaller and smaller until she completely disappeared from Amelia's sight.

CHAPTER 11

A spasm of fear locked tightly around Amelia's throat as she burst into tears. One minute she was happy and all was well, she thought she had learned all about dealing with fear, but now sheer panic gripped her chest and the silence surrounding her was filled with a high pitched ringing in her ears. Dizzy and lightheaded, she sat down. How could Äsha abandon her like this? Didn't she care about what was going to happen? Amelia didn't know how to get back to the base on her own, she didn't even know where she was, and now she would never be able to reach Matthew in time.

Lying on her side with her head on her arm, Amelia couldn't stop crying. The pain in her throat worsened as she struggled to breathe. All was lost. Even if she could find her way, the base was in lockdown. How would she get in?

Imagining Matthew trapped in unconsciousness, and forced to survive on life-support, she cried until there were no tears left to cry. At last, she fell into a helpless, exhausted sleep and later woke to a nagging pain in her hip. At first she thought she was lying on a stone, but soon realized it was something in her pocket. She rolled onto her back and dug out the strange object that Admiral Byrdie had slipped into her hand in the cafeteria.

Lying on her back and holding the object with outstretched arms, Amelia was shocked to see it was quite old and made of twenty-four karat gold. It was round and flat, about three inches in diameter, and looked similar to a pocket-watch. It was beautifully crafted with emerald cut diamond studs embedded all around its outer edge.

Strangely, there didn't seem to be any way to open it, nor even a hairline crevice indicating that it could be opened. The lid looked like a map of the Earth, but the shapes of the continents looked completely unfamiliar until she realized the map was from the perspective of the North Pole, which was represented by crushed diamonds at the center. Amelia sat and stared for a few minutes. She had never seen all of the continents from this perspective and it seemed a much more logical way to view a map of the world. The only continent missing was Antarctica – but who ever visited Antarctica?

Amelia wondered why the Admiral had given this to her? It was obviously a treasured possession, maybe even a priceless antique, yet he was adamant that it was to be hers. It was so thick she felt there had to be something inside, but there was no way to open it. Why would the old man have given her something so precious and rare if it didn't have a purpose?

Looking up, Amelia saw a massive yacht-like ship with three masts and a square rig sailing down the river. She jumped to her feet, stuffed the object in her pocket, grabbed the flask and slung it over her shoulder as she ran down the path hoping to reach the dock in time.

Running with far more ease than she could have imagined possible, she bounded down the hill toward the river. To her surprise, when she arrived at the dock she wasn't even the slightest bit out of breath.

Amelia sat on a bench near the dock and got her bearings. The climate was somewhat balmy, but not too hot or sunny, it felt perfect. The river must have been ten miles wide and though it was obviously very deep she could still see all the fish and other creatures swimming below with perfect clarity. As she took it all in she realized that oddly, there wasn't a single fishing boat, nor were there fishermen for that matter.

All this made Amelia wonder if it really was possible to live without money as Äsha had suggested. On one hand the concept was inconceivable, how could a world exist without money? But she had seen it before in her game-lifetimes as a Vedruss and now everywhere she looked she saw all manner of fruits and vegetables growing in abundance. There were banana, avocado, papaya and mango trees, bushes laden with berries and fruits, and all kinds of vegetables growing freely, rather than in structured, farmed rows. And just like within the Vedruss communities, there were no fences, no farms and no *Private Property - Keep Out* signs.

Then, much to her surprise, Amelia heard singing. She looked toward the sound and saw the ship coming into view as it passed a large island in the middle of the river. It sounded as if thousands of people were singing together as one phenomenal chorus – their voices echoing from bank to bank filling up the entire universe with their hauntingly beautiful song and intricate harmonies. When the adults stopped singing the children began and it sounded like a choir of angels.

With perfect grace the ship pulled up to the dock. A gangplank was lowered and smoothly dropped into place with a soft hydraulic *whoosh*. High above, a smiling middle-aged man with curly grey hair waved to Amelia from the top deck encouraging her to come onboard. She smiled and waved back as she stepped onto the walkway and climbed onto the ship.

Once onboard, a man who seemed to be the captain approached her and said something in a language she couldn't understand.

"Do you speak English?" she said hopefully.

"English? No," he said smiling and shaking his head.

Then he yelled to a nearby man with pure white, thick, wavy hair. Due to the color of his hair, Amelia assumed the man to be quite a bit older, but as he turned around she saw he was extremely fit, his eyes were bright, his skin luminous and appeared to be only in his early to mid-thirties.

"English! English! Over here!" the captain yelled to the man, as if *over* and *here* were the only other words he had ever mastered. The man called, *English*, laughed and smiled as he walked over to them.

"Hello," he said warmly, "I'm Richard. As you may have guessed I happen to speak English… which is where my extra name came from. You can call me whichever name you prefer."

The captain then said something in his native tongue and Richard said, "The captain is wondering where you're headed."

"Oh," said Amelia, taken aback, "I need to go to Utah, but I'm not really sure exactly where I am… so I don't know when I would need to get off the ship."

"That's all right," said Richard with a peculiar expression, as if he had something to say, but didn't quite know how to tell her, "we'll figure out the best place." Then changing the subject slightly he said, "Would you like a tour of the ship?"

There was nothing Amelia could do to get back to Matthew any sooner, but she was still worried. "Yes," she said politely, "but you will make sure I get off at the right stop for Utah?"

"Of course," said the man kindly.

Amelia relaxed a bit as they strolled along. There were several hundred people onboard and she had an awkward moment when she realized just how much she stood out in the crowd. While everyone on the ship wore simple white clothing – everything from pants and tunics to flowing dresses and robes; there she was in olive green, military cargo pants, a long-sleeved grey knit shirt and army issue boots. But she quickly realized she needn't have worried, every person who saw Amelia went out of their way to be kind and thoughtful. She was struck by how happy and healthy everyone appeared to be, and they all had such beautiful complexions it was difficult to tell their age.

Richard turned to Amelia and said, "Earlier you told me you didn't know how to get to where you're going. Have you thought of using that compass tucked in your pocket?"

Amelia's shirt was draped loosely over her pants and she knew it was impossible to see the object. "How can you tell what's in my pocket?" she said surprised. "How do you know it's a compass? I don't even know what it is."

"I didn't mean to make you uncomfortable," said the man apologetically. "For us... here in this place... it's as easy to *see* what's in your pocket as it is to recognize the color of your eyes. I wouldn't have mentioned it except I think it will help you on your journey."

Amelia pulled the treasured object out of her pocket. "I don't know how to use it. I think I'm supposed to open it, but I don't know how," she said, chewing on her lower lip as she concentrated.

"Does it not have a code?" said Richard.

Amelia shook her head. "I don't know. The man who gave it to me didn't say anything about a code."

"Are you talking about Admiral Byrdie?"

Shaking her head in astonishment she said, "Yes! How did you know?"

"You were thinking loudly," he said smiling.

"I have no idea why he even gave it to me."

"I suspect he believed you would have more use for it than he would."

Amelia tried to remember something – anything that might be a clue. She went over and over in her mind everything she could remember the old man saying to her. Nothing made sense. Finally she closed her eyes and thought, "IF I knew the answer, what would it be?" And then Amelia remembered something so obvious she suspected it wouldn't work, but since she could think of nothing else she said, "Minus 74 point 85 16 16... Minus 102 point 59 zero 33 zero."

The top of the compass, with the map of Earth, softly clicked and opened gently in a sliding, horizontal motion revealing a second-Earth – but this was a *living*, 3-D, holographic image.

In the center, was the Inner-North Pole, but it wasn't icy, it was tropical with an ocean portal that clearly flowed into the ocean at the point that would be Earth's North Pole. The holographic map showed every portal and tunnel that connected the two Earths. Carved around the outer edges of the disc were the words, "As above, so below."

As she continued staring at this holographic Inner-Earth, Amelia saw a brightly glowing reddish sun suspended in midair. Clouds were moving in the holographic sky and she could clearly see mountains, oceans, forests, rivers, rolling hills, beaches and plains. To her surprise, all she had to do was focus on a particular area and instantly she would see the area close up, hovering right before her eyes. She discovered this feature quite accidentally when she looked at a mountain while at the same time wondering what it would be like at the top – the image instantly zoomed in to a field covered with wildflowers. As she wondered what the flowers were like, the image zoomed-in even closer and she experienced a close up of the flowers, fragrance and all. Amelia discovered she could see all the way down to their subatomic level.

As she pulled her attention back, the flower zoomed out until it was a few feet away. Amelia then turned her gaze slightly to the left and realized she could see the view from the top of the mountain as if she was standing there in person looking out over the ocean – even a slight breeze ruffled her hair. Ancient trees, fifty to one hundred feet in diameter, led down to rolling green hills with a sandy beach below extending into the clearest blue ocean she had ever seen.

Entranced, Amelia focused on the water and though she didn't move physically, she felt as if she was in the midst of the holographic image swimming with sea turtles as they surfed the gentle waves. She could feel the exact temperature of the air and the water as if she were actually there.

Astonished, she looked up at Richard and said, "This is the most incredible thing I've ever seen in my life! Is this really what it's like here?"

"Yes," said Richard smiling warmly.

Amelia followed his directions and saw that the holographic Earth was an exact duplicate of planet Earth, at least the continents were laid out the same way, but up close nothing looked familiar.

With a sigh she said, "I don't understand how this compass works. How will it get me back to where I need to go? I can see everything on this map, even something as small as a flower but I don't see planes or buses or trains or cars."

A bemused look crossed the man's face. "You still don't really understand where you are, do you?"

"What do you mean? I'm right here on the ship standing next to you." Then a wave of shock passed over Amelia's face as an unsettling memory crossed her mind. "Oh! I forgot. All transportation is down because of the terrorists! Well, what's the closest you can get me to Utah? I'm just in a really big hurry. There's an emergency and I have to get back," she said nervously.

"My dear," said Richard kindly, "you are no longer on Earth's surface."

"What do you mean?" said Amelia looking around, "I see sunlight, I see the sky and grass and trees and the river. I just came from being in an underground cavern and I can tell the difference."

"No, that's not what I mean," said Richard patiently. "You're not on Earth – at least not the Earth that you know. Some people call this the Inner-Earth, but it is actually a parallel world. The Earth you know is actually a duplicate of this world."

Amelia looked puzzled.

"Do you understand that Earth is a virtual reality?" he said good-naturedly.

Amelia nodded.

"Well, think of it this way... what you see here is the Earth just as the Creator of The Game originally imagined it." Then, Richard pointed to the engraved words and said, "*As above, so below* means that Inner-Earth is a match to your Earth. The pristine beauty you see here is what Earth was like in the very beginning – and it is what your Earth can return to because the Inner Earth is a living blueprint."

"Do you call this Inner-Earth because it's inside Earth?" asked Amelia.

"No. We are not *inside* Earth. Inner-Earth refers to the blueprint you carry within you. What you see here," said Richard with a sweeping gesture, "is not just an *other-dimensional reality* – it's embedded in your DNA and the DNA of every person playing The Game – and that's why Earth's original blueprint can never be lost. That's why human beings will always long for what you see here – not just the untouched magnificence of this place, but also our way of life – people living in harmony with each other and with nature.

"Our two worlds are sort of like identical twins separated at birth. One baby is raised by loving parents, the other is raised in a dysfunctional family, but as they grow up separately they both feel something or someone is missing… until they are ultimately reunited."

"Well, having a blueprint in our DNA doesn't seem to be doing us any good," said Amelia glumly.

Richard held out his hand and said politely, "May I hold your compass for a moment?"

Amelia nodded and placed the compass in the palm of his hand. Richard then held the outer edges of the compass with the golden side up and the holographic side down. "You see how both Earth's have sort of a belly-button at the center? What you would call the North Pole, is in fact, right in the center of your world."

"No, you don't understand," said Amelia, "that is the farthest north you can go."

"Well, that's only because you've been taught that Earth is a sphere, and the really cold parts are the farthest north and the farthest south."

"What do you mean? Earth is round. It is a sphere…

everyone knows that."

"You've been shown pictures, and you've been told what to see and believe. I know this will be hard to grasp, but even though the universe is filled with spheres, Earth is not one of them," said Richard plainly.

"Oh my God, I have no idea what you're talking about. You clearly don't know the facts. Maybe it's something you don't know about here," said Amelia, feeling both frustrated and a bit sorry for Richard, since he was obviously quite ignorant. "Listen, wherever we are, I just need to get back to Utah. Can you help me do that?"

"Yes, of course," said Richard warmly. "Where exactly do you need to go?"

"I don't really know the exact location," said Amelia hopelessly. "It's an underground military base somewhere in the Utah desert."

"Do you know what it looks like outside or inside?"

"I've been inside, but I don't know what it looks like outside."

"If you have a clear picture in your mind, we have the technology to transport you any place in the universe."

"You mean I can go from here directly into the base?" said Amelia, completely stunned.

"Yes."

"Well, then where do I need to go to get access to your... transportation?"

"I'm headed there actually. It's right here..." he said pointing to the holographic map. Then using his mind he caused the compass to zoom in. "It's called The Portal. I'll take you there if you'd like."

Amelia sighed with relief. "Oh thank you! Yes, please!"

As she looked at the holographic map Amelia suddenly thought of Admiral Byrdie and how adamantly he kept telling her to go to the library. "I know this is an odd question, but do you have any libraries here?"

Richard laughed, "The Portal is the largest library in the

universe."

"Really?" said Amelia thinking it didn't look very large.

"It looks small because you're looking at the entrance. The Portal has underground storage that spans over 456 square miles. It holds living records of everything that has ever occurred anywhere in the Universe – throughout time, space, in all dimensions, parallel worlds, and all realities.

"Any question you may have, The Portal will show you what truly happened – down to the smallest detail… even the thoughts, feelings and true motives of those involved. But more importantly, it is literally a portal to anywhere in the universe, including Earth. We call it, *'Think and Go,'*" said Richard smiling.

Amelia smiled as she remembered Äsha using that term. "You mean all I have to do is go to your library, think about where I want to go and I'll just show up there?"

"Yes, there are special chairs, somewhat like the Montauk Chair, but infinitely more advanced."

Though Amelia didn't want to take her eyes off of the holographic Inner-Earth, she wanted the compass to be safe.

As if reading her mind Richard said, "Use the same code to close the compass whenever you're ready. You can open and close the compass telepathically or out loud."

Amelia didn't fully trust that she had any telepathic abilities so she said the code aloud and the compass closed silently. She stared at it for a moment and said, "Why do you call this a compass? It seems more like a map to me – I mean, an incredible, holographic map, but still a map."

"Didn't you notice that your thoughts could take you anywhere you wanted to go and show you anything you wanted to see?" asked Richard.

"Well, yes, but it doesn't tell me how to get there," said Amelia.

"It would tell you if you asked," said Richard.

"Oh, you mean it's like a GPS – except this compass is a GPS times infinity!" said Amelia grinning. "Okay, I have one more question for you. Where is Antarctica?"

"Why don't you ask that question when you're at The Portal? You'll be able to see everything for yourself," said Richard encouragingly. "Come with me, we'll be docking soon."

When they disembarked Richard said, "From here we'll take the hovercraft. It's just a five minute walk. It will take about an hour to get to The Portal, so feel free to pick some fruit or anything you'd like before we get onboard."

"For some reason I'm not really very hungry," said Amelia.

"That's normal," said Richard, though he didn't explain any further.

As they walked Amelia saw bright green rolling hills dotted with colorful gardens. There were plenty of people walking and riding horses, but there was an odd lack of homes or businesses, and no one seemed to be doing work of any kind.

"Where are all the houses?" asked Amelia curiously.

Richard smiled and said, "Look again, you'll see."

As Amelia looked more closely she realized everything was built underground with vegetable gardens on the rooftops and colorful flower gardens in front of each house. But because there were no fences, only windows and doors facing out into the world, all of the buildings blended flawlessly into the hillsides.

"Are all of your homes built into hillsides?" Amelia inquired.

"No, there are many options, but whatever we do, whether it's a building, a road, or a pathway – we tread lightly. We live in harmony with nature," said Richard warmly.

"So do you mainly sail and use hovercraft to get around?" said Amelia.

"Most people here have the ability to teleport or bi-locate, some use hovercrafts, but it's more for our own enjoyment, just like sailing or horseback riding. But for those who don't teleport and need to go a long distance we have underground trains that move through tubes using only electromagnetic energy. We can be anywhere in less than an hour.

"Here we are," said Richard as they stepped up onto a platform that blended so perfectly and naturally with its surroundings Amelia never would have noticed it.

"This is beautiful… the way it blends in… but don't you have a hard time finding things?" said Amelia inquisitively.

Richard smiled and pulled a compass very much like her own, out of his pocket. "Not at all! We can simply think of where we want to go and the compass communicates telepathically."

"Do you mean it talks into your mind?" asked Amelia.

"It really depends on the person receiving the communication. Some people hear words, others see images, some people receive telepathic communication through their feelings, and sometimes it's a combination. Personally, I feel the communication. So when we were walking along I suddenly felt like turning left, and then right and then I had the feeling to walk up the stairs."

"That's incredible!" said Amelia enthusiastically.

"You can use your compass the same way. You just have to trust your feelings," said Richard.

Amelia wasn't sure if she was quite at that level of trusting, so she was happy when she saw a thin golden frame gliding along the soft hills. As it got closer she noticed a large, blue crystalline sphere radiant with etheric energy protruding from beneath. Two parts splayed outward away from each other behind the sphere and met at a point up front, like two equal halves of a wishbone.

Atop the sphere hovering always just a few feet above the ground was a long platform with a polished wooden floor that seemed to glow a light-colored amber. And this is where she and Richard stood with the other passengers watching as hills and grass morphed into a placid ocean waterfront stretching far into the distance with just a sliver of a beach.

From a distance they silently passed houses that were round and translucent and must have been created with some very advanced form of technology. From the outside Amelia could see through the structures so they were barely noticeable and blended perfectly into their environment, but Richard assured her that the inhabitants had complete privacy.

Small, white, furry creatures with big, black eyes and large ears stared at them as they chewed on strands of grass, their eyes following the craft as it passed for a moment over a small channel.

They followed the running water through a valley and then on into a massive cavern, capable of containing a small city, composed of crystalline rocks and gemstones.

Light passed through carved crystalline archways rising hundreds of feet high, causing rainbow colors to sparkle throughout the interior and across a massive healing temple built with precious jewels, crystals and gold.

As they passed through to the other side of the cavern the earth turned a tender green like the grass of early spring and brilliant flowers spiraled out of it. Luminous and colorful the flowers burst from curling vines low to the ground, but she noticed that as the wind blew they would stand up to dance gracefully, as if they were dancing just for her enjoyment.

Small crystalline bugs darted from flower to flower, sometimes rising in sparkling, diamond waves with the rolling of the wind, and then lightly splashing back down into the curls of plant life, where they hid beneath the petals of the flowers. Then the wind picked up again and they all rose together in a crystalline cloud, this time lighting up all at once and shooting out a brilliant display of red, blue and green. Accompanied by a loud BRZSRRRRZT! the lights disappeared with the loud sound that came with them.

The hovercraft moved gracefully up a steep incline then down the other side of the hill where it stopped to pause at the edge of a multi-colored forest. Then suddenly, a barely noticeable density began to fill the air. And though there was still blue sky and clear air an unseen world seemed to be emerging directly in front of them, as if it had been there the whole time and Amelia just hadn't seen it – but then she did: Lots of little lights dancing all around or maybe it was just a feeling and she was seeing them in her mind's eye as an overlay atop the scenery surrounding her.

At their stop Amelia and Richard stepped onto a broad pathway as the craft silently moved along toward its next destination. Sunlight filtered down through immense trees with leaves in every conceivable shade of green, yellow, orange and red. The trees were spaced a good distance apart and Amelia could see a nearby field bathed in sunshine and filled with the most superbly colored flowers. Many of the flowers were in full bloom, and although she was familiar with some of them, the vast majority she had never seen before. Everything seemed to exhale pure life-giving energy.

"Do you have any military or police?" asked Amelia.

Richard shook his head.

"Aren't there any bad people here?"

"There is no dishonesty. Remember how easily I could see that compass in your pocket? Everyone here is telepathic, so there's no sense in lying and no need for laws. No one takes more than they need and everyone shares. There's plenty of space for everyone, every view is beautiful, so you simply need to decide what you like best. There's no winter here, and though our sun is dimmer than the one you see on the surface it shines all the time, so fruits and vegetables are constantly growing and available to all. We barter with each other, so there's no need for money. Children are educated differently. They grow up in happy, loving families and they have the freedom to be themselves."

Richard noticed Amelia trying to understand how all of this could be possible. "Your world has been complicated and you've been educated to believe that you have no choice but to obey the laws, pay for property, pay for housing and food. But if you look at nature it carries the blueprint of what your world is meant to be like. In nature, no animals possess property, they're not stressed out, or warring with each other.

They don't take control of fruits and vegetables, or hoard them while others starve. There's a natural balance and it's always there as a reminder for anyone willing to pay attention."

"Well, what about people from Earth invading you? Don't you need a military presence to stop them, or has no one ever tried?" asked Amelia.

Richard laughed, "Oh they've tried! But there are energetic barriers created with technology far beyond what anyone knows on the surface. This is also a different dimension from your third-dimensional reality. Our technology allows us to move back and forth instantly, but if you had come here instantly, rather than gradually acclimating to this dimension, you would not have survived the sudden change."

As Richard spoke, the forest path opened into a meadow with lush grass, flower gardens, and tall, graceful shade trees amidst circular clearings with benches, tables and chairs set up for both privacy and small gatherings.

"Here we are!" said Richard beaming. "Welcome to The Portal!"

CHAPTER 12

As they walked across an arched bridge Amelia looked over the railing and saw perfectly clear water flowing above sparkling multicolor quartz crystals, semi-precious and precious stones.

"Are you thirsty? Would you like a drink of water?" asked Richard.

Amelia stepped off the bridge and scooped a handful of water out of the creek. The moment she touched it an exhilarating feeling flowed from her hand and up into her arm. She experienced the same effect as she drank the water, a feeling of being totally relaxed, yet fully energized and alive at the same time – as if she would never experience the need to sleep again.

Seeing the look on Amelia's face, Richard said with a smile, "We need very little sleep because our bodies are harmonized and constantly being regenerated by our crystalline surroundings, as well as by the water we drink and bathe in. We mature, but we don't age. There are people here who are hundreds and even thousands of years old."

As they headed toward The Portal entrance they walked through an archway composed of diamonds and bathed in sparkling rainbows. "In this library anyone in the Universe can access and study the records of The Game," said Richard.

"But what can you learn from us?" said Amelia as they climbed a crystal staircase leading into the main part of the library. "Earth is a mess! Clearly we don't know what we're doing!"

"Recognizing what doesn't work can be just as effective as observing what does work," said Richard. "Here at this library we have access to the entire Universal databank. So we can look at any problem that arises in The Game and access the best solution for solving it. We then record the problem and the solution – as well as how to prevent the problem in the first place. In this way anyone can quickly access the highest and most positive outcome for any event. Every conceivable problem and answer exists here – and that's mainly because of every brave person, like you, who plays The Game… we learn from your mistakes!"

Amelia certainly didn't feel very brave – stupid, scared to death and *what the hell was I thinking* had come to mind many times, but brave? Not so much.

They reached the top of the crystal stairway and found themselves in the midst of a hologram. Not only did they see the Milky Way Galaxy, but stars and suns and entire solar systems were floating overhead.

"Oh my God, I feel like I'm lifting off the floor and about to float away!" exclaimed Amelia breathlessly.

"That's partly because there are crystals embedded all throughout the library," said Richard. "Well, actually, everything in the library is crystalline. In the same way that you have quartz crystals in your computers, all information here is held and accessed with crystals as well.

"This library is an Inter-dimensional Portal. It will take you to wherever you project your thoughts. Whatever you intend to see – you will have a first-hand experience – on any and every level."

The library appeared more like an elegant park with

rainbow light glittering on the trees, flowers, streams and waterfalls everywhere the eye could see. Amid this stunning beauty people were walking and talking, some were studying or reclining in the most comfortable looking chairs imaginable. Others had their eyes closed and were day-dreaming and quite a few were *wired up* and connected into the library operating system, which took them anywhere they chose to go without ever leaving the comfort of their reclining chair.

There were mini-theatres throughout the library where history not only came to life, but when Amelia stepped inside she felt as if she was actually living it – as if she was really there in that exact period of time. But more than that, she felt as if she was part of everything that had ever existed or ever would exist anywhere in the Universe.

Richard led Amelia on to an alcove with one of the reclining chairs. She sat down, stretched out and leaned back luxuriously. She lay there as if she were floating without a care in the world.

"The Portal will not only transport you to any place in the Universe, it can also answer any questions you may want to ask. But may I make a suggestion?" said Richard supportively.

"Of course!"

"The trick to getting the most out of The Portal is to ask high quality questions."

"What do you mean?" asked Amelia.

"Well… for instance, if you ask *'why am I trapped in this experience?'* you would be shown a series of things that you said or did or thought that brought you to that moment of being trapped… which would only magnify the problem. Whereas if you ask, *'how can I free myself from this situation?'* you would receive solutions rather than more problems.

"Now think of the question, *'Who am I?'* … this question has been going round and round in the mind's of players for as long as The Game has been in existence, yet no one has ever found a definitive answer. But if you ask a high quality version of that question, you would have a very different result."

Amelia thought for a moment then confessed, "I can't think of a different way to ask that question."

"How about... Who am I when I'm not getting my way?" said Richard, smiling broadly.

Amelia burst out laughing. "Oh, I see what you mean," she said as several ideas popped into her mind in quick succession.

With a warm smile Richard said, "I will now take my leave of you."

Amelia bounced out of her chair, hugged Richard and kissed him on the cheek. "Thank you so much. I hope to see you again someday!"

"That would be my wish as well," he said affectionately. "Oh, and don't forget to ask your question about Antarctica!"

Amelia smiled and nodded enthusiastically. She sat on the chair, leaned back and felt as if she was floating on a warm, luminous cloud of energy, but the energy felt like a part of her rather than something separate or outside of herself.

Amelia took a deep breath. "I have sort of a compass-map type thing in my pocket. It shows Earth from the perspective of the North Pole – and it shows all of the continents except Antarctica... where is it?" said Amelia digging the compass out of her pocket.

"Antarctica does not exist as a separate continent... it extends all the way around the Earth's playing field. It's represented on your compass by the diamonds surrounding the outer edge."

Amelia looked at the compass in the palm of her hand and said, "I don't understand what you mean. Antarctica is a small continent at the South Pole."

"Well, that's certainly what you've been taught."

"Maybe because you're inside the Earth you just don't understand what it looks like from outer space," said Amelia. "But trust me it's round, not flat… I've seen pictures."

"Your belief will cause you to see whatever you say is so."

"No, you don't understand. The Earth can't be round *and* flat – it's either one or the other," said Amelia definitively.

"You see whatever you believe."

"But you're saying that Earth is flat and I don't believe that!" said Amelia emphatically.

"That's why you perceive Earth as a planet rather than a plane," said The Portal. "But both versions exist simultaneously."

"I don't see how that's possible?" said Amelia skeptically.

"Well, you believe Earth is round… so the only way to experience both versions simultaneously is to open your imagination to see the version where Earth is flat."

Taking a deep breath, Amelia said hesitantly, "Okay… how do I do that?"

"Imagine that you and your parents were raised believing that Earth is just as stationary as it appears to be – NASA, your government and educational system are all in agreement with the information you receive from your senses.

"Now imagine trying to convince people that Earth is not stationary – that it is spinning at 1,000 miles per hour – and moving forward through space thirty-two times faster than a bullet shot from a rifle. But no one feels anything because of gravity."

"At least I know gravity is real!" said Amelia confidently.

"Maybe in some version of reality… but in your version gravity has never been scientifically proven to exist… and yet its so-called magnetism is responsible for keeping everything and everyone from flying off of the planet… it's strong enough to hold people, buildings, oceans and the atmosphere tightly stuck to the surface, yet it's just weak enough so that birds are able to fly and smoke rises upward.

"Do you think you could convince the entire world that this is an established fact that doesn't require any scientific proof?"

"When you put it that way," said Amelia taken aback, "it sounds bizarre! But then how do you explain all of the pictures of Earth from outer space?"

"Can you tell the difference between a real photo taken in outer space and a picture created with computer generated imagery?"

"Well… no," said Amelia thoughtfully. "But there are astronauts that walked on the moon! That happened for sure!"

"How do you know that happened… for sure? How do you know anything for sure?" said The Portal. "What would you think if you knew that all of the Apollo 11 videos and audios suddenly *disappeared* and every contractor managed to mysteriously lose the prints and plans for the Lunar Rover, LEM Lander and Apollo Ship Engines?"

"Really? I didn't know that!" said Amelia stunned. "But why would anyone pretend we had been to the moon and create fake images of Earth from outer space if it's not real?"

"Why indeed? What if it's all part of the fun and games you signed up for?" said The Portal.

"What do you mean?" asked Amelia.

"Imagine you could create your own virtual reality game… what would you want to experience?"

Amelia thought for a moment and said slowly, "Well, first I'd want it to be 100% believable with an infinite number of choices and levels of challenges so the game would basically never end... I hate it when I find a really good game… I play for three days straight and then I have to wait for the next game because I already know the whole storyline so it's boring if I play it again.

"Sorry, off topic," said Amelia laughing. "Um…I'd want to be able to choose any timeline; past, present or future. Oh... and I'd want a vacation part! I mean a real vacation, not one where I'd be at the beach and have to keep an eye out for snipers! I'd want to be able to come home from school and do anything I wanted… ride horses, go mountain climbing, visit another country… stuff like that.

"And I'd want a storyline that can go in any direction," she said, her imagination gathering steam, "but especially things that are mysterious and intriguing. I like figuring things out. You know, things that aren't obvious where you have to do research and piece things together.

"Oh… and I'd want a boyfriend," said Amelia a bit sheepishly. "I know that's kind of weird… a cyber boyfriend and all, but it would be fun to have a little romance thrown in with the mayhem!"

"So what are you experiencing now?" said The Portal.

"Well, not the virtual reality I have in mind… that's for sure," said Amelia rolling her eyes.

"My dear, you designed the virtual reality that you're currently playing and all the intrigue and conspiracy theories that go with it!"

"But what about the Big Bang and evolution? I mean, people WAY smarter than me believe in that event!" said Amelia.

"Every possibility exists – but in the reality you designed, does The Big Bang make sense? The theory begins with nothing, then somehow there's an explosion out of nowhere and instead of destroying things like every other explosion,

THIS explosion somehow manages to create space, time and all matter – in an instant, for no reason at all.

"Debris flew outward at over 670 miles per hour for fourteen billion years! Then some of that debris turned into bubbling ooze that ultimately became planet Earth. Magically, single-celled organisms appeared, then they became multi-celled, then conscious, then everything multiplied, divided, mutated, adapted, evolved and finally crawled onto land, replacing gills with lungs… tails were lost… and then voila - opposable thumbs!"

"You're right, it sounds crazy… it is crazy!" said Amelia in complete shock. "How come people can't see this? Why does everyone believe it without question?"

"It doesn't matter…" said The Portal, "it's part of what you designed."

"Okay, look. Here's the problem," said Amelia, suddenly worried about what was to come. "When I get back to the base, I don't know what I'm going to do – these are real people and they're unbelievably powerful."

"Certainly all those *powerful* players would be delighted to know you think that way. But the truth is that every person playing has equal power. Those in *authority* have no more power than you – unless you choose to give your power away by believing you have no power.

"The prime directive is '*Thy Will Be Done*.' If you feel and believe '*I'm trapped… there's nothing I can do…*' the program is designed to give you more experiences that confirm what you believe."

Amelia shook her head. "I understand what you're saying but I don't think I can do it. I don't think I can make myself feel differently than I do."

"You are now recognizing that two seemingly separate realities can exist at the same time… so can you understand that reality is flexible…that it moves according to your focus and beliefs?"

Amelia nodded her head. But if she was being perfectly

honest she would have to admit that she wasn't sure who The Portal was, where it came from, or if it was telling the truth. And from that perspective she also wondered whether or not the Inner Earth was part of her own game, if The Game existed at all. But that was just one more distraction. The only thing she knew for sure was that she needed to get back to the base.

"I know where I need to go, but can you help me understand what I'll be dealing with when I get back to my reality? I need to see things… related to me… things going on in my world… so I know how to help Matthew."

Instantly, Amelia found herself out-of-body and hovering unseen in front of Thomas.

CHAPTER 13

For a moment it seemed that Thomas was looking directly at her, but then his attention turned to five men seated at a long, highly polished cherry wood table. He picked up a remote control and a large screen lit up with video images of burning rain forests.

"Images like these capture people's attention, but the real problem is a lot less visible and far more serious. At least 30,000 species vanish every year. Right now we're living in the midst of one of the greatest mass extinctions in Earth's history. Our planetary ecosystem is collapsing. Environmental toxins are bringing about new patterns of disease, and pollinating insects are on their way to extinction, leading to widespread crop failure. This ongoing loss of biodiversity may have consequences we'll never think of, until it's too late.

"First we're going to focus on one aspect of this collapse. Albert Einstein said, '*If the honey bee disappears from the surface of the earth, man would have no more than four years to live.*' Bee colonies are disappearing at an alarming rate. Earth would instantly begin to thrive again without the human race. But WE cannot live without pollinating insects. In the past five years we have lost 30 percent of the honey bee population.

And there is no doubt that in a matter of years all of the bees WILL die and then the entire human race will die within four years. The paradox is that if a large portion of the human race were to die off first, not only would it save pollinating insects, our entire planet would quickly begin to recover.

"We know the problem. We know the solution, but no one is doing anything about it. So who's to blame? The corporations, the chemical industry, the government, the farmers, the consumers? The truth is… it doesn't matter," said Thomas emphatically. "No one is taking responsibility, not even The Brotherhood, and by the time everyone starts to wake up and see what's really happening, it will be too late.

"For years we've been working to subtly reduce the population by degrading human health with specific chemicals added to food, air, water and pharmaceutical drugs, but we're out of time. We need to be prepared to drastically reduce the population if we're going to stop the collapse of our ecosystem. If the bees die everything will be lost. No government will legally be able to take these steps. It's up to us. Are we in agreement?"

The men all nodded gravely.

"There are two methods we will be employing… activating natural disasters and manipulating human consciousness." Nodding toward a man with black, curly hair and a neatly trimmed beard, Thomas said, "Carlos will explain the latter."

Standing up, Carlos said, "Our research has shown that the power of the human mind can be directed and manipulated to create strong beliefs, even convictions, as well as diseased conditions that lead to death with nothing more than fearful thoughts."

A split screen video sprang to life showing Amelia and Matthew as they reacted emotionally to the newscast they had watched only days earlier. "The video you're seeing is nothing more than a combination of past newsreels showing natural catastrophes and movie clips that were edited out of recent disaster films. We then created a narrative and added time-stamps. Though none of it was actually happening, these teenagers fully believed what we told them to believe. They both accepted their fate and unquestioningly cooperated with everything we asked of them."

Though she was out-of-body Amelia was dizzy with shock. How could that be? Why would anyone do something so appalling and cruel?

"The intention of our experiment with these teens was to isolate them and give them totally inaccurate, but convincing visual and audio information, then observe the level at which they could be controlled. Even though the female is particularly intuitive, psychic even, we've had complete cooperation and they've both become passive even in areas where they're required to submit to activities they wouldn't ordinarily do."

A man in his early-thirties with short-cropped, brown hair interjected, "So what are you suggesting, Thomas, false flags or some form of mass hypnosis via the media?"

"That's what you and the others are here to discover," said Thomas. "In the lab we have thousands of case files. We maintain complete control of the stock market so you have an unlimited budget - you can acquire whatever you need."

Motioning to a grey haired man who seemed to be the oldest one in the group, Thomas said, "Maksim will now explain our natural disaster program."

Standing up and walking over to a large map Maksim said, "One of the fastest ways to covertly reduce the population is by triggering natural disasters. We started this process quite some time ago by triggering seismic and volcanic activity using Tesla technology in this area." Pointing to a map of the Pacific Ocean he said, "The Ring of Fire has been created by oceanic tectonic plates getting stuck on continental plates. Volcanoes erupt in this region when the oceanic plates slide deep beneath the continental ones, eventually the temperature and pressure become so extreme the rock above them melts.

"This volatile area runs from New Zealand up through Indonesia and Japan, across the ocean to Alaska, and down the west coast of the Americas to Chile. Japan, Indonesia, Alaska, and Chile have already experienced earthquakes at magnitude 9 and above.

"Our plan is to activate a fault line which is part of the Ring of Fire, but has been completely ignored." Maksim then pointed to a map of California. "Just north of the San Andreas fault line lies another fault line known mainly to the geological community as the Cascadia subduction zone. It begins here, near Cape Mendocino, and runs for seven hundred miles off the coast of the Pacific Northwest, along Oregon and Washington... terminating here," said Maksim pointing to southwestern Canada, "around Vancouver Island.

"As you may know we've been developing Nikola Tesla's research and designs since the time of his death in 1943," said Maksim, picking up a small mechanical device and holding it out in the palm of his hand. "This device generates a frequency that resonates at Earth's frequency. The concept is much like a high pitched sound resonating with the frequency of a crystal glass. At first the glass will hum, but when the amplitude is high enough to exceed the strength of the glass – in other words the sound becomes too loud for the glass to vibrate – the crystal shatters.

"Waves of any sort set up sympathetic vibrations in the materials they impinge upon, and devices like this one have been planted along the Cascadia subduction zone and the San Andreas fault.

"When the time is optimal we will activate the devices and a massive earthquake extending over 1,600 miles will take place on the San Andreas fault and the Cascadia subduction simultaneously. One end will hit the entire northern coastline and trigger a tsunami of epic proportions, but it won't be like a Hokusai-style wave rising up from the surface of the sea and breaking from above. The entire ocean will be elevated at least one hundred feet as it overtakes the land.

"Activating the San Andreas fault would damage half the buildings in Los Angeles and destroy the city's water supply.

But as you know the 1906 earthquake is not what devastated San Francisco, it was the ruptured gas mains that started fires which ultimately burned the city to the ground. With this in mind we are planning to create the *'perfect storm'...* which is to say that we will activate the Tesla devices to coincide with gusting winds."

The picture before them changed and Maksim said, "This map of the Santa Ana winds in SoCal is constantly being updated. Yellow is marginal risk, orange is moderate, red is high and purple is extreme. As you can see, the map currently indicates red from Santa Barbara all of the way down the coast to San Diego, but the prediction over the next few days turns into purple. And this is what we've been waiting for... extreme, hot, gusting winds which will cause fires to burn intensely and move at phenomenal speeds.

"A series of 9 point earthquakes combined with the resulting tsunami to the north and fires to the south will cut back substantially on the population in this area... the entire coastline will remain all but uninhabitable for several years... with no electricity, drinking water, sewer services, health care facilities and major highways. Interstate 10 will be torn apart making it impossible to receive supplies from the south.

"This will cut back substantially on the human population while allowing our honey bee population to thrive. Even though this area has some of the richest soil for farming, no one will be focused on planting and poisoning crops when they have no electricity, sanitation, roads, hospitals or homes," said Maksim as he returned to his seat.

"An additional part of our plan is to activate the Wasatch fault here in Utah," said Thomas, pointing to the map. "This fault line is long overdue for an earthquake which means that it will be activated with the slightest provocation. Not only would this cripple the Wasatch Front urban area with over two million people, but as you can see these east-west Interstate highways 80 and 70 plus I-15 running north and south will be destroyed at these points," he said pointing to Salt Lake City and highway connection points both north and south. "These three highways are surrounded by mountains so when they are crippled, it will be extremely difficult for disaster supplies to reach Utah, Nevada and California and most transportation will come to an immediate halt."

A grey haired man raised his hand and said, "Isn't the southern portion of the Wasatch fault dangerously close to our location?"

"It's close, but we won't activate any devices south of the I-15 / I-70 convergence," said Thomas.

"But as you said, an earthquake is long overdue… couldn't the earthquake effect us here?" said the man narrowing his eyes.

"It's very unlikely given how deep we are underground. And the fact that our facility is composed of manmade caverns and tunnels built into the bedrock," said Thomas, "but to be on the safe side I've created a map for each of you so you can be sure that you're out of harm's way."

"Wouldn't it be best if we just took a train to one of the other bases where it's safe?" said the man.

"Well, there have been some unexpected developments, so let me explain," said Thomas. "As you know, our military has been trying to reach the Inner-Earth ever since Admiral Richard Byrd actually flew inside through the North Pole in 1947 returning with a full report. There are untold amounts of gold, diamonds and other important elements that we want to control. And though we immediately became a presence at the North Pole and in Antarctica back in forty-seven, we've never been able to penetrate the Inner Earth defenses – their technology is light-years ahead of ours.

"However, our remote viewers discovered a *back door,* an underground cavern that opens into a series of tunnels that lead into the Inner Earth. It's completely unguarded. In fact I've sent a test-subject to the cavern via the Montauk Chair. Our best remote viewers have been tracking her movements and she has successfully reached the Inner Earth in a remarkably short period of time," said Thomas with a restrained smile, but it was clear to Amelia that he was extremely pleased with himself.

"Though we will continue to do our best to reduce Earth's population and save pollinating insects, regardless of what happens, our Brotherhood will not be forced to live underground if Earth is ultimately destroyed. My alternate plan will allow the six of us to live inside the Inner Earth. It's a utopian world where everyone is in perfect health. They live for hundreds or even thousands of years. They've managed to stop our military, but I'm now confident we can make it through."

Amelia was fuming. He wasn't just testing her – he had been using her without her knowledge *or* permission. Adding insult to injury, he didn't even give her a name or any credit whatsoever! He called her a test-subject, as if he deserved all of the credit for picking her and she had done nothing!

If she hadn't been viewing him out-of-body she would have hit him over the head with his coffee cup – and the prison time would have been totally worth it! But all she could do was stare at the cup, willing it to fly off the table and hit him in the head. Yet as Amelia stared at the stubbornly unmoving cup she realized she was looking at an emblem of the flat Earth. It looked exactly like the map on her compass, with the North Pole at the center. She couldn't believe her eyes. She moved closer and saw that it was the flag of the United Nations.

Amelia didn't know what to think. She had seen the United Nations emblem before, but nothing registered at the time. Could the design be a coincidence? Or was it an inside joke shared by an elite few who knew Earth was a flat playing field and laughed at all the rest who believed it was actually a sphere?

Thomas continued. "Though the Tesla device is being utilized to activate earthquakes, the resonant frequency can also be moderated, allowing us to tunnel through virtually anything. We're very close to breaching the cavern that leads into the Inner Earth, but just recently we hit an igneous layer that required us to intensify the frequency of the Tesla device, which in turn set off an earthquake.

"This has happened before, but in the past the tremors have been insignificant and fairly brief. However, this time, though the movement is barely noticeable at this level… miles below us there is a great deal of movement and it appears to be increasing.

"We're pressing on and doing everything we can to reach the cavern, but our instruments have indicated a fast buildup of magma underground and it would appear we have awakened an ancient super-volcano. It's impossible to know if or when it will erupt, but this type of buildup occurring at this rate of speed generally precedes a massive eruption.

"If this happens there will be an emergency evacuation of this facility. This evacuation is not to protect those leaving, but to be sure that everyone left in this facility can easily survive, even for generations. So all of you need to stay here… you'll be far safer underground whether or not the tunnel is finished."

"Once again," said the grey haired man interrupting, "wouldn't it be safest to evacuate by train and then return when we're sure it's safe?"

"If the super-volcano erupts there will be no escape anywhere on Earth," said Thomas ruefully. "Even if you were to take the train to another base and try to get home from there, this type of eruption would cause a ten foot layer of ash that would spread up to 1,000 miles away. And when the ash plume rises up and reaches the stratosphere it releases sulfuric gases that when mixed with Earth's water vapor would cause all air transportation to cease and a volcanic-winter would ensue as ash in our atmosphere spreads around the world. We would be facing a small ice age with very few, if any, survivors."

"But doesn't this mean it's even more dangerous to activate the Wasatch fault, given how close we are?" said the man emphatically.

With a conciliatory sigh Thomas said, "I admit there is a small possibility that the earthquake could activate volcanic activity, but given the tunnel work below that may be the result regardless of whether we activate the fault line or not. And if we want to make it extremely difficult for the west coast to survive and rebuild it's more important that we do everything we can to stop transportation from reaching as many cities as possible.

"My plan is to finish the tunnel to the Inner Earth," said Thomas, "and continue working on everything we've discussed. When we've implemented our strategies and we know the population will be sufficiently decreased, then our job is complete and you are all welcome to journey with me to the Inner Earth.

"In case of an unforeseen emergency you'll find your gear is already packed and waiting in your rooms for those who would care to trek to the Inner Earth," said Thomas as he handed each man a small metallic device. "These devices will give you access to any place in this facility and also the GPS coordinates that will lead you to the safest possible location – either in this facility or leading you to the Inner Earth tunnel when it's finished."

Suddenly, Amelia felt a strange pulling motion and in the next moment she was back in her body at The Portal. She was horrified by the cold, calculating methods Thomas was planning to implement and even more shocked by the fact that she and Matthew were actually being shown video clips of what could very well take place within days – and now that she knew it was actually coming she had no way to stop it.

"This is terrible! What am I supposed to do?" she asked desperately.

The Portal responded, "Life is but a dream."

Before she could respond Amelia suddenly felt utterly exhausted, as if all of the energy had been drained from her body and was being replaced by a light tingling feeling. She was falling asleep, but it was happening so quickly she couldn't even force her eyes to open. And then she found herself standing in a very ordinary looking room with a highly set, square window, a red, exterior door, four white walls and a square, wooden table with four wooden chairs set neatly around it.

But this was unlike any dream Amelia had ever dreamed before, because she was fully aware that she was dreaming and that her body was actually lying in a lounge chair at The Portal. Amelia looked at the table. She knew for a fact that the table wasn't solid and it wasn't real. With this in mind she walked up to it and knocked on the surface. The table behaved just as any table would. It felt solid to the touch, made the appropriate sound given the size of the room and the height of the ceiling, and it even had color and texture and the faint scent of pine. Yet, Amelia knew for a fact that it wasn't there. She knew her mind had created everything, down to the smallest detail – even details that never would have occurred to her.

She decided to go outside and without even needing to open the door she found herself instantly standing in the yard smelling freshly cut grass and astonished to see a perfectly clear blue sky overhead. She thought, '*Since I know I'm dreaming I might as well fly.*' In an instant she was high in the sky, lighter than air, laughing out loud from the thrill of it all.

She decided she should go home and check on her parents, and immediately began flying toward home, but then she realized she was in the Inner Earth and had no idea how to find her way. Immediately she was back on the ground and no matter what she did she couldn't get herself to fly again.

Amelia guessed that it was her fear that had grounded her, but even when she decided she didn't need to be afraid, she simply couldn't get her body to fly again, as if her fear had somehow anchored her to the ground.

When she woke up Amelia had complete awareness of her dream; it was as clear and real to her as if it had just happened in her own reality – only everything had happened in a split second.

"You see?" said The Portal. "As I told you, your dreams are far closer to actual reality than the world you believe is solid and real. When you awaken from your dreams you are in a highly believable hologram projected by your avatar. In The Game program, nothing is as it seems."

"Look, I don't know how to get this through to you," said Amelia exasperated, "I'm talking about real problems, not some hologram, not a game. We have real problems on Earth… but you can't understand that because… well, I mean, you're a library… or something like that." Amelia wished she had taken a class on how to communicate with artificial intelligence.

"My intelligence is not artificial. I am connected to the Universal Intelligence of All That Is," said The Portal.

"Okay… all right, whatever," said Amelia sighing and not wanting to offend The Portal – clearly it wasn't programmed to know the truth of its existence. "Um, I get that you're trying to show me that even when I know, for a fact, that something isn't really there… like that table in my dream… that the illusion-of-a-table is still going to act like a table.

"And I understand that you're trying to tell me that nothing is really real in my world – everything is a hologram projected by my avatar…" Amelia paused as she tried to put everything together, "And, um, I think you're saying that even if I consciously know I'm in a hologram… and even if I know that what I see isn't really there – it is still going to *act* as if it's real. Right?"

"Yes."

"Well, that's just confusing! Can't you just give me a *'For Dummies'* version? I mean, something for human beings… something that will really help me when I get back?" said Amelia praying The Portal was actually programmed for such a thing.

"Yes, I can. Imagine a mirror hanging on the wall. It is neutral. It's not good or bad, it's just a mirror. Now, when you stand in front of the mirror you're no longer perceiving it as neutral… in fact, if you think about it, you no longer see the mirror… you only see yourself.

"But even then, you aren't actually seeing yourself… at

least not in a neutral way, the way you originally saw the mirror as it was hanging on the wall… you're seeing your perception of yourself. Do you understand?"

"I think so…" said Amelia hesitantly.

"The Game program itself is neutral. Just like the mirror on the wall it mirrors back whatever you are thinking and feeling. And there are countless reasons why you perceive yourself the way you do and every reason is connected to something you've experienced before… either in the game you're currently playing or in games you've played prior to this one.

"We'll call these perceptions, imprints. Some imprints you're consciously aware of, but most imprints come to you unconsciously – yet they are still imprinted in your avatar-mind whether you remember them or not. And these imprints determine your experience."

"You mean I'm attracting certain people or experiences because of these imprints?" said Amelia, confused.

"You do not attract anything. You are creating everything. Your focus creates an imprint. The imprint is projected by your avatar and shows up as your holographic world."

"But how does that help me?" said Amelia impatiently. "Do I have to learn how to fight off an imprint?"

"No. You can't fight or destroy an imprint. But you can create new imprints that are more powerful than the old imprints."

"How?" said Amelia abruptly.

"The only reason things don't appear differently, according to your desire, is because your fear that what you want WON'T happen is stronger than your desire for what you want. You can have anything you can imagine if you can *wish without worrying*," said The Portal.

Wish without worrying. Amelia had never contemplated whether or not her wishes included worrying, but now that she thought about it she did have the tendency to worry when she really had her heart set on something. As she contemplated what she might wish for, that wouldn't cause her to worry, she couldn't think of anything. So she decided to wish for whatever she wanted, and worry about the worrying part later.

Amelia took a deep breath and said, "I want to help Matthew escape so we can go home and help our families too… and well… I guess I want to save everyone on the planet from what's coming…" she added, "whether it's Thomas's plan of destruction or the extinction of bees and everyone dying four years later ….or whatever the next catastrophe may be.

"And… well… I know how to save the Earth! I remember being a Vedruss… I wish people would listen to me and that people could live that way again… I mean, if they want to." Amelia paused. "Okay, that wish went on a bit," she conceded, "and it's not very realistic."

"Being realistic is highly overrated. You wouldn't have the desire to do all of those things if there was nothing you could do about it," said The Portal.

"Okay, but here's the thing," Amelia confessed. "I'm not very good at wishing without worrying."

"That's okay, here's a solution. Think of someone else who wants what you want, and then help them get it."

Amelia laughed. "I don't know anyone crazy enough to think that they can save the Earth and all of humanity… I think I was on a bit of roll thinking it was just a wish," she added sheepishly. "But even if I could find someone like me who had the mother-of-all-wishes… how could I possibly help them when I don't know what to do myself?"

"Remember that *'wish without worrying'* part?"

Laughing, Amelia said, "Oh… yeah."

"So don't worry. There will be someone you can help, and it doesn't matter whether you accomplish what you set out to do or not. You are simply creating an imprint and ninety percent of the imprint is your intention to help someone else."

"Okay… " said Amelia, hoping there would be something more substantial that she could do.

"Think of anything good you're doing to help others and that will take all of the worry out of it."

"That's it?"

"Yes."

"Oh."

Amelia took a deep breath. Growing up, people her mom's age used to always say, "Oh, you're such a little Pollyanna." She had to look it up in the dictionary to find out what it meant. Actually there were two words. Pollyannaism was excessively or blindly optimistic, whereas Pollyannaish was unreasonably or illogically optimistic. Amelia never was completely sure whether she was an *'ism'* or an *'ish'* but either way she outgrew that phase when her best friend died in sixth grade. After that she didn't see life quite the same way anymore.

If The Portal was right and the answer to getting whatever she wanted was by helping someone else get what they wanted first, why hadn't anyone ever mentioned that before? It was so simple it couldn't be a total secret. But then it occurred to her that maybe Pollyannaism had been programmed into The Portal or the library needed some serious updating when it came to the reality of human existence – at least where she came from.

So Amelia focused on her real reason for being at The Portal in the first place. "Can you deliver me to the military base where I came from – the secret, underground base in the Utah desert?" she said, figuring there couldn't be more than one. "Oh, and I want to be inside the base…" And then as she thought about the size of the base she added, "and in a spot where I can easily reach Matthew."

"Yes, I can."

"Good, please send me back," said Amelia, unconsciously gripping the arms of the chair.

"You do understand you will not be able to find your way back to the Inner-Earth."

"Yes."

"And you want to do this without asking anymore questions?"

"Yes… NO! WAIT!" said Amelia quickly as she remembered

leaving too hastily when Äsha asked her the same question, more or less. "If I don't have the time or ability to help someone else get what I want, is there something else I can do so I won't worry?"

"Imagine what you want and say to yourself, *This or something better.*"

In the next moment Amelia disappeared from the Inner-Earth. But she didn't have much time to be grateful for the fact that she had been able to access technology capable of delivering her directly to the underground base because she materialized in a logical but inconvenient place.

It was logical because every form of transportation was within walking distance. But it was highly inconvenient because it was also the command center for the entire base.

CHAPTER 14

Amelia materialized and found herself kneeling on the floor next to a waist high, metal railing with glass panels. Disoriented, it took her a moment to adjust to where she was, but just seconds later she ducked down as low as she could, scooting away from the railing, her eyes wide open. She was on a small balcony with nothing but a wooden podium. At the back of the space a staircase led down to the main room below, but it didn't seem that the stairs got much use or that people came up to the balcony very often.

Lying on her stomach she moved slowly back to the railing and looked carefully into the large room below. There were men in military uniforms milling about, but more than anything it reminded her of a huge university lecture hall. The space was filled with people in white collared shirts sitting at computers facing the front of the room. But instead of a blackboard there was a massive screen showing the Earth. At first glance it looked like something she would see on the news with satellite coverage showing clouds and a bunch of tiny lights where it was obviously nighttime, but as she looked more closely she realized she was seeing the Flat Earth with the North Pole at the center, just like the cover of her compass. Amelia couldn't believe her eyes. They knew! All these people knew the truth.

Amelia slid carefully away from the railing. She didn't know what to think, let alone what to do or where to go. Nothing The Portal had told her was going to help. First of all, there was definitely no one in the command center who wanted what she wanted, and since she had no idea of what to do, *'this or something better,'* wasn't an option. So she moved toward the back wall until she could stand up without being seen by the people below. Crouching down she walked cautiously over to the podium when suddenly a hologram popped out asking for a fingerprint scan and showing the same map she had seen on the wall below. Frantically she drew away in a complete panic, praying that no alerts had been activated.

When no alarms went off and she felt quite sure no one was coming for her, Amelia contemplated the possibility that the hologram had a map of the facility, or at least something to give her an idea of where she was, but it wasn't worth the risk even in the unlikely event that she could somehow access the map. So she moved to the top of the stairway and moved carefully and quietly down the metal steps.

Amelia had no solid plan and was hoping that maybe she could just blend in when she got to the main floor by acting as if she belonged there and had some kind of a mission. But in truth she knew that once she got to the bottom of the staircase there would be no way to get past the swarm of soldiers and officers below. Coming to her senses she turned to climb back up to the balcony when she noticed an unusual patch of light.

Looking up she saw a slightly opened, metal framed window which was part of a large façade formed of flat glass panels. Climbing up on the railing Amelia was able to look beyond the window, which seemed to have been cracked open for ventilation, into a luxuriously decorated office. In the middle of the room there was an elegant dark, polished wood desk and a large, brown leather couch and matching armchair, atop a somber red and white oriental rug with large, green plants in the corner.

The room was empty, so without a thought, Amelia pushed the window fully open, grabbed the bottom of the window frame, pulled herself up the short distance and jumped into the room. Quickly she closed the window, leaving it open just a crack, and then she hurried across the room to the door. But immediately she heard footsteps and loud voices moving quickly in her direction, so she rushed to the other side of the room and squeezed herself between the wall and the sofa.

The door opened and she heard a man's voice as he stood in the doorway giving orders. "No, absolutely not! Find out right now what caused the alarm," his voice boomed.

"But sir," said a younger male voice, "we checked... the cameras weren't on."

"Whatever happened... I want to know about it," said the older man as he closed the door.

Walking heavily across the room, the man sat down at his desk and started typing on his computer. Amelia was lying on her back, but the couch was over six feet long so she knew the man wouldn't see her unless he was looking for her.

She tried to listen intently as he spoke on the phone, but she wasn't sure what he was talking about and in moments her exhaustion caught up with her. Every cell in her body wanted to sleep and suddenly she found herself drifting through time and space until she found herself once again in her Russian home. The day was perfect, the sky was crystal clear and she was lying on the grass feeling a faint tingle from the earth below. She was so happy to be home. It felt as if she had never left, as if she had simply woken up from a bad dream and was now relieved and grateful to discover that none of it was real.

And then she felt something pressing uncomfortably into her hip, but as she felt around nothing was on the ground beneath her. Suddenly, she realized that she wasn't dreaming. She was in two places at once and she desperately needed to get back into her body before she fell soundly asleep.

Amelia imagined herself back in the office and found

herself hovering above her body as she lay with her eyes closed behind the couch. She didn't know how to get back into her body and she was afraid that if she did, she would be unable to wake up. So she imagined herself opening her eyes. Her body jolted slightly as adrenaline rushed through her veins, but in the next moment she was in her body looking up at the ceiling.

She listened carefully to see if her movement had alerted the man at the desk, but nothing happened. Then she realized the pain in her hip was being caused by the compass in her pocket and she suddenly remembered Richard telling her she could use it telepathically.

At the time, she doubted her abilities, but now she had no choice, so she thought, "Minus 74 point 85 16 16... Minus 102 point 59 zero 33 zero." And then, "Show me where I am and how to safely get to Matthew."

Instantly she saw herself in the office and then she discovered that she could see out into the hall. In her mind's eye she could see the placement of objects and the movement of people who looked like little lights moving along the corridor. Nothing significant happened for a while, and she was about to unwillingly fall asleep when she heard the man stand up from his desk. Instantly alert she was able to see a little light which represented him as he walked out the door.

Amelia waited until he turned the corner and went down another hallway. She then wriggled out from behind the couch and paused at the door until she could see that the corridor was clear. Just as she was about to open the door she heard, or rather felt, the feeling to wait. She could see someone walk out of one office and into another, and then in about ten seconds she was compelled to go.

But Amelia wasn't totally sure of her feelings so she hesitated and listened at the door a moment longer until a voice spoke clearly in her mind, "Go, now!"

Amelia quickly slipped out into the passageway, quietly closed the door and then walked as inconspicuously as possible down the hall in the direction she was being guided.

Miraculously she could hear, "Go left, turn right, stand in the doorway, walk, stop, bend down, tie your shoe." She could feel herself getting closer and closer to Matthew, but it seemed as if he was below her. She waited in front of two elevators. One door opened and closed, but she waited for the next elevator and then chose the fourth floor without waiting to be guided.

The minute she stepped out into the hall and the elevator door closed behind her, Amelia knew she had made a mistake. She turned to get back on the elevator but before the doors could open alarms were blaring and armed soldiers swarmed out of every hallway. Adrenaline shot through her body and her mind began spinning in blind panic as she realized she could no longer see, hear or feel what to do next. In moments she was surrounded by soldiers with their weapons pointed directly at her.

Terrified, Amelia put her arms in the air, but she had the presence of mind to telepathically lock her compass by thinking of the code. As she suspected, she was searched and the compass was confiscated. Her heart sank, but there was nothing she could say or do as she was escorted immediately down the corridor and into a large electric transport vehicle with no doors. As she climbed in with a guard right behind her, she saw another guard was waiting on the other side of the seat with handcuffs in his lap forcing Amelia to sit between them. After being cuffed a dark nylon hood was placed over her head and Amelia's world went black.

The vehicle drove over several different types of ground. At first it felt smooth then very uneven, the way it felt when their bus drove over a wash, and then really bumpy as if they were crossing over cattle guards. Once again it was smooth and the vehicle came to a stop and the motor was turned off. But no one moved or got out they just sat there. And then Amelia realized they were moving, but they were going down inside an elevator.

Down and down she felt herself dropping, but after

awhile she had no sense of speed only that they were going down for what felt like forever before coming to a slow stop. Amelia heard the elevator doors moving open with an oddly familiar *'ding'* as if she were in a hotel and not in some deep, underground military outpost.

The strong hand of her guard grasped her right arm firmly, guiding her out of the humvee, then along a cement walkway and ultimately into a large echoing chamber where her handcuffs were removed. Then she heard the solid, thudding stride of the guard leaving the chamber and the bang of a heavy door.

Shaking, Amelia removed the hood from her head only to find herself in pitch black darkness. Like a small animal sensing a nearby predator she strained to listen for a sound, every muscle tensed, ready to take flight. But there was only ringing in her ears.

Amelia tried to walk, but instantly felt dizzy and slowly dropped to the floor. She crawled cautiously until she came to a wall. For a moment she sat there trying to calm herself, her heart pounding heavily in her chest and a feeling of panic rising in her as nausea brought bile up the back of her throat. A voice coming through a loud speaker caused her to jump.

"Strip down" said a man's voice echoing in the expanse of the room.

"I will NOT!" yelled Amelia incensed, her anger quelling the panic she'd been feeling. But she couldn't say anything more. In the dark she heard the sound of boots marching toward her and though she tried to fight off the hands that reached for her she couldn't resist them. Her arms were held as her cargo pants were removed then her underwear. Her shirt was yanked off in the next moment. And almost before it began Amelia was left sitting on the floor in the dark shivering and completely naked.

A mist filled the room and though she couldn't see it Amelia felt an ultra-violet light surrounding her as if she were being sterilized then the room lit up with a red glow. The voice said, "Put on the clothes."

Amelia saw a heavy, blue jumpsuit lying on the ground. Shuddering tears of rage and anger welled up in her as her body shook uncontrollably. Through sheer force of will she tried to make her body appear calm and defiant, but she felt like a shivering small animal, her body weakened by fear as if she was nothing more than a puppet dangling from strings with no control over anything, not her body or her emotions. Her breath came fast and shallow as she grew dizzy and dropped to her knees. With all the determination she had she forced herself to focus and with a deep breath she tried to steady herself as she reached out to grasp the jumpsuit then stood up and stepped into it.

The suit was a bit too big and the sleeves were laden with heavy bracelets sewn into the fabric of the suit that immediately tightened to the size of her arms. Instantly a dull sensation came over Amelia. Her brain fumbled to make a connection with her emotions, but she felt nothing. All of her anxiety and fear slipped away leaving her in a grey lifeless world where nothing mattered. And then as if she had no will of her own she thought maybe this world was better, less complicated and that it felt good to feel nothing at all.

The door to the chamber swung open. Two specters stood waiting in the hall – ghostly psychic soldiers. But she wasn't afraid of them she simply knew what they were without harboring any feeling about them whatsoever.

The guards seemed more like shadows than human beings waiting for Amelia in their out-of-body forms. She felt drawn to walk between them her mind unquestioning and her heart still as they escorted her down a dimly lit corridor of roughly hewn stone. They seemed to drift on either side of her, but Amelia did not question what she was seeing nor where they were headed.

After some time they came to a massive metal door that opened into an immense subway system. A train was just leaving. It appeared as if it were moving through a body with no organs along a spine surrounded by a perfectly round ribcage lit sporadically with lights. In a moment the train shot like a flash of light down the tracks – one track above and one below - until it was nothing more than a tiny spark in the distance evaporating into a black hole the size of a pinprick.

Like a shaft of light slipping under a doorway fear gripped Amelia and she tried to run, but her body was instantly beset with an extraordinary sense of fatigue. At the same time she had the feeling that her escorts were pleased to see that she had the ability to overcome the suit's suppression of her emotions, even if only for a moment.

Droning electromagnetic energy could be heard from a distance growing louder and louder on her left side until a single train car appeared and slammed to a dead stop in front of them in what seemed to be a single moment. Doors silently opened and the three of them stepped into the empty car.

In moments the train was rocketing down the railway instantly enveloped in darkness like a terrifying ride in an amusement park. Amelia felt herself swallowed in hiccupping blackness as the interior light of the car flashed off and then briefly on again.

Moments later the train passed into a remote hole, high up in the wall and stopped in front of a building which she quickly realized was a prison. Yet she felt nothing. It was as if she were marking off the events on a notepad in her mind: boarded the train, went to prison, walking to my cell…

Amelia was locked in her cell, but she felt totally apathetic.

"Hey, I designed those suits! … you know…" exclaimed an old man's voice from an adjacent cell.

Amelia put her hands on the bars of her cell and peered kitty-corner across the hall where she saw the wild visage of a grey haired man.

"Interesting model you're wearing though," he said thoughtfully, stroking the small growth of stubble on his chin. "Yes, yes, they must be afraid of you. That, or they really don't want you to escape… high priority… yep… hmmm."

"What do you mean?" asked Amelia, her mind fighting back a confusing haze that had her wanting to drift into sleep instead of speaking, thinking, or doing anything at all for that matter.

"You can still talk... and ask questions, no less!" the man replied in astonishment. "Well, it would seem they made a wise choice! Most people would be a drooling mess by now." Then noting Amelia's puzzled expression he added, "That is a psycho-suppressive, hyper-suggestive outfit meant to strip you of your free-will even as it clothes you in a 100% cotton lining... everybody around here wears them, even I am locked in a fibrous jail of my own construction... But yours! Yours is special – it was made for extra strength psychic distortion!"

Amelia put her head in her hands. It was getting more and more difficult for her to think straight and now she felt such an urge to fall asleep she could no longer stay standing. As her knees gave way she slumped to the floor in a mental miasma, her strange world drifting away to the sound of the old man's voice chattering blithely onward as she was slipping out of his world and into a place somewhere beyond consciousness where hopefully, she thought, she'd be able to finally rest.

When Amelia awoke the man was still talking, seemingly unaware that she'd been asleep. She heard his voice before her eyes had even opened.

"So I gave him two fingers and a twist, and I said, *'that's soddin' right you'll go get your own alien doomsday device! I'll have nothing to do with this insane business!'* Then I stomped out of his office and into the welcoming arms of his guards... ahh yes. I suppose I could have handled that better... But anyways, that's how I got to be here with... Oh, you're awake!" he added as he saw Amelia open her eyes and look at him.

"Oh..." Amelia groaned, looking around dazedly. "What time is it?"

"Ooh, that's rough, kid. Here... I've got something for you."

The old man threw Amelia a small package which landed

just outside of her cell. Reaching groggily for the object she half expected something horrible to happen as her arm passed between the metal bars framing her cell, but there was nothing, no electric shock, no alarm – just the eerie silence of the prison as she pulled the paper and twine wrapped package into her cell.

"It'll help… trust me," he said, then musing quietly, almost to himself he added, "What an odd thing to say… *'trust me,'* as if those two little words should satisfy your… discernment… The only people who need to say *'trust me'* are probably people you have no business trusting."

Grimacing, Amelia said, "You aren't making a very good case for yourself."

"Aha! But you see, I am the exception!" he declared jauntily, "Perfectly trustworthy!"

Amelia opened the package and found a small glass bottle padded around the outside with cotton. She removed the lid, unsure of what to expect, only to find it was a horrible smelling liquid and her nose rankled at the pungent scent. Immediately she decided to put the lid back on the bottle and throw it out, but an illogical, intuitive feeling somehow made it past the grey, non-feeling world she was in. She put the bottle to her lips and drank the bitter, foul tasting liquid as quickly as possible.

Watching her the man chimed, "Oh, by the way, my name's Phil."

Before Amelia could say a word she started coughing. The liquid was having an immediate and startling affect. Her head felt like it was detaching from her body, as if she needed to reach up and pull it down to reattach it to her neck. Then suddenly she felt trapped, an emotion she had not felt since putting on the jumpsuit, and her mind was dashing around her cell like a wild bird trapped in a cage moving up and down, bashing herself against the bars of her cell, trying wildly to get out. But her body remained motionless until bile shot up the back of her throat and she vomited until there was nothing left and she passed out.

Amelia's essential-self left her body and she flew from her prison cell like a bird set free. Up, up into the sky and then shooting like a star into the south until she found herself drifting down, down, down, deep into the Amazonian rain forest. In her underground prison she'd lost track of time, but here in this place it was late at night and she found herself hovering in front of an elderly man with a deeply lined face painted with red, circular lines.

His brightly colored feathered headdress, countless strands of multi-colored beads, and an unusual feathered ornament through the piercing on his face, indicated his status as a tribal shaman. He was tending a small fire, brewing a plant spirit potion in a pot hanging above the fire. As if expecting Amelia, he looked up for a moment and motioned for her to sit across from him.

"You have drunk ayahuasca," he said in a deep voice, crinkling with age as he puffed mapacho, wild jungle tobacco. "We call it the vine of the soul... teacher of the teachers," he added as he blew the smoke down onto the crown of Amelia's head then into the palms of her hands. "We use this to access higher dimensions and higher knowledge," said the shaman telepathically. "But it is not wise to take this medicine without proper ceremony," he added as he poured a cup of an acrid smelling thick, brown liquid and ceremoniously handed it to Amelia. He then said a lengthy prayer in a language Amelia did not understand, but she felt a tingling vibration move through her body as he spoke.

Acknowledging the shaman, feeling that she had known him before, and had somehow done this before, she bowed her head and when he finished the prayer she reverently took a sip from the cup. It tasted exactly like the tea Phil had given her in prison, the same bitter after-bite that caused Amelia's face to scrunch up involuntarily as she swallowed. Though her physical body had reacted violently, it was different for her essential-self; she could taste the ayahuasca, but it didn't make her nauseous, and rather than leaving and flying away, she immediately moved inside herself while connecting to everything around her.

For a few minutes she sat quietly listening to the sounds of the jungle. A lone owl hooted, cicadas whirred and rustled in the leaves with a thousand other unseen insects, a bird whistled sharply and frogs croaked in the nearby river. Snakes slithered through the leaves on the ground only inches from where she was sitting.

Gradually a warm, buzzing began gliding smoothly through her veins. Simultaneously the shaman shook his shacapa, a rattle made of leaves, and began singing ancient tribal medicine songs in a language no longer spoken, but full of feeling. The vibration of the song painted pictures in the air, and called down spirits from the plant, animal, bird and insect kingdoms to guide Amelia through her visions. As the buzzing vibration became stronger she felt as if she'd been infused with the spirit of the ayahuasca.

Complex patterns spun through her mind as animal and insect silhouettes appeared then blurred into unrecognizable shapes, then reappeared as tiny snakes in bluish hues darting in and out of her vision. Her in-breath sounded like wind howling through trees in a cold desolate place.

Suddenly everything went black and Amelia felt a hard, cold surface beneath her body and through closed eyes she became aware of a strange flickering light. As her eyes opened, torch light from a golden holder on the wall to her left revealed a shadowy chamber of smooth stone blocks rising around her in the angular, sloping shape of a pyramid with a ceiling so high it dissolved into eerie blackness.

CHAPTER 15

Immediately Amelia knew four things: She was in a different game-lifetime, she was a man named Alex, a prisoner inside of a massive stone pyramid, and she was dying.

With death close at hand Alex's memories traced back over his lifetime, Amelia was shocked to recognize the pond and surrounding forest, but there wasn't yet an orchard or a garden or the raspberry bush fence. Then she realized Alex must have lived there before it was a homestead so she must be experiencing a lifetime that took place prior to the game she played as Sasha.

As the memories continued, Alex remembered meeting the woman who would become his wife. He took her to the forest glade and they sat together every evening imagining where they would plant a garden and an orchard as well as fragrant flowers that would fill their home with sweet scents no matter which direction the breezes blew. They imagined planting a long row of raspberry bushes, side by side, surrounding their property – a fence that would last forever, give them fruit and privacy while keeping deer out of their gardens, yet this fence would feed their neighbors and passersby as well.

When the vision of their homestead was complete, Alex

and Jenica visited every home in each of their villages and invited all of the families to their wedding. As they were enthusiastically welcomed into each home they complimented the owner on something they admired: a particularly beautiful tree or hardy plant, even an animal that served their host's family.

Alex, sitting on the cold stone floor of his cell, remembered his wedding day with such perfect clarity it could have happened the day before despite the fact that it was countless years earlier. In his mind's eye he saw the wedding guests all dressed in soft, woven clothing carrying seedlings or saplings from a plant or tree that Alex and Jenica had especially appreciated on their visit to each person's home.

Some of the guests brought animals. There was a puppy and a colt as well as bear, fox and wolf cubs, and baby squirrels too. All of the young animals came in pairs with their mothers and they were put in one pen together. As Alex recalled that day his memory paused upon the babies and mothers together harmoniously in one pen; then his memory jumped ahead to the time when all the babies were first taught by their mothers to respectfully wait until they were called upon for a task or to be stroked.

This may seem odd by modern standards especially given that these were mainly wild animals, but the Vedruss people had a very different relationship with animals as well as with plants and insects for that matter. No one really knew when this kinship began nor did they question the time honored practice of putting the baby animals together so they'd always be friends. No one remembered when mother animals first began training their off-spring to serve humans or how that came to happen in the first place.

This was not forced servitude, in the way that animals today are treated. (And the idea of eating an animal to the Vedruss would be like eating your family pet). The animals lived happily and freely, and more than anything they all loved being given a task. At the snap of a finger a dozen squirrels would rush down from the treetops with the enthusiasm of a dog playing fetch. The young ones especially would push and jostle each other hoping to be the one who'd be noticed first and invited to come closer with their pine nuts.

The wolf, fox and bear cubs learned how to protect the family and gently play with children. In addition, the bear cub learned how to dig holes for root cellars and how to prepare the ground for a garden in the spring. The puppy was trained by its mother to bark with discernment and come when called, among other things.

Alex's memories returned to his wedding day. He remembered standing on a small hill speaking of the vision he and Jenica had for their land and pointing to the place where they envisioned each tree, plant and shrub. As Alex spoke, a wedding guest, holding the corresponding sapling or seedling, walked to the spot he mentioned. When the guests were in place they each planted their gifts and in less than half an hour all of the trees and bushes had been planted on the homestead. And since everyone from each village participated in this way at every wedding, there was never any envy or jealousy toward a neighbor because they all felt directly connected to the beauty of each property. Any time a neighbor would pass by they would particularly notice the flourishing tree or bush they had planted or how much everything had grown since that first day.

The only thing left to plant was their vegetable garden. The fruit and vegetable seeds were given to them, but never planted by others because every family would put a few seeds under their tongues and let the seeds soak for nine minutes. This allowed the seeds to absorb the DNA of each family member. When planted, these seeds would communicate to the rest of the garden the unique hereditary needs of the family. Disease was nonexistent among the Vedruss because their food prevented illness and therefore any need for medicine.

Although families often shared with each other, no one grew fruits or vegetables to sell to others nor would anyone dream of stealing from a neighbor. Their plants were meant for their family's needs specifically. Every family had only the property they needed. Alex and Jenica, like every other young couple, settled on about four or five acres of land. This gave them the space to have a forest, an orchard, a garden and a pond. And because the Vedruss only took care of their own families, no one worked—there was no need. All of their needs were provided for effortlessly by their natural surroundings.

Alex remembered standing with Jenica after their wedding and seeing their home for the first time: It had been erected by the most talented carpenters in their villages in just two days.

As Alex's bright memories continued in the midst of his cold, empty chamber he remembered a bright spring day with his son cradled in his arms. Singing as he walked through the garden radiant with love for his newborn son, Alex noticed a solitary, ruby colored bud sprouting from a rosebush. In that moment he felt an intense desire for his son to smell the fragrance of a rose. Without thinking, Alex closed his eyes as he sang and imagined the rose in full, fragrant bloom and when he opened his eyes a few moments later, much to his surprise, the rosebud was completely open with a fragrance as delicate and sweet as he'd imagined.

Though he didn't understand how such a thing was possible, Alex was nonetheless delighted and sat next to the rose hoping his sleeping son would dream of fragrant roses until he awoke to see the real one. Smiling at the thought, Alex closed his eyes once more. Still singing softly, he imagined his son's delight in a few months hence when all of the wildflowers would be blooming like radiant, colorful stars bursting all around the pond. He was so caught up in this vision that he didn't realize he'd fallen asleep until his son stirred in his arms. As Alex opened his eyes he was awestruck by the display that lay before him; all the wildflowers were in full bloom. The meadow seemed to have been kissed by a rainbow and flecked with white flowers glowing like captured starlight amidst the explosion of color.

It was not unusual for Alex to close his eyes and imagine something, but this was the first time that *something* had physically appeared before his eyes; not once, but twice in a matter of minutes. Over the next few days Alex tried to understand what he'd actually done. Suddenly he realized he was feeling more love than he'd ever felt before as he held his infant son and found himself singing at the same time.

At this point Alex's memories began to move more swiftly. Day after day he practiced creating through imaging and deeply feeling and singing until he had it down to a science. Imagining himself across the pond, he would instantly disappear from where he stood and immediately reappear on the opposite side of the pond. But it was more than just imagining himself to be elsewhere.

First, Alex visualized all the cells in his body and then imagined the cells dispersing into out into space and gathering back together in the place he desired. This took diligent thought and practice because he had to visualize every single aspect of his body down to the most microscopic detail—and in a single moment visualize the cells dispersing and gathering back together perfectly. Even the tiniest error in mentally re-picturing his body, all the way down to the atomic level, would prevent his body from reforming properly after being dispersed into space.

Once Alex understood every aspect of teleportation he realized he could go anywhere on the planet, in fact anywhere in the universe. To avoid materializing at the bottom of the ocean, for instance, Alex traveled as his second-self first, then decided whether or not he needed to teleport. Finally, he practiced going to other planets, though initially as his second-self, which was unaffected by lack of oxygen or any other unsuitable environment. But if the planet would sustain human life he could materialize on the planet as well.

Alex recalled in great detail teaching the Vedruss how to create using thought, feeling and sound; and then he moved on to teleportation. His memories were so detailed he could remember what he'd taught word for word and so did the Vedruss who continued his teachings until his lessons in mental creation and teleportation spread throughout all of the settlements in Russia.

But then a painful memory began to stir. In Alex's second-self travels he began to see a world filled with violent battles and constant destruction. He believed with all of his heart that if he could manage to share what he knew with others they would benefit the way the Vedruss had and their lives in turn would be happy and prosperous, because in truth there was an infinite supply of everything – anyone could materialize anything they desired.

And then he suddenly realized that the only way to protect his family, the Vedruss settlements, and further generations was to help others in the world find relief through the same methods he'd been teaching. The day he left his family he knew he might never return home.

With his understanding of the Science of Imagery – which in the simplest terms would be understanding how to work with the vibration of thought, feeling and sound all at once – Alex was able to bring together six of the most powerful warring tribes.

First he showed each leader his unparalleled abilities, and then promised that he would teach one priest from each tribe how to do what he had demonstrated. He showed the leaders the fruitlessness of trying to dominate each other and helped them see what would happen if they joined together using the tools he would teach them.

He taught the science of imagery to the six high priests. Using these techniques, along with their combined mental force, Alex and the priests built the pyramids of Egypt; without slaves and without physical force. Thought, feeling and sound were all that was required to create and move the massive stones into place to form the majestic structures.

The permanence of the pyramids was due to the potency of Alex's thought. The priests could create in the short-term, but Alex could create so powerfully his creations literally withstood the test of time.

Alex's eyes opened slowly as the torch flickered dimly by a tiny breeze caused from a single brick being removed from a doorway that was otherwise completely sealed with smooth, granite bricks.

A low voice, solemn and haunting said quietly, "Tell us how to create in perpetuity and we'll tear down the wall and save your life."

Weakly, Alex replied, "You cannot save my life for it is not yours to give or take. I gave you the answer before you sealed me in this dark place and it hasn't changed. The power to create lasting creations, creations that will be here for thousands of years in the future… and to create more powerfully than any other man… is simply the power of love… desiring only to benefit all of mankind, not only your selfish lust for power. I shall abide here. Do not touch me, or remove these walls."

Amelia knew there was a message in what she was seeing, it had deeply penetrated her body, trying to get her attention, but she couldn't seem to grasp what it meant. Why was she seeing this?

She opened her eyes and looked at the shaman, hoping he'd have an answer for her, but there was a black hole where his face should have been. As if reading her mind the shaman reached for her hand, grabbed it and began shaking her arm with an energy so intense her entire body began to vibrate – drawing her spirit back into her body.

In the next moment Amelia saw a white light glowing all around the shaman as he sang hypnotic notes filled with complex patterns; at times sunny and joyous, while at other moments frightening and mournful.

When he stopped singing the shaman turned to Amelia and said telepathically, "Remember who you are and create with Love as you were meant to. Know that you don't have to join the chaotic dream of others… create your own world as you want it to be."

Bile inching its way up the back of her throat brought Amelia violently back into her body. She didn't know whether she'd been gone for seconds or hours as the old man said loudly, "... Yep, it's quite a thing this journey... Oh, don't worry about the hurl, it just comes with the territory. You're getting rid of a lot of stuff right now... things you've carried with you, emotionally and physically... not just your lunch."

Amelia lay on the floor feeling desperately ill, while Phil kept talking. Despite her wretched physical state, her mind was clear and as she listened to Phil his story made a strange and horrifying kind of sense.

"You see... I know and you know that you shouldn't be here! For God's sakes you're just a kid," said Phil thoughtfully. "And what's worse is that I've seen what happens to kids here."

"What do you mean?" asked Amelia weakly.

"You don't know anything about this place do you?"

Amelia shook her head feeling queasy as she did.

"Alright, I'll tell you," said Phil with a pained look in his eyes. "This is a military base, but it's black ops. It's funded secretly and regular military, the CIA and the FBI know nothing about it.

Phil paused for a moment, vomited loudly, cleared his voice and said, "Hah!! Now that's better! Ok, where was I? Oh yes... well, there are hundreds of secret underground military facilities around the world, but this place that we're in... we call it the HUB, not very imaginative, but it's like all roads leading to Rome. Actually, I like to think of HUB as an acronym for Hellish. Unbelievable. Bullshit. I think that kinda puts what we do here into a nutshell."

"How are they connected?" Amelia asked weakly.

"By electromagnetic trains... those trains can move at the speed of Mach 1. And they can go anywhere in the world without having to refuel because they run off the electromagnetic energy of the planet."

Oh hey... I'm starting to see things, little visions are poppin' into my mind... and man if I'm not seeing you! Huh... you are special aren't you?"

Amelia vomited again, not feeling special at all.

"Oh wow," he said in a tripped-out voice, "you really need to get out of here before you get killed. Alright then," said Phil with the energy of one trying to pull himself together under dubious circumstances. "Here's the deal. There is no such thing as regular warfare… what you see on CNN are just little skirmishes to make you think the world is still the same… a little warring here, a little terrorism there… but the real war is being controlled right here in the HUB."

Amelia picked her head up off the floor and looked at him.

"The real war my friend, is created through what you think are natural disasters… but there is nothing natural about those disasters. Everything from hurricanes and tornadoes to volcanic eruptions to earthquakes and tsunamis… we control it all from here.

"I can't begin to explain how it's done… but the reason might be to show a particular country that we can do whatever the hell we want thereby forcing them to support that desire or face the consequences… something like a hurricane or tsunami might be a way of moving public attention away from something the military doesn't want them poking their noses into… and instead shift their focus onto a disaster.

"There's something in Alaska called HAARP… well, you probably don't want the details, but we are capable of controlling not only the planet… we have devices set up all over the world that can influence people in an entire city. We have the ability to control the mood of thousands of people or we can focus down to one individual. There are secret military psychics – it's hard to escape from them around here and they can make your life a living hell inside or out.

"But I want you to know I am not proud of that," said Phil, "and one thing you have to understand is that anyone who comes to work at this facility doesn't know what they're getting themselves into… and they never leave… when they die they're cremated here."

"You're telling me I'm going to die here?" said Amelia weakly her whole body trembling.

"No, I'm not saying that you're going to die… at least not right away. But I do know one thing," said Phil, "pretty soon you're going to pass out… I gave you one powerful dose of this stuff… I'm sorry… you're gonna be really sick. But that means they'll have to take you to the infirmary and there they'll remove your suit. But you'll understand soon…

"Now listen to me," he added with a new strength in his voice, "this facility is protecting something. I don't know what it is, but I've heard the sound of exotic birds and I've smelled flowers coming through the ventilation system. We're far, far underground, but if you get the chance to escape," he said, something in his voice hinting that there would be no chance involved, "get yourself into the ventilation system. You'll feel a breeze so just go toward it. I don't know what's there, but I know there's something.

"I know we're protecting something… whatever it is… And I would try myself, but, well… I have an implant that makes me easy to track... But you don't have an implant yet because the suit you're wearing is all they need to keep track of you."

"But you don't understand," said Amelia desperately, "my friend is in a coma… it's a medically induced coma… and if I don't get back to him he might die."

"So you're planning to find him, sneak into his room and wean him off of the chemical cocktails streaming through his veins… without being seen and with harming… or God forbid… killing him accidentally. And even if you pulled that off… do you have a plan for how you'll escape?"

"No," said Amelia, her eyes focused on the floor.

"Well, maybe you'll find help if you follow that fresh air I told you about," said Phil. "Like I said, I don't know what's there… but it has to be better than no plan at all." With that last effort Phil suddenly passed out.

Everything was hopeless. Nothing she learned from Äsha

or The Portal could help her now. Phil was right: There was no way that she could find Matthew and help him now. If she somehow managed to escape, her only choice would be to find the tunnel with fresh air and try to get help. But even if she could get out, what were the chances that she'd be able to find her way through the desert, get help and then get back inside?

Amelia lay on her side in a fetal position with her head on her arm wishing she would just die.

CHAPTER 16

Opening her eyes, Amelia became aware that she was now in a dimly lit hospital room. Terrified, she forced herself to focus and suddenly recalled how she had come to be there.

As Phil had predicted her blue jumpsuit had been removed and she could once again feel her own feelings. She also remembered Phil telling her to find the air ducts. She looked up at the ceiling and saw nothing, and though she couldn't see the floor from her position, in her mind's eye a metal grate materialized and she found she could move through it and down a shaft and into the main system. Had the drug Phil gave her made her super psychic, she wondered, or was she making it all up?

In that moment a short, Hispanic man dressed in grey scrubs with a shaved head and intense dark eyes walked in with a needle and syringe in his hand. Amelia's body tensed in preparation to receive a shot, but instead he looked over his shoulder, drew the bed curtains around Amelia's bed, capped the needle with a plastic lid, and slid it into a pocket of his lab coat as he pulled out a key from the other.

He swiftly unlocked her manacles and handed Amelia a note:

"Don't talk. Phil sent me. None of us can escape from here. Everyone is either wearing a suit that can't be removed or has an implant. But we knowingly chose this life; not like you… and I know it will ease some part of my conscience for the horrors that have taken place here if I am able to help you escape. Phil thinks you can make it. I believe in you, too…

There's a grid in the floor that leads to the air ducts. There's enough light to see and no cameras. But once they know you're gone they'll send psychics into the tunnels to find you. I've blocked the camera in this room, but you'll only have a few minutes. I removed the screws already and I'll be on look-out while you climb in there. Your clothes and shoes are under the bed.

Run as far and as fast as you can. The minute they know you've escaped from here, they'll be looking for you. No one has ever escaped. Just go in the direction from which the air is coming. If there's more than one choice, go where the air smells fresher. I'm not sure what's there, but it's where our air comes from, and no military personnel are allowed in there, not even the out-of- body psychics. So if you make it, they won't be able to follow you.

If you somehow get back to the surface…will you mail a letter for me?
Angel
P.S. I had to guess your size, and sorry I couldn't get you any underwear at the commissary without being noticed. In the pockets there's a penlight, a screwdriver and a bunch of different heads, a Swiss army knife, and protein bars."

After reading the note Amelia looked up at Angel and nodded that she understood. As she held out her hand palm up Angel handed her an envelope with an address and took the note back from her stuffing it in his pocket. He then stepped outside of the curtain to give her some privacy. Shakily she got out of bed in her hospital gown and kneeled on the floor. She had a fever and wanted to just lie on the cool tile, but she forced herself to keep going. She had already seen the clothes in her mind's eye, hanging from the metal springs. Without even looking she reached down to the exact spot and pulled on the clothing with a brisk jerk. Army fatigues and a pair of regulation boots landed on the floor with a slight thud.

She quickly put on the pants and a tank top that clung tightly to her body, while tying the arms of the shirt around her waist. The pants were a bit big, but the belt held them up – which was a good thing because the pockets were heavy – and the shoes were snug, but Amelia would have left naked and barefoot if that had been her only choice.

When she stepped out from behind the curtain Angel was holding the metal grid open for her in the exact spot she had seen in her mind's eye. He handed her a small bottle of water contained in a pouch and helped her secure it to her belt. With a flashlight he silently showed her foot and handholds where she could climb down.

Amelia surprised Angel with a quiet kiss on his cheek and then climbed down into the shaft. As he was replacing the grid and screwing it back into place Amelia descended carefully downward. When she reached the bottom of the ladder she found herself in something that made her think of an immense drainage pipe – the floor was flat, but the sides and top were round and about 12 feet high. It was strangely clean and fresh smelling and Amelia headed in the direction of what she hoped was a breeze, but she couldn't tell for sure, except for the fact that in her mind's eye she was seeing nature; tall trees, singing birds and blue sky – not at all like the desert, but still, it seemed to be the way she should go.

She began running slowly at first, expecting that she might not be completely over her drug induced nausea, but just as Phil had said, it was as if she had gotten rid of a weight in her mind and body and now she was beginning to feel alive and free. It felt incredible to run, though a bra would have been nice, but at least her tank top was tight so that helped a little.

She didn't know how close she was getting, or how she would know when she got there – she just knew that the air would smell fresh. And for a moment that's exactly how it seemed. She would have sworn she could smell eucalyptus trees, something she remembered from a trip to California with her grandparents. But there weren't any eucalyptus trees in the desert, so that made no sense.

But what else could she do? Amelia ran and ran. With every split in the tunnel she could sense and feel, and smell the proper direction to go. She knew without doubt that she was on the right path and getting closer and closer to her destination.

She paid no attention to the tunnels passing by until she came to an unusual split in the pathway, one branch leading into total darkness. She thought it must be for an area that was no longer in use, but just as she had walked by it, a sudden image of Matthew flooded into her mind. Instantly she felt overwhelming pain and shock and she knew something horrible was happening, or was about to happen.

As she stared into the darkness, there appeared a subtle golden glow of light about 30 feet away. And though several times she had to fight the urge to go back the way she came, she soon arrived at the source of the light – a round, metal grid, a bit larger than a manhole. Amelia forced herself to slide her fingers through the square holes in the grid and take a deep breath; then, with a stiff tug she got it to move. Still, it took all of her strength to shift the grid; back and forth, pushing, pulling, heaving until a metal lip on one side released and she was able to drag the grid across the floor of the air duct, just enough so she could see more clearly what was below.

The grid was easier to move now that it was sliding along the floor – though it did so with a disconcertingly loud scraping noise that echoed in the tunnel – and Amelia opened it enough so that she could squeeze through the opening and then hang on the grid.

A loud stuttering bang reverberated loudly down the air duct, as if an entrance to the tunnel above was being accessed, and bright lights were switched on. There was no going back. Her only hope was to stay ahead of whoever was coming. Moving as quickly as she dared until at last her trembling body reached the solid rock floor, Amelia found herself in a low, hand carved tunnel dimly lit by a flickering light from a round room about ten feet away.

Slowly, tentatively, she bent down to walk beneath the low tunnel ceiling, clinging to the wall for security, until she found herself in a taller chamber, also hand carved out of red rock, where she could finally stand up. An amber colored electric light was flickering brightly from a metal and glass casing that hung on the wall, as if it would go out at any moment. Just below the light was a staircase, hand carved out of stone.

Standing completely still, Amelia counted thirteen steps down to the next landing. She took a deep breath and told herself she just had to take one step at a time, which seemed almost comical to her until she saw a rat shoot past, and, with a barely stifled squeal, nearly fell down the entire stairway.

She was so focused on avoiding rats, she didn't pay attention to where she was placing her hands on the wall until they came to something soft and sticky. And with a slow settling terror, she realized she had put her hand into a massive spider's web.

Involuntarily, she let out a horrified scream, and screamed again, even louder, when she saw the hideous, black, fist-sized spider that lived on the web, only an inch from her where her hand had previously been only seconds before.

In the same moment, she was sure she could hear drumming coming from somewhere beyond the landing below. Shaking uncontrollably, Amelia pressed onward, the sound of drums becoming clearer as she reached the bottom of the stairs. She found herself in a long, narrow passageway with no lights. Amelia reached into her pocket and pulled out the penlight. She was standing on a dirt floor and though she tried to move quickly in the direction of the drumming, the ground was uneven and the yawning tunnel that stretched endlessly before her seemed to swallow the tiny beam of light, making it difficult to move without tripping or falling.

Amelia could see light coming in through a series of holes in the wall which allowed her to take in the view of an immense cavern from different positions without being seen. The cavern was lit up by giant torches, each supported by black metal bases that had been molded into grotesque shapes. Rows of benches that could potentially seat hundreds of people filled the space below a ceiling that was so far out of sight, it was literally enveloped in darkness. As Amelia continued carefully along the passageway, peering through various holes in the wall, she observed crude tribal masks and relief carvings depicting horrible acts of violence.

Erratically placed statues of smiling skeletons, snakes, gargoyles, and other hideous looking creatures all with vicious faces molded out of gold, silver and copper caused ghostly shadows to dance eerily across the cavern walls. Farther down the passageway she was finally able to see the drummers, their eyes closed, heads bobbing and swaying, all bare-chested and black skin shining with sweat.

Then, chanting began and the voices of hundreds of men erupted from a location Amelia couldn't see. Soon after it began, she saw a man walking in a slow, ceremonious manner down the center aisle between the benches, wearing a black robe and covering his face was the head of a mountain goat with a black candle burning between the ram's three-foot horns.

Following him were four girls. They seemed to be in a hypnotic trance, wearing necklaces laden with gold and dressed in long, sheer, black dresses silhouetting the forms of their naked bodies beneath as they passed by the torchlight.

The first girl wore a snake with blazing emerald eyes the next wore two salamanders with deep-set ruby eyes and linked at the tail with their heads meeting to form a V around her neck. The third girl's necklace displayed the figure of a man's full body, with the head of a goat and huge wings splayed out upon his back. Between the horns of the goat head was a golden torch and the flame of the torch was represented by a diamond. The last girl wore a necklace with the sun, the moon and the planets. Small diamonds, emeralds and rubies represented stars and dangled from a golden collar held by gold threads.

The girls walked slowly down the aisle carrying black velvet pillows. Each pillow held a different object: the first, an ebony handled dagger; the second, a sword; the third, a wand; and the fourth a five-pointed star.

Hundreds of men wearing animal costumes oozed into the cavern temple, down every aisle, clamoring and crying, climbing over benches, howling, grunting and snuffling as they shuffled unsteadily forward, swaying wildly. As the freakish congregation assembled, the girls all lined up around a wide, central platform.

Removing the goat's head, the priest placed it upon a darkly imposing altar. He then began the mass by holding an up-side-down cross in his right hand and making the sign of the cross with his left. The congregation also used their left hand to make this sign and they all repeated aloud, "Ghost Holy the and Son the and Father the of name the in." They then repeated the Lord's Prayer backwards with the exception of the opening line where they said, "Our Father which art on Earth."

The high priest raised his arms over his head as the congregation sat back in their seats. Some fell off the benches and struggled to get back up. When they were finally all seated the priest walked around the altar and down to two circles on the floor. Without a word, the four girls followed him and stood just outside the circles.

Removing the five-sided star from one of the pillows, the priest stepped into the middle of the center circle and placed it on the floor. One at a time, in succession, each girl leaned forward proffering a pillow. First the priest took the ebony handled dagger and thrust it in the leather strap he wore around his waist. Then he removed the sword with his right hand and the crystal wand, wrapped in copper, with his left. The girls all moved in one accord backward to the altar as the priest held the wand and sword over his head and began chanting. "Belial, Belial! To you I sacrifice the blood of innocence. I give you the blood of life for the blood of my enemy's life!"

Still in a trance, the girl wearing the snake necklace walked stiffly up to the stone altar. With a flamboyant swirl, the priest removed his robe revealing a broad well-defined chest and narrow-waist with impeccably toned muscles, which instantly aroused a deafening cacophony of animal noises from the crowd. Like a performer drinking in his audience's mounting cries for more, he whisked the girl off the platform and into his arms and then reverently laid her on the sacrificial table.

He stopped momentarily, taunting his devotees with the twisted promise of what was to come, and everyone went wild, their anticipation exploding in a fit of screaming, dancing, yelling and jumping as the drummers drummed louder and louder, faster and faster as he pulled out his ebony-handled dagger.

The priest then threw both arms in the air and the room dropped into a dead silence as he chanted, "This blood sacrifice is the atonement between man and Prince Lucifer." The congregation began to chant his words over and over again as the priest swayed back and forth in a trance.

Suddenly the priest stood still, and in one fluid motion he poised the dagger over his head, ready to plunge it into the girl's breast. In that moment, Amelia found an opening, hidden from the temple worshippers by a heavy drape, and she burst out from behind it screaming STOP!

"AMELIA!" shouted Matthew in a clear, strong voice. He was wearing a black hooded cape and threw off the hood when he yelled for her and tried to run in her direction, but he was quickly caught by several pairs of hands as he struggled to get to her. As whinnies, grunts and other animal noises erupted from the congregation, all eyes turned back and forth between Matthew and Amelia. The drumming stopped and the priest whirled around to see what was causing this disturbance. Upon seeing Amelia his face lit up, "Ah, there's my true prize. I was hoping you would come… Won't you join me at the altar?"

In that moment Amelia realized she had no plan. Even if she could disappear the way she had in her lifetime as Alex, it wouldn't help Matthew, or the girl who was about to be sacrificed. What did she think she could she do? What was she thinking?

But it was too late to go back over her actions and try again. In little more time than it took her to regret her decision, she was roughly seized by two towering men, their faces masked by paint and tribal ornamentations, Amelia was paraded through the maniacal hordes. A man dressed as a horse and using his hands as hooves, reared up whinnying and pawing into the air like a stallion. But like a man, he made violent pelvic motions showing her his dark intent. Yet no one touched Amelia, or even tried, and she was delivered to the priest, and held tightly in front of the altar.

The priest did not address Amelia, nor did he even acknowledge her presence, instead he began to chant in a deep, rasping voice, his eyes turned upward as if peering into his own skull. "I conjure and command thee, oh Belial, to appear forthwith and show thyself to me, here outside this circle, in fair and human shape, without horror or deformity and without delay. Speak to me visibly, clearly and without deceit. Possess my mind and my body. Answer all my demands and perform all I desire. Do not linger. The King of Kings commands thee."

Immediately the priest fell into a deep trance, his chin dropping to his chest. A moment later his head jerked up, eyes opened wide, and he stepped outside of both circles without touching either one as two men joined him at the altar.

One man handed the priest a piece of chalk and he proceeded to draw a triangle on the floor. The other man put evergreen boughs around the outside of the triangle along with some skulls from horned animals.

The congregation began chanting as the priest took a drink of wine and then sprinkled it over the triangle. In the meantime one man ground up some herbs and powder with the mortar and pestle and handed it to the priest who placed it in the triangle.

"I work to the destruction of YOU – AMELIA!" the priest hissed, fury seething from him as he pointed his dagger viciously at Amelia, who had been brought within a few feet of the altar. His voice was softer now, like a feeble old man, yet filled with venom, as he took a chunk of clay and began molding it while saying Amelia's name over and over again. When he finished, the priest engraved something into the doll and chanted, "In the name of Belial, and the spirit of destruction and revenge - Oh creature of clay I name thee Amelia."

He then took the doll and placed it at the tip of the triangle. Next, using a scarlet candle, he dripped wax around the triangle and began chanting. Finally he stood at the tip of the triangle, crossing his arms over his chest and chanted, "It is not my hand which does this deed, but that of Belial." He then took a long needle in his left hand, viciously stabbed the doll with the needle, and yelled, "SO MOTE IT BE!"

CHAPTER 17

Gasping for breath, searing pain exploding in her body, Amelia's world turned black. She knew this was death. And with that realization an intense rush of emotion swelled beneath her, raising her up until she found herself hovering above her own limp body. She saw herself being lifted up by two hooded men and placed carefully on the stone altar as Matthew struggled in a futile attempt to escape his captors and reach her side.

From above Amelia tried to get Matthew's attention. "I'm right here, I'm fine… please don't worry," she begged, but she was slipping further and further away as Matthew gave up and stood stricken with shock and overwhelming dread.

A wave of loss swelled beneath her suddenly lifting her higher and higher until it seemed that time and space could no longer contain her as she plunged into the depths of an unknown, yet strangely familiar realm. She knew she was both *dead* and alive and she wondered what she should do.

As if summoned by Amelia's thoughts her best friend, Delilah, who had died in a car crash when they were thirteen, was instantly standing by her side. The moment Amelia saw her familiar dark hair, boyish haircut and looked into her beautiful, warm brown eyes the emptiness in her heart vanished and she found herself staring in disbelief.

"I can't believe you're here! I thought I'd never see you again! And you're not a kid anymore… you look more like you're twenty! And you're so beautiful! Did you turn into an angel or something?" said Amelia bubbling with excitement as she hugged Delilah. "Wait! You can't be an angel – you're solid! I just hugged you," she added in amazement.

Delilah burst into laughter. "You're no longer in The Game program, Amelia! There's a whole new world waiting for you now," she said her eyes bright.

"What about Matthew? He's so sad, he has no idea I'm alive," said Amelia, looking at him longingly.

"You can stay here as long as you'd like, but there's nothing you can do… he can't see or hear you," said Delilah, gently taking Amelia's hand.

As Amelia continued staring at Matthew she suddenly became aware of a blue-white light surrounding her and permeating everything as far as she could see. Then to her amazement she watched as the light gathered itself into an immense sphere of concentrated white light that turned sapphire as it radiated out.

As if she was watching a holographic, educational film, Amelia was shown how this blue-white sphere propelled each player's soul into their avatar body while in their mother's womb, and a small amount of this light existed within each player, connecting every player to this source of light and to each other throughout the entire game.

This invisible light-force gave life to each player, beating their hearts, healing their wounds and breathing each breath until they died out of the game. And in that final moment, the light within each player was drawn out of the avatar-body by the blue-white sphere which then launched the player's soul-essence into the Spirit world.

Amelia understood this is what happened every time. And though she could stay as long as she cared to she felt suddenly disconnected from the Earthly scene and ready to let go. Delilah understood her wishes immediately.

"Here, take my arm, or you can put your arms around me. This might seem a bit overwhelming, so it's okay if you close your eyes, but I promise you there's nothing to fear."

As Amelia took Delilah's arm and closed her eyes, a floating sensation drifted through her body as if she was dissolving and expanding all at once with every moment holding infinite possibilities. Her mind was perfectly clear and alert and she had the sense that they were moving rapidly, but after a short while their movement slowed down and soon after Amelia felt solid ground beneath her feet.

"Open your eyes," said Delilah, giving Amelia's hand a light squeeze.

They were in a large park standing on soft, green grass facing a huge sign.

"What's this?" said Amelia.

Delilah laughed, "It's a little between-lifetimes reminder you created for yourself! Read it, see if you can remember!"

Amelia read the sign aloud.

"Game Reminders: Details Every Player Will Forget

The Game is known throughout the Universe as The Great Experiment.

Forgetting who you are and your purpose for being there is part of the Experiment.

Just like any drama, the more that goes wrong, the more you like it. (Note: Please remember, this is only true in the playwright phase - your enthusiasm for problems will shift dramatically when you are playing the part you wrote for yourself.)

Dramas that change you are essential for playing at higher levels.

You will be afraid of change.

And things change.

"Is there any way I could take that with me into the program next time?" said Amelia laughing. "I think it would help me a lot more there than here!"

"Well you rememorize it every time you're between games

– who knows," said Delilah giggling, "it might just stick one of these times!

"Where are we exactly?" asked Amelia.

"Many people call this the Spirit world, because everything we experience here is created instantly in the *spirit* of how we think, act and feel."

"So that's why everything's so beautiful!" exclaimed Amelia finding it hard to believe her eyes.

"In this place, yes," said Delilah, "but this isn't the only place that exists. There are places here that accommodate all thoughts and beliefs because the Spirit world is a world of *thought-that-takes-immediate-form*. In other words… whatever you believe you will see instantly.

"Come! There's so much I want to show you!" said Delilah holding out her hand. "We can travel as quickly as we're able to imagine where we want to go. But since you're new at this and you've never been where we're about to go, we'll hold hands."

Amelia smiled, nodded and took her hand. In the next moment they were standing in front of several stately buildings. But unlike cities where the buildings stand side by side with little space between them, each building was surrounded by magnificent gardens with tall trees and glittering, crystal clear pools of water which reflected all the colors of the rainbow, as well as colors never seen on Earth.

"These are the Halls of Learning," said Delilah, spreading her arms wide. "This entire city is devoted to the study and practice of the arts. Everything is free and available to everyone. Would you like to start with the Hall of Painting?"

Amelia nodded her head enthusiastically as Delilah took her arm and excitedly led her inside. They stepped into a long gallery where every masterpiece known on Earth was hanging before them.

"These paintings are the direct result of the thoughts of the artist," said Delilah. "Each painting created here is an exact duplication of the artist's imagination… what they envisioned… prior to actually transferring their ideas to canvas on Earth. So if the artist was imagining a certain color that wasn't available at the time, the color shows up here exactly as imagined."

As they walked to another part of the building they stopped to watch the art students.

"Being an artist takes on a whole new meaning when you can create easily, effortlessly and quickly," said Delilah enthusiastically. "You'll discover that you already know every method and technique necessary."

"How is that possible?" asked Amelia.

"There are no Earthly-restrictions or physical limitations here!" said Delilah happily. "Whatever you can imagine you can create!

"Come on! I know how much you like to read and write… I'm taking you to the Hall of Literature," said Delilah taking Amelia's hand.

Instantly they were standing in a light-filled library composed of small rooms. "You can read the books, or you can simply hold a book and *feel* the contents," said Delilah.

"What does that mean?" asked Amelia.

"Well, try it… here," said Delilah taking a book off the shelf. "Don't look, just hold it and tell me what happens."

Blinking, Amelia said in astonishment, "It's a history book, but it's not like any book I've ever read. It's in two parts. The first part is American history… I know a lot of this from school, but I feel like I'm a computer that could answer any question you ask and ace any test I had to take.

"But the strange thing is that right along side the history I'm familiar with, is the actual truth of what happened," said Amelia amazed that she was comprehending everything all at once.

"Some of Earth history has been passed on by those who are ignorant of the facts, but more often than not, the truth has been suppressed through deliberate intent. Every word contained in the books is literal truth. Concealment is impossible, because nothing but the truth can enter into the

Spirit realm," said Delilah.

Amelia smiled and said, "I can't believe what I'm seeing... the people responsible for historical *misinformation* on Earth are the ones who write the true history in all of these books!"

"Yes! And they're always happy to do it and set the record straight!" said Delilah.

Then as if she had just received a message in her mind, Delilah said, "Oh, there's a concert that's about to begin!"

Taking Amelia's hand she led her out the door, across an expansive lawn and past a vast amphitheater sunken down beneath the ground like a gigantic bowl. Looking over the edge Amelia could see the concert hall surrounding the stage with hundreds of rows rising upwards and seating for thousands of people.

The seating farthest away from the performers was on the lawn at ground level and the entire area was surrounded by the most beautiful flowers of every color and hue, while the outermost borders had magnificent trees.

"Let's sit here on the grass. I know it's far away from the performers, but I think you'll be happily surprised," said Delilah with a mysterious smile.

Leaning back on her elbows she added, "Just like the Hall of Painting, the College of Music has a library containing every masterwork ever created on Earth, as well as altered versions created by the original composers based on newfound inspiration. You can learn every branch of music from theory to practice."

"That sounds wonderful... I love music, I really do," said Amelia, "I always wanted to just sit at the piano and start playing, but as you remember I never made it past chopsticks! I think it's just that I don't have the patience to be a beginner."

"Well, you're going to love being a musician here!" said Delilah grinning. "You'll discover that you already have the necessary dexterity in their hands and you know every technique... so you can skip right to the creativity part! Before you know it, you'll have the mastery to join an orchestra or you can be a solo performer… or just play for the fun of it!"

Almost as if by magic a great audience materialized all at the same moment, and then over two hundred musicians took their places as the conductor stepped up to the podium.

"How does the audience manage to appear just like that?" said Amelia, fascinated by the timing and precision involved.

"The organizers simply send out their thoughts to the people who are particularly interested in this concert… that's how I got the message… and everyone just shows up at the appointed time," whispered Delilah.

The moment the music started a sheet of bright light began rising up from the orchestra and continued until it was level with the uppermost seats. The light then grew in strength and intensity and rose up until it looked like a solid dome ceiling of iridescent, shimmering light covering the entire amphitheater and the park itself.

Because the amphitheater was below ground level Amelia couldn't see the audience or the players in the symphony, but she could see, hear and feel music as never before. She lay back on the grass and watched as the coloring of the dome responded like a chameleon and changed from one shade to another, as if it knew how to intuitively blend a number of colors according to the theme or movement of the music.

Even when the music ended the rainbow colors continued interweaving with one another, then finally faded away in the same amount of time it would take for a rainbow to disappear from Earth's sky.

Quietly, Delilah said, "Here, all music is color and all color is music. Students don't just learn about music acoustically, they learn to build light and color architecturally!"

Amelia smiled and was already imagining herself studying at the Hall of Music.

"Come, I want to show you something," said Delilah, leaping to her feet and offering Amelia her hand as she led her to some nearby flowers.

They knelt together in front of the flowers and Delilah

cupped her hands around a yellow lily. "Do it like this," she said as Amelia mirrored her.

Amelia's face lit up. Not only was the lily vibrant and fragrant, but she could hear a lovely tone that emanated from the flower. The combination filled her with a gentle, yet life-giving force. Amelia tried this with other flowers and discovered every color had a matching tone and all the colors and tones harmonized perfectly with one another.

Delilah then led Amelia to a bubbling brook which was singing too and exhaling a life-giving force that perfectly combined with the colors and sounds from the grass and flowers on its shores, even the rocks were singing.

As they walked along the brook Delilah pointed to a large, elegant building and said, "That's the Hall of Science. There you'll find every scientific study and discovery, and solutions to every unsolved Earthly mystery. All scientists are men and women of vision. Every new invention, every new discovery originates here and is sent, via thought-form, to open-minded scientists on Earth. Sometimes humanity benefits, but because these inventions have often been perverted or used against mankind in some way the inventions have been held back until only recently. However, an entirely new generation of game players has been coming to Earth over the past twenty to thirty years. They aren't trapped in the old paradigm, their hearts and minds are balanced, and that's why you may have noticed so many teenage prodigies making phenomenal discoveries."

Delilah took Amelia's hand and said gently, "You do know you need to go back, right?"

"Go back?" said Amelia puzzled, "go back where?"

"Back into The Game," said Delilah.

"Oh no... no, no, no," said Amelia fervently, "there's nothing I can do if I go back... it's impossible to do anything... or change anything... or help anyone... And besides, I love it here! It's better than any heaven I could ever have imagined.

"I mean, I was afraid of death... I was afraid that Matthew would die... but now I'm not afraid."

"Amelia, everything that has happened to you is all part of what you programmed before playing The Game, even your trip here to the Spirit world. But you planned to go back to help Matthew... because you see, he won't die for quite some time."

"What will happen to him?" said Amelia desperately.

"I can't tell you that... but it won't be anything like your experience here." Noticing the horrified look on Amelia's face Delilah said, "I wasn't going to tell you this... because this is something you only discover when you're fully out of the program with no chance of going back in to your lifetime. But this is important.

"Right now, there are parallel versions of you playing out the character of Amelia. There is a version of you that died on that hike and came back here. There's a version that went back and experienced past lifetimes, or more accurately, past games you've played. And so on. There's no limit as to how many parallel games you can play at the same time.

"Everything happens simultaneously... but it's even more than that," said Delilah slowly. "You are capable of playing every character in your game simultaneously... with no knowledge that you're doing it... at least while on Earth."

Amelia narrowed her eyes, "That's not possible! I don't know what other people are thinking or doing... how could I play the game for them... even if I could get my head around it?"

Delilah smiled and said, "Okay, I'm going to tell you, but only because you won't consciously remember any of this when you return to your physical avatar." Taking a deep breath she continued, "When you are in your avatar body you completely forget that there's another aspect of you that's multidimensional. This real you, is like the ocean, and the part of you playing the game would be equivalent to a drop of sea water."

"You mean like same qualities, different capabilities?" asked Amelia, shaking her head.

"That's it exactly!" said Delilah, laughing. "So the quantum-player that you are is capable of playing every character in your game… in multiple realities, all at the same time. Sort of like the way the ocean can handle every drop of water!"

"Okay, that's totally tripping me out!" said Amelia.

"Alright, I'll make it simple," said Delilah. "Pretend you and your quantum-player are like identical twins going out onto the ocean in a glass bottomed boat. You put on all the necessary equipment for deep sea diving and jump in while your *twin* stays in the boat and observes what's happening below. She might suggest that you turn to the left to see a pod of dolphins or she might warn you to be careful of the sea urchin you're about to step on. But it's up to you what you want to do."

"Are you saying that this *quantum me* has been playing the role of every person I've ever met?" said Amelia wincing.

"I'm saying the *quantum-you* is capable of playing all those parts… but that doesn't mean that's what you choose every time. Sometimes you might kick back and play as a *drop of water*, or a *puddle*, or a *stream*… or a *lake*… and sometimes you might want to be the entire *ocean*. You are completely unlimited!

"When you're on Earth, your thoughts and feelings create your experience, but there's a time-lag… usually about a month, which gives you the opportunity to make new choices and refocus… you can observe cause and effect, and the program teaches you how to play while you're actually playing the game.

"Here in the Spirit world your thoughts, feelings and beliefs are created instantly. It's as if you broadcast a signal – and everything you see, every experience you have, is a match to that signal."

"So everywhere you go here it's beautiful like this?" said Amelia admiring the view.

"Well, everything for you is beautiful… but every person creates their own experience, so the environment that surrounds each individual is a perfect match to what they deeply believe at the time of death. They instantly see an *out-picturing* of where their attention is focused and what they truly believe. And they see and experience others with matching thought-forms.

"For instance, if a person was cruel or cared nothing for others, no matter how religious or powerful or successful they may have appeared to be on Earth – when they come here they live in a world of their own making – a world that is uncaring or cruel. *Thy will be done* is the prime directive in the Spirit world as well as on Earth – but here everything happens instantly. There's no *pretending*. You are who you are – and you see a world that perfectly mirrors whatever you deeply believe.

"And this is what Thomas is afraid of. He can send remote viewers anywhere within The Game program but he can't penetrate the Spirit world. That's why he sent you."

"But I'm sure that Thomas was behind the satanic ritual… he wanted me dead! That's why I'm here," said Amelia fervently.

"Yes, Thomas wanted you in the Spirit world, but if you think about it, your body is unharmed. And that's because he wants you back."

"I refuse to do anything for him!" said Amelia angrily.

"He knows that," said Delilah knowingly. "But you would do anything for Matthew."

CHAPTER 18

Instantly Amelia saw herself in a game she had once played growing up as an only child in a small town in the Welsh countryside. She didn't know the exact year, but she was wearing a long, fitted dress and boots that laced up the front that were dusty from walking on the dirt roads in the village. She was holding a package from the market wrapped in brown paper and tied with string.

In this lifetime her father was a retired professor and her mother was the only teacher in a one room school house. Amelia immediately recognized Matthew when he showed up in her memory. They had known each other since childhood. He was the oldest in a family of six boys and he was bright, charismatic and handsome, but more than that he adored Amelia, and she never loved anyone else.

Amelia had the ability to feel everything in an instant. Even so, she found it surprising that she was able to fast-forward and see events unfold more quickly as well as slow them down so she could focus on the specific details. So she moved ahead to their wedding day.

It was springtime. They were outdoors on soft, green grass beneath a canopy of ancient oak trees. Sheep dotted the hillsides and clouds drifted like wisps of white smoke. Each person in the wedding party held a single, silky ribbon of a different color. Women and girls were skipping and dancing clockwise around a 20 foot pole while the men and boys moved counterclockwise; everyone ducking under the ribbons coming toward them. As they danced around the pole a beautiful rainbow colored pattern was woven from the top of the pole down to the very lowest point where they could all still move in and out while holding the sparse remnants of remaining ribbon in their hands.

Amelia discovered that she could zoom-in on the tiniest details from that day. She could see the embroidery on her dress, the roses on her wedding cake and even Matthew's unabashed gaze as they said their vows to each other. Though his eyes were different—hazel, flecked with gold—and more widely set beneath heavier brows, there was no question this was Matthew.

The scene shifted quickly to their move to England as Amelia watched the verdant countryside, speckled with brightly colored wildflowers, speeding by from the train window. Once they arrived at the main terminal in London they managed to make their way a bit farther on to their new home amidst the hustle and bustle of the city. It was a humble dwelling, but they were not poor by any means and her father had leant his financial assistance as well as extended his business and social connections.

Amelia observed the quiet elegance of the horses, their riders and the many carriages traversing in Hyde Park, where she and Matthew often walked together, hand in hand and radiantly in love. And then, quite unexpectedly, time began moving forward swiftly.

Amelia saw every nuance of their life together. Her father's money and connections combined with Matthew's brilliance and charismatic nature landed him at the top of his class in London's best college. When he graduated he was already well-connected socially as well as in business. Amelia saw herself dancing and dining with him at elegant parties where he was sought after for his acumen on a variety of subjects. Yet regardless of the amount of attention he received, nothing changed Matthew's humble nature or his deep love for Amelia.

However, everything in the sparkling world of Matthew's rising star paled in comparison to the day Amelia gave birth to their daughter. Even at night after a long day of work and study, Matthew would untiringly hold his infant daughter in his arms and sing lullabies to her until she fell soundly asleep. He would then return to bed gently placing the baby between himself and his wife and though he should have felt exhausted he could barely sleep from all the love he felt for his wife and daughter. Surely he was the luckiest man in the world.

And then she saw a memory of a time when their daughter was two years old. The little girl could have been her mother's twin at the same age; angelic with her pink cheeks, rosebud lips and eyes the shade of bluebells. Matthew commissioned a portrait of her as a cherub complete with a halo and feathery wings which hung prominently in their parlor.

On this particular day, Matthew was galloping two-legged through Hyde Park with his daughter perched on his shoulders, her shiny, blonde, ringlet curls bouncing in time with his stride. He whinnied and snorted, shaking his head like a stallion while pausing to paw the ground as his little rider giggled in delight. Amelia saw herself basking in the pleasure of that moment. Then all at once pain gripped her entire body so intensely she doubled over in anguish.

Amelia then saw herself hovering above a graveyard as Matthew, numb with grief and sorrow, buried her body at the family's church in Wales. Though the daughter he so loved and cherished was crying and clutching at his leg, it was as if he was in another world and had forgotten all about her. But Amelia could see that their daughter reminded him agonizingly of his wife and he couldn't bear to look at her.

Before the ceremony was even over, Matthew wandered away from his family and friends, leaving the churchyard in a state of silent shock. He mindlessly boarded a train bound for London, but didn't go home. Instead he wandered aimlessly through the city streets, eating nothing, sleeping in doorways or under bridges until at last, mercifully, he died.

But in the next moment a new set of images came into focus as if there was more for her to understand about who she and Matthew were to each other.

From what she could tell it seemed to be the late eighteen hundreds in England. Amelia was seventeen and her father was a widower raising his daughter alone. Although they lived in beautiful, modest estate, he had lost his fortune and was living off of past credit that was quickly running out. To save them both from poverty Amelia had agreed to marry Matthew, a wealthy landowner nearly twice her age and crippled from birth.

Matthew was a capable man, but his mother had been running the estate all of his life and had decided it was time for him to marry so she could train his wife to eventually take her place as mistress of the estate. Amelia watched the scene unfold before her on the day she arrived at her new home riding in a carriage through miles and miles of property surrounding an immense three story stone manor with over one hundred rooms. Nearly twenty staff members were lined up in the driveway to greet her, but there was no sign of the man she was to marry – or his mother.

Amelia had no idea what to expect because she had agreed to marry him sight unseen. In fact, Matthew was so reclusive no one outside of the estate had any idea what he looked like – and this led to much speculation and many harsh rumors amidst the elite social circuit linked to both his physical appearance and his demeanor. She had prepared herself for more of a monster than a man.

Amelia was ushered into the study where Matthew was sitting in a wheelchair with his back to her, but even as she approached him she could tell he hadn't been confined to a wheelchair for long. Unlike people who had been crippled for quite some time he still seemed remarkably robust and his legs were not yet emaciated. As he turned to greet her she was shocked. He looked much younger than she'd expected and was quite handsome with full lips, intensely blue eyes and softly curling ginger hair. But even more surprising was the strange recognition she felt when he first looked at her… they both seemed to recognize the inexplicable connection that existed between them. The intensity of it took her breath away.

In spite of the fact that they were about to be married, Amelia knew it was impolite to continue gazing into Matthew's eyes and yet she struggled to look away. He matched her stare unwaveringly as well. Suddenly, a loud, "Ah hem!" broke the spell as Matthew's mother entered the room. Matthew quickly turned away. At first Amelia felt confused, then embarrassed – thinking she must have imagined the whole thing. And then she mistook his reaction as one of arrogance.

But from her current perspective, lifetimes away from that moment, Amelia realized that Matthew wasn't being arrogant or egotistical, rather, he was intensely shy. And then she discovered she had access to his mother's thoughts and it was clear that his mother had manipulated him from childhood as a means of maintaining control. Amelia became aware that this woman had taught Matthew to believe that his birth defect, a minor malady which could have been highly improved if not cured over time, would cause any woman to reject him. This belief was so firmly engrained from his childhood that Matthew was uncomfortable looking any woman in the eye so he was as shocked as Amelia when they each held their gaze with unexpected recognition.

Yet, as Amelia stood next to him on the day of their wedding, idly listening to the minister repeat a marriage ceremony that he had doubtlessly given until it was rote, Matthew withdrew into a lonely world of his own without the slightest glance in her direction. Amelia forlornly recalled her girlhood fantasies and what she dreamed her wedding day would be like – the carriage and horses, the splendor, the dancing and royal guests, but just as quickly she banished the thought, determined to make the best of her new life.

In that lifetime Amelia had been raised by a wonderful and loving father. She had always been kindhearted and in some ways Matthew seemed like one of the many stray animals she'd taken in over the years. As his wife, she felt she'd have the opportunity to love him and that he'd soften. But Matthew wanted nothing to do with Amelia. She was young and beautiful, and even though they were married he knew Amelia would have nothing to offer him other than pity; and he was too proud for that.

Bound by etiquette, tradition and the laws of the day, feelings were mostly kept privately within but as Amelia watched that lifetime unfold, every single thought and feeling was laid bare before her.

In her science class she'd learned that light travels into infinity, never ceasing to exist. So was it possible that human thoughts, feelings and events continued unchanged as well? It was strange and disturbing to think that her own thoughts – thoughts she believed were completely private, might be accessible in the future and that she couldn't lie or try to make up a good story, because the truth would still be there somewhere amidst all the other infinitely shining light. Anyone accessing the information would know the truth – exactly as it happened.

Immediately following their wedding ceremony Matthew retreated directly to his bedroom suite. Amelia was assigned a room at the opposite end of the house and Matthew's mother wasted no time as she proceeded to instruct Amelia in regard to her duties as mistress of the estate.

A profound sadness washed over Amelia as she watched years go by with the knowledge that at another time and in another place, they had once been deeply in love. She could see that even though they had no conscious memories of other games, there was actually some level of unconscious emotional transference from one game to another. Matthew treated her politely in passing, but never entertained an actual conversation with Amelia. She couldn't understand why he was so distant and why he had no desire to have a child.

Amelia felt like a caged bird, but the door to that cage flew open and set her free when Matthew's mother suddenly fell ill and was bedridden in a wing of the house far from the daily activities. In the end, there was nothing any doctor could do for her so the staff was advised to keep her as calm and quiet as possible for the remainder of her days. Amelia now found herself as mistress of the estate and at once, effectively turned the household staff upside down and inside out with her new plans for the life she wanted to live.

Much to the initial shock and dismay of the head butler, Amelia no longer sat alone at the mahogany dinner table that seemed to reach out to infinity, instead she began dining with the household staff. This of course was unthinkable and frankly never done – there was no protocol for such behavior. When she first appeared in the servant's dining area everyone felt awkward and uncomfortable but by the end of their meal, echoes of gay laughter pealed through the halls of what had previously been nothing short of a mausoleum.

Amelia began singing and playing the piano, which had never been allowed by Matthew's mother. She fell in love with gardening and learned all about the farm; insisting she be present for the birth of the farm animals, even if it was the middle of the night. In no time at all she was able to deliver a calf or a colt as easily as milking a cow.

She learned to ride and hunt and jump horses, but she dispensed with the side-saddle and donned britches so she could ride astride the horse like a man. In this particular game she had been married into the highest position in society yet she wasn't socially inclined to have friends that would criticize her. Everyone on staff adored her so it really didn't matter to her what the outside world thought.

As she played her part in this game, Amelia assumed Matthew simply didn't care for her, but now, as the observer of the game, she could see what had been invisible to her in that lifetime. Every night Matthew ordered his meal to be delivered to his room but he would secretly sit at the top of the stairs in his wheelchair listening and smiling as laughter erupted from below. He had sworn the staff to secrecy as he moved from room to room watching Amelia as she worked in the garden or as she rode the horses or played with the young farm animals. He would close his eyes and listen with delight as she played the piano and sang. In truth, he adored her and longed to be a part of her life, but he was afraid to show his true affections for fear that she would find him repulsive and that he would lose her in the end.

As the years progressed Amelia watched as her desire to love Matthew and have his child transposed into love for the farm animals and nature. Every spring she poured love out to all of the new babies on the farm and spent the summer and fall delighting in their growth. Even though she had become quite content to finally let go of what she thought her life was supposed to be, she felt a profound sadness that Matthew never opened his heart and allowed for her to love him.

And then, one beautiful summer day, Matthew became extremely ill. The doctors predicted he would die within a week, but Amelia sat with him resolutely day and night. She ate her meals in his room and though he was unconscious she read poetry and prose and sometimes sang songs. Believing he was unable to hear her, Amelia shared everything she held in her heart. She spoke of her favorite flowers blooming in the garden and described how the sunlight magically glittered on the pond as she watched the swans sail elegantly throughout the day. She told him charming stories about the staff members and all of the animals on their farm.

Then one day his eyes flickered open and for the first time he smiled at Amelia. His smile was weak but it was genuine, and love filled his watery eyes as he said, "You've been with me all this time. I heard every word and I felt every beat of your heart."

Amelia dissolved into tears and laid her head on Matthew's shoulder as he reached out tentatively to stroke her hair.

Miraculously he was in remission. They didn't know how long they would have together so they made every moment count. They shared poetry and painting, Matthew joined Amelia in the garden in his wheelchair, and for the first time they ate their meals together. At night Amelia would lie in bed next to Matthew with her head on his shoulder and her arm across his chest as he stroked her hair.

Then, one morning upon waking and feeling his hand gently resting on her shoulder, Amelia saw the light in Matthew's eyes flicker as he gazed upon her with unfathomable love and in the next moment he was no longer there.

CHAPTER 19

"I'll do it! I'll go," said Amelia in tears as she reached out for Delilah.

The moment Amelia's hand touched Delilah's they were instantly standing in a place with very little color, the sun had already sunk below the horizon, and looming grey clouds hung heavily overhead. Ill-nourished flowers, faded and sickly, were here and there in the midst of parched, yellow patches of grass. Everywhere they looked the countryside surrounding them was in a gradual state of deterioration.

As they continued on, the sad-looking vegetation gave way to barren rocks. The light steadily diminished and everything surrounding them appeared in dismal shades of grey, even their clothing looked grey. Before them a rocky pathway wound its way downhill through massive boulders and on into what appeared to be a land of deep, black, impenetrable darkness.

Looking deeply into Amelia's eyes Delilah said, "I can't go any further with you than this. You won't get lost… just keep heading downhill. You will eventually come to a place that is at the very bottom of a deep crater."

"And that's why Thomas sent me here? That's what he wants me to see… some crater?"

"Yes. It's the place he fears above all else. He doesn't know for sure what it's like there… but he's heard rumors and he's terrified."

Amelia's body shivered uncontrollably. "I have to go?"

"If you don't go now, Thomas will find a way to send you back again," said Delilah. "But I have two gifts for you. One is this rose quartz," she said, handing a polished, pink heart-shaped stone to Amelia. "It will protect you, so don't lose it. My second gift is that you won't consciously remember any of this when you come back to life in your avatar body."

"But if I can't remember… how will I tell Thomas what I saw?" said Amelia anxiously.

"Thomas will pick up your experience telepathically," said Delilah, wrapping her arms around Amelia and hugging her tightly.

Hanging on for dear life, Amelia closed her eyes tightly and wished away whatever was to come, but in the next moment Delilah was gone.

Amelia's heart sank as she walked along a hardened pathway that crossed over barren, colorless land. A dull, grey sky loomed lifeless overhead and the temperature was dropping quickly. When she was in the realms of light surrounded by beauty the idea of doing this on her own had seemed viable, heroic even. But now she was all alone and her feelings of vulnerability and helplessness gathered strength as she climbed to the top of a rocky hill and found nothing below but a towering bank of mist. She looked around desperately for another way down, but the fog spread out as far as she could see.

Fear seized her all at once as she followed the path into mist that wrapped itself around her like a death shroud. Amelia could barely see the ground as she slowly and carefully picked her way down the slick, rocky hillside. The fog gathered in density until it transformed into swirling, damp, heavy clouds that pressed upon her like cold dead weight. Nervously, Amelia wrapped her fingers around the pink, heart-shaped stone in her pocket and to her surprise she felt suddenly warm and a bit less frightened as well.

Gradually the clouds dissipated until they vanished altogether, revealing a bleak landscape with no trees or grass or plants of any kind, leaving only small, square houses that looked completely uninviting and even a bit sinister in their utter plainness. Every home stood solitary and forlorn without a single adornment, as if each were housing people who lived in extreme poverty.

As she passed by the houses Amelia saw a middle-aged man standing on his porch dressed in clothing that might have been worn in the 1800's by someone very wealthy, but each piece was completely tattered and threadbare leaving him with nothing more than an air of faded prosperity.

With no effort at all, Amelia clearly saw an overlay that showed her the kind of person he was while on Earth. He had been a very successful business man and though he made sure that everything he did was legal, he was ruthless in his treatment of others. At home everyone was subservient to him. He gave generously to charity and his church, but only if he saw a financial or social advantage for himself. He was solely motivated by selfishness and greed.

Though the man didn't seem to notice her, Amelia gave him a wide berth as she walked quietly past his house. Even so, she could hear him muttering to himself about the injustice of it all and how much he was forced to suffer in this place. Suddenly his eyes narrowed and shifted upward until he was staring suspiciously in Amelia's direction. Instinctively, she stopped in her tracks. He stared for a moment longer and then looked away and continued ranting about his pathetic existence.

Amelia knew that the stone was protecting her from the cold but was it causing her to be invisible as well? Testing the situation, she carefully drew her hand away from the crystal in her pocket. The instant she lost contact with the stone the man's head jerked up. Licking his lips, he stared greedily at her as if she was about to be his next meal. Jamming her hand back into her pocket Amelia grabbed the stone. Instantly the man's eyes went blank, as if she had been nothing more than a figment of his imagination.

Silently, Amelia continued on. She was still unseen by the man but she was able to hear him grumbling for quite some time. Gradually, the path seemed to disappear as she picked her way through rocky formations. The grey light diminished rapidly from the darkening, heavy, black sky. There wasn't a soul or any sign of life whatsoever. Everything surrounding her was colorless and empty as if she had just wandered into another world.

Dimly ahead she could see some dwellings as she passed through rocks and nothing else. Here and there she saw people sitting silently, their heads bowed down, filled with gloom and despair. These structures were nothing more than shacks, so utterly worn down and disheveled it was distressing just to look at them. But it was infinitely more unsettling that these repulsive places were the end result of someone's lifetime on Earth.

Amelia jumped as a man suddenly appeared out of the darkness and spoke to her.

"I'm sorry if I frightened you," he said gently, "but my dear, this isn't where you belong. If you continue in this direction you may not return to the world of light for a very long time."

Amelia stood quietly for a moment staring at him. "Are you someone who tries to help these people?"

"Yes. There are many of us who continually attempt to rescue those who end up here – but we find it impossible to succeed if they don't want to be rescued."

"How do you know they don't want to be rescued? Why would anyone want to live like this?" said Amelia aghast.

"If the person doesn't have a glimmer of light in their mind, or even the slightest desire to step forward onto a different path, then nothing – literally nothing, can be done. The desire to change has to come from deep within that person. People here are revealed for being exactly who they are – and so they punish themselves – choosing over and over to be right.

"But there always comes a time, even if it takes thousands of years, where they finally realize they've punished themselves long enough with their own thoughts and convictions. And when the darkness they've created no longer holds any attraction to them… they finally choose to let go. And in that moment they are immediately transported out of the darkness and into a place where they can begin to heal.

"It takes time because they have to acclimate to the light realms… but we've never lost anyone," said the man smiling as he answered Amelia's unspoken question.

"But why did you say that I might not be able to get back to where I came from?" asked Amelia anxiously. "If I came in this way, why couldn't I get back out?"

"Let me explain," said the man kindly. "Have you noticed that there's nothing keeping these people here? There are no walls, no prisons… no restraints of any kind."

"So, why don't they just leave and go to where it's beautiful?" asked Amelia as she thought of how miserable life must be in this place.

"Think of the Spirit world like a mountainside. When a person exits The Game they instantly find themselves on a part of the mountain that matches their most deeply held beliefs on Earth. But no matter what level you are on… if you try to enter a level that is higher than your own frequency, it would be very much like trying to climb Mt. Everest without acclimating to the lack of oxygen. You simply come to a point where you can't breathe… and this causes everyone to turn around and go back to where they came from."

"But if I came from a *higher part of the mountain*… then why couldn't I go back?" asked Amelia.

"My dear, the reason I suggest you don't continue any further is because you are empathic. The discomfort you experience is caused by your ability to feel the thoughts and beliefs of others. It's manageable now but it will get far worse the deeper you go and you're not trained to be here.

"I, too, am empathic and I understand your reasons for being here but please listen to me. If you continue on you will be surrounded by people who are drowning in their own misery and if they see you, if they have any awareness of your presence… they will grab hold of you and energetically take you down with them. You will forget who you are and how you came to be there. Their world of darkness will become your only reality."

Petrified, but trying not to show it, Amelia thanked the man for his concern and continued walking, afraid she would lose her nerve if she stayed with him for even a moment longer.

Gradually she became aware of rancid odors smelling like rotting meat. Large bands of malevolent souls passed her by, all with hideously malformed bodies reflecting their distorted minds. And though Amelia held her crystal heart tightly in her hand and was therefore completely invisible to them, she knew everything about each person that passed by. Some of them had been there for centuries, but their ghastly appearance wasn't caused by the passage of time – it was their ongoing, malicious thoughts which appeared etched on their repulsive faces.

As the sounds from the groups matched their horrendous surroundings – everything from mad, raucous laughter to shrieks of torment inflicted by others as demented as the person being tortured, Amelia clearly saw an overlay hovering around each person. Everything was completely transparent. Whatever was created and held to be true on Earth was now *outside* for all to see and though a person may have escaped moral justice while playing The Game – in this place there was a self-created, strict, unrelenting justice.

Trembling with fear, Amelia continued walking unseen through the roving bands until they eventually diminished and she found herself enshrouded in darkness. Without thinking, she pulled the heart-shaped stone out of her pocket and discovered she could see in the dark with perfect clarity. Grasping the stone tightly, she climbed down over large rocks and boulders covered in a revolting, noxious smelling, dirty green slime hoping desperately the stone would protect her from falling.

After climbing down for about a mile she looked up. Towering above her, treacherous and menacing with a circumference of several miles, Amelia realized she was inside a massive crater. Rocks and boulders were strewn everywhere, as if there had been an enormous earthquake and everything had hurtled into the depths below scattering in all directions, forming natural caverns and tunnels.

In the center of the crater a dull cloud of poisonous vapor rose up as if a volcano was churning below on the verge of erupting. Dimly through the haze Amelia saw what might have been human beings at one time, crawling on all fours over the surface of the upper rocks; hovering above each one she saw the regrettable lives they had lived on Earth.

With her heart hammering frantically in her chest and her legs shaking with exhaustion, Amelia forced herself to keep moving until she reached a part of the crater that was more densely populated. Each person was frighteningly distorted from their limbs to their faces. Some were seated on small boulders conspiring together with a clearly evil intent. Others were lying face down on the ground as though exhausted. Small groups tortured those who had fallen out of favor, delighting in their victim's unbearable shrieks. Everywhere she looked there was unspeakable cruelty and she was not yet even at the bottom of the pit.

Horrified, Amelia stepped back, tripped over a rock, and as she fell backwards she opened her hands to catch herself. The pink stone dropped to the ground, skittered across a large, flat rock and as Amelia desperately reached out to save it, the crystal fell into the cesspool with a heart-stopping plunk.

The moment the protective stone left her hand the man's eyes flashed open. Suddenly able to see her, he focused on Amelia with laser-like attention as she struggled to get up. Slowly and laboriously he inched his way up the slimy incline edging his way toward her. On hands and knees Amelia tried to scramble out of his way but instead, she slipped on the rocks and tumbled down the incline toward him landing on her back. The man reached out and grasped her ankle with a fierce, crushing grip. Amelia screamed as she flipped over with her hands on the slimy rocks and struggled to pull her foot out of his grasp. But he was unbelievably powerful despite the deplorable state of his physical body. Amelia burst into tears as unbearable pain shot through her ankle and up her leg, as if she was bound by an iron shackle.

The man looked up at her with beady, penetrating eyes peering out of a monstrous face. His repulsive mouth was more like a gaping, cavernous opening with yellowed, dripping fangs rather than teeth. He exuded the odor of rotting flesh, and the remnant of clothing he wore was nothing more than a filthy rag hanging so precariously from his body that Amelia could see most of his grey, lifeless looking flesh. His skin was paper-thin and she expected to see his bones pop out at any moment. His hands were talon-shaped like a bird of prey, with fingernails more like claws. Everything about him was so distorted and malformed he seemed barely human.

Screaming and yelling only made the man more powerful so Amelia did her best to stay calm and quiet despite the lightning pain shooting up her leg. Though she tried not to look at the man she couldn't help but see images of the mental and physical torture he had caused hovering all around him, floating in the mist. She could see that every crime he had committed against others he was now experiencing himself, living daily with the indelible memory of everything he had done while feeling all of the pain and anguish he had callously caused, both directly and indirectly. His body and spirit were the visible expression of cause and effect. Yet even with all the pain he suffered daily, it was also clear that given the strength and opportunity he would continue tormenting others, herself included. His mind was creating a self-fulfilling prophecy over and over again.

Desperate to escape, Amelia tried to grasp the slick, coated rocks beneath her while attempting to gain some leverage to help her stand but her fingers slipped through the festering slime. Although the man was lying on his belly without the strength to move any further, it seemed he had the ability to channel all of his strength into and through his hand and there was nothing she could do but fight back the terrifying feeling that she would never escape and no one would be coming to save her.

Amelia tried to remember what she'd been taught and took a deep breath, only to gag on the putrid air weighing her down, constricting her breath and causing a terrible squeezing pressure in her chest.

Tears welled up in her eyes from the searing pain in her ankle. "Let me go!" yelled Amelia with as much authority as she could muster.

A hideous sound gurgled out of the man's throat and she realized he was laughing.

"It's been so long since I could taste and touch… and suck the life out of one as innocent as you. Rare birds like you never land in this place."

Anger and disgust twisted through Amelia and even the smallest movement on her part sent needles of pain searing into her ankle as the man tightened his talon-like fingers, digging his claws into her flesh.

Laughing at the expression of intense pain on Amelia's face the man said in a deep, ominous tone, "You think you're such a little lamb don't you? You don't even think you belong here. But even lambs lose their innocence – sooner or later they're taken from their mothers and slaughtered. For you it came sooner… that's why you're dead. That's why you're here."

Furious, Amelia hissed, "You're wrong. I'm not like you. I don't belong here. I came here for a reason."

A sputtering laugh erupted from the man's throat as green mucous dribbled from the corner of his ghastly mouth. "You are what you see – all of this is you!" he said, indicating their disgusting surroundings with a slight nod of his head.

A swollen, nauseating wave of grief and anger threatened to overtake Amelia. What if this repulsive thing was telling her the truth? How long would she be doomed to stay here? But then a thought flickered through her mind, *Thy will be done.*

"NO!" she screamed. "You're wrong! I don't belong here!"

"No? You're saying you don't hate the man who killed you – you don't despise him for what he's done to you, all that he's taken from you?" said the man with a monstrous, satisfied grin. "Oh, wait…" he said as if reading her mind. "Don't tell me you believe that you are a multi-dimensional being capable of playing within multiple avatars at once. That's such an amazing con. If you were really playing the part of your opponent then what if you are me and I am you? Isn't that a horrifying thought?" he said with revolting delight.

"Does that mean you're not the least bit infuriated that I can do whatever I want with you? That I have the little tigress by her tail!" he said jerking her leg with such intensity Amelia shrieked in pain as her entire body scraped along the rocky surface.

Shaking and filled with rage, Amelia bit her lip and wordlessly glared at the man wishing he would explode on the spot.

"Yes!" he said in a low, hissing voice. "There you are! The angry little lamb… the self-righteous, judgmental little lamb! Ah, let's see the vindictive-you come out!"

Amelia shook her head, nauseous with anger and disgust. "I'm not staying here. I only came to get information," she said vehemently.

A gurgling chuckle bubbled out of the man's throat. "Oh I'm quite sure you'll be staying," said the man slowly and deliberately, "I'm afraid no one's coming to save you."

Amelia could feel the man's strength returning to his body as she was being drained of hers. Black, all-consuming hatred rose from her stomach and up into her throat as suddenly everything before her eyes turned a dark, muddy red. As much as Amelia loathed this revolting creature before her, she despised Thomas even more. But now was not the time to worry about getting back at him. She needed to escape.

And that made her wonder, "If *Thy Will Be Done* works in the dark realms just as it did in The Game... then my deepest wish is for these two monstrous men to spend eternity suffering over and over again for every bit of the suffering they've caused."

"Ah... Little Lamb... be careful what you wish for! I told you that you belong here with me! And this is where you'll stay – I can guarantee it!"

He gripped her ankle so tightly Amelia screamed in agony.

"And fear will keep you here. You are in MY world now."

Sucking the life out of Amelia, the man gained more and more strength as she thrashed about trying to kick him and free herself, yet she found herself utterly powerless. Burning pain coursed through every inch of her body as he dragged her slowly over the rocks. Amelia flapped about helplessly like a bird with a broken wing until he drew her fully into the cesspool. With one last gasping breath, Amelia was drawn below the surface and into the depths of the foul, fetid liquid.

How was this even possible? She was a good person. How could this wretched excuse for a human being, or whatever he was, manage to drown her? After a short period of struggling Amelia involuntarily exhaled and in one spasmodic breath the decaying liquid filled her mouth and windpipe, completely flooding her lungs.

Half-conscious, Amelia did everything in her power to claw her way to the surface – anything to stop the horrific sensation of being smothered to death, but darkness closed in on all sides. Her body went limp, her lungs gave out, her mind was blank and there was nothing to do.

The man released her body as she floated lifelessly far below the surface. Amelia couldn't move or breathe, she wanted to die and it seemed her body was dead, but now she fully understood the truth: Death did not exist in the Spirit world and it would just be a matter of time before she regained her strength and then that hideous creature would be waiting to drown her again, and again, and again.

Minutes felt like hours, but finally she could move her eyelids and without thinking Amelia opened her eyes. Somehow in the dense liquid she was seeing the ghostly grey faces of people who had fallen into the cesspool. Their flaccid bodies were alive, but barely moving as they drifted about staring aimlessly into the grey depths waiting for the strength to crawl out. The grotesque man floated nearby. He had used all of his might to hold her underwater until she drowned, and now he was waiting to have enough strength to overpower her again.

Rage ate its way through Amelia's body, consuming her from the inside out. This was all because of Thomas. He had her killed and he was planning to indiscriminately kill as many human beings as possible in the future. She could only imagine the Machiavellian schemes he was responsible for in the past.

He knew *he* was the one who deserved to be here – this was *his* hell, not hers. But he sent her instead. Apparently he thought he could keep avoiding this place, but Amelia did feel a certain satisfaction knowing there would come a day when Thomas would no longer be able to hide behind his power, position, or politics, and he would suffer like this for eternity, if she had her way. And she would happily watch.

A woman drifted by underwater with a hungry look in her eyes, as if she was craving the anger exuding from Amelia's body hoping to suck in the sensation while she waited until the time was right. Amelia closed her eyes tightly. She couldn't breathe, she couldn't think, a grey mist clouded her mind and yet somehow she knew she had to remember something. What was it? How had she come to be in this place? Remember. Remember. Remember.

Amelia felt nothing but dark, dank liquid surrounding her and filling her lungs. She barely remembered her own name, but she knew one thing for sure – she was powerless to change anything. Slowly her leaden, numb body sank through thick, murky layers until she settled on the slimy bottom, face down, arms outstretched, but she was beyond caring. Then, to her surprise, a gentle sensation pulsed through two of her fingers. She pressed them in the direction of the warm current of water and felt something hard and small. She had just enough strength to pick it up. A soft, tingling feeling spread through her hand, up her arm and flowed into her entire body. In the palm of her hand was the heart-shaped stone!

Amelia's mind suddenly became perfectly clear and alert. "Help me!" she screamed silently. Instantly she saw a vision, almost like a dream of herself standing next to Thomas, but rather than seeing physical features she saw energy radiating from both of their bodies, swirling around them in muddy colors.

Around her own body she saw variations of dark reds and browns and the words, *Angry, Vengeful, Hateful.* Black and red light erupted from her heart as the words *Guilty* and *Vindictive* floated on the surface of the colors.

None of it made any sense so she focused instead on the dark, rusty colors that surrounded Thomas' head accompanied by a strange halo of words. She could literally see words such as: *Prideful, Indifferent, Demanding, Scornful,* floating in and out of the dark, muted colors. Blackish-brown colors enveloped his body along with the words, *Shameful, Despised, Miserable, Humiliated.*

These words describing Thomas made sense, except maybe the humiliated part, but she didn't understand what she was seeing around herself. She wasn't a vengeful, vindictive person. Well, perhaps a little when it came to Thomas, but he certainly deserved to suffer for all the terrible things he had done and was about to do.

Still, there was that energy of guilt flowing out of her heart, but she had no reason to feel guilty, she hadn't done anything wrong. So it had nothing to do with her. Instead, Amelia focused intently on Thomas' faults and knew for a fact that her anger was completely justified, so she had every right to be vindictive and he deserved pain and suffering.

As her rage bloomed Amelia discovered that she felt better, yet she couldn't help but notice that the colors swirling around her own image were becoming darker and darker until suddenly she was sucked into the image and found herself standing inside a massive clear, glass globe. But this globe wasn't filled with lovely, white fake snow. She was standing in raw sewage up to her knees with rats paddling around madly looking for refuge. She let out a blood curdling scream as the rats began climbing up her legs, but she couldn't move because her feet were glued to the bottom. Terror and rage stormed through her body shaking the globe furiously as sewage and rats rained down on her.

CHAPTER 20

"**P**lease! Help me!" she screamed desperately. "PLEASE!"
Instantly Amelia found herself standing in a
blackened tunnel. Petrified, she spun around looking for a way
out and saw nothing. But as her eyes adjusted to the dark she
noticed a tiny golden light, as if someone was holding a candle
at the far end of the tunnel and walking slowly away.

Amelia followed the light steadily downward as the tunnel
spiraled deeper and deeper into the earth. At last she caught
up with the light as it expanded and she found herself standing
in front of two massive and very old, wooden double doors,
each with their own round iron handles.

She didn't know where she was or what she was supposed
to do so she grabbed one of the handles with both hands and
pulled with all her might. The heavy door swung silently open
revealing Thomas sitting with his back to her in front of a
huge holographic image playing what appeared to be a video
game. Amelia stepped cautiously into the dark room lit only by
the light emanating from the hologram. She quickly realized
she was invisible to him so she moved closer and stood right
next to him, watching as he ran a series of game programs at
lightning speed.

Gradually, the images slowed down and she realized Thomas was watching himself play The Game through a single lifetime that somehow spanned across thousands of years. It quickly became apparent to Amelia that he was trying to locate and fix a problem he had created in the past because he kept saying over and over, *causal seed, causal seed,* as past games flashed back and forth showing different scenarios. It seemed as if he was trying to achieve a different outcome by going back in time and choosing an alternate path that would take him into a parallel reality.

Unable to find an answer and completely exasperated, he focused on a moment in time prior to being born into The Game. To her surprise, Amelia watched as the Spirit world flashed onto the image a vision of Thomas walking through a gorgeous park and talking with the most exquisite woman Amelia had ever seen.

She had thick, shiny, black hair that fell to her waist and a golden light encircling her head like a halo. Her hands and feet were adorned with jeweled rings and bracelets and she wore a long, flowing dress studded with emeralds and rubies that seemed to be lit up from within causing the dress to sparkle and glow as she moved at a walking pace, floating just above the ground. Her face was so beautiful and luminous it seemed as if a goddess from India had come to life.

"Naia, I know what I want to accomplish and this time I'm going to end all human suffering," said Thomas wholeheartedly.

Shaking her head gently Naia said softly, "Thomas, I understand your desire to choose a game lifetime that has the potential for you to understand how to navigate the program, but with power comes great responsibility… and as you know, you won't remember your original intentions.

"There's a much better chance that your new found power will cause you to manipulate the program rather than try to benefit mankind – and if you do, you will become irrevocably disconnected from any feelings of empathy for your entire lifetime. Do you see the problem?

"Without empathy you won't care what happens to anyone else – you'll make selfish decisions from your mind, not your heart. And you could very well create the opposite of what you're now intending."

"But The Game is an illusion," said Thomas emphatically. "It's temporary, there are no victims or victimizers – there are only pre-game agreements that are fulfilled or unfulfilled. You yourself have taught me that every action and reaction has a purpose, so what does it matter whether I disconnect from empathy or not? Nothing happens without a prior agreement and even if there is… unavoidable pain… suffering isn't necessary, it's always a choice."

"Thomas, that's easy to say from the perspective of the Spirit world with light shining all around," said Naia knowingly. "But as you well know, suffering doesn't feel like a choice when YOU are the one suffering."

"Well, that's true and I should know," said Thomas, "I have certainly had more than my fair share of suffering! All those lifetimes as a woman where I had plenty of empathy, but no power," said Thomas indignantly. "It didn't help me or anyone else, just suffering and more suffering… and then there's childbirth, but I won't even get into that!"

Amelia burst out laughing, clapped her hand over her mouth and then remembered Thomas had no idea she was there. Just the thought of Thomas choosing multiple lifetimes as a woman was enough to make Amelia's head spin and though she knew he had been a woman, she still had the image of him going through all of the inconveniences of pregnancy and childbirth as a man – it was the most entertaining thought she'd had in a very long time.

"I understand what you're saying," said Naia kindly, "but I'm talking about what your life will be like when you return to the Spirit world after a lifetime with no empathy. You must remember, Thomas, you have never played a game where you're a man with power and authority. Whatever you believe and feel when you return will show up instantly – and you know nothing of the dark realms."

"Really, how bad can it be? No one stays there forever. Everyone can change their mind at any time. People get rehabilitated all the time. There's a hospital right over there," he said, nodding to a gleaming building just beyond a sparkling lake at the opposite end of the park.

"Yes, but before anyone is brought to the hospital they must have a willing change of heart. And sometimes people would rather be right than happy for very, very long periods of time," said Naia thoughtfully.

"I know I'm taking a chance on this, but I've spent over a hundred years in Earth-time researching The Game program, as well as past games I've played, and I'm certain I can change what's happening on Earth. I've even devised a way to stay alive in a human body… mine or some else's… for as long as it takes to get the right outcome. And I'm not talking about a longer life I'm talking about being able to stay for hundreds or thousands of years!"

"Staying in human form for longer periods of time is not necessarily better. There's a very good reason players have short lifetimes and fully disconnect from their avatar body. You need time away from the illusion to learn from your mistakes and to assimilate new solutions before you return and play again. A fresh start and a new body can be very helpful… even if you *are* required to forget."

"But in the end, we're just talking about two different experiences because the entire program is an illusion – a very convincing one, but still, an illusion that's no more powerful than a dream. Of course most people dream unconsciously, but there are lucid dreamers who know how to wake up inside the dream and then they use their thoughts and feelings to manipulate what's happening. I'll have the ability to be fully aware that I'm living in an illusion… a waking dream if you will… and that awareness will allow me to manipulate the entire program and help everyone on Earth!"

"It's a very slippery slope, Thomas," said Naia with a

penetrating gaze.

"Well, isn't the whole idea behind The Game – to sally forth, going where no man has gone before… while making colossal mistakes along the way?" said Thomas jovially. "How else will everyone in the universe be able to sit back, watch the games we play and know what NOT to do? How else will they come up with answers if WE, the game players, don't create new problems to be solved? My idea is to find a way that we can create and solve problems without suffering."

It took a moment for Amelia to fully connect with the idea that this was Thomas talking. He was funny, lighthearted, and to her amazement, joyful. More like a person planning a trip to a theme park than someone contemplating a lifetime on Earth.

"I agree with you, Thomas, and many players share the same sentiment. But this brings us full circle back to the original problem – you will have a full mental understanding of the program, but you will lack empathy. It isn't just a matter of what you will do for others, what happens to you is just as important, especially when you exit the game."

"I know I'll probably lose my ability to feel empathy, but I'll be able to feel love… and combined with my knowledge I think there's a very good chance I can create a world without suffering."

"Thomas, you have never managed to do that for yourself in any of your lifetimes. Remember *Rule Number 1? If it doesn't work stop doing it.* What makes you think you could accomplish this for everyone playing on Earth when you haven't yet managed it for yourself?"

"Well, we know that the program causes energy to slow down and appear as matter – according to the feelings of each player… which means each player creates their own world… their own reality," said Thomas. "The illusion only exists when players see energy moving very, very slowly and perceive it as physical reality. However, perception is not the truth. There's a greater Truth that's not subject to perception and *It* runs the program.

"You see, most computer programs have a back door created by the architect but The Game program is just the opposite. The backdoor IS the program itself.

"I've been thinking about this and there's a way that I could alter the program so that it's more like the Spirit world – likeminded players playing together rather than a few players dominating the rest." Thomas paused for a moment.

"Go on," said Naia with the faintest hint of a smile.

Enthusiastically, Thomas continued. "Energy is the combination of Universal Intelligence and Universal Love which creates, connects and IS everything – including The Game program itself!

"The Game is programmed to cause a feeling of separation – how else could a player have an experience? If you know and love everything that has ever happened or ever will happen – nothing new can occur… there would never be the feeling of expansion or growth or creativity. So players perceive Intelligence and Love as two separate energies and spend each game period trying to put the two back together.

"So, as I was saying, the program itself IS the backdoor. You don't have to hunt around for the backdoor or figure out a special passcode. The program is pure energy and it responds to resonant frequencies – just like a crystal glass humming along with a particular sound."

"Alright, Thomas," said Naia. "But tell me, how do you get the program to *hum* along with you?"

"Well, it's something you always tell me between lifetimes…" said Thomas grinning.

Naia smiled, *"If you would only love more…"*

"All limitations in your life would vanish," said Thomas finishing the statement.

"And how will that help you when you can't remember it?" said Naia thoughtfully.

"Well, like I said, the program itself is the backdoor – so you don't have to know anything about it. Every player has access to it at all times. But of course, we forget everything so I just have to have a compelling reason to love and then I could work around my lack-of-empathy problem."

"Alright… I'm listening… what's your plan?" said Naia supportively.

"In my research I've discovered a game where I can be a high priest who learns how to perfectly navigate the program… to the point that I could even manipulate it… with love, of course," Thomas added quickly.

"Did you research all of the variables as well?"

"Yes. And you're right, the failure rate – at least in regard to my plan – is about 99.999 percent," he said rolling his eyes in acknowledgement of Naia's warnings. "But here's my idea. I will have a daughter that I dearly love. And to be sure of that… I have picked someone who I have loved in every game we've ever played, no matter what parts we've played. And she has always loved me as well… of course other things have gone wrong…" Thomas admitted, knowing it was a complete understatement, "but I really believe this will work!

"Even though I won't feel empathy, I will consistently and powerfully be feeling love. I can't help but love her more and more as she grows up. And when a player loves like that the resonant frequency in the avatar body will oscillate with the program automatically overriding all limitations!" said Thomas, so proud of himself he was practically glowing.

"Thomas you seem to be forgetting all of the things that can go wrong. You're planning to play a game as a wealthy, powerful man in ancient Egypt. You've never lived in that time period before. You can't possibly know how you will react.

"On top of that you are talking about loving a child. Yes, that kind of love can last a lifetime, but human emotions can change. Children change. They grow up. They move away. They can disappoint you. And you don't know how you will feel when that happens."

"I know, I know… but that's not going to happen. I've already taken everything into account! I have contracts with everyone I'll be playing with as well – so there are certain things I know will happen," said Thomas with the enthusiasm of a child on Christmas morning.

Patiently Naia said, "Every time you've played as a man you have plans to enlighten all of humanity, and then your ego kicks in – someone does something you don't like, or something happens that you can't control and you suddenly FEEL separate and disconnected. And you feel this so powerfully… your experiences go from bad to worse as the program quickly and powerfully out-pictures the intensity of what you feel."

"I know I've made mistakes in the past, but I've learned from them!" said Thomas earnestly. "I've calculated the perfect time to go back and make changes. My idea will change everything – I even have more than one alternate ending. And yes, there's a chance it won't work – but what if it does work? The alterations to the program would stop human suffering. I could make The Game fun again," Thomas said smiling hopefully.

"Naia, think about the real purpose of The Game. It was designed to make us forget who we are. How much adventure could you have - how courageous would you be if you knew there was nothing to fear? People who want to play it safe stay here in the Spirit world! They go to concerts and paint and write poetry. They never have to worry about ending up in the dark realms because they never go anywhere or do anything challenging.

"Game players are the cosmic, bad-ass renegades of the entire universe!" said Thomas laughing. "We don't go to Earth to play it safe! We don't go there afraid of screwing things up."

"Alright, Thomas, imagine you have manipulated the program and created this perfect world you're aiming for. People love each other, they play with other likeminded players… everyone shares the bounty of Earth equally and fairly, there is no lack and you have no limitations. Everything and everyone is in perfect balance. Love prevails. Now, given eternity, how long would it take for you to get bored? How long would it take before you wanted a challenge?"

"Not long… given eternity," said Thomas thoughtfully.

"That's why I'm telling you… again… you don't need to fix The Game. The program isn't broken – it works exactly as it was intended to work."

Smiling warmly Thomas said, "I do thank you for your advice, Naia. Your words of wisdom are always something I take to heart," he added, putting his hand on the middle of his chest. "But I'm sure you know that I've already made up my mind."

"Yes, of course, Thomas," said Naia smiling affectionately. "You are indeed a cosmic renegade and you have a beautiful, kind and strong heart. As you can see," she admitted graciously, "I am one to stay securely in the Spirit world and give advice. I'm happy to leave all of the audacious experiences to *bad-ass* adventurers like yourself!"

Instantly the scene disappeared. Thomas sat back in his chair contemplating what he had just seen. Then a holographic image appeared as if responding to his thoughts and showed Thomas playing out the lifetime he had been so eagerly anticipating.

Everything went as planned. As predicted, his ability to feel empathy was no match compared to his desire for power, but that was not unusual for an imposing, high-born man in ancient Egypt and clearly it didn't slow down his progress. He was rich, brilliant, charismatic and very well-connected.

After his marriage, and with their combined fortunes, Thomas became one of the wealthiest, most influential men in Egypt. When his young wife died in childbirth just nine months after their wedding, she left him with a healthy, beautiful baby girl – and that was all he really wanted. He didn't remember why he wanted a daughter so badly, nor did he question his utter devotion to her.

Standing quietly next to Thomas, Amelia watched as the years passed quickly, and though she didn't focus upon any specific point in time, she could see the energy exchange between Thomas and his daughter and it was just as loving and pure as he had predicted. His life was going better than he could possibly have planned and Amelia wondered if maybe he was right. Maybe there was something his daughter could teach him about loving and caring for others.

Then the images slowed down and Amelia saw Thomas' teenage daughter, Juliana, standing on a balcony looking out over the ocean. She was a tall, stunningly beautiful and graceful young woman with vivid green eyes and long, wavy auburn hair. And then a sudden, shocking recognition swept over Amelia as she realized she herself had played the part of Juliana in that lifetime.

CHAPTER 21

Juliana adored Thomas – and he couldn't have loved her more. He continually gave her anything and everything she wanted, so when she fell in love with her father's champion chariot driver Juliana wasn't the least bit concerned, because even though the object of her desire was low-born he had brought the attention of Egypt's most elite families to Thomas' door, and consequently more money, power and prestige came to their own family. So Thomas loved this handsome chariot driver like a son and had promised to help him rise up through the ranks to the highest position possible, given his birth.

In the meantime, there had been offers for Juliana's hand in marriage. But Thomas was in no rush to lose his beloved and only child. Juliana took advantage of this by convincing her father to let her choose the perfect man who would not only make her happy, but also add to their status. That left Thomas more than content to build a palatial home next door for her and her future husband.

Though Juliana knew her father was at least, on the surface, looking for acceptable suitors, she also knew that sometimes parents would *surprise* their offspring with the happy (or not-so-happy) news that an engagement had been arranged. Juliana thought arranged marriages were barbaric and much closer to her father's breeding program for his race horses than the way a young woman should be expected to enter into a marriage. Besides she was already madly in love – so she chose to take matters into her own hands.

Early one evening after the horses had been fed and while no one was paying any attention to her, Juliana snuck out of the house and wandered through the barn until strong arms surrounded her and pulled her into an empty stall. She threw her arms around a devastatingly handsome young man in his twenties with dark eyes and hair, angular features, curly, black hair and a muscular, tanned body.

Though Juliana had no idea she was playing a game, Amelia instantly recognized that Matthew was the soul inhabiting the avatar.

Juliana knew that if she told her father she wanted to marry Matthew, he would say no, and there was a good chance that she would never see him again. But if she told her father how much she loved Matthew and that she was already pregnant with his child – her father could hardly say no. He had never said no to her, ever.

Besides, her father was in a position to elevate Matthew's standing in society and could easily allow them to marry. And then, of course, they would simply move into the house next door. Her father would happily spoil his grandchildren and Juliana would have the best of both worlds – her father's love and the love of the man she desired more than anything in the world.

She and Matthew became secret lovers; regularly meeting in deserted places or swimming naked in the ocean whenever she could successfully sneak out in the middle of the night. She was so in love with Matthew, the time between their clandestine meetings seemed to drag on forever and she could hardly wait until they were married and could sleep together each night and wake every morning in each other's arms. So she was completely thrilled when she discovered she was pregnant. But this was the moment when Naia's predictions began to play out.

When Juliana revealed her pregnancy and plans for marriage she expected that her father might be a bit surprised, maybe even temporarily upset, but never in her life would she have considered the possibility that her own father, her hero and the person who had always loved her unconditionally from the day she was born, would treat her in the most horrendous way.

Thomas was in such a rage and so humiliated he had Juliana locked in her bedroom and because of his pride and lack of empathy he never saw her or spoke to her again for the rest of her life. Matthew was hauled into the streets and publicly beaten to death. But rather than going to the Spirit world, when his soul-essence left his avatar body, Matthew returned to find Juliana. He quickly discovered it was impossible to communicate with her, because even though he could see himself and hear his own voice, he may as well have been in a different world.

Gradually he realized he was living in some kind of strange parallel existence. He was as close to Juliana as her own breath, but he couldn't make his presence known to her. He could see the future, but nothing good was coming and he was powerless to change any of it.

Then, one night as he sat watching Juliana sleep she popped out of her body and for the first time she was actually able to see him. Bursting into tears she threw her arms around his neck and to Matthew's complete and total astonishment they could physically *feel* each other. That night they made love all night long, but in the morning when Juliana awakened she burst into tears when she realized it was only a dream. Her heart was breaking all over again.

Though Matthew was invisibly present with Juliana all day long he decided it was best to leave her room after she fell asleep. And despite the fact that he wanted nothing more than to be her lover again he didn't want to upset her, knowing that she would wake up in more pain than ever thinking it was all a dream.

So that night he drifted down to the local tavern where inside it was business as usual: Prostitutes clinging to men who had the means to pay for their services. Some patrons were gambling while others began to raise their voices as they became progressively more inebriated. However, being out-of-body, Matthew saw everything from an entirely new and strange perspective.

Hovering around the men in the tavern were dark entities; those who had once inhabited human avatars, but who now were mere shadow-like versions of who they had been prior to their deaths. As Matthew took in the scene it appeared they were all waiting for something to happen; as if they were dark moths who had been drawn to the flickering flame inside a lantern. In spite of their relentless efforts they weren't able to get close due to an ethereal egg-shaped energy field surrounding each person. This energy wasn't the multi-colored light that Matthew was used to seeing emanating from avatar bodies; it was more like a barely visible, protective shell. However, many of the shells surrounding the avatars in this place had become dull and somewhat opaque, with dark holes or tears on their surface.

Matthew observed one man in particular who was becoming progressively more inebriated by the minute as dark entities gathered around him with great anticipation. The moment the man passed out the most powerful entity among the group forced its way into his body through one of the tears in his protective shell. It was at that very moment that Matthew clearly understood the attraction. This menacing being was savoring the feeling of inebriation and even more than that, it was able to take control of the man's body as well. When the man eventually regained consciousness he became angry and mean, but what he didn't know was that he was literally not himself; the entity was controlling all of his words and actions. By the morning the man would remember nothing other than a pounding headache and a hangover to prove he had had far too much to drink the night before.

From his current, non-physical perspective Matthew had already seen what was coming for Juliana. He knew their baby daughter would be taken from her and given to a trusted, older shepherd who would then leave the helpless newborn on a remote hillside to die. Matthew also knew there was nothing he could do without his avatar body. But that night in the tavern he'd suddenly had an idea and the next day Matthew began following the shepherd who always had a flask of wine at his side.

Every time the man got drunk Matthew attempted passing through a hole in his protective shield so that he could practice controlling the man's words and actions. To his surprise, passing through the shield and getting control wasn't all that difficult under the right circumstances, but getting the man's body to do what Matthew wanted it to do was like getting on a horse and trying to ride with no experience or training.

Day after day he continued to practice until he was able to completely control the man whenever necessary, but in order for his idea to work his timing would have to be perfect. The man had to be drunk enough for Matthew to project himself through the shield, but not too drunk for his avatar to function properly and there was a limited amount of time that he could stay inside before he was automatically ejected by the program.

When Juliana gave birth to their daughter, just as Matthew had seen, the tiny girl was torn from her mother's desperate arms and given to the shepherd with instructions to let the child die on a hilltop far away. The man always did as he was told, but he had never been asked to do something this barbaric, therefore, he began to drink in earnest as he carried the baby along a familiar, winding pathway next to a river and then climbed to the top of a distant hill.

This was far enough away from human ears that no one would ever hear the baby's cries and though he knew she was going to die no matter what he did, he gently laid the sleeping newborn on the ground as the full moon began to rise. It was a deep, blood-red moon and he would have walked quickly away, but he'd had too much to drink so he sat down heavily on the ground next to the child and in a few moments he was sound asleep.

Matthew instantly shot into the man's body but the shepherd was so drunk he could do little more than wait for the man's head to clear. Finally, he managed to open the man's eyes and then Matthew noticed coffee plants growing nearby, so he stood up carefully and after a few unsteady paces he gathered some beans and returned to his sleeping baby. There was little he could do in his current condition, so he sat in the moonlight chewing on the beans one at a time until his mind finally began to clear.

The moon lit up the landscape with a pinkish glow as Matthew gently gathered his sleeping daughter into his arms and carried her carefully down the hillside. He knew exactly where to go as he followed a path along the creek and on into a dense forest. Though he had drifted along this path many times out-of-body, it was far more difficult being inside the body of a fairly drunk shepherd with poor eyesight and moonlight that was barely able to penetrate through the treetops, so he was grateful he had had the foresight to spend plenty of time memorizing the path.

The trail wound its way into a clearing of ancient, slender grey stones towering ten to twelve feet tall. They appeared to be strategically placed into a large, perfect circle and stood looming like immense, silent guardians. In the center of the circle was a gnarled, old tree adorned with all kinds of offerings; everything from flowers to food to crystals; all laid carefully at its base or in the hollows and crevices of its trunk. Matthew had been visiting here, out-of-body, for months on the evening of each full moon.

He knew this was a sacred place and that a small group of forest women would soon be gathering together to dance naked in the moonlight. For months he had whispered into the mind of the most sensitive woman in the group that a baby was coming soon and would be left in their care on the next blood moon. And so when he placed his precious daughter in the center of the circle he knew he was fulfilling the prophecy he had created. And he had already seen that she would be raised with love and care in this hidden, woodland world and would ultimately possess a great deal of carefully concealed magic.

Matthew stayed in the shepherd's body long enough to observe the women as they discovered his daughter sleeping under the sacred tree bathed in moonlight and then he moved as quickly as possible until he reached the stables at Thomas' estate in the dead of night. Moonlight streaming through cracks in the walls provided just enough light for Matthew to climb up a ladder into the hay loft. He sat down with his back against the wall and then exited the shepherd's body. Matthew knew that even if the man happened to recall some strange memories in the morning, or wonder how he had come to be in the barn, he certainly wouldn't hike back to see what had become of the baby.

Leaving the shepherd's body sleeping comfortably, Matthew was able to fly quickly back to Juliana just as she was secretly being taken out of her home in the dead of night. The next day her clothing, possessions and portraits were all burned.

Matthew stayed with Juliana night and day as the small caravan journeyed south along the Nile. Though she was young her body was weak and never had the time to recover. But what was even worse was all of the pain she carried inside. The loss of Matthew had been unbearable on its own, but losing their child and knowing her daughter was surely dead was more painful than Juliana could bear.

By the time the caravan reached the Temple of Hathor, Juliana was more dead than alive. Her body was unceremoniously dumped in the dirt in front of the main steps leading inside. Several priestesses came to her rescue and though Juliana recovered to some degree over time, she never regained her strength nor did she leave the temple until several years later on a beautiful autumn day.

The merest breath of wind blew puffy white clouds gently across an indigo sky as her body was ceremoniously curled into the fetal position and buried deep in the sand. As her soul lifted from her lifeless body, Juliana saw Matthew and realized he had been with her all along.

Intense love intermingled with guilt and shame as Amelia felt a deep and ancient aching in the very core of her heart. In her lifetime as Juliana she had been completely selfish, careless and had caused much suffering. The truth was that she had known what would happen if a lower class man was caught in an intimate relationship with an upper-class woman, but even so she had only been focused on what she wanted, she had never considered what the fate of Matthew might be if her assessment of her father's good will was inaccurate.

Instead she had convinced Matthew to trust her, reassuring him that she knew how to handle her father. But in the end she had betrayed Matthew's trust in the most horrendous way. She had been utterly selfish and irresponsible with the fate of someone she loved as if he shared her very heart and soul. She was well aware of the social norms and of the fact that people in her social class supported people like Matthew only so long as they stayed in their proper social and much lower position.

In that lifetime Amelia had hated Thomas for what he did, but she hated herself even more for her own self-serving choices and for all of the pain she had caused for those she loved the most. Thomas had reacted violently, but that was the way any father would have reacted in that time period. She was his dearest possession – that's all he knew.

After her death, Amelia came immediately back into the game, though she was cautioned to wait until she was ready. But she didn't listen and chose to be born into the Alex avatar and programmed herself to choose Thomas to be a high priest hoping desperately that her love would change him. But his heart was completely closed off from the time she was his daughter and instead of relieving humanity of its suffering, as he had intended before being born into the program, he ultimately made everything worse.

Thomas had relied upon her to play her part by helping to remind him how to love others, but she had failed him. And whatever would ultimately happen to humanity was now her responsibility as well.

Thomas had genuinely believed that he could stop human suffering. He believed that his love for her would be an antidote to his disconnect from empathy. He had convinced himself that everything was just a game and that his choices to help or harm made no difference in the long run.

She also knew that by staying alive for thousands of years he had never had the chance to step away from the *playing field* to observe his mistakes or reflect upon how he might have corrected them. Then, the strangest thing happened. Amelia was able to feel the one thing Thomas had never been able to feel – empathy. In the beginning he'd had all the confidence in the world, he possessed a knowing that love would prevail and that together they would play out their parts to end the suffering of humanity as they had agreed to do before ever being born.

Amelia wondered if everyone who entered The Game did so with only the best of intentions, just like Thomas had done. How could she have forgotten that everything about life on Earth was completely unpredictable? It was more like a wild and rickety roller coaster ride where the chances were far better that a player would crash and burn than survive gracefully – and yet she had willingly jumped back on that ride over and over again.

Amelia suddenly felt her body moving backward rapidly as if she was being sucked into a vortex, only this time without the putrid liquid that had been previously surrounding her. She had absolutely no control over her own movement as she felt her body race past all the realms beginning with the darkest and continuing on until she flew past people dressed in white. She thought she saw Delilah and desperately wanted to stop and tell her she was okay, but she wasn't able to slow down. And as she reached the outer limits of the Spirit world, her mind began to reconnect with Earth time. Although she could still see Delilah, her body appeared frozen as if Amelia had pressed the pause button while watching a movie. Amelia was now out of sync with time in the Spirit world and was connecting once again with Earth time instead.

As if diving from a high cliff into water, Amelia shot between the dimensions and back into her body.

CHAPTER 22

I nstantly Amelia found herself back in her avatar body with no memory of what had happened. But just like a stone being thrown into a still pond, her entrance from one dimension to another caused a ripple-effect in the program which translated into a deep, ominous trembling in the cavern.

Amelia's eyes opened. Above her loomed the high priest swaying in a trance, his unseeing eyes rolling back in his head as the drumming surrounding them intensified into something powerful and dangerous.

But suddenly the music cut off and a panicked roaring filled the cavern amidst anguished yelling as a violent shaking was accompanied by stones and boulders crashing down from the ceiling above as bones cracked and bodies shattered beneath immense stone slabs.

Ear-splitting screams pierced through a massive surge of panicked bellowing as the shaking intensified and torches fell from the walls igniting those trapped below, their faces contorting in pain. Within moments the drug-laced smoke was mingled with the putrid scent of burning flesh and hair.

Amidst the chaos, Matthew's captors dropped his arms and

fled as the sinister celebration transformed into a sea of men running, stampeding, shoving and trampling one another until there was nothing but an immovable wall of bodies pressed tightly together. Pushing his way past men with glistening, crazed eyes, Matthew moved in the opposite direction of the hoard climbing over rocks and stricken bodies.

When Matthew was just a few feet away from Amelia the earthquake intensified. The high priest stumbled backward and tripped over a thick slab of rock that had fallen directly behind him. His arms pinwheeled momentarily until he landed flat on his back, hitting his head with a sickening crack. His body jerked once and then went completely still as dark, red blood spread slowly over the rock beneath him.

Matthew wrapped his arms around Amelia, protecting her with his body as he helped her sit up and slide to the floor and then under the altar for protection.

"It's okay, you're alright," he said holding her shaking body in his arms. "How did you get in here?"

Amelia's head was spinning but she managed to collect her thoughts. "There's a hole in the wall behind that curtain," she said pointing, "and a tunnel."

When the tremor subsided Matthew helped Amelia stand up, wrapped an arm around her and steadied her as they climbed over a massive rock slab and down the other side. He followed her along the wall until they came to the hidden opening. Terrified, Amelia kept looking to see if any one was following them, but the cavern was now so dark it was impossible to tell.

Matthew climbed upon a bench and yanked a torch from its holder. Amelia held the curtain open as he thrust the torch into the tunnel and quickly moved inside pulling her in directly behind him as the drape fell heavily back into place.

"It's this way," yelled Amelia over the chaos.

Matthew grabbed her hand and they raced along the passageway until the frantic screaming behind them gave way to silence, infused only with the sound of their own labored breathing. They slowed their pace a bit, but Amelia's entire body was still on high alert, adrenaline pulsing through her as she scanned the cracks and crevices for any shapes that might suddenly materialize out of the darkness.

Finally they slowed down and stopped at a point where their path branched out into three separate tunnels. Gulping in the dank air, Amelia knew she had come from one of the tunnels, but at the time she was following the sound of drumming, and with only a small flashlight she hadn't noticed the other tunnels coming out of nowhere.

Matthew held the torch aloft and walked slowly past the openings, but nothing looked familiar to Amelia as each tunnel swallowed the flickering light in shadow.

"Do you recognize anything?" he said anxiously.

"Give me a minute," said Amelia breathlessly.

Trying not to panic, she closed her eyes and took a slow, deep breath, breathing in through her nose. From one direction she noticed a musty infusion of things-rotting and rodents, both dead and alive.

Pointing to the tunnel on the left she said definitively, "It's not that tunnel. We're looking for a tunnel with fresh air."

"You think there's fresh air down here?" said Matthew bewildered.

"I know that sounds impossible," said Amelia, "but I was told to look for it... and I know it's here somewhere."

She then focused on the middle tunnel as Matthew stepped closer to the passageway on the right.

A moment later Matthew said, excitedly, "I think this is it!"

Amelia moved to the other tunnel and held still for a moment. It was nothing more than the tiniest breath of air, but there was a hint of something fresh and alive.

"This isn't the tunnel I was in before, but I think it's where we need to go," said Amelia breathlessly.

The passageway sloped down steeply and within a few hundred yards came to a dead end in front of a massive ventilation system at least eight feet high with a small vented doorway.

Matthew turned the handle and opened the door. "You're sure this is the way?" he asked.

Amelia poked her head inside. "I think so," she said hesitantly.

Two rows of tiny lights ran along the ceiling. It wasn't bright, but they could definitely see, so Matthew put out the torch on the tunnel floor and pushed it out of sight in a small crack beneath the vent.

Tentatively they crawled through the small opening one at a time and then stood up inside as Matthew pulled the door tightly shut and twisted the handle securely back into place.

Amelia was already facing the direction of the breeze and said, "It's this way... I'm sure of it."

"Do you think this could be taking us to one of those parks we saw when we first arrived here at the base?" asked Matthew pensively.

"Maybe..." said Amelia hesitantly, "but I was told there would be a tunnel with fresh air... and that it would lead to a place where none of the soldiers were allowed to go."

"Well, if it is outdoors, let's hope we can get out when we get there," said Matthew anxiously. "For now, let's walk as fast as we can. If we run it'll make too much noise and we need to distance ourselves from that doorway."

Amelia nodded in agreement and after walking quietly for about fifteen minutes she said, "I don't think anyone's coming after us, do you?"

"If soldiers start running we'll hear it echoing through the vent," said Matthew as he stopped and looked carefully around. "As far as I can tell there are no cameras or sensors in here... do you need to rest?"

"Maybe we could just sit down for a few minutes," said Amelia wearily.

Sitting side by side Matthew held Amelia's gaze and said softly, "I thought I'd never see you again."

"I know," said Amelia, blinking back hot tears.

Matthew's fingertips skimmed across Amelia's forehead, outlined her ear, traced along her cheek and down her neck. Moving onto his back he gently pulled her down and into his arms. Amelia lay on her side with her head on his chest and her arm around his waist. Warmth blossomed and swirled through her body as she placed her hand on his stomach accidentally touching his bare skin. Matthew unbuttoned his shirt as she skimmed her hand along the unfamiliar landscape of his flat stomach and over his muscular chest feeling the heat of his skin and his response to her touch.

Everything about his body was so beautiful and breathtakingly different from her own. Matthew pulled Amelia up onto his chest, their bodies pressing together as his warm hands slid under her shirt and along her back. Then he gently kissed her in a way she had never been kissed before. His lips, full and soft, barely touched hers, and every nerve in her body lit up the moment his tongue traced along her lower lip.

Melting into him she returned his kiss and her heart beat as if tiny hummingbirds were fluttering through her body, transforming into light as they escaped through her chest. Nothing existed but the softness of his lips pressing into hers as he held her tightly.

Suddenly Matthew stopped kissing her and pulled back. "Listen," he whispered urgently.

At first there was only silence, but then Amelia heard something too. Looking at him puzzled she said, "I'd swear it's a bird singing!"

"Are you okay to keep going?" said Matthew with concern.

Smiling a bit awkwardly as she looked into his eyes, Amelia nodded and said, "Yeah, I'm ready."

Holding her hand as they walked, Matthew said quietly, "I haven't seen you in days... where have you been? How did you end up at that satanic ritual... or whatever the hell that was?"

Without going into too much detail, Amelia did her best to explain everything that had happened to her, from her experiences in the Montauk Chair, to the moment she appeared in the cavern yelling for the high priest to stop.

"Of all the things I've been through," said Amelia, "the strangest thing was Äsha telling me that I could imagine the world of the Vedruss into reality… I mean, she said it would be my own version of that reality, and that I have to focus on what I want… instead of what I don't want.

"Honestly I don't even know how that could be true… but if it is, I'm obviously much better at creating what I don't want," said Amelia, feeling like a total failure.

"Do you know how to drive a stick shift?" said Matthew out of the blue.

Caught completely off guard Amelia laughed and said, "Um… no."

"Well, I read about it online, I watched my dad, and I thought it would be really easy. But it took more practice than I thought to get to the point where I could just drive on autopilot. So maybe what you're talking about is kind of the same thing… maybe it just takes practice… and then one day you'll be doing it without thinking," he said kindly.

Amelia smiled warmly at him and said, "I guess you're right. I do overanalyze things sometimes."

"I can relate," said Matthew laughing gently.

"So tell me what happened to you? How long did they keep you in a coma?" said Amelia anxiously.

"A coma?" said Matthew surprised. "I was drugged and unconscious for a while," he said thoughtfully, "but I don't think I was ever in a coma."

"But I saw you," said Amelia emphatically. "You were on life-support!"

"Well, here's what I remember," said Matthew. "When I went with Trevor, she told me that instead of further testing I could choose to be involved in a brief research project. She said I would be paid $20,000 and that you and I could both live in military housing rather than the psych ward, but that it was a one-time offer because their test subject had just dropped out and they needed someone right away.

"She told me I would be temporarily unconscious, but that it would be harmless in the end. It was supposedly research being conducted on how we perceive time without seeing the sun… and they would keep track of when I naturally slept and wanted to eat… stuff like that. And she said she would tell you so you wouldn't worry."

"What did they do to you?" said Amelia uneasily.

"I was taken to a room loaded with hospital equipment… they had me lie on a bed and gave me a shot. I don't know what they did after that," he said. "Maybe they hooked me up to life-support and then disconnected me. All I know is that when I came to I was in a padded room… like I was in a psych ward again. I felt a bit lightheaded but I don't think I was out for long, and all of the equipment was gone.

"I couldn't hear anything, not even sounds in the hall. When I was ready to sleep I turned off my light and when I woke up I turned it on. If I wanted a meal I put my dishes in a doorway in the wall. And then I'd close the door on my side and it would automatically open with a meal. If I didn't do that I wouldn't get fed."

"How did you end up in that… cave… temple place?" asked Amelia.

"I totally lost track of time, but at some point I found a black cape in the cubby hole where they put my meals. I took it out, and I wasn't going to put it on… but then they wouldn't feed me. So I put the cape on and then meals appeared. I quickly figured out that if I wanted to eat I had to be wearing the cape… which was just bizarre. And then one time I put the cape on, but rather than a meal appearing the door to my room opened.

"I walked out and it was like a hospital corridor… you know like with florescent lighting and tiled floors, and everything smelled like a hospital… but all of the rooms were closed and it seemed like everything was completely deserted. And then I heard this steady drumming. I followed the sound, but I didn't feel like I was running away or leaving the experiment because there was no place else to go. I felt like some rat in an experiment, but anything was better than being stuck in that room," said Matthew shaking his head.

"And then I came to these two metal doors... double doors... just regular doors, and the drumming was coming from the room beyond. But when I opened the door there was a thick curtain hanging about six feet in front of me, and when I went inside and opened the curtain I saw the temple and ceremony going on.

"At first I couldn't see a thing. But now that I think about it... it just seems so bizarre that these double doors in a hospital wing would open up into a cavern," said Matthew at a complete loss. "I saw men in cloaks that matched mine, so I pulled the hood over my head and went further in. But then I saw those four girls down by the altar... and even from where I stood I could tell they were hypnotized... or drugged... or something.

"I didn't know what to do, and I didn't know if it was part of some weird experiment, but I was afraid of what was going to happen to the girls, so I just started walking down the aisle. No one paid any attention to me... until I saw you and yelled out your name. And everything else from that point you know."

Amelia shook her head and said, "That ritual must have been some kind of bizarre set up... how else would you have a cape and then suddenly your door just opens and the cavern is the only place you can go?"

Matthew was quiet for a moment. "You know... if you think about it like a story problem – you have to strip away the story to understand the equation. So if we forget about the ritual... how I got there... how you got there... and we only focus on what happened, there was one major occurrence. You died and came back to life."

"Oh my God," said Amelia in a shocked tone, "death is really just a *trip* to another dimension... it's just that people rarely come back... but still, that's exactly what Thomas did with the Montauk Chair. He was trying to see if I could go to another dimension and return with information... *and* with my mind intact.

"And since the Chair was destroyed, what if he created the ritual not to kill me... but to send me into another dimension with the idea that I would come back with information?"

"That's pretty risky," said Matthew, "how could he have known that you would come back to life?"

Amelia closed her eyes. "Maybe he had plans to bring me back to life but I came back first."

"You and an earthquake!" said Matthew. "That can't be a coincidence."

"I'm not sure if I'm right or just making this up," said Amelia, "but when I imagine Thomas... without... you know... an opinion... I feel this horrendous fear. Not like I'm afraid of him... but it's as if he's desperately afraid of dying... or afraid of what he'll find when he gets there.

"What if he set up the whole ritual to kill me so he could pretend to save me... and then ask me questions after?"

"Do you remember anything at all?" asked Matthew.

"I don't have any visual images," said Amelia, "but I have a feeling I was there for a long time... and I think I know what he's afraid of but it's only a feeling, not an actual memory I could describe."

"What you're saying makes sense. And here's something else... Thomas can see the past and the future with remote viewing. He's capable of knowing everything we say or do. What if it's all smoke and mirrors and everything has been orchestrated with nothing left to chance?" said Matthew. "What if we're meant to think we have choices... but we really don't?"

"It's just like you said... we're like rats in a maze!" said Amelia, freaking out. "Thomas can close and open doors until we go where he wants us to go – and every step of the way we'd do everything thinking *we* were choosing it... when in fact, we have no choice!" Stopping, she turned to him and said, "What should we do?"

"I don't know," said Matthew shaking his head.

As they stood there quietly contemplating what to do next they suddenly heard songbirds singing all at once.

"Oh my God, it's not just a bird trapped in the tunnel! Those birds must be outdoors!" said Amelia excitedly.

"Wait!" said Matthew, his head cocked, listening.

Then he dropped onto his stomach with head turned to one side and his ear against the metal floor.

Jumping up he grabbed Amelia's hand and whispered loudly, "Run! They're coming!"

Weak and light-headed Amelia tried desperately to keep up with him. Though she could barely breathe as pain ripped through her body, Amelia raced on with Matthew pulling her along.

Within minutes she heard voices growing louder in the tunnel and the pounding, ringing sound of boots running on metal, then a voice yelling, "This way!"

Running full out they came abruptly to a dead end and were met with a vented doorway. Matthew skidded to a stop and examined the door. There was no handle, so he tried kicking the door open with his foot, but it was securely bolted shut.

Frantically Amelia spun around trying to find another exit point as beams of bright, halogen light zigzagged across the tunnel walls dazzling her eyes. But then she saw a small, red, glowing light on the wall next to what appeared to be a dark mirror.

Amelia punched the button with her fist as the soldiers bore down on them with huge, blinding lights. She knew there was no way they would make it past a facial scan, but there was nothing else she could do but stand there petrified as a long, slender light moved slowly from the top of her head to her chin and back.

With the commotion of at least ten soldiers running heavily toward them Amelia never heard the quiet click or realized the door was opening until Matthew yelled, "Amelia! Come on!"

as he grabbed her hand.

"Halt! Stay where you are!" a voice echoed from twenty feet away.

Matthew pulled Amelia through a round portal that was in the process of spiraling open. Squeezing through the exit they found themselves on a narrow cliff in a world they could never have imagined.

CHAPTER 23

One of the soldiers, racing at top speed, beat the others to the open portal but stopped dead as the portal began spiraling closed. Though he could easily have stepped through the opening, he stood there gradually joined by others, as they all stared dumbfounded at the scene before them.

Terrified and unable to move, Amelia waited for the soldiers to come after them but instead, the opening continued to close in its spiraling motion and to her surprise blended perfectly with the surrounding rocks and moss.

"Why aren't they coming after us?" asked Amelia confused.

Matthew shook his head, took Amelia's hand and said, "Come on, I see a way down."

"Where are we?" said Amelia in astonishment.

"I have no idea," said Matthew as he led her quickly along the edge of the cliff.

Overhead an intensely blue sky was layered with white, cumulous clouds tinged with dusty rose. Even the dense forest canopy nearby was dotted in pink, but it was the hot pink of a raucous bunch of Australian galah parrots gabbling like hundreds of ladies at tea with their feathery white hats, speaking a language all their own.

A trembling sensation shook the ground and the flock rose all at once, circling above the tree tops as they spun out of sight. Amelia and Matthew clung fast to the rock wall for support as stones and small rocks skittered down the hillside above and below them.

As they headed down a winding path Amelia said, "This can't be the desert…"

Matthew shook his head. "I've hiked here since I was a kid. I've never seen a forest like this and where did those tropical birds come from unless they all escaped from a zoo?" Looking at Amelia he confessed, "I'm as confused as you are. We did a lot of traveling underground in the base, but even if we traveled hundreds of miles in any direction we would either be in the desert or the mountains."

The trail led them to a point where it crossed over a bubbling brook wending its way along the edge of the forest. Whether it was safe to drink the water or not, they both dropped to their stomachs and scooped cold handfuls from the creek until they were fully satisfied.

Amelia sat on the soft grass bordering the creek. She took a deep breath and closed her eyes as the warm sunlight filtered down through the trees turning the leaves bright green as it danced across her face. Her body hadn't felt relaxed in days but now the sun was shining, the birds were singing and everything felt fresh and new. Amelia opened her eyes and smiled at Matthew and then began sobbing with relief.

Matthew gently put his arm around her and said quietly, "Are you okay?"

"Yes," she sniffled, "I'm just so happy…" She wiped her nose on her sleeve and blurted, "Okay… we're like totally lost… but we're alive!" And then in the midst of her meltdown she burst out laughing. "Oh God, I'm sorry… I'm so weird… it's just that sometimes when I'm really… you know… relieved… and then I cry…" and then she laughed even harder and said, "and I don't know why I laugh… it's really awkward…"

Matthew's eyes were glowing as he looked at Amelia then he wrapped his arms around her and burst out laughing. They laughed together until finally they just stretched out in the grass and closed their eyes. Amelia felt her body drifting off to sleep when suddenly she was sitting bolt upright, fully alert. Matthew too sat up at once as they heard the thundering sound of galloping hoof beats.

They both jumped to their feet and moments later a pure white stallion with a long mane and tail jumped over the creek and came to an abrupt halt in front of them. Astride the horse was a freckled faced girl of about thirteen years old, with penetrating blue eyes and long, dark auburn hair riding with no bridle or saddle.

"I'm Sophia," she said, jumping off her horse.

"Um… I'm Matthew and this is Amelia," said Matthew with polite confusion.

"Yes, I know, Father sent me to get you," said the girl sweetly. Then without any further explanation she added, "You're safe here… the soldiers won't come after you but we need to hurry, there's not much time. Follow me," she said as she walked purposefully to the trail that bordered the forest.

"Where are you taking us?" said Matthew walking quickly to catch up.

"It's right down that hill" said the girl.

"What's down the hill," asked Amelia confused.

"The settlement," said Sophia, "but we have to hurry… we've been having earthquakes … and they're not stopping. We all need to be someplace safe."

"But aren't we safest being outdoors?" asked Amelia.

"We're not outdoors," said Sophia walking even more quickly, "this is a biosphere."

"What?" said Matthew shocked.

"It's one hundred and fifty miles in diameter. The sky is holographic, but there's a layer of rock above that… that's why we're not safe! Hurry!" she said as her horse jogged slowly next to her.

A few minutes later the forest just sort of dropped away and before them were velvety rolling hills bearing vast stretches of wildflowers ranging in color from sapphire blue to the most luminous yellows stretched out before them. In the distance stood dense mountain forests that seemed to embrace and protect the valley below.

The girl stopped suddenly, patted her horse on the neck and then with the slightest motion of her hand the horse took off at a gallop down a narrow, grassy path. Following Sophia, Amelia and Matthew ran along the crest of the hill until they saw a sweeping, emerald valley complete with a languid river running through it to a point where at last it poured itself into a sparkling clear lake.

They climbed with ease down a wide path of soft, grassy mounds squishing beneath their feet as they stepped carefully over small rocks and around colorful wildflowers. At the base of the hill they found a variety of tropical fruit trees and wild berries growing everywhere.

Matthew surveyed the scene and said quietly to Amelia, "You'd have to make an effort to starve here!"

"If you're hungry," said Sophia, "Father will have plenty of food for you. It won't be long until we're there."

They continued running for a few more minutes until they came to a settlement nestled within the valley. Widely spaced plots of land dotted with houses were surrounded by trees and gardens. Amelia recognized everything she was seeing and wondered how the world of the Vedruss had been reborn in this place.

When they reached the small community, children ran up to greet them peppering Sophia with questions and staring wide-eyed at the newcomers.

Sweetly, but firmly Sophia said, "Father is waiting for us. You can talk to our new friends later. Now go back inside where you're safe."

Obeying her, the children ran quickly into the nearest house.

Finally, they came to a homestead at the outer edge of the settlement. Sophia called out in a happy voice, "Father! Father!"

"Sophia!" a voice sang out from the orchard, as a tall man with a large mustache waved from beneath a tree where he was gathering apples. Striding toward them with long, purposeful steps, the man approached, grinning from ear to ear.

"Here you are!" he said heartily to Sophia, Matthew and Amelia, all at once, as if he had been expecting them.

Amelia noticed that the man was a good five or six inches taller than Matthew – who was over six feet tall himself. He had a long nose, angular jaw and short-cropped, jet-black hair, parted down the middle, framing deep-set eyes and black, bushy eyebrows. There was a certain intensity about the man's appearance, but all of this was softened by his dark-brown eyes, sparkling with kindness and permanently creased at the outer edges by smile lines.

Matthew leaned toward Amelia and whispered, "He looks exactly like Nikola Tesla when he was young!"

The man beamed at Matthew, "That's because I AM Nikola Tesla."

Matthew's jaw dropped. "The Nikola Tesla I'm talking about was born in the mid-eighteen hundreds…"

"Eighteen fifty-six to be exact," said the man warmly.

Matthew stared at him skeptically, "The Tesla I'm talking about died as an old man in the nineteen-forties."

"I know. That's what most people believe…" he said enigmatically. "Will you excuse me for just one moment?" he said as he motioned to Sophia. "If there's a tremor, just run inside the house," he added. Then he began talking quietly to the girl as they walked together to the main pathway.

When they were out of earshot Matthew spoke excitedly to Amelia. "Do you know who Nikola Tesla is?"

"I've heard the name… but I don't know anything about him," said Amelia, shaking her head.

"I wrote a paper on him last semester. He's one of the

most brilliant men who ever lived … he's like the Father of electricity!" said Matthew, his voice filled with admiration.

"If this man is Tesla, he's the one who invented the first radio, the AC motor, vacuum tubes, and hydroelectric generators. He developed a way to give free electricity to everyone in the world – but the funding was pulled out and the power plant he was building was closed down before he was able to finish – then the plans disappeared.

"Supposedly all of his papers and experiments were stolen by the FBI when he died… but maybe everything just came here," Matthew added in amazement. "I mean, it makes a strange sort of sense, given everything else going on here.

"The military wanted his work. Tesla's technology and discoveries are connected with missiles, particle beam weaponry, satellites and nuclear fission... It makes sense that he'd be here and they'd cover it up by faking his death."

"Isn't he the one who created an earthquake machine?" asked Amelia.

"Apparently, he didn't create it on purpose – he was experimenting with resonant frequencies and accidentally caused an earthquake… nearly flattened an entire city block."

"But that doesn't explain how he could be a hundred and fifty years old and look like he's forty – at the most," Amelia said emphatically.

"I know – that's the part I don't understand either," confessed Matthew.

"But if he is telling the truth," said Amelia, "what could explain him becoming young?"

"Well… Tesla won a Nobel Peace Prize in medicine," said Matthew thoughtfully.

"I thought he was a scientist, not a doctor," said Amelia, now feeling even more confused.

"It had something to do with deep-heating tissues with high frequency, alternating currents. I don't remember exactly, but I think it was all about increasing blood circulation in a specific part of the body and getting rid of tumors."

"Very good," said Tesla as he rejoined them. "Now you can guess my secret! The truth is that your body has brand new cells replacing old cells constantly. Some organs are completely replaced in weeks – your brain requires only a year to replace itself.

"A perfect cell gives birth to another perfect cell. The problem is that cells begin to malfunction, and then they pass along this misinformation to the new cell. And that's where disease and aging come from. I discovered a way to identify the resonant frequency of a diseased or aging cell, then with alternating current I matched the frequency…"

Tesla paused for a moment and said, "Think of it this way… When a high-pitched sound carries the same resonant frequency as glass… the glass shatters when the sound is loud enough. In the same way, I *shattered* the cells carrying misinformation, and left only perfect cells to create more perfect cells.

"Because I was already eighty-six, I had to go slowly – gradually building up the healthy cells. But within a year I looked the way I do now. Needless to say… the man found dead in my apartment wasn't me. The powers-that-be arranged for my supposed-death and subsequent cremation so no one could ever prove it wasn't me. And then I was given full control over this biosphere. There is no disease," he added enigmatically. "Infants and children mature, but they don't age."

Looking around Amelia said, "Have you ever heard of the Vedruss?"

"Yes," said Tesla smiling, "everything you see is based on the world they created thousands of years ago."

"Did you read about them somewhere?" said Amelia curiously.

"No… there's no recorded history of the Vedruss," said Tesla. "I discovered their culture quite accidentally through remote viewing."

"And that's how you created all of this," asked Amelia in amazement.

"Yes. This biosphere is the most highly guarded secret in the world," said Tesla using both hands to indicate everything around them. "Only a handful of people know this exists."

"Are you planning to share your secret with the world?" asked Matthew.

"I had hoped to create a perfect utopia... and that's exactly what this is. But we've had an unforeseen turn of events," he said miserably. "I'll explain what's happening with the earthquakes as we walk but we need to hurry... it's not safe out in the open. Come with me."

Quickly, they walked across a grassy meadow to the edge of a tall cedar forest just as the sun was nearing the horizon.

"I'm going to try to answer your questions and fill in some gaps." Then, as if reading her mind, Tesla looked at Amelia and said, "You're wondering how you got in here... yes?"

Smiling, Amelia nodded.

"With remote viewing I knew you were coming and I programmed the scanner to let you in," said Tesla.

"Why?" said Amelia grateful, but confused. "Why did you let us in if this is such a big secret?"

"Well, some highly unlikely events have been occurring... and to be honest, we need your help," said Tesla frankly.

"But how did you know exactly what was going to happen?" asked Matthew. "Aren't there alternate or parallel timelines that would have taken us someplace else?"

"Yes, of course," said Tesla, "but there are certain timelines that hold the most potential. Remote viewers follow those timelines while keeping track of what is actually occurring in real time.

"So you might turn left in a situation where going right held the most potential... a remote viewer would psychically follow you down your path to the left and then continue on the most likely path into the future. So there is a lot of adjusting that's constantly taking place. And that's how it works... at least most of the time.

"There are exceptions... and Amelia, you are one of those

exceptional people. Do you know that you actually died and came back to life during the satanic ritual?"

"You know about that?" said Amelia in a shocked tone.

"Yes, as I was tracking you, I saw the ritual remotely," said Tesla.

"Do you work with Thomas?" said Amelia horrified.

"I don't work with Thomas – the biosphere has been mine to create without interference – but he's the one behind it. He created the biosphere… I don't know where the technology came from, I only know that he brought me here and gave me the freedom to create everything based on the world of the Vedruss. If it was successful the plan was to show its success to world leaders and bring this way of life to the rest of the planet. But now the biosphere is on the verge of collapse."

"What's happening?" asked Amelia fearfully.

"Well," said Tesla with a wry smile, "it actually has something to do with you."

"With me!" said Amelia shocked.

"You may not remember this, but when you died you visited the Spirit world and returned to your body in a matter of minutes."

"I was really dead!" said Amelia, still unable to fathom the idea.

"Yes," said Tesla. "Of course you didn't feel dead, because there is no such thing as death, but you were in another dimensional reality and unable to connect with anyone or anything on the third dimension."

"I do remember being above my body," said Amelia, "but I don't remember anything else."

"That's not unusual," said Tesla. "I don't know exactly what happened to you. But wherever you went, the frequency of that dimension caused a great deal of disturbance upon your return.

"You mean I'm the reason the biosphere is collapsing?" said Amelia horrified.

"No, your entrance was more like the straw that broke the

camel's back," said Tesla lightly. "You see, Thomas has been using my technology underground."

"He's trying to access the Inner Earth," exclaimed Amelia.

"I know!" said Tesla exasperated.

Suddenly, Amelia felt strangely lightheaded and off-balance and then rocks and stones began falling from the sky above.

CHAPTER 24

"**R**UN!" yelled Tesla, "Under the trees! Right up against the trunk!"

They raced into the forest and Amelia stood directly under a large branch with her arms around the tree for support as Matthew wrapped his arms tightly around her, sheltering her with his body. Rocks and boulders crashed down through the treetops around them and exploded a few feet away in the field. They both hung onto the tree as the ground beneath them swayed and surged with an unstoppable force.

Even as the final tremor settled to a stop and no more stones were falling from above, Amelia was still shaking and holding tightly onto the tree.

Rubbing her back, Matthew said gently, "It's okay, Amelia, I think we're safe now."

"Come," said Tesla briskly. "There's a much safer place ahead… it's not far."

As they began climbing a small hillside Tesla said, "At the lowest level of the biosphere we're several miles underground and very close to Thomas' tunnel. The tremors that he set off were barely noticeable on the desert surface, but we felt it here right away and every part of the biosphere was affected. I warned him to stop immediately, but he wouldn't listen.

"Thomas used remote viewing to see the future, but the probability of what happened was so small, he never looked for it or even considered it."

"But what exactly happened?" asked Matthew.

"Well, in the same way that a high pitched resonant frequency can cause glass to vibrate and eventually shatter when the frequency is loud enough… my device causes the earth to vibrate. If the vibration is controlled they can easily dig out the tunnel – but if the frequency gets too *loud* everything collapses instead.

"When Amelia passed between the dimensions, her entrance created a resonant frequency… a sound wave that instantly magnified the frequency of my device to the point that it collapsed the tunnel. And though the device was buried it's still running."

"But can't they dig it out and stop it?" asked Matthew.

"No," said Tesla, "the tunnel would just continue collapsing."

"But then why are we here?" asked Amelia in a complete panic. "What can we possibly do?"

"Come with me a little further," said Tesla. "I'll explain everything."

With only a few more steps they reached the knoll of the hill and on the other side, in the valley below, there stood a magnificent, golden pyramid hundreds of feet tall. Amelia and Matthew both stopped in their tracks, staring wide-eyed at the spectacle before them.

Tesla looked at them and said, "Thomas built this pyramid out of solid gold over seventy years ago before I ever came to the biosphere. Everything he's accomplished, along with all of his current plans, is directly connected to this pyramid. For years he's tried every frequency known to man to activate the gold… but with no success."

"What do you mean… how do you activate gold?" asked Matthew.

"Imagine you lived in the North Pole and only knew of water in the form of ice. That would be similar to what we know of gold. Now imagine all of the things you can do with water and steam. Well, that's the idea of what happens when gold is activated.

"Come this way," he said leading them down the hillside. "Everyone from the biosphere is meeting here tonight."

"But you said that Thomas built the pyramid seventy years ago. How's that possible when he's only in his forties," said Matthew. "That is… unless he's been using your technique with alternating currents to stay young."

"No, that's not Thomas' secret," said Tesla. Then pausing for a moment he looked at Amelia and said, "Do you remember the high priests you trained in your lifetime as Alex?"

Amelia nodded. "Yes… how do you know about that?"

"I've been using remote viewing to piece together Thomas' plans for quite some time," said Tesla frankly. "Thomas was one of the priests you trained and taught to build the pyramids.

"He looks quite different now, but not because he's been born into the program repeatedly like most players. The truth is that he has played one single game for thousands of years by taking over different adult bodies."

"I don't understand," said Amelia.

"Well, there's more to The Game than you realize. Because life on Earth holds the possibility for a great deal of pain… physically and emotionally… and players are never forced to stay in the program. If you want out badly enough the program will arrange for you to leave one way or another… an accident, a fatal disease, war… things like that…

"But if the player's exit takes place without destroying the avatar-body… it's possible for another soul to *jump* into the avatar at the exact moment the original soul exits and before the avatar-body has a chance to die.

"It will often appear that the person *exiting* was on the verge of death and has had a sudden, miraculous recovery… when in fact the original soul is no longer there and has been replaced by a completely different soul… but only the most advanced players are capable of such a thing… they're sometimes referred to as walk-ins."

"But wouldn't people notice the difference in their personalities… even though the body looks the same?" said Amelia.

"The new soul… the one who steps into the avatar," said Tesla, "retains the memories and abilities of the original soul, but you're right… the personality will be different. And for this reason all walk-ins have a unique, unbreakable agreement.

"Much like your agreement to forget everything when you're born into the program… they agree to only change their circumstances in a gradual way. And this is because people who know them will accept a change in personality as long as there isn't a radical, immediate change in their outer world. This protects the new player and also helps to assure that no one will suspect there has been a soul exchange.

"The high priests, and Thomas in particular… mastered this ability and they've been able to take over unwanted bodies as needed. That's how they've managed to control and manipulate the program all this time."

"But then why are we here?" said Matthew.

"Have you ever had a plan, but then everything turned out quite differently?" said Tesla.

"Of course," said Matthew.

"Well, I don't collaborate with Thomas or agree with most of his methods, and he reveals very little to me," said Tesla, "but from what I've seen remotely it seems that everything is somehow connected to this pyramid. As far as I can tell, Thomas is convinced that when you died as Alex, you took the secret of the true purpose of the pyramids with you.

"I also believe that Alex used the Science of Imagery to project the world of the Vedruss thousands of years into the future," said Tesla, "and that this is the time and place where he sent the energy. This pyramid was built to be a portal into that reality."

Tesla opened the door as they all stepped inside to walk along a glowing, golden corridor lit sporadically with beeswax candles in small, carved wooden holders on the floor. Considering that everyone in the biosphere was supposed to be there already, Amelia thought it was surprisingly quiet. She couldn't hear anything but the sound of their own footsteps echoing down the passageway.

Finally, they came to an immense doorway that swung silently open. As they stepped inside Amelia was shocked to see hundreds of people sitting on the floor silently meditating. But what surprised her even more was the fact that everything was glowing and light was streaming through a clear capstone at the top of the pyramid.

Amelia's body involuntarily shivered from the energy that was surrounding her and coursing through her body as Tesla led them onto a platform that rose a few feet above the floor.

Whispering she said to Tesla, "With rocks falling from above, won't the glass break?"

Tesla replied quietly, "It's not glass. The capstone is a single, flawless diamond."

"But the base of it must be at least six feet across," said Matthew incredulously.

"That's right," said Tesla.

As a tremor shook the building Tesla said, "Just sit right where you are, you'll be fine."

Matthew sat with his arm protectively around Amelia. Light still poured through the diamond capstone, but nothing happened, they only heard the muffled sounds of large rocks crashing onto the capstone.

Amelia leaned in to Matthew and whispered, "You know when we first arrived in the biosphere… I was thinking… oh my God I'm so awesome… I created this… just like Äsha said I could. Here it is… the world of the Vedruss. I thought I had finally gotten it right," Amelia confessed quietly. "But now we're in this perfect place that's everything I imagined… and the sky is literally falling… and it's because of me!"

"It's okay, Amelia," said Matthew holding her close. "It's not your fault."

"But it is!" she whispered desperately. "If I had just stayed dead and not come back that earthquake wouldn't have happened and Tesla's device wouldn't have been buried… and this biosphere wouldn't be collapsing.

"And those people are all looking at us like we're going to save them," said Amelia anxiously. "But I don't know any secrets and I have no idea what to do."

Walking over to them Tesla said, "Everyone in here is perfectly safe." Then, reaching out for Amelia's hand, he asked, "Can you both stand up for a moment?"

Taking Tesla's hand Amelia stood up and looked tentatively at Matthew. All eyes were instantly focused on them.

"These are the two I promised you," Tesla announced to the audience, "Amelia and Matthew."

Amelia shot a worried glance at Matthew as everyone in the pyramid smiled warmly at them. Strangely, no one seemed concerned about the boulders dropping out of the sky. If she didn't know better she would have thought she was attending a family reunion – just a really, really big one.

Directly in front of the platform was a group of children. They didn't look the least bit frightened, in fact, it seemed they were eagerly anticipating what was about to happen. Amelia wondered if the opportunity to hear Tesla speak was a rare occasion, because the children's eyes were all lit up as they looked up at him with excitement.

"As you all know, it's impossible to stay here any longer. It may seem like a loss, but our biosphere has really been more like a cocoon. Admittedly, we didn't see this coming," Tesla conceded, "but what caterpillar would spin its cocoon if it knew it would turn into liquid before becoming a butterfly?" he said, smiling broadly and winking at the children in front of him. "So, sometimes… not knowing… is part of the bigger plan… it gets us where we need to go!"

The adults smiled and nodded as the children giggled.

"We thought we could continue living here indefinitely and that, in time, we could move to the surface and share with others. But humanity is still not ready to live this way.

"So of course, you may be wondering where we'll go and what we'll do in a world that is now completely foreign to us. None of us knows exactly how this is going to work out, anymore than a caterpillar can conceive how it will ever be capable of flying... There's nothing to do but trust the process.

"In our meditations we've seen clearly that this pyramid is a portal. And though we don't understand the mechanics... I believe these two," indicating Matthew and Amelia, "carry the memories that will lead to activating the portal."

Amelia had no idea what Tesla was talking about. Looking past him she saw that all eyes were focused in her direction. Heat rushed up her neck turning her face bright red with embarrassment as she realized that she would personally be letting down hundreds of people eagerly anticipating some kind of miracle that she could never deliver.

Quietly, Tesla spoke to Amelia and Matthew, "Please sit down where you were."

They sat down Indian-style a few feet from the edge of the platform facing the audience as Tesla spoke to them quietly, "I know that neither of you have a conscious memory of how to activate the pyramid, but I believe you hold the information unconsciously in your DNA... which holds the records of every game you've ever played.

"So just trust that you already know and silently say to yourself, *'IF I knew how to activate the portal – what would I do?'* That's it. Just allow yourself to make something up.

"You won't need to say a word to anyone here – just let images flow in and out of your mind – everyone will telepathically recognize the answer when it comes through – even if it makes no sense to you, they will understand."

At first Amelia couldn't stop worrying. All of these people were depending on her and to make matters worse if they were all telepathic then they certainly knew that she was clueless. Of course they could survive in the pyramid when the biosphere collapsed, but they'd have no food or water. Everyone would die and it would be her fault for not being able to remember anything useful.

Taking a deep breath, Amelia tried to remember everything she had learned from Äsha and Richard and The Portal, but her mind was a complete blank. Drawing a deep breath she tried to remember the cheat code that Äsha had taught her. What was it? It was so simple it probably wouldn't work, but everything else she had been thinking definitely wasn't going to help. But whatever it was, the cheat code was gone.

Then, to her surprise, Amelia felt Matthew slide his hand beneath hers. Opening her eyes she saw him sitting directly in front of her gazing deeply into her eyes without looking away. At first she felt awkward and embarrassed, but then she found herself looking steadily back into his eyes. Suddenly, it seemed as if Matthew's face was shape-shifting into someone familiar, yet completely different with deep, brown eyes, smooth, dark skin, and thick, black hair. It seemed as if he was staring at her through an opening which became smaller and smaller until, to her horror, he slid a single brick into the opening and sealed the wall shut.

CHAPTER 25

Amelia blinked. Suddenly she remembered him from her lifetime as Alex. Matthew had been Ammon, the high priest who sealed Alex into the pyramid prison thousands of years earlier.

Then, to her surprise, Amelia was shown an overview of Ammon's lifetime after the moment when he had sealed Alex into his tomb. It was bizarre but not... like watching a movie only the movie would automatically speed up through unimportant events and then slow back down for anything she needed to see.

She was in awe as she observed her mind-movie begin to play out quickly. It was initially focused on the time period that Ammon was becoming more and more powerful and as the years went by she watched him selfishly take possession of one body after another. But then the movie slowed down to a time when Ammon had been living for well over one hundred years. Even though he didn't appear to be any more than thirty-five or forty, he knew it was time to let his current body go.

Ammon desired the closest genetic match possible, so he waited patiently for a son who possessed the qualities he most desired and when that son was ultimately born he made him heir to his entire fortune – leaving everything to him exclusively. However, he was unable to take over his son's body, unless his son's soul wanted to leave voluntarily, so Ammon waited until his son was deeply in love, then covertly brought about so much emotional devastation his son refused to eat or drink and was waiting longingly at death's door to be released from his broken spirit and heart.

Ammon made a tremendous show of begging "God" to take his own life… so that instead, his son might live. And that is exactly how it appeared to the general public but in reality his son did die and as the young man's soul left his body, Ammon's soul *stepped-in* to his son's place.

To those looking on, Ammon appeared to be dead while his son miraculously came back to life – inheriting all that had been his father's. But in truth, Ammon simply carried on with life only now it was in his son's body and for this reason Ammon was never close to his sons. The women he married were chosen for a specific purpose and nothing more, love had nothing to do with it. But this time, when Ammon took over his son's body, he had devised an extraordinary plan.

Over a span of hundreds of years the six priests sent out their minions to sow the seeds of fear, and obedience to authority, into the minds of mankind. And though they eventually accomplished this, no matter what they did they could not influence the minds of the Vedruss. Alex had taught them well, even as he taught the priests themselves.

Ammon telepathically scanned the future until he saw a window of opportunity. He'd waited over one hundred years for this opening and now, having his son's young, healthy body would make the event he had planned even easier.

Using his psychic abilities Ammon was able to witness the battle between the Vedruss and the Roman army. He saw Sasha and knew she would tend to the wounds of the Roman soldiers. Ammon's son was extraordinarily handsome, so the fact that Ammon had taken possession of his son's body gave him even more confidence in his ability to attract Sasha's attention.

But the moment Sasha looked into Ammon's eyes something happened that he had not expected. A feeling arose deep within him. Sasha reminded him so much of Alex that even though Alex had been dead for hundreds of years, Ammon felt pain rip through his soul as if he'd been stabbed in the heart.

He had never wanted Alex to die. Alex had been his teacher and mentor for years. They had different desires, and Alex stood in Ammon's way from time to time, but he never, ever wanted Alex to die. It was only a ploy to manipulate information from a man facing death.

Sasha had Alex's eyes. Ammon couldn't take his eyes off of her, and he knew that at some unconscious level she recognized him too. He followed Sasha as he had planned. His idea was to infiltrate the Vedruss by marrying Sasha and having a child with her.

Ammon knew Sasha would be capable of reading his energy, and this was the very reason he took his son's body as his own. Ammon's face and body, prior to his *death* exuded cold detachment, but in his son's body, the look in his eyes still carried the vibration of one who knew what it was to be deeply in love – something Ammon had never experienced.

The plan Ammon had projected across his *window of time* unfolded exactly as he expected it to. Sasha fell deeply in love with him. He had successfully kept his true thoughts and intentions from her. But in pretending to be a part of her world, Ammon never expected that he would fall in love with her and the world in which she lived.

His focus had been on taking over a body with the best possible genetic match, but his son's heart was full of love for his beloved, and that feeling of love continued without abating, even after his son's soul had left his body and Ammon had taken over.

The beautiful simplicity of Sasha's world and the depth of

her love for him astounded Ammon. He had infiltrated the enemy camp, only to discover that his own life and ambitions were meaningless. He had no desire to go back.

On their wedding night, Sasha asked Ammon if he would like to have a son. He smiled warmly at her, knowing that he would never decline any wish that Sasha put before him. The next morning Ammon felt as if he was floating above the ground. He kept looking down to assure himself that his feet were still planted solidly on terra firma. As he remembered kissing Sasha the night before the most extraordinary feeling took over. Although he tried he wasn't able to stay in his body and as he rose up into the night sky, Sasha rose with him, radiant like a star. A blur of light shot toward them and materialized as a young boy who looked exactly like his son did in Egypt.

Ammon instantly felt the horror of what he had done – he was responsible not only for his son's broken spirit, but for the death of the woman his son had loved so deeply. For the first time in his life Ammon wanted to apologize, he wanted his son's forgiveness, but before he could say anything his son spoke.

"Father, do not fear. Love has its own plan – I see it more clearly than you do. If you and mother will invite me to be your son… a new star will light up in the heavens. And as we live together, our combined light will go up to our star on the wings of love and be reflected back to everyone on Earth. A single glance at our star will fill hearts with unimaginable love."

Ammon's heart was ready to explode with joy, but the next thing he remembered he was waking up to the most glorious morning he had ever experienced. He thought it would be impossible to love Sasha more than he already did, but when their son was born Ammon's heart was as big as the universe and he loved Sasha even more. He would have stayed forever and been content to be buried in the forest near their little pond. But once again the Roman army was planning to invade the Vedruss colonies.

Ammon saw a plan which involved Sasha and his son. He knew the plan would work. He had anchored it across the *window-of-time* and saw the outcome clearly.

And then Amelia saw Ammon's side of a shared memory.

It began with Ammon staring into the night sky until the stars blinked out and a rosy hue from the unseen horizon was mirrored in the pond. He gently moved his arm from beneath Sasha's head and laid their sleeping son in her arms. As he kissed Alexei's curly head Sasha opened her eyes. It was as if he was seeing her, truly seeing her, for the first time and yet somehow feeling as if he'd known her throughout all eternity.

Tears filled Sasha's eyes as Ammon smiled and looked at her with all the love in the world shining from his own glistening eyes. In that moment he knew why the priests would never understand. They were surrounded by the answer, but they would never see it, because they didn't know what it was to love, they only wanted more and more power.

But as Ammon looked proudly at his sleeping son, all-aglow after his day of battle, he suddenly understood. His son was only a young boy, yet there was already a look of nobility and accomplishment about him. Even in the boy's sleeping face it was evident that something had irrevocably changed in the way he saw himself.

If he, Ammon, had faced the Roman commander on his son's behalf – his son would have looked up to him and seen his father as a hero. But as his father, Ammon wanted Alexei to see himself as strong and brave and incredibly capable and that was why he and Sasha agreed that she would pretend to be Alexei's sister and only the two of them would meet the Roman commander.

Suddenly it occurred to Amelia that The Game was set up the same way. Every challenge was actually an opportunity for players to experience themselves as more than they thought they were capable of being and because games often spanned multiple lifetimes – perspective was everything.

The instant the idea of perspective came to mind, Amelia

saw herself outside of the pyramid gazing upwards. But she wasn't looking into the sky, she was gazing up at the apex just above the capstone along with hundreds of other people.

Blinking she blurted out, "I see it!"

Matthew smiled, squeezed her hand and said, "I see it too!"

Simultaneously they both turned to face the audience, but the pyramid was empty.

Tesla smiled warmly and said, "They're all waiting for you outside."

"I don't know exactly how it works," said Amelia anxiously, "or what's going to happen… but that's all I can see."

"You never have to worry about how something will work out," said Tesla warmly, "you already know far more than you realize!"

Standing up, Amelia and Matthew jumped off the platform, ran down the corridor and rushed out of the door. Amelia saw her vision taking form. Everyone was already standing around the pyramid, but even though there were hundreds of people, including all of the children from the biosphere, except for babies and very young children being held by their mother or father, there were large gaps between all the people.

Amelia watched in amazement as everyone followed the images she'd seen in her mind. They all looked up to a point just above the apex of the pyramid and began to sing AUM. The sound Ahh…Ohhhm resonated up the sides of the pyramid and into the enveloping night sky bejeweled with sparkling stars. Every face was alight and not just in the reflected glow of the candles, but radiant with love and joy as they sang. Suddenly a fiery, glowing sphere of light, fifteen feet in diameter, white at the core and sapphire as it radiated out, appeared directly above the diamond capstone as the thoughts and intentions of every person converged into one place.

The energy was so powerful Amelia felt light-headed and a bit dizzy, yet she continued staring at the glowing ball as it grew in size and intensity. In her mind she heard the words, *"union of opposites…you need opposite modes of thinking."*

And then to her surprise Thomas appeared strangely dressed in the robes and jewels of an ancient Egyptian high priest along with soldiers clad in army fatigues. Amelia turned to see streams of dotted candlelight flowing toward them from high on a hill above them as hundreds of soldiers walked down the various paths that led to the pyramid.

Like Tesla, it seemed that Thomas had also seen these events unfold through remote viewing and he knew that soldiers were meant to fill the gaps with their opposite modes of thinking.

With perfect precision the soldiers stepped into the spaces between the men, women and children, and though they looked around uncertainly at first, they appeared to have been told what to do because as most of them eventually gazed upward at the fiery sphere of light above the pyramid, which had now doubled in size and they began singing *Ahhh-Ohhm*.

The soldier who stepped into the empty spot next to Amelia seemed so uncomfortable she reached out to hold his hand and smiled warmly at him when he looked uncertainly at her. For a moment he seemed to relax, but then he quickly looked away. Amelia understood his mixed emotions. Though she'd had many new experiences between her Vedruss lifetimes and everything leading up to this moment, even for her the energy swirling around everyone and penetrating them was more intense than anything she'd ever felt.

Some people experienced the energy as intense heat, others were freezing cold, while some were shivering and sweating at the same time. And though some of the soldiers, like the one standing next to Amelia, remained rigid and seemingly unmoved by the intensifying energy, the vast majority of the troops and all of the others began feeling strong emotions as the dreams that mattered most to each of them, many long forgotten over the years, flowed into their imaginations. Some were laughing, some were crying, yet everyone continued singing to the best of their ability.

As they all stood, shoulder to shoulder, one of the soldiers looking into the intense, glowing light above the pyramid, was so completely overwhelmed by the energy that now flowed through, and seemed to radiate out from, his body, tears began to silently roll down his cheeks. In that moment a little boy with curly brown hair, looked up at him and reached out to hold his hand. The soldier looked down at the boy and smiled as tears of delight flooded down his cheeks, but he didn't seem to care. All he knew was that he had never felt love like this in his entire life, and it was what he wanted more than anything in the world. Then a little girl reached up and held his other hand.

And if he had been hovering above the pyramid and looking upon it, he would have seen that children and adults both were reaching out to the soldiers until everyone was holding hands all the way around the pyramid, and most of the soldiers were feeling very much the way he did – a deep feeling of love and peace they had never known before, but which had been in their nature all along.

When this happened, a whirling vortex of golden light began spinning around the base of the pyramid and formed into a tornado-like funnel. Light poured into the ground, into the sky and into the top of Amelia's head filling up every cell in her body. The energy then exploded out of her as radiant golden light.

CHAPTER 26

I n the next moment Amelia found herself standing next to Matthew in front of their high school just as an empty yellow school bus was pulling out of the parking lot. On the ground in front of them lay their backpacks as a couple of kids drove past yelling, "Bye!" "See you Monday!"

Then Mrs. Caldwell hollered from the doorway of the school, "Do you two need to call your parents for a ride home?"

Matthew and Amelia stared at each other for a brief, shocked moment, and finally Matthew yelled, "Uh… thanks, Mrs. Caldwell, we're all set."

Then looking at Amelia, Matthew said, "Do you remember what I remember?"

"You mean the underground base, a solid gold pyramid and teleporting… though I have no idea how we ended up here!" said Amelia. Then she grabbed Matthew and hugging him tightly said, "YES! I remember everything!"

When they finally released each other from their marathon hug Matthew said, "I live just a few blocks away… I'll give you a ride home."

"Okay," said Amelia, though she was fairly sure she was

dreaming the whole thing.

As they walked Amelia said, "I'm so confused. No one seems to realize that anything happened. I mean, they obviously didn't miss us…"

"I know," said Matthew. "I can't even think of a single quantum physics principle to explain that."

They walked quietly for a couple of minutes until Matthew stopped and said, "This is me."

They were standing in front of a completely fenced in wooded property with an elegant metal gate that swung silently open when Matthew punched in the code. On the other side of the gate was a three bedroom white stucco cottage with a grey shingle roof.

"Oh I love this cottage," said Amelia, "Was it built in the 1800's?"

"1866," said Matthew smiling.

"Do you think your parents are home?"

"I'm pretty sure someone will be home, but we live a bit further along the drive," he said.

"Oh! I see," said Amelia, now completely unsure of what to expect.

The cobblestone driveway wound its way past wooded areas, gardens, lawns, a magnificent greenhouse and a huge stone carriage house complete with a clock tower. Finally they came to a three-story stone house with two towers standing like sentinels on either side of the front door and the upstairs balcony.

"This was originally my great-grandparent's home," said Matthew. Then with a sweeping gesture toward the front door he said, "Come on in. You can *Meet-The-Parents*," he added, mysteriously raising one eyebrow.

"Does this mean you're taking me on the guided tour?" said Amelia as she ventured up the front steps.

"Of course!" said Matthew as he flung open the front door with a grand gesture. "You can just leave your backpack here on the porch."

Amelia set her pack down and stepped into the house. The magnificent entrance was a room unto itself with high ceilings, paneled wood walls, an immense hand carved fireplace and hardwood floors beneath Persian rugs with a stairway rising three-stories above them. Beyond the stairway Amelia could see French doors leading into a huge solarium which overlooked a sweeping lawn and gardens that led down to a lake with sailboats moored at the dock.

In a mock hushed and ominous tone, Matthew said, "I think we'll start off with the darkest, most depressing room... get it out of the way. I call it the Lion's Den since my dad has all of his safari conquests pegged to the mahogany paneling. He likes it dark and gloomy... to reflect his mood."

They walked through a paneled library with floor to ceiling bookcases, a fireplace, and a huge bay window. Matthew opened the double doors leading into the den and exclaimed, "I don't believe it!"

The room was full of light. In place of wood paneling the walls were painted a soft, sandy color and lined with white molding. There were no animal heads or skins, no guns hanging on the walls. Instead, there were potted orchids in a variety of colors and delicate watercolor pictures. The room was decorated with beautiful white furniture and glass tables with a thick pastel Persian rug in the center of the room.

Amelia said, "This is it?"

"Apparently, Mother did some fast redecorating," he said incredulously. "Unbelievable!"

At that moment Mrs. McKinley entered the room. She looked considerably younger than Amelia would have expected and was wearing a tennis outfit with her long, light brown hair up in a ponytail.

Smiling affably she said, "What's unbelievable?"

"Oh, hi, Mom! This is my friend, Amelia," said Matthew quickly.

"Hello, Amelia," said his mother smiling broadly. "It's a rare treat when I get to meet any of Matthew's friends."

"Uh, Mom, I was wondering how you managed to redecorate this room so quickly."

She laughed and said, "What on earth are you talking about? This room hasn't been redecorated since you were ten years old."

Matthew looked at Amelia, then back at his mother. He said, "Alright, then. Tell me where the safari animals are... and all of Dad's guns?"

His mother paused for a moment looking intently at Matthew. "Are you feeling alright honey?" she said as she put her hand on his forehead.

"Yeah... "he replied. "Why?"

A bit puzzled, she said, "Well, you know your father hasn't touched a gun in his life. He can't bear to see an animal harmed. The only time he ever shoots an animal is with a camera."

Then turning to Amelia she said warmly, "Would you like to see the animals his father shoots?"

They walked into a long hallway with windows on one side overlooking the lake. The opposite wall was lined with spectacular pictures of animals and wild flowers from around the world.

Mrs. McKinley said proudly, "Matthew's father took every one of these pictures. He's traveled all over the world and this year there's even going to be a wildlife calendar composed exclusively of his work."

Amelia said enthusiastically, "He's fantastic!"

Matthew whispered to Amelia, "I've never seen these pictures in my life!"

They walked quietly down the hall, exchanging puzzled glances, as Matthew's mother led them outside. Matthew's father was leaning over the garden when his wife waved and yelled, "Darling, look who's here!"

He straightened up with a bouquet of flowers in his hands and smiled broadly. With long, swift strides he headed toward them. He was vibrantly healthy with a glowing complexion and rosy cheeks like Matthew's.

His eyes sparkled as he hugged Matthew and said, "It's great to have you home, son!"

Matthew said, "Dad, this is my friend, Amelia."

Mr. McKinley smiled, graciously handed her an exquisite yellow rose and said, "I'm delighted to meet you." Then he said confidentially, "I have to cheat a little in the spring, these flowers are from the green house."

He then handed his wife a bouquet of multi-colored tulips and said sweetly, "These are for you my angel."

Mrs. McKinley hugged him and whispered, "I love you so much."

Mr. McKinley winked at Amelia and said unabashed, "This is what it's like to be on a honeymoon for twenty-two years!"

Amelia smiled, and Matthew said, "I really should get Amelia home. It's been an awfully long trip."

"Lovely to meet you, Amelia," said Mrs. McKinley.

"Come back any time!" said Matthew's father gregariously.

As they headed back to the house Amelia glanced over her shoulder and saw Matthew's parents strolling through the garden with their arms around each other.

"Your parents are really in love with each other," said Amelia.

Matthew shook his head slowly and said, "I don't understand. I've never heard him say a kind word to my mother, let alone pick flowers for her."

He looked at Amelia intently and said, "My father has been sick for years. He was skinny and pale a few days ago. Now he weighs at least twenty pounds more. He's healthy and happy. And my mom has always had short hair, and dark circles under her eyes... she's never been athletic in any way."

As they walked out the front door Matthew grabbed Amelia's backpack, led her down the steps and across the driveway. He opened the door of his red, 1967 convertible Corvette for Amelia. She climbed in and he closed her door then threw her pack behind the seats.

"No trunk!" he said with a grin. "I have no idea who came

up with that idea!"

As he started the engine he said, "Alright… let's see if there are any surprises at your house!"

Amelia laughed and wondered the same thing as they drove into the countryside and arrived at a quaint, ranch style log cabin. She led Matthew into the screened-in porch and through the back door to the mudroom.

"Hi Dad, I'm home!" she yelled.

Her mother pushed through the swinging doors that led into the kitchen and said, "What? You don't say hi to your mother anymore?"

Matthew could see where Amelia got her looks. Her mother was tall and beautiful, with a glowing complexion, and smiling, deep blue eyes.

"Oh… hi, Mom. I just didn't expect you to be here," said Amelia slightly taken aback.

Her mother laughed and said, "Well, I live here don't I? Where else would I be?"

Puzzled, Amelia said, "Uh, Mom, this is Matthew."

"Hello, Matthew… why don't you come into the kitchen? I'm teaching Amelia's father how to make applesauce." She looked at Matthew, smiled and said with a wink, "We're an equal opportunity household!"

They stepped into the kitchen and there was Amelia's father perched on a stool wearing a frilly Christmas apron while he pared apples. Amelia smiled broadly at her dad as she introduced Matthew.

"Alright, I don't want either of you laughing at my brush with domestication," said Amelia's father, "I pledged to your mother I'd do whatever she wanted for our twentieth anniversary and look what she has me doing!" He dumped a pile of sliced apples into a big pot on the stove and added with a grin, "Ah, the cost of true love!"

Amelia's mother wrapped her arms around him lovingly, kissed him on the cheek and said, "What dedication!"

Amelia's father winked at Matthew and said slyly with

a twinkle in his eye, "When you get married, son, never underestimate the fringe benefits of understanding... and complying with... the marital chain of command!"

Going slightly pink over her dad bringing up the subject of marriage with Matthew, Amelia giggled awkwardly and deftly changed the subject.

"Dad, are you going to let us sample the finished product?" said Amelia grinning.

"Sure. This should be done in about half an hour. In the meantime, why don't you take Matthew down to see the pond?"

"Okay," said Amelia.

She and Matthew held hands as they walked down the lawn behind her house.

Matthew smiled, raised his eyebrows and said innocently, "Anything different at your house?"

Amelia laughed and shook her head. "Are you kidding? Three days ago... or something like that... my parents were thoroughly divorced. They've been living in separate houses for over a year. On top of that, they look more like they did in their wedding pictures twenty years ago... and my dad has never had a sense of humor in his life!"

Sitting next to each other on a small hill overlooking the pond with weeping willows dotting the edges and a small waterfall directly across from them, Amelia looked into Matthew's eyes and said, "I have to confess something... I know we must have done something to bring this about... but I have no idea what it is."

Matthew smiled and said, "I've been thinking about this, and what's happening strangely ties in with some quantum theories. Of course I can't prove anything, but I can tell you what I know."

"Please do!" said Amelia enthusiastically.

"One of the latest theories in quantum physics is called, MIW, which stands for Many Interacting Worlds. The theory is mathematical and on the quantum level, but if it's true in the infinitesimally small world of the microcosm then it should be true in the macrocosm… which would be our world.

"Anyhow the idea is that for a long time quantum reality has been regarded as energy moving in waves, but MIW suggests that rather than being a wave, quantum reality is a collection of parallel worlds, but they aren't linear, they're more like bubbles, and many scientists are now beginning to believe in the existence of hidden universes… but that gets us into what Einstein referred to as *spooky* quantum entanglement," said Matthew laughing, "and, well, that would be like… way too much information."

Amelia laughed, "Okay, give me the *for dummies* version."

"I can do that!" said Matthew smiling. "Imagine that each game player is playing in their own bubble… or better yet, think of yourself playing on the surface of a bubble."

"Okay…" said Amelia hesitantly.

"So every player is floating around on their own little bubble-of-reality. And sometimes these bubbles come together and stay there for any length of time and then they detach and float away… some come back together regularly, and some you never see again. And that's kind of the idea of Many Interacting Worlds."

"That makes sense, but I still don't understand what caused everything to change? I mean if we're floating around on interactive bubbles, why did everything in our bubbles change? And why do we know there was a change, but no one else realizes it?"

Matthew shook his head. "I haven't quite figured that out yet, but you know those entangled particles I mentioned? Well, the idea is that particles remain connected so that even when an action is performed on one particle, it instantly affects the other particle as well, even when they're separated by great distances."

Amelia thought for a moment and said, "Well… then how could time and space be real?"

Matthew nodded. "Exactly! Time and space are just

illusions… and I think that's why Einstein called it *spooky*!" he said laughing.

Matthew sat quietly for a moment then said, "Do you think this has anything to do with your trip to the Inner Earth? I know I'm grasping here, but it's all I can think of. I mean, you didn't tell me much about it."

"Well, they have this library called The Portal… And get this – it has 456 square miles of storage underground and not a single book."

"What kind of library has no books?"

Amelia smiled mischievously, "Everything is stored in crystals – you sit in a chair, ask a question in your mind and instantly you're shown whatever you need to know. And you can go anywhere in the UNIVERSE with just the intention to go!"

"Anywhere… in the universe?" said Matthew amazed. "Where did you go?" he asked.

Amelia smiled, "I didn't go anywhere – I came back for you."

Matthew wrapped his arms around Amelia and she felt herself dissolving into him as he bent down to kiss her. More than anything Amelia had longed for this moment. They were home, they were together and finally they weren't facing some life or death situation. But still, the moment was bittersweet. It seemed so unfair that she had to choose between the man she loved and living some place she had only ever dreamed of – why couldn't she have both?

Sensing her feeling of loss, Matthew said, "Well, we'll just have to go there and do some traveling together."

With a slightly pained smile Amelia said, "I'm afraid we can never go there. There's an entrance at the North Pole but there's no way back in… at least not for us."

"My family has plenty of money. That stupid car I have in the driveway is what my dad gave me when I told him I just wanted a *used car* and that I didn't want to stand out in the school parking lot. The car my dad gave me is a 1967 L88

Corvette. Only twenty of them were made and the car is worth over four million dollars – that's why I always walk to school," he said, shaking his head and rolling his eyes. "I would be so happy to sell the car and my father would know how to set up an expedition."

"You're so sweet," said Amelia with a sigh. "It's just not that easy. There are powerful people who don't want anyone to know this other world exists – and when people try to go or set up an expedition they're stopped by military planes."

"What could you possibly be worried about?" said a sweet child's voice.

"Äsha!" exclaimed Amelia and Matthew at once.

"Oh my God, are we dead or about to die or something?" said Amelia wide-eyed.

Äsha tilted her head back and laughed. "No, Amelia! You live in a new world – and new rules apply!"

"Well, where do you live when you're not appearing out of nowhere?" said Amelia.

"Oh!" said the little girl laughing merrily. "I'm multidimensional. I am wherever I think myself into being."

Matthew and Amelia looked at each other and burst out laughing.

"Okay," said Amelia shaking her head and quickly changing the topic. "So, tell us what happened? Nothing's the same. We don't even know how we made it out of the base. And what happened to the days and time and everything…?" said Amelia, her words unable to keep up with her thoughts.

Äsha giggled, "Don't you remember what you wished for?"

"What wish?" said Amelia.

Äsha looked at her silently.

"Oh, you mean that crazy wish where I was going to save the Earth?" she said rolling her eyes. "The one where I was supposed to wish without worrying?"

Äsha smiled and said, "Well, did you worry?"

Amelia burst out laughing as she thought about everything that happened after she left The Portal. "No… I was kind of busy! Actually I forgot all about it. But wait a minute, I was supposed find someone else and help them first. I never did that part."

"Yes, you did," said Äsha waiting patiently for Amelia to remember.

"Who? Who did I help? There's no one else crazy enough to think they could save the Earth and people…"

"And the bees?" said Äsha knowingly.

Taken aback Amelia said, "You're talking about Thomas! I didn't try to help him."

"But you did," said Äsha.

"But that doesn't explain what happened at the pyramid or how we ended up back here or why our families are completely different?" said Matthew incredulously.

"You're both still playing The Game but you're in an alternate, parallel reality that has never been part of the program before."

"But how did that happen?" said Amelia.

"Well, as you may remember, every player in the game has the same amount of power… but the reason it appears that some players arc more powerful than others is because most of the players have been coerced into giving their power away through fear," said Asha. "The high priests knew this and cooked up every fear-based institution… government, the monarchy, war, religion, politics, education and their most brilliant creation – money.

"As Alex, you saw this coming. You knew the high priests were going to stay in their bodies and take control for thousands of years and that's why you built the pyramids in Egypt. The priests never guessed that the true purpose of the pyramids was to allow hundreds or thousands of people to stand at the base and look up at the apex, simultaneously gathering everyone's focused thoughts and intentions into one place.

"And this conscious unity was the one thing that could instantly stop the high priest's domination of Earth. But as

Alex you envisioned far more than that. You envisioned all players playing the game of their choice with likeminded players, and without interference or domination, something that has never happened before in the history of The Game."

"Why hasn't that happened before?" asked Amelia curiously.

"Even the most well practiced players tend to get stuck in duality... seeing other players as right or wrong, good or bad... worthy of punishment or praise. Instead, just like the Vedruss, your vision included everyone."

"But how did that ball of light appear?" asked Matthew dumbfounded.

"The human avatar-body has electrical currents throughout every cell, all of which have the strength of lightning, and each cell produces light from its DNA... which means your bodies are literally swimming in an ocean of light.

"When all of you gathered together in a circle around the pyramid and began singing, you created a symmetry of mathematics... what you might call a perfect circle of sound. The light you saw was very similar to atomic energy."

"But where's the math part?" said Amelia.

"Math is everywhere," said Äsha merrily. "But in this case, without realizing it, everyone surrounding the pyramid was singing at 528 hertz which is mathematically consistent with nature and the universe."

"What does that mean?" asked Amelia.

"Well, if you think of music as the universal language and love as the universal healer..." said Äsha, "you were all singing in the key of love. 528 Hertz is the same tone that emanates from the sun, it's the frequency of chlorophyll... and therefore the frequency of every green, growing thing, it's the tone emanating from the middle of the rainbow... which is green, and the sound emanating from the human heart.

"So, this perfect circle of sound, along with the atomic energy above the apex activated the gold pyramid and eliminated planetary dissonance by regenerating the original harmony… the original sound frequency that created The Game in the first place.

"And in the same way that your DNA has a unique frequency that identifies you in every game you play… no matter where or when… The Game takes place in countless different dimensional realities, what you might call parallel worlds… with each dimension vibrating and creating its own unique music.

"So in the simplest terms, your musical celebration tapped into the science and mathematics of love, literally vibrating your inner awareness of life as you choose it to be… into physical reality.

"And when you both combined your thought-force with everyone else focusing at the apex of the pyramid… you were no longer focused on other people's version of reality. In other words, you both stopped adding your power to someone else's creation, and started creating – imagining – the world YOU wanted to see.

"And that's how you both changed the entire programming of The Game… forever!

"But why did just the two of us remember what happened?" said Matthew. "We saw our teacher and some of the kids from our camping trip… but we're the only ones who seem to know that anything happened."

Looking back and forth between Matthew and Amelia with a knowing look and a suppressed smile, Äsha said, "A long time ago Plato said this… *when one of them meets with his other half, the actual half of himself, the pair are lost in an amazement of love and friendship and intimacy and one will not be out of the other's sight even for a moment.*

"And that's the part of The Game you love and hate the most. You love it when you find each other, and you hate it when you spend a lifetime looking for each other!

"You two are like the embodiment of *spooky* quantum entanglement. You can't be separated… not by time, space or game-lifetimes. So when Amelia felt deeply connected to the

Vedruss… you instantly felt the same way, Matthew," said Äsha looking intently at him. "You both will always experience what the other is experiencing, even if you aren't fully conscious of it."

"So do you think I can tell people about the Vedruss and they'll actually listen?" said Amelia hopefully.

Äsha looked directly at Amelia and smiled, but she didn't say a word.

Matthew reached out and held Amelia's hand as she smiled at him.

"Äsha, I know this is impossible, but I really want to go back to the Inner Earth… and I want Matthew to see it too," said Amelia.

"Impossible? Nothing's impossible! For goodness sake," said the little girl blinking incredulously, "do you really think that the Intelligence that created the human avatar-body needs the Montauk Chair or some other device to travel?!

"Amelia, don't you remember anything about being Alex? You know… all that teleporting and the Science of Imagery… and now it's even easier because you're not in the third dimension anymore!

"Wish without worrying," Asha said as her body began to shimmer, "you can go anywhere in an instant… and come back too!"

And then she was gone.

Matthew and Amelia looked at each other, but before either could say a word the dinner bell rang out loudly from the porch.

Amelia's dad shouted, "Homemade applesauce – are you guys coming?"

"Yeah, Dad!" Amelia yelled back, "You and mom go ahead and get started, we'll be there in a few minutes."

"Alright, sweetheart! Take your time, we're making dinner – there's no rush!"

Amelia looked at Matthew and held her hands out. He took her hands in his and she said, "There's only one way to find out if we really have access to the Inner Earth."

"I'm ready," said Matthew. Then dropping her hands, and wrapping his arms tightly around her he added, "But I'm not taking any chances!"

Amelia held Matthew and said, "I'll imagine the Inner Earth and you imagine coming with me." They closed their eyes and Amelia envisioned the place she first saw on her Inner Earth compass.

There was no feeling of movement, but even before they opened their eyes they felt moisture in the air. Then they heard flocks of birds singing their evening songs. They opened their eyes to hundreds of different species in the treetops and high overhead like a living rainbow that had splintered off into tiny, colorful flecks darting through the air.

Matthew and Amelia were holding each other exactly as they were a moment earlier, but now they were standing on a grassy knoll with an ancient stand of towering sequoias behind them. They both looked down in awe at the sparkling ocean below then looked back at each other.

Yelping with joy, Amelia jumped into Matthew's arms, wrapped her arms around his neck and her legs around his waist. "I didn't lose you this time!"

"Nope!" he said smiling warmly.

"And my dad said we could take our time…"

"Yep," said Matthew with mock-seriousness, "I think it's very important to obey your parents – and he did say *don't rush.*"

Amelia leaned in and whispered in Matthew's ear, "I think we have all the time in the world."

EPILOGUE

Not everyone in the biosphere had the same experience. The soldier standing next to Amelia had no idea why he was there; in fact, he'd had no idea that the biosphere even existed. Though he'd been named Dylan after a famous singer whose first name was Bob, he didn't consider himself to be much of a singer, and the idea of singing to a pyramid was the most ridiculous, un-soldierly thing he had ever heard of, let alone having to walk around with a stupid candle when he had a perfectly good flashlight in his room.

Never before had he been ordered to wear army fatigues while being asked to leave his weapons and equipment in his locker. His latest orders had taken him to the deepest level underground that he had ever been. There were hundreds of other soldiers milling about and, oddly enough, several people who looked completely out of place including four teenage girls, a prisoner, a male nurse, and an old man and middle-aged woman who appeared to have escaped from the psych ward, based upon the green scrubs they wore and her pink, fluffy slippers.

They had all ended up in some kind of expansive chamber with thirty foot ceilings composed almost entirely of cement.

There was a massive vault-like metal door at its far end and florescent lights emanated an eerie, unnatural glow throughout. It felt as claustrophobic and lifeless as a mausoleum.

Strangely enough, their commanding officer ordered them to follow every instruction issued by a man called Thomas. Dylan was sure his CO couldn't be serious when he saw this man dressed in a white linen tunic with a collar of precious and semi precious stones set in a flexible gold mesh that extended eight inches out from his neck and draped slightly over his shoulders while covering his chest and upper back. Dylan thought the man looked like an ancient Egyptian priest who'd just walked off a movie set, and when he looked to his commanding officer to see if this was a joke, he was met with a grave look that communicated he was serious.

As candles were passed around and lit one from another, Thomas told the group that they would be walking to a pyramid. He then ordered them to fill in the gaps between the people and follow whatever the people were doing.

As the vault-like door began slowly swinging open Dylan immediately heard the sound of a towering waterfall crashing into a pool of water approximately twenty feet away. In single file they marched over the threshold, as Dylan realized they were in a cave which was completely hidden behind the waterfall. In moments the rumbling sound was replaced by the light splash of water falling in small streams, glinting in what appeared to be the soft silvery glow of moonlight. As the streams became mere droplets, the water below drained so that only a light shimmer of water remained on the rock floor.

As he stepped out beyond the mouth of the cave and up onto the land, Dylan was shocked to see moonlight filtering down from overhead through an evergreen forest wrapped in the delicate scent of pine. The air was fresh and filled with floral fragrances and the sounds of whirring insects and the occasional croaking frog. He would have sworn he was outdoors, but he knew that wasn't possible. Even so he felt incredibly alive. Maybe it was the air, he thought, or maybe it was because he was no longer wearing his regulation jumpsuit... but that seemed crazy, how could a jumpsuit change a person's feelings?

The men's commanding officers led them along separate pathways, allowing them to descend quickly down the hillside. At first Dylan could only see the forest and moonlight filtering down through the trees; and though they knew they were heading toward a pyramid, no one was prepared for the size and scope of what they saw.

A large group of plainly dressed men, women and children circled around the magnificent pyramid and as Dylan stepped into an empty spot next to a tall, beautiful young woman, she looked at him and smiled as she reached out to hold his hand. Part of him hoped he would never have to go back to his post and that he would be ordered to stay in this magical place forever, but he reminded himself that he was a soldier and snapped his mind to back into the present moment.

As he began to take in the sights and sounds around him, Dylan realized that everyone was gazing up at this weird ball of light that was hovering just over top of the pyramid and they were all singing some weird sound, yet he just stood there, tight-lipped and waiting for whatever it was that was going on to be over. Any magic he had seen in the place didn't seem worth the embarrassment of being there at that time, but at least he had the comfort of knowing that he would soon be back at work and could forget the whole thing ever happened.

But he never did make it back to work. He would never admit this to another soul, but as he gazed up toward the top of the pyramid, the ball of light was growing larger and larger until it seemed to explode into an intense sapphire blue-white light and Dylan was suddenly overwhelmed with a feeling of love beyond anything he had ever felt in his entire life. Nothing he'd ever experienced compared to this feeling – nothing. And in the next moment Dylan burst into tears and instantly fell to the ground. What had happened? He struggled to get to his feet, but the entire ground beneath him was shaking violently.

He looked desperately around for a place to take cover as huge chunks of the biosphere came crashing down from above. He tried to take the young woman and some other people with him, but they all seemed to be in some kind of trance. So he ran into the pyramid entrance and was joined by just a few other soldiers when a gigantic block of cement crashed in front of the doorway.

Dylan wasn't practiced in prayer nor did he talk to God – he didn't even believe in God – but as Death was staring him in the face he really had no one else to turn to, so he begged that his life be spared. And in that moment the strangest thing happened.

He heard a voice speak directly into his mind saying, "No one will ever change your destiny against your will. All that you desire for yourself will be allowed."

"Then I desire to walk out of here alive," Dylan whispered, his eyes shut tight as he huddled next to a wall with his hands covering his head, "… and in one piece," he added wanting to be sure he covered all of his bases.

When the earthquake had subsided, the soldiers cautiously climbed over the rubble and discovered that the dome ceiling had fully collapsed. Everything was silent. Apparently there were no other survivors. They could see the edge of the earth several miles above and blue sky beyond that. Dylan stood and stared for a moment, unable to remember the last time he'd seen the sky. He felt lucky to be alive.

But at the same time he wondered what it was all for. As a soldier he'd seen plenty of death, and he'd caused some of those deaths as well, but something had changed within him, and he began to question the purpose of a life that would only end in death. And though all the physical evidence pointed to the fact that everyone was dead and buried in the rubble, Dylan kept seeing images of everyone alive and well - but surely that was just wishful thinking on his part.

Dylan and the other soldiers tried to return to their barracks, but the cave with the waterfall had collapsed. The only way out was to climb up to the top of the biosphere.

It was twenty miles to the nearest wall and from there it was six miles high. Though they didn't have proper climbing equipment, they were able to salvage ropes and other things they needed by picking through the rubble at some of the homesteads.

Clearly everyone had perished at the base of the pyramid, because they didn't see a single person, dead or alive; yet in contrast there was so much life everywhere. Birds were singing high in the trees, and all kinds of animals, large and small, appeared around them – but they bore neither fear nor aggression. Dylan was secretly relieved that they had been ordered to leave their weapons behind. He wouldn't have said anything, but he would have felt awful if the others had killed these beautiful, harmless creatures for food.

Life reemerged so quickly, he was amazed to witness the way that nature continued unperturbed, as if nothing had happened and all was well. Water moved gracefully around the new obstructions, departing from old streambeds and creating new ones, but the underground source still provided an abundance of the most delicious, invigorating water Dylan had ever experienced – and combined with the fresh air and eating the most delectable raw fruits, nuts and vegetables each day, he felt more alive and energized than ever before in his life.

Once they had what they needed for climbing, it took them several more days to reach the desert floor, yet when they finally arrived Dylan felt a tug in heart as he looked down. He would miss this woodland world but he was a trained soldier and knew he had the responsibility of reporting to a new commanding officer as soon as possible – his, it seemed, had perished in the earthquake.

After discovering that the surface entrance to the military facility had collapsed, they hiked out to a road looking for water and food. Here and there they managed to find enough to keep them going, by digging in a garbage can at a deserted campsite or a water pump that was still functioning.

As time went on they met a few more soldiers who also seemed to have been cut adrift, and somehow their circumstances had separated every single one of them from their weapons. Even so, as a band of trained soldiers, they were prepared for hand to hand combat. But there really wasn't much to fight for. Everywhere they went houses had collapsed and people had left the towns. The occasional stray dog or cat seemed to be the only things alive.

But the soldiers had no trouble surviving. They rummaged through the rubble of collapsed homes and restaurants and raided pantries for food. They found plenty of canned goods that they shared with each other. Ultimately they found all kinds of necessities, flashlights, batteries, even maps of the country. But due to the state of the roads after the earthquake they had no transportation, and they were in a small desert town, miles and miles from any other town. Their solution was to hike out with food and water, store it and hike back. They stock piled their resources until everything was in place and then set out again, going farther and farther each time, ultimately coming to another vacant town, and starting over again.

It was slow going, hiking back and forth and back and forth with supplies. They began to lose track of time, but soon winter was upon them and there was nothing to do but wait it out until spring. When they began their slow process again, they came to a town where frightened looking men and women peered out from behind stone walls or boarded up windows with a shotgun aimed straight at them. Having a gun was a tempting thought, but they discovered if they kept walking no one bothered them, so they decided to wait. And sure enough, one day they came across a shotgun and ammunition in a deserted barn.

They had rabbit for dinner that night, and because there was more ammunition than they could carry they took turns shooting bottles and cans off of fence posts. It was the most fun they'd had in over a year since their journey began. The next morning they started their trek once again. They were headed for Denver, but who knew how long that would take? And then, like another miracle, they saw a barn, and grazing in a nearby pasture was a horse, a sturdy looking little palomino with a shaggy white mane and long tail. The little mare didn't look like much, but somehow she'd been well cared for and she was plump from eating the lush grass of early summer.

As they walked toward the pasture, a boy came out of the house and onto the porch. He was obviously surprised to see them because he yelled out in a panicky voice, "Papa!"

But when he turned to go inside the soldier carrying the shotgun readied the weapon and yelled, "Stop or I'll shoot!"

The boy froze in his tracks. The soldier yelled more gently, "We don't want to hurt you, kid, we just need your horse."

Without any fear at all, the boy screamed, "No! No! She's mine, you can't have her." But as he realized there was nothing he could do he withered onto the porch in tears crying out, "She's all I have left."

Dylan was the one soldier who'd had a horse growing up. He felt for the boy as he now realized the child had no father, he just wanted the soldiers to believe he wasn't all alone, but they really did need a horse to haul food and water if they were ever going to make it over the mountains and down the other side to Denver. And, of course, what they were doing was for the greater good. So he grabbed a halter and lead rope and walked quietly up to the horse holding his hand out coaxingly. The mare looked up at him inquisitively, but didn't move away when Dylan reached out to stroke her neck as he gently looped the lead rope around her neck and put the halter on.

In the barn, her tack wasn't in very good shape, but the saddle would only be used to strap on bags of food and canteens of water. As he led the horse along the road behind the other soldiers, the land seemed to be bursting with the magic of summer. Flowers bloomed alongside the road, in a way he'd never noticed before. They weren't planted, and they seemed to have a carefree feeling to them, as if they enjoyed growing wherever they pleased.

Finally they camped for the night. They had rabbit again for dinner, and it was such a delicious treat after months of canned food. Dylan walked with the little palomino as she grazed on the long grass growing intermittently in the forest. He didn't dare allow her to graze by herself since they were still close enough that she might gallop back home. But after a day of walking, and now to stand and wait for the horse to eat, he decided he was just too tired. So he jumped on her back while holding the lead rope that was connected to the halter. The mare didn't seem to mind and continued grazing.

Reminded of his childhood days and his own horse, Dylan leaned back and stretched out on the horse's rump looking up at the clouds tinged with pink in the early evening sky. "I think I'll call you Dusty Rose," he said. "I know you're a palomino," he added with a note of apology, "but Dusty Rose was my horse growing up… and she was a fine horse… so it really is a compliment," he added, stroking her side as he enjoyed the warm, horsy smell of her.

As he lay on the mare, her rump for a pillow, Dylan was reminded of a day in his childhood growing up in Kentucky where he'd done exactly the same with his own horse. The sky had been so very blue and polka-dotted with puffy little clouds. There was no breeze and the clouds barely moved, but he played a game where he saw dragons or faeries or monsters in the clouds and then enjoyed watching them transform into something new.

He was in a beautiful, hidden place that he'd discovered all on his own and right in the middle of a corn field the land suddenly dipped down into a little pond surrounded by red-winged black birds swaying on reeds rising sturdily from the water. To one side was a forest and as he rode slowly down to the water he saw a mother fox emerge from the cover of the trees with her kits, and after they left, a mother skunk appeared with her young clan; tails high in the air like striped banners proudly marching to the pond. There were baby cottontail rabbits too, but they were just here and there without a mother, and Dylan was relieved that the red-tailed hawk flying lazy circles in the sky above him seemed to take no notice. But then again, there was plenty of cover between the reeds and the undergrowth and the tall forest trees.

As the twilight sky began to darken, there was a moment when Dusty Rose suddenly jerked her head up and looked quickly to one side, pulling Dylan out of his childhood reverie. He thought she was about to bolt so he jumped off and hung onto the lead rope while giving her a quick yank to get her attention. He was tired and it was time to sleep, so he led her to a tree near their camp and tied her up for the night. A few times during the night Dylan sat up out of a deep sleep, his heart pounding, but each time he could still make out Dusty Rose standing at the tree. He could tell the night sounds were making her antsy as well, yet he knew how to tie a solid knot and that gave him the confidence to go back to sleep each time.

But then something woke him. It wasn't a frightening sound it was more of a low, soft stirring in the air. Dylan's eyes gently opened. The moon had set and the sky was just a bit lighter than the dark of night so he knew the dawn was approaching. He heard a twig snap. None of the men stirred, and Dylan told himself he wasn't going to sit up this time, and that Dusty Rose was still tied to the tree, so he lay there for a moment, just listening. But then he heard the soft sound of a horse walking quietly away.

Dylan leapt to his feet and took off in the direction of the horse's hoof beats, but her walk turned into a trot, and though he could hear her trotting away he couldn't see her in the dark grayness of the early morning. On and on he ran. It wasn't hard because the mare was following a forest path that had been created by other animals, deer perhaps. Dylan realized he'd never been in better shape in his entire life. He wasn't breathless, and though he hadn't caught up with the mare, he could still hear her enticingly just ahead of him, slowing for a moment to grab a mouthful of grass and then trotting on, as if she knew he was still following her. Gradually it became lighter. He'd been running for miles, but finally, just ahead in a clearing he saw her. Like a round, little golden Buddha surrounded by a sea of the greenest, most lush grass he had ever seen that rippled in the early morning breeze, Dusty Rose didn't even look in his direction as she flicked her long, white tail in the early morning sunshine.

Dylan stopped to catch his breath as he admired the scene, but then a familiar sound rang out through the woods and the next thing he knew he'd been knocked flat on his back sensing warm blood oozing from the buckshot holes spreading out across his shoulder and onto his chest. He didn't know who had shot him. He guessed it must have been the boy as he sat up to try to see for sure. But this action only made his blood gush more quickly, and no matter what he did or didn't do, he knew he'd be dying alone. No one knew he'd left the camp to run after the horse, and he'd run for several miles. Even if they heard the shot and started running he would die before they could get to him.

But as he lay on his back watching shafts of sunlight angling through the aspen leaves as they sparkled a soft light green above him, and as he listened to the faint breeze rustling through the trees while songbirds trilled in the air above, Dylan suddenly remembered how much he had loved the forest in his childhood.

He'd grown up on little Kentucky farm with a stream out back, and a swimming hole where he and his friends used to climb an immense oak tree and swing out over the hole, dropping in with a huge splash. His family had chickens, two milking cows, a few goats, and even a llama which his mom brushed daily to collect its hair. She then spun the wool which she knitted into sweaters and wove into blankets. He basked in the joy of reflecting upon these memories of his boyhood but as much as he loved all of them, the ultimate love of his life was his horse.

He fed her every day, except for in the summertime when the grass was long and lush, and even now he could remember the warm smell of the hayloft and the light coming down in shafts through holes in the roof. He always loved sweeping out the loft prior to getting a new load of hay, because he'd end up with a huge pile of loose hay below. He and his friends spent many happy hours jumping out of that loft and into the hay and then climbing back up the ladder. He'd sit in his mare's cement feed bin on top of her hay and she would nibble around him as he scratched her ears and spoke softly to her of what a wonderful friend she was to him.

But the most fun he had was just riding through the fields and jumping over anything that got in their way. They'd typically end up at a quarry where he and his Dusty Rose would swim in the warm water together. Quarry water was completely different than river water, which was often cold and polluted. The rock walls kept the water in one place where it spent the summer being warmed by the sun, and because there was no pollution he could see right down to the very bottom which had to have been eight feet below. Swimming with his horse was one of the most cherished memories in his entire young life. He had to hang onto her mane because he was riding bareback so his body would float up to the top of the water as her body undulated below the surface. And then, as she stepped back onto land, he had to hang on tight as her body suddenly rose up beneath him. Nothing in his entire life had ever compared to all his days in nature, riding his horse and playing with his friends... How had he managed to forget something he'd loved so dearly?

Ever since the biosphere collapsed he'd spent all of his time in nature, first in the biosphere, then the desert and most recently in the forest, but never, not once did he simply relax and enjoy the peace and splendor of being surrounded by this completely natural world. No one would mourn the loss of him, and no one would be there in time to save him, if they even found him. For all he knew his body would just rot where it lay in the dirt. And then he wondered something he'd wondered a year earlier when everyone was buried at the base of the pyramid... What was it all for?

And then he laughed. It wasn't a hearty laugh, it was more of a tiny chuckle, but even so it caused wracking pain to tear through his body. Still it was funny to realize that this was the most superb moment of his entire life, even though it wasn't lush and moist like Kentucky, the Colorado forest had its own beauty. But what made this moment different from his childhood was that he truly, deeply appreciated everything around him, he took nothing for granted.... How had he missed it? Where exactly did he think he was going?

As a soldier, Dylan liked to think of himself as a peacekeeper and to keep the peace sometimes you had to go to war. But there was no war. There was nothing going on at all, really. They were headed to Denver in the hope that there would be some kind of civil disturbance or at least something to do. But suddenly the whole idea was preposterous. No one in Denver was waiting for a ragtag band of soldiers to come marching into town; he knew it, they all knew. Still they marched every day, and if he was really honest with himself, Dylan would say it wasn't so much about being a soldier or a peacekeeper – they just didn't know what else to do with themselves.

But as the smell of grass mingled with the bark on the trees, the leaves and rich soil, Dylan knew there was no feeling that ever compared to the Earth beneath him while gazing up into a canopy of emerald leaves, dotted with blue sky. As he lay there he heard soft steps and then felt a blow of warm air coming from Dusty Rose's nostrils as she sniffed him gently.

"Just like a woman to go and run off on me," he said with a weak smile, being careful not to laugh even a tiny bit. "It's ok, I forgive you," he said as he stroked her velvety nose with his left hand.

In that moment, as he touched the mare with genuine love and appreciation, expecting nothing from her – finally, finally he knew what he'd been searching for his entire life. Never had he felt more fully alive. It was as if every cell in his body was singing. But he wasn't alone. The Earth was singing, the trees and rocks and flowers, the sun and the clouds were all alive with the sound of life.

The song was around him and inside of him. It reminded him of what he heard at the pyramid… it seemed like years ago… It didn't make sense at the time, but now that song was *singing him* and this time he heard it with his soul. He closed his eyes, happy, truly happy for the first time in recent memory. He smiled as he saw that he'd been searching and searching for something all his life, going from person to person and then from one place to the next, but just like some cosmic joke, one he was loath to laugh at under his current painful circumstances, he'd finally come full circle.

He had spent his life wanting to feel something, anything, yet it didn't matter what he did. He'd been with countless women, felt the thrill and agony of killing in battle, he'd tried drugs and gotten as drunk as humanly possible, but it was all fleeting; nothing more than a momentary thrill – a rush of adrenaline and the moment dissipated back into some distant dream of happiness that never, ever materialized… at least not for any length of time.

Lying on the ground feeling what he could only have described as a divine sensation flooding through him, it seemed like a strange cliché that he should find the feeling he'd been looking for at the very last possible moment, and though he'd known it as a child, he'd forgotten and it had been buried inside him all along. Yet, he thought to himself, "I'm ready to die."

He closed his eyes and waited. Dylan knew there was death, he'd seen it, he'd caused it, and now he was about to experience it himself. Definitively he thought, "No. When you're dead you're dead and after that you're just a rotting corpse until you turn into dust… but maybe there would be a tunnel of white light… that would be interesting," he mused.

But as he lay there waiting to die, there was no tunnel of light, no smiling family members as his mother had once assured him… there was just this strange sensation that he was drifting in and out of a dream.

After some time, he began to feel as if he was waking up. He opened his eyes to see why it was taking so long to die but what he saw only confused him further – the setting sun was golden and low on the horizon, and he realized that a few hours must have passed. Everything else was exactly the same, except the colors seemed brighter somehow, and the song that had been singing through him and around him seemed more like a vibrant humming in the air.

Carefully he picked his head just slightly off the ground, thinking he must have misjudged how bad his wounds were. Dusty Rose was nowhere to be seen, but sitting next to him was a little girl with luminous blue eyes and golden ringlets falling around her round, pink-cheeked face. She sat cross-legged, gazing at him, as if she'd been there for quite some time and she was holding a bouquet of tiny, colorful wildflowers in her hand.

"I'm Anastasia," she said, "well, at least that's the way you would say it. The proper pronunciation is Ana-sta-SEE-ah… but everyone just calls me Äsha. Are you hungry?" she said, offering him the bouquet. "Would you like to come to my house for dinner?"

A faint smile flickered across Dylan's face. "Thanks kid," he said, "But I'm kinda bleedin' to death here."

The girl silently stared at him with a puzzled look on her face. Finally he used his left hand to indicate the blood on his right shoulder. Still she seemed not to notice. So he turned his head to glance at his shoulder. There was no blood. He sat up. There was no wound. Had it all been a dream, or was he dreaming now?

Dylan scrambled to his feet and the child reached up to hold his hand. "Am I in heaven?" he said. The child looked at him puzzled and said, "I don't think so. We call this Earth."

Together, they walked through a meadow dotted with wildflowers of every color imaginable, then splashed through a stream before taking a path to a small settlement nestled deep in a forest of aspen and cedar trees. Though he was dressed in raggedy military clothing, and knew he must be frightening to look at and smelled even worse, no one seemed afraid of him. Mother's didn't shoo their children into the house, and in fact, as they walked along, people waved and said hello, smiling at him with kindness while waving to Äsha and offering them some extra fruit or vegetables from their gardens.

Unlike the other houses he'd seen, which all appeared to have been through an earthquake if they were even still standing, the log homes around him looked solid and in perfect condition. He marveled at the peace and serenity he felt as they passed by one home after the next. Each homestead had fragrant colorful flowers, a vegetable garden, a pond, an orchard and a forest, and oddly enough, most seemed to have fences surrounding the property composed of raspberry bushes.

What a clever idea, Dylan thought, as he remembered how they were constantly mending fences on the farm where he grew up, a fence that will last forever, will feed your family and your neighbors and never needs to be repaired... how about that!

Between each home was a wide ribbon of rolling pastureland where horses and ponies were grazing. But this wasn't the type of space that was owned by the rich with signs posted saying 'No Trespassing.' It was land that was open and free to all, Äsha informed him.

It struck Dylan that every homestead had the most extraordinary colors and fragrances. He had never seen so many diverse and unique designs in the landscaping surrounding a home. And rather than feeling that these homesteads were private and cut off from each other, he had the feeling of spaciousness. The homesteads had plenty of space, but no more than they needed, just enough to provide for their own families with plenty of open land in between.

As they continued walking Dylan noticed that everyone seemed to have everything they needed. Clearly no one was working and the children didn't appear to be in school. Yet he could tell that Äsha was uncommonly intelligent, so he asked her if she went to school.

Äsha cocked her head but looked confused. Dylan said, "Do you know how to read and write?"

Äsha laughed gaily, "Oh I see what you're asking. I can read or write if I need to, but it slows your brain down. We pass stories down through oral traditions… it's much more challenging to remember every single word down to the tiniest detail, and that causes our brains to move more quickly and this builds momentum in the mind of the thinker."

"Do you know math?" asked Dylan, now very curious, and hoping he might be able to actually test her abilities.

Äsha nodded enthusiastically.

Fumbling through his pockets he finally found what he was looking for. "This is a calculator… don't really know why I kept it… guess I just figured it would come in handy one day. I'll show you how it works."

First he showed Äsha that it was solar powered and then he tapped in two numbers and showed her the button to touch for multiplying numbers, then he tapped in two more numbers, but in the moment he tapped the 'equals' button Äsha told him the answer before the number appeared on the screen.

And this kept happening even when he was finally up to multiplying six digit numbers. Äsha was faster than the calculator every time. But oddly enough she didn't seem to be having any fun, nor did she seem in the least bit pleased with herself, in fact, she appeared to be rather bored.

Dylan said, "How do you calculate all of these numbers in your mind?"

Äsha shrugged and said, "Calculations are always the same on a dead dimension."

"What do you mean, a *dead dimension?*"

"Well, nothing changes… the numbers are always the same… it's just not that much fun. I'd rather calculate numbers in a living dimension."

Dylan looked at her skeptically and said, "A living dimension? What does that mean? One plus one will always equal two."

"That's true on a dead dimension," said Äsha, "but not in a living one."

"Can you show me how one plus one would equal something other than two?" asked Dylan.

Äsha nodded and holding up her fist she unfurled her pointer finger and said, "Momma," then unfurling her next finger she added, "plus Papa," then straightening her third finger, she said, "equals me." Äsha looked at Dylan ingenuously and said, "So one plus one equals three… and in a living dimension it could be even more."

Dylan was stunned and couldn't help but wonder if there was anything this little girl didn't know. Responding directly to his thoughts she said, "I don't know what we're having for dinner." Dylan burst out laughing.

As they continued walking Dylan realized that he recognized the landscape from the day before. "This is odd, but I'd swear I just came through here and this doesn't look at all the same. Where did all of these houses come from?"

"Well, it's the same scenery, but you're not exactly in the same place," said Äsha.

Dylan shook his head, blinking in disbelief. "What does that mean? Where did I go?"

"You didn't really *go* anywhere…you changed your frequency… sort of like tuning in to a different radio station," said Äsha, looking at Dylan and noticing that he didn't quite understand. "You changed how you were feeling… right? And when you sort of *fell in love* with everything… that feeling caused you to wake up here."

He nodded, his eyes moist as the remembrance washed over him. He wasn't sure he understood, but the evidence was all around him, so he didn't disagree.

"Then… what happened to my friends?" asked Dylan.

"They're on a *version* of Earth that matches the frequency… or *vibration*… of their thoughts and feelings… and they're experiencing what they most believed would occur."

For a moment Dylan was taken aback, but as he thought about what Äsha was saying, an image appeared in his mind and he saw how the world he came from had felt as empty and aimless as he did at the time, and how this world felt as loving as he did while dying. Like a puzzle piece changing its shape, he understood that he no longer fit into that old reality; but just as he had become a match to this world, his friends were still a match to theirs.

"So, when I woke up and you were sitting there next to me, if I had gone back to where I was camping, what would have happened? I mean, could I have brought any of the others here with me?"

"If you had gone back, you would have found the place where you camped, but you wouldn't have found your friends or any evidence that they had ever been there," said Äsha.

"But I know there are others who would love this world…" said Dylan, "it seems unfair that they didn't have the same opportunity that I did."

"They do have the same opportunity, everyone does, but in order to experience a new reality they have to let go of everything that keeps them in the *old* reality."

"How could they possibly know what to let go of?" asked Dylan.

"They just let go of anything that doesn't feel good," replied Äsha simply.

"I guess that's what I did…" mused Dylan thoughtfully to himself.

During the past year, he had watched the things that he believed in lose their meaning completely. As a soldier, he had described himself as a *defender, peace keeper,* and *protector of our liberties.* But in a world without war, without people, without government, it was only a matter of time until he realized that none of it meant anything anymore, and with that, there was nothing left to fight for.

But still he had held on, struggling to keep his sense of identity, and for what? He smiled to himself, wondering why he hadn't let go sooner. It felt like the most natural thing in the world.

"Are you sure I'm not dead?" said Dylan, grasping for any reason that he might be having this experience, short of a very long dream.

Äsha burst out laughing. "You say the funniest things!" she said, her eyes filled with delight as if she were being entertained by a kitten. "Why don't we go have dinner?"

The little girl smiled up at him adoringly. Her eyes sparkled as she led him happily to her home. They lived in a modest log cabin, but he sensed they didn't spend much time indoors. A gentle breeze was blowing past the house and Dylan could smell the sweet, combined fragrance of the jasmine and magnolias that surrounded their home, and when they arrived at the front door the lavender colored roses were as glorious as their soft scent.

To Dylan's surprise Äsha's parents welcomed him inside, warmly. The little girl was the image of her tall, beautiful, blonde mother, with the same full lips and intensely blue eyes. But there was something about her father in her too, something in her eyes or in the expressions on her face. He was taller than his wife and ruggedly handsome, and they both appeared to be in their mid-twenties, just a bit younger than Dylan. But what struck Dylan the most was how much they loved each other as they laughed and giggled while preparing the simple, but extraordinarily delicious meal they would all share that evening.

They sat outside on the soft grass next to the pond to eat their dinner. Countless songbirds sang their evening songs as translucent dragonflies flitted in the golden, early evening light and danced just above the surface of the pond.

They didn't ask him questions like where he'd come from or how he'd come to be there – it was as if they already knew everything about him. They casually discussed things at dinner like the dragon that was nesting in their forest and how the earth faeries moved out of that vicinity and the fire faeries moved in.

Äsha was so excited to have a real guest over for dinner that she became an explosion of information. She told Dylan that she had befriended a unicorn earlier that summer and she explained what delicacies it liked to eat and how she planted everything in the garden with love so it would feel her love even more when it ate the carrots she planted.

He thought this was a childish game with her parents playing along, until a living, breathing unicorn stepped out of the forest and walked gracefully up to the girl, bowing its head as she smiled and gave it a carrot.

Äsha giggled and said, "He didn't like carrots in the beginning… he thinks they're *horse food*… but I told him that was the easiest thing for me to plant, so he learned to like carrots… but he always says he just comes for the love."

Dylan laughed and suddenly found himself looking at Äsha's mother unable to take his eyes off of her. "There is something so familiar about you," he said candidly. "I know that's not possible…"

She smiled and said, "Yes, it is possible. You were standing next to me in the biosphere at the base of the pyramid."

"Oh my God," said Dylan taken aback. "You're absolutely right! I remember now! But what happened?" he said, looking back and forth between Amelia and Matthew. "I mean, I'm not dead, right?"

Amelia shook her head, "No, you're not dead."

Dylan bit his lip and went on, "I understand about being on a different frequency – at least I think I understand – but what triggered all of this? I mean what was it about the pyramid and the singing and looking up… and where did that ball of energy come from? I thought everyone died – but here you are – and you seemed so young, did you have your daughter then?" he blurted out, his words tumbling over themselves.

Amelia laughed, "Well, time doesn't function quite the way you might think. This will probably be hard to understand, but everything happens all at once. All events and every possible outcome of every situation occurred in a single moment."

"Whoa," said Dylan, his mind reeling, "I don't think I'm quite ready for this conversation, how about if you tell me about the pyramid instead?"

"Okay," said Amelia gamely, "We'll get back to that later. The pyramid in the biosphere was an exact replica of the Pyramid of Giza. The shape allows hundreds or thousands of people to gather at the base and focus on a single point, just above the apex, where everyone's thoughts and intentions come together for whatever they desire."

"We were all singing *AHH-OHM* because AUM is the Original Sound that sparked everything into existence," Amelia paused for a moment, looking at Dylan and said, "That's a little confusing, isn't it?"

He nodded.

She smiled understandingly and said, "Why don't you close your eyes for a moment and see if you can imagine this – try not to figure it out – just allow pictures to flow through your mind."

Dylan nodded again, smiled and closed his eyes.

"Though you can't hear it," said Amelia continuing, "every organ in your body and every cell emits a unique sound or vibration. And this is true of the entire universe... everything is connected through harmonic frequencies... much like the way you can pluck a guitar string and if it's the right frequency another string will vibrate or *sing* at the same time."

With his eyes still closed, deeply immersed in his imagination, Dylan smiled and nodded, as he remembered this phenomenon from playing his guitar as a child.

"Now imagine these sounds as different colors, and the sound AUM is equivalent to white light. So in the same way that white light contains all imaginable colors, AUM contains every vibration, every harmonic frequency that now appears in physical form. And in the same way that you dream and see a world instantaneously before your eyes, all that is was created in a single moment with the sound AUM."

Dylan leaned back on his elbows and finally lay down on the soft, fragrant grass behind him. And then, without another word from Amelia, he saw it himself. There had been hundreds of people singing AUM around the base of the pyramid, and though that included soldiers who had no idea what they were trying to achieve, the sound itself clearly carried the vibration of the Earth as it was created in the beginning, and the intention to return it to its original state was magnified through a single point of focus.

Suddenly Dylan saw himself at the beginning of time, and felt the sound AUM vibrating everything and every possibility into existence in a single moment, like a dream world to be entered into at the will of the dreamer, each dreamer becoming real in the dream they were choosing.

In the next moment, Dylan heard a deep snuffling sound and something wet and warm touched his cheek. He opened his eyes and instantly launched himself into the air and shot backwards so quickly he frightened Blossom, the family's massive bear, so thoroughly she ran several feet away, hackles up and then turned around to look at this strange, terrifying creature, unsure of what she should do.

Äsha ran over to the bear and threw her arms around Blossom's neck as she whispered into her ear the way someone might try to calm a startled horse. Finally she convinced Blossom that Dylan was a friend and they walked up to him so that bear and man could try their greeting again.

Dylan's head was spinning. He'd given up trying to understand anything at all. In fact, he decided he knew nothing, and it was much better that way. He was looking forward to going to sleep because he hoped that in the morning everything would make more sense. And then he saw little lights that appeared to be floating in the distance.

"Oh come look, come look!" yelled Äsha as she ran ahead down a path through the forest, constantly looking over her shoulder, beckoning him as she skipped and ran.

By the time they reached the end of the path it was nearly dark, but they could easily see the broad river before them flowing along languidly with tiny, handmade wooden boats, with a candle and a piece of fruit in each.

"Oh how sad," said Dylan, "somebody must have died."

Äsha giggled, "No… nobody died… these boats are sent from girls upstream who haven't found the man of their dreams yet."

"You mean it's sort of like a wish… like throwing coins in a fountain?"

"No…" said Äsha with a sigh of laughter, and then she began to talk to him as if she was explaining the *birds and the bees*. "You see when a young woman is ready to get married, she'll sometimes meet a man in her village or at one of the festivals we have where lots and lots of people come together. But sometimes she hasn't found the right man. So about once or twice a year, all the girls in the village who are of marrying age and still looking for their beloved… Well, they get together and make these boats with candles they've made themselves and fruit from a tree that grows on their own land. They send the boats downstream and any man who hasn't found his… goddess yet," she added with a smile, "goes into the stream, takes the boat he's drawn to, and then journeys along the shore up the stream to find his beloved."

"What if she doesn't like him, or vice versa?" said Dylan thinking the idea was both intriguing and terrifying, at least from his perspective.

"I've never heard of any couple not falling in love that way… there are no coincidences you know."

"Well how does he know who she is? Is her name and address on the boat?"

Äsha howled with laughter. "No…" she said with another

sigh. "He takes a journey up the river and he can tell from the fruit in the boat which tree it grew from."

"Wow!" said Dylan, genuinely impressed.

"Or sometimes he'll just feel which woman it is… and when he sees her, he gives her back her little boat. And he'll say something really romantic like… *You are the Goddess of my dreams…* stuff like that… and then she'll say something that lets him know she's interested… and then they talk for a while… and then they walk around until they find the perfect land on which to build their home."

"How do they afford the land?" asked Dylan, especially curious because it seemed that no one ever worked.

"No one has to pay for land," said Äsha, "If no one lives there you can build a home and plant everything you need and start a family."

"So you're saying," said Dylan slowly, "that if I just walked into that river right now and plucked out a boat… the woman who made it would most likely fall madly in love with me?"

Äsha nodded.

"Well that's just the craziest thing!" he said, feeling a bit stupid for even mentioning such a ridiculous idea.

"You'd only say that if none of the boats were meant for you."

"So what if I grab a boat anyhow, just to prove that you're wrong?" he said tickling Äsha as she squealed in delight.

"Well, as my Mama says, *would you rather be right or happy?*" said Äsha smiling broadly.

The boats had all bobbed past them in a merry procession and were now quite a bit further downstream, but there was one little boat that was tagging along at a slower pace and now it was stuck on a rock with the current going past it. Dylan could see it wouldn't come loose by itself and he felt sad to think that there might be a damsel somewhere waiting for her beloved and wondering why he never came. So he waded out into the river and picked up the little boat with the idea of sending it on its way. But the minute he held it in his hands he felt a charge of warm energy flow up his arms and into his heart. The warmth was so powerful he felt it flooding through his entire body, even causing his cheeks to flush.

Dylan decided right then and there that he didn't care whether she was attracted to him or if he was attracted to her he simply had to meet the woman who made the boat. Just holding it made him feel like he was madly in love. And though he didn't know how it was happening he'd have sworn he saw her face, heart-shaped, rosy cheeks, and bright green eyes, smiling lovingly at him saying, "Come to me, come to me…"

It was crazy, he knew, but it was a far superior *crazy* to the life he'd been leading until now. So with boat in hand and the apple that came with it in his pocket, he held the candle in one hand and Äsha's hand in the other, and they walked back up the path to her home.

That night everyone slept outdoors. The air was cool and fragrant with night blooming jasmine, and the scent of magnolias drifted by tantalizingly when the breeze shifted slightly and came a bit more from the east. He was given the softest bedding and he laid it in the grass a good distance from the rest of the family, just in case he snored. Äsha brought him a fluffy pillow and sat down next to him as he stretched out on his back with his head on the pillow and turned to smile at her.

As if she was telling him a bedtime story Äsha said quietly, "The stars and the planets and the moon are all reflecting the love we feel here on Earth back to us. So we sleep outside every night that we can see the stars and moon, and send love back to them." With that she gave him a goodnight kiss on his cheek and walked over to her parents where she burrowed under the covers between them.

The man looked up at the twinkling night sky, and indeed he felt the love the little girl had predicted. As he lay there, eyes open, gazing into the sky, he heard, or rather felt, the heavens singing. The flowers and grass and trees joined in the chorus. He could hear the pond and all the nighttime creatures singing as well. And then without thinking he began singing with them the low, deep, resonant sound of AUM.

As Love surrounded him and shone upon him, sparkling across the ripples in the pond and on the dew dropped tips of grass he yawned and stretched, and felt that marvelous feeling of being so tired his bed felt like a cloud carrying him off to dreamland. He opened his eyes dreamily one last time to see everything drenched in moonlight, and said to himself, "What a beautiful space of love." Then he reached out for the little boat and held it in his arms as he fell asleep dreaming of an apple tree and a beautiful green-eyed maiden beckoning him to come home.

MORE BY HEATHER NOËL

If you relate to the concepts in this book and want additional, simple tools, Heather has created a Free 60 day eCourse at: **TheGivingGameFoundation.com**

For more information on THE GAME AUDIOBOOK Please visit: NavigateTheGame.com

AFTERWORD

Here is further information for those who suspect that *'the truth is stranger than fiction'* and want to dig a bit deeper:

• **Vedruss of Russia**: Most of the information about the Vedruss is based on the teachings of Anastasia in <u>The Ringing Cedars of Russia</u> - a 10 book series by Vladimir Megre, originally published in Russia.

• **528 hertz**: After including 528 hz in the storyline, I woke up the next morning with the song, "Imagine" by John Lennon, singing itself in my mind. I listened to the song and was amazed by how much the story and song are in alignment. But I was even more astonished to discover that John Lennon apparently sang the original version in 528 hertz.

[Note: <u>The Book of 528: Prosperity Key of LOVE</u> gives detailed information on the topic of 528 hz. When it was translated and published in Japan the book was retitled: <u>The Frequency that Killed John Lennon</u>.]

• **Inner Earth**: Admiral Richard Byrd wrote a journal about his experience flying into (what I refer to as) the Inner Earth in 1947, including the exact coordinates at the North Pole where they entered. From what I understand, it was his wish that his journal be published posthumously, but the day it was to go on sale every copy was immediately purchased and the book was never seen again. However, it is still possible to find limited information about his journey online.

ACKNOWLEDGEMENTS

Two people were instrumental in transforming this book from a caterpillar into a butterfly! First is my 'twin' (we share the same birthday) Kelly Cavanaugh. Kelly patiently, persistently and expertly edited this book (and the companion novella as well) and offered her assistance as a gift. I know from experience that not all editors are created equal. Kelly, you are the BEST!

The second person who helped me immensely (and was the cause of many rewrites and over 100 deleted pages!) is the very talented author and writing teacher, Ted Dekker. Thank you, Ted, for sharing your insights and excellent advice, and thank you, Kelly, for patiently re-editing all of the subsequent rewrites!

Though I enjoy sci-fi movies, I rarely read science fiction, and for this reason, I would find myself getting thoroughly stuck when it came to describing something like a hovercraft! I am so blessed that my son, Andrew Macauley (who was 2 years old when I wrote the first draft of the original story, <u>Children of Light</u>) grew up to be a brilliant science fiction writer. Whenever I got stuck Andrew would say, "What do you need, Mom?" and usually within an hour or so he would send me a few terrific paragraphs. I'd pull out the descriptions I needed, tuck them into the story – and voila' I'd be unstuck and back to writing! (Andrew, if writing is a game, thank you for being my own personal cheat-code!)

By the time I started writing <u>The Game</u>, most of my high school memories were fairly irrelevant. I'd like to thank my daughter, Amelia, for inspiring me (always) and turning seventeen at the perfect moment so I could base my main character on a real, live-in, teenage girl that I know so well!

Thank you for being the very first person to laugh and cry over this book, and for every time you yelled, "Mom, that's SO me!" from the couch! And also, thank you (times infinity!) for jumping in and doing the tedious work of editing the audiobook with me. (I would have put off the audiobook for years if it hadn't been for your mortal support!)

Thank you to my husband, Don, for always holding down the fort and supporting me in all of my wild endeavors – everything from writing this book to creating a free website to owning horses and home schooling Amelia in Guatemala!

For years I have been compelled to find ways to share ebooks, audiobooks and programs (like thegivinggamefoundation.com) that are free to all. One person who took giving to a whole new level is my sweet friend, Carla Hess, a true visionary and philanthropist. Thank you Carla for all you have done to help me help others! I love that you've had the courage to trust life (even when it doesn't seem to be behaving properly)!

ACKNOWLEDGMENTS
PART II

This is for all of the people who helped me 20 + years ago with the original story, <u>Children of Light</u> (long before it morphed into <u>The Game: Nothing is as it seems</u>).

I especially want to thank my friend, Dr. Ted Conger, who had so much faith in me, he gave me the keys to his chiropractic office so I could use his computer after hours (often until 3 a.m.) and type the COL manuscript. Though I never asked Ted for support, he offered to help me over and over again at the exact moment when I could go no further on my own. Ted funded the production of the original Children of Light audiobook (way back when audiobooks were still on cassette tapes!) which is how Enrico Melson, M.D. heard the story while commuting, and subsequently shared it with Deepak Chopra, M.D. (who later endorsed the book!)

To Al Robbs and to Janine Groth for their faith in me, and their financial assistance in publishing the book version of <u>Children of Light</u> (most of the copies - nearly 5,000 – were given away to a variety of charitable groups in one week.) But one copy in particular was given to a man named Thomas, who was the director of the dolphin area at an ecological park in the Yucatan called X-Caret. I was four months pregnant at the time (November 1996) with my daughter, Amelia, and as I handed him the COL book, I told Thomas that I wanted to write about the connection between dolphins and the human fetus and asked if I could have his permission to swim by myself with dolphins on a daily basis. In five minutes he gave me a pass to the park and *my own* dolphin, Itzel, to swim with each day before the park opened. (I swam with Itzel every day for a month, and this has never been allowed before or since). When Amelia was 12 years old, we journeyed back to the Yucatan and she was allowed to swim by herself with Itzel. Al and Janine, thank you for being such a big part of that magic, as well as the charitable gifting of the books!

Ram Dass for inviting me to join his 7-day retreat, which helped me to bring my vision into reality.

Madeleine L'Engle (author of one of my all-time favorite books, <u>A Wrinkle in Time</u>) for reading my first draft of <u>Children of Light</u> and being kind enough to send a very thoughtful, handwritten two page letter (in 1994) with support, encouragement and excellent advice!

Jean Huston for her Colorado Mystery School where I learned to bend spoons... among other things!

ABOUT THE AUTHOR

Heather Noël and her daughter, *the real* Amelia (who is also the model on the cover of this book and the companion novella) currently live in Sedona, Arizona.

For more about the adventures that preceded this book, please see "About the Author" at:

NavigateTheGame.com